A *Regency* Collection

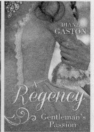

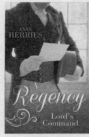

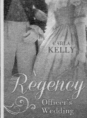

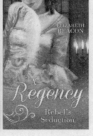

A
Regency
Gentleman's Passion

DIANE GASTON

MILLS & BOON

All rights reserved including the right of reproduction in whole or in part in any form. This edition is published by arrangement with Harlequin Books S.A.

This is a work of fiction. Names, characters, places, locations and incidents are purely fictional and bear no relationship to any real life individuals, living or dead, or to any actual places, business establishments, locations, events or incidents. Any resemblance is entirely coincidental.

This book is sold subject to the condition that it shall not, by way of trade or otherwise, be lent, resold, hired out or otherwise circulated without the prior consent of the publisher in any form of binding or cover other than that in which it is published and without a similar condition including this condition being imposed on the subsequent purchaser.

® and ™ are trademarks owned and used by the trademark owner and/or its licensee. Trademarks marked with ® are registered with the United Kingdom Patent Office and/or the Office for Harmonisation in the Internal Market and in other countries.

Published in Great Britain 2015
by Mills & Boon, an imprint of Harlequin (UK) Limited,
Eton House, 18-24 Paradise Road, Richmond, Surrey, TW9 1SR

A REGENCY GENTLEMAN'S PASSION © 2015 Harlequin Books S.A.

Valiant Soldier, Beautiful Enemy © 2011 Diane Perkins
A Not So Respectable Gentleman? © 2012 Diane Perkins

ISBN: 978-0-263-91763-5

052-1115

Harlequin (UK) policy is to use papers that are natural, renewable and recyclable products and made from wood grown in sustainable forests. The logging and manufacturing processes conform to the legal environmental regulations of the country of origin.

Printed and bound
by CPI Group (UK) Ltd, Croydon, CR0 4YY

Valiant Soldier, Beautiful Enemy

DIANE GASTON

Diane Gaston always said that if she were not a mental health social worker, she'd want to be a romance novelist, writing the historical romances she loved to read. When this dream came true, she discovered a whole new world of friends and happy endings. Diane lives in Virginia, near Washington DC, with her husband and three very ordinary housecats. She loves to hear from readers! Contact her at www.dianegaston.com or on Facebook or Twitter.

Prologue

Badajoz, Spain—1812

A woman's scream pierced the night.

Countless screams had reached Captain Gabriel Deane's ears this night, amidst shattering glass, roaring flames and shouts of soldiers run amok. The siege of Badajoz had ended and the pillaging had begun.

The marauding soldiers were not the French, not the enemy known to live off the bounty of the vanquished. These were British soldiers, Gabe's compatriots, prowling through the city like savage beasts, plundering, killing, raping. A false rumour saying Wellington would permit the plundering had sparked the violence.

Gabe and his lieutenant, Allan Landon, had been ordered into this cauldron, but not to stop the rioting. Their task was to find one man.

Edwin Tranville.

Edwin's father, General Tranville, had ordered them to find his son, who'd foolishly joined the marauders. Once inside the city Gabe and Landon had enough to do to save their own skins from drunken men in the throes of a bloodlust that refused to be slaked.

The scream sounded again, not distant like the other helpless cries of innocent women and children—this woman's cry was near.

They ran in the direction of the sound. A shot rang out and two soldiers dashed from an alley, almost colliding with them. Gabe and Landon turned into the alley and emerged in a courtyard illuminated by flames shooting from a burning building nearby.

A woman stood over a cowering figure wearing the uniform of a British Officer. She raised a knife and prepared to plunge its blade into the British officer's back.

Gabe seized her from behind and wrenched the knife from her grasp. "Oh, no, you don't, *señora*." She was not in need of rescue after all.

"She tried to kill me!" The British officer, covering his face with bloody hands, attempted to stand, but collapsed in a heap on the cobblestones.

At that moment another man stepped into the light. Lieutenant Landon swung around, pistol ready to fire.

"Wait." The man raised his hands. "I am Ensign Vernon of the East Essex." He gestured to the unconscious officer. "He was trying to kill the boy. And he attempted to rape the woman. I saw the whole thing. He and two others. The others ran."

The two men who passed them? If so, it was too late to pursue them.

"The boy?" Gabe glanced around. What boy? He saw only the woman and the red-coated officer she was about to kill. And nearby the body of a French soldier, pooled in blood.

Gabe kept a grip on the woman and used his foot

to roll over her intended victim. The man's face was gashed from temple to chin, but Gabe immediately recognised him.

He glanced up. "Good God, Landon, do you see who this is?"

Ensign Vernon answered instead. "Edwin Tranville." His voice filled with disgust. "General Tranville's son."

"Edwin Tranville," Gabriel agreed. They'd found him after all.

"The bloody bastard," Landon spat.

Vernon nodded in agreement. "He is drunk."

When was Edwin not drunk? Gabe thought.

Another figure suddenly sprang from the shadows and Landon almost fired his pistol at him.

The ensign stopped him. "Do not shoot. It is the boy."

A boy, not more than twelve years of age, flung himself atop the body of the French soldier.

"Papa!" the boy cried.

"Non, non, non, Claude." The woman strained against Gabe's grip. He released her and she ran to her son.

"Good God, they are French." Not Spanish citizens of Badajoz. A French family trying to escape. What the devil had the Frenchman been thinking, putting his family in such danger? Gabe had no patience for men who took wives and children to war.

He knelt next to the body and placed his fingers on the man's throat. "He's dead."

The woman looked up at him. *"Mon mari."* Her husband.

Gabe drew in a sharp breath.

She was lovely. Even filled with great anguish, she was lovely. Hair as dark as a Spaniard's, but with skin as fair as the very finest linen. Her eyes, their colour obscured in the dim light, were large and wide with emotion.

Gabe's insides twisted in an anger that radiated clear to his fingertips. Had Edwin killed this man in front of his family? Had he tried to kill the boy and rape the woman, as the ensign said? What had the two other men done to her before it had been Edwin's turn?

The boy cried, *"Papa! Papa! Réveillez!"*

"Il est mort, Claude." Her tone, so low and soft, evoked a memory of Gabe's own mother soothing one of his brothers or sisters.

Fists clenched, Gabe rose and strode back to Edwin, ready to kick him into a bloody pulp. He stopped himself.

Edwin rolled over again and curled into a ball, whimpering.

Gabe turned his gaze to Ensign Vernon and his voice trembled with anger. "Did Edwin kill him?" He pointed to the dead French soldier.

The ensign shook his head. "I did not see."

"What will happen to her now?" Gabe spoke more to himself than to the others.

The woman pressed her son against her bosom, trying to comfort him, while shouts sounded nearby.

Gabe straightened. "We must get them out of here." He gestured to his lieutenant. "Landon, take Tranville back to camp. Ensign, I'll need your help."

"You will not turn her in?" Landon looked aghast.

"Of course not," he snapped. "I'm going to find her a safe place to stay. Maybe a church. Or somewhere." He peered at Landon and at Ensign Vernon. "We say nothing of this. Agreed?"

Landon glared at him and pointed to Edwin. "He ought to hang for this."

Gabe could not agree more, but over fifteen years in the army had taught him to be practical. He doubted any of the soldiers would face a hanging. Wellington needed them too much. General Tranville would certainly take no chances with his son's life and reputation. Gabe and Landon needed to protect themselves lest Tranville retaliate.

More importantly, Gabe needed to protect this woman.

"He is the general's son." His tone brooked no argument. "If we report his crime, the general will have our necks, not Edwin's." He tilted his head towards the woman. "He may even come after her and the boy." The captain looked down at the now-insensible man who had caused all this grief. "This bastard is so drunk he may not even know what he did. He won't tell."

"Drink is no excuse—" Landon began. He broke off and, after several seconds, nodded. "Very well. We say nothing."

The captain turned to Vernon. "Do I have your word, Ensign?"

"You do, sir," the ensign readily agreed.

Glass shattered nearby and the roof of the burning building collapsed, sending sparks high into the air.

"We must hurry." Gabe paused only long enough to extend a handshake to the ensign. "I am Captain Deane. That is Lieutenant Landon." He turned to the woman and her son. "Is there a church nearby?" His hand flew to his forehead. "Deuce. What is the French word for church?" He tapped his brow. "*Église?* Is that the word? *Église?*"

"*Non.* No church, *capitaine,*" the woman replied. "My…my *maison*—my house. Come."

"You speak English, *madame?*"

"*Oui, un peu*—a little."

Landon threw Edwin over his shoulder.

"Take care," Gabe said to him.

Landon gave a curt nod before trudging off in the direction they had come.

Gabe turned to the ensign. "I want you to come with me." He looked over at the Frenchman's body. "We will have to leave him here."

"Yes, sir."

The woman gazed at her husband, her posture taut as if she felt pulled back to his side. Gabe's heart bled for her. She put an arm around her son, who protested against leaving his father, and Gabe felt their struggle as if it were his own.

"Come," she finally said, gesturing for them to follow her.

They made their way through the alley again and down a narrow street.

"*Ma maison,*" she whispered, pointing to a wooden door that stood ajar.

Gabe signalled them to remain where they were. He entered the house.

Light from nearby fires illuminated the inside enough for him to see the contents of a home broken and strewn across the floor: legs from a chair, shards of crockery, scattered papers, items that had once formed the essence of everyday life. He searched the large room to be certain no one hid there. He continued into a small kitchen and a bedroom, both thoroughly ransacked.

He walked back to the front door. "No one is here."

The ensign escorted the mother and son through the doorway. The woman's hand flew to cover her mouth as her eyes darted over the shambles of what had once been her life. Her son buried his face into her side. She held him close as she picked her way through the rubble towards the kitchen.

Determined to make her as comfortable as possible, Gabe strode into the bedroom and pulled the remains of the mattress into the large room, clearing a space for it in the corner. He found a blanket, half-shredded, and carried it to the mattress.

The woman emerged from the kitchen and handed him water in a chipped cup. The boy gripped her skirt, like a younger, frightened child.

He smiled his thanks. As he took the cup, his fingertips grazed her hand and his senses flared at the contact. He gulped down the water and handed her back the cup. "The—the *Anglais,* did they hurt you?" What was the French word? *"Violate? Moleste?"*

Her long graceful fingers gripped the cup. *"Non. Ils m'ont pas molester."*

He nodded, understanding her meaning. She had not been raped. Thank God.

"Can you keep watch?" he asked Ensign Vernon. "I'll sleep for an hour or so and relieve you." He'd not slept since the siege began, over twenty-four hours before.

"Yes, sir," the ensign replied.

They blocked the door with a barricade of broken furniture. The ensign found the remnants of a wooden chair with the seat and legs intact. He placed it at the window to keep watch.

The mother and child curled up together on the mattress. Gabe slid to the floor, his back against the wall. He glanced over at her and her gaze met his for one long moment as intense as an embrace.

Gabe was shaken by her effect on him. It did him no credit to be so attracted to her, not with the terror she'd just been through.

Perhaps he was merely moved by her devotion to her child, how she held him, how she gazed upon him. Gabe had often watched his own mother tend as lovingly to his little sisters.

Or maybe her devotion to her son touched some deep yearning within him. The girls had come one after the other after Gabe was born, and he had often been left in the company of his older brothers, struggling to keep up.

What the devil was he musing about? He never needed to be the fussed over like his sisters. Much better to be toughened by the rough-housing of boys.

Gabe forced himself to close his eyes. He needed sleep. After sleeping an hour or two, he'd be thinking like a soldier again.

The sounds of looting and pillaging continued, but it was the woman's voice, softly murmuring comfort to her son, that finally lulled Gabe to sleep.

The carnage lasted two more days. Gabe, Ensign Vernon and the mother and son remained in the relative safety of her ransacked home, even though the forced inactivity strained Gabe's nerves. He'd have preferred fighting his way through the town to this idleness.

His needs were inconsequential, however. The woman and child must be safeguarded.

What little food they could salvage went to the boy, who was hungry all the time. Ensign Vernon occupied the time by drawing. Some sketches he kept private. Some fanciful pictures of animals and such he gave to the boy in an attempt to amuse him. The boy merely stared at them blankly, spending most of his time at his mother's side, watching Gabe and Vernon with eyes both angry and wary.

None of them spoke much. Gabe could count on his fingers how many words he and the woman spoke to each other. Still, she remained at the centre of his existence. There was no sound she made, no gesture or expression he did not notice, and the empty hours of waiting did not diminish his resolve to make certain she and her son reached safety.

On the third day it was clear order had been restored. Gabe led them out, and the woman only looked back once at what had been her home. Outside, the air smelled of smoke and burnt wood, but the only sound of soldiers was the rhythm of a disciplined march.

They walked to the city's centre where Gabe supposed the army's headquarters would be found. There Gabe was told to what building other French civilians had been taken. They found the correct building, but Gabe hesitated before taking the mother and son inside. It was difficult to leave her fate to strangers. In an odd way he did not understand, she had become more important to him than anything else. Still, what choice did he have?

"We should go in," he told her.

Ensign Vernon said, "I will remain here, sir, if that is agreeable to you."

"As you wish," Gabe replied.

"Goodbye, *madame*." The ensign stepped away.

Looking frightened but resigned, she merely nodded.

Gabe escorted her and her son through the door to the end of a hallway where two soldiers stood guard. The room they guarded was bare of furniture except one table and a chair, on which a British officer sat. In the room were about twenty people, older men, once

French officials perhaps, and other women and children whose families had been destroyed.

Gabe spoke to the British officer, explaining the woman's circumstance to him.

"What happens to them?" he asked the man.

The officer's answer was curt. "The women and children will be sent back to France, if they have money for the passage."

Gabe stepped away and fished in an inside pocket of his uniform, pulling out a purse full of coin, nearly all he possessed. Glancing around to make certain no one noticed, he pressed the purse into the woman's hands. "You will need this."

Her eyes widened as her fingers closed around the small leather bag. *"Capitaine—"*

He pressed her hand. "No argument. No—" he pronounced it the French way "—*argument.*"

She closed her other hand around his and the power of her gaze tugged at something deep inside him. It was inexplicable, but saying goodbye felt like losing a part of himself.

He did not even know her name.

He pulled his hand from hers and pointed to himself. "Gabriel Deane." If she needed him, she would at least know his name.

"Gabriel," she whispered, speaking his name with the beauty of her French accent. *"Merci. Que Dieu vous bénisse."*

His brows knit in confusion. He'd forgotten most of the French he'd learned in school.

She struggled for words. *"Dieu*...God..." She crossed herself. *"Bénisse."*

"Bless?" he guessed.

She nodded.

He forced himself to take a step back. *"Au revoir, madame."*

Clenching his teeth, Gabe turned and started for the door before he did something foolish. Like kiss her. Or leave with her. She was a stranger, nothing more, important only in his fantasies. Not in reality.

"Gabriel!"

He halted.

She ran to him.

She placed both hands on his cheeks and pulled his head down to kiss him on the lips. With her face still inches from his, she whispered, "My name is Emmaline Mableau."

He was afraid to speak for fear of betraying the swirling emotions inside him. An intense surge of longing enveloped him.

He desired her as a man desires a woman. It was foolish beyond everything. Dishonourable, as well, since she'd just lost her husband to hands not unlike his own.

He met her gaze and held it a moment before fleeing out the door.

But his thoughts repeated, over and over—*Emmaline Mableau.*

Chapter One

Brussels, Belgium—May 1815

Emmaline Mableau!

Gabe's heart pounded when he caught a glimpse of the woman from whom he'd parted three years before. Carrying a package, she walked briskly through the narrow Brussels streets. It was Emmaline Mableau, he was convinced.

Or very nearly convinced.

He'd always imagined her back in France, living in some small village, with parents...or a new husband.

But here she was, in Belgium.

Brussels had many French people, so it was certainly possible for her to reside here. Twenty years of French rule had only ended the year before when Napoleon was defeated.

Defeated for the first time, Gabe meant. *L'Empereur* had escaped from his exile on Elba. He'd raised an army and was now on the march to regain his empire. Gabe's regiment, the Royal Scots, was part of Wellington's

Allied Army and would soon cross swords with Napoleon's forces again.

Many of the English aristocracy had poured into Brussels after the treaty, fleeing the high prices in England, looking for elegant living at little cost. Even so, Brussels remained primed for French rule, as if the inhabitants expected Napoleon to walk its streets any day. Nearly everyone in the city spoke French. Shop signs were in French. The hotel where Gabe was billeted had a French name. *Hôtel de Flandre.*

Gabe had risen early to stretch his legs in the brisk morning air. He had few official duties at present, so spent his days exploring the city beyond the Parc de Brussels and the cathedral. Perhaps there was more of the cloth merchant's son in him than he'd realised, because he liked best to walk the narrow streets lined with shops.

He'd spied Emmaline Mableau as he descended the hill to reach that part of Brussels. She'd been rushing past shopkeepers who were just raising their shutters and opening their doors. Gabe bolted down the hill to follow her, getting only quick glimpses of her as he tried to catch up to her.

He might be mistaken about her being Emmaline Mableau. It might have been a mere trick of the eye and the fact that he often thought of her that made him believe the Belgian woman was she.

But he was determined to know for certain.

She turned a corner and he picked up his pace, fearing he'd lose sight of her. Near the end of the row of shops he glimpsed a flutter of skirts, a woman entering a doorway. His heart beat faster. That had to have been her. No one left on the street looked like her.

He slowed his pace as he approached where she

had disappeared, carefully determining which store she'd entered. The sign above the door read *Magasin de Lacet.* The shutters were open and pieces of lace draped over tables could be seen though the windows.

A lace shop.

He opened the door and crossed the threshold, removing his shako as he entered the shop.

He was surrounded by white. White lace ribbons of various widths and patterns draped over lines strung across the length of the shop. Tables stacked with white lace cloth, lace-edged handkerchiefs and lace caps. White lace curtains covering the walls. The distinct scent of lavender mixed with the scent of linen, a scent that took him back in time to hefting huge bolts of cloth in his father's warehouse.

Through the gently fluttering lace ribbons, he spied the woman emerging from a room at the back of the shop, her face still obscured. With her back to him, she folded squares of intricate lace that must have taken some woman countless hours to tat.

Taking a deep breath, he walked slowly towards her. "Madame Mableau?"

Still holding the lace in her fingers and startled at the sound of a man's voice, Emmaline turned. And gasped.

"Mon Dieu!"

She recognised him instantly, the *capitaine* whose presence in Badajoz had kept her sane when all seemed lost. She'd tried to forget those desolate days in the Spanish city, although she'd never entirely banished the memory of Gabriel Deane. His brown eyes, watchful then, were now reticent, but his jaw remained as strong, his lips expressive, his hair as dark and unruly.

"Madame." He bowed. "Do you remember me? I saw you from afar. I was not certain it was you."

She could only stare. He seemed to fill the space, his scarlet coat a splash of vibrancy in the white lace-filled room. It seemed as if no mere shop could be large enough to contain his presence. He'd likewise commanded space in Badajoz, just as he commanded everything else. Tall and powerfully built, he had filled those terrible, despairing days, keeping them safe. Giving them hope.

"Pardon," he said. "I forgot. You speak only a little English. *Un peu Anglais.*"

She smiled. She'd spoken those words to him in Badajoz.

She held up a hand. "I do remember you, *naturellement.*" She had never dreamed she would see him again, however. "I—I speak a little more English now. It is necessary. So many English people in Brussels." She snapped her mouth closed. She'd been babbling.

"You are well, I hope?" His thick, dark brows knit and his gaze swept over her.

"I am very well." Except she could not breathe at the moment and her legs seemed too weak to hold her upright, but that was his effect on her, not malaise.

His features relaxed. "And your son?"

She lowered her eyes. "Claude was well last I saw him."

He fell silent, as if he realised her answer hid something she did not wish to disclose. Finally he spoke again. "I thought you would be in France."

She shrugged. "My aunt lives here. This is her shop. She needed help and we needed a home. *Vraiment,* Belgium is a better place to—how do you say?—to rear Claude."

She'd believed living in Belgium would insulate Claude from the patriotic fervour Napoleon had generated, especially in her own family.

She'd been wrong.

Gabriel gazed into her eyes. "I see." A concerned look came over his face. "I hope your journey from Spain was not too difficult."

It was all so long ago and fraught with fear at every step, but there had been no more attacks on her person, no need for Claude to risk his life for her.

She shivered. "We were taken to Lisbon. From there we gained passage on a ship to San Sebastian and then another to France."

She'd had money stitched into her clothing, but without the *capitaine's* purse she would not have had enough for both the passage and the bribes required to secure the passage. What would have been their fate without his money?

The money.

Emmaline suddenly understood why the captain had come to her shop. "I will pay you back the money. If you return tomorrow, I will give it to you." It would take all her savings, but she owed him more than that.

"The money means nothing to me." His eyes flashed with pain.

She'd offended him. Her cheeks burned. "I beg your pardon, Gabriel."

He almost smiled. "You remembered my name."

She could not help but smile back at him. "You remembered mine."

"I could not forget you, Emmaline Mableau." His voice turned low and seemed to reach inside her and wrap itself around her heart.

Everything blurred except him. His visage was so

clear to her she fancied she could see every whisker on his face, although he must have shaved that morning. Her mind flashed back to those three days in Badajoz, his unshaven skin giving him the appearance of a rogue, a pirate, a libertine. Even in her despair she'd wondered how his beard would feel against her fingertips. Against her cheek.

But in those few days she'd welcomed any thought that strayed from the horror of seeing her husband killed and hearing her son's anguished cry as his father fell on to the hard stones of the cobbled street.

He blinked and averted his gaze. "Perhaps I should not have come here."

Impulsively she touched his arm. "*Non, non,* Gabriel. I am happy to see you. It is a surprise, no?"

The shop door opened and two ladies entered. One loudly declared in English, "Oh, what a lovely shop. I've never seen so much lace!"

These were precisely the sort of customers for whom Emmaline had improved her English. The numbers of English ladies coming to Brussels to spend their money kept increasing since the war had ended.

If it had ended.

The English soldiers were in Brussels because it was said there would be a big battle with Napoleon. No doubt Gabriel had come to fight in it.

The English ladies cast curious glances towards the tall, handsome officer who must have been an incongruous sight amidst all the delicate lace.

"I should leave," he murmured to Emmaline.

His voice made her knees weaken again. She did not wish to lose him again so soon.

He nodded curtly. "I am pleased to know you are well." He stepped back.

He was going to leave!

"*Un moment,* Gabriel," she said hurriedly. "I—I would ask you to eat dinner with me, but I have nothing to serve you. Only bread and cheese."

His eyes captured hers and her chest ached as if all the breath was squeezed out of her. "I am fond of bread and cheese."

She felt almost giddy. "I will close the shop at seven. Will you come back and eat bread and cheese with me?"

Her aunt would have the *apoplexie* if she knew Emmaline intended to entertain a British officer. But with any luck Tante Voletta would never know.

"Will you come, Gabriel?" she breathed.

His expression remained solemn. "I will return at seven." He bowed and quickly strode out of the shop, the English ladies following him with their eyes.

When the door closed behind him, both ladies turned to stare at Emmaline.

She forced herself to smile at them and behave as though nothing of great importance had happened.

"Good morning, *mesdames.*" She curtsied. "Please tell me if I may offer assistance."

They nodded, still gaping, before they turned their backs and whispered to each other while they pretended to examine the lace caps on a nearby table.

Emmaline returned to folding the square of lace she'd held since Gabriel first spoke to her.

It was absurd to experience a *frisson* of excitement at merely speaking to a man. It certainly had not happened with any other. In fact, since her husband's death she'd made it a point to avoid such attention.

She buried her face in the piece of lace and remembered that terrible night. The shouts and screams and roar of buildings afire sounded in her ears again. Her body trembled as once again she smelled the blood and smoke and the sweat of men.

She lifted her head from that dark place to the bright, clean white of the shop. She ought to have forgiven her husband for taking her and their son to Spain, but such generosity of spirit eluded her. Remy's selfishness had led them into the trauma and horror that was Badajoz.

Emmaline shook her head. No, it was not Remy she could not forgive, but herself. She should have defied him. She should have refused when he insisted, *I will not be separated from my son.*

She should have taken his yelling, raging and threatening. She should have risked the back of his hand and defied him. If she had refused to accompany him, Remy might still be alive and Claude would have no reason to be consumed with hatred.

How would Claude feel about his mother inviting a British officer to sup with her? To even speak to Gabriel Deane would be a betrayal in Claude's eyes. Claude's hatred encompassed everything *Anglais,* and would even include the man who'd protected them and brought them to safety.

But neither her aunt nor Claude would know of her sharing dinner with Gabriel Deane, so she was determined not to worry over it.

She was merely paying him back for his kindness to them, Emmaline told herself. That was the reason she'd invited him to dinner.

The only reason.

The evening was fine, warm and clear as befitted late May. Gabe breathed in the fresh air and walked at a pace as rapid as when he'd followed Emmaline that morning. He was too excited, too full of an anticipation he had no right to feel.

He'd had his share of women, as a soldier might, short-lived trysts, pleasant, but meaning very little to him. For any of those women, he could not remember feeling this acute sense of expectancy.

He forced himself to slow down, to calm himself and become more reasonable. It was curiosity about how she'd fared since Badajoz that had led him to accept her invitation. The time they'd shared made him feel attached to her and to her son. He merely wanted to ensure that Emmaline was happy.

Gabriel groaned. He ought not think of her as Emmaline. It conveyed an intimacy he had no right to assume.

Except she had called him by his given name, he remembered. To hear her say *Gabriel* was like listening to music.

He increased his pace again.

As he approached the shop door, he halted, damping down his emotions one more time. When his head was as steady as his hand he turned the knob and opened the shop door.

Emmaline stood with a customer where the ribbons of lace hung on a line. She glanced over at him when he entered.

The customer was another English lady, like the two who had come to the shop that morning. This lady, very prosperously dressed, loudly haggled over the price of a piece of lace. The difference between Emmaline's price and what the woman wanted to pay was a mere pittance.

Give her the full price, Gabe wanted to say to the customer. He suspected Emmaline needed the money more than the lady did.

"Très bien, madame," Emmaline said with a resigned air. She accepted the lower price.

Gabe moved to a corner to wait while Emmaline wrapped the lace in paper and tied it with string. As the lady bustled out she gave him a quick assessing glance, pursing her lips at him.

Had that been a look of disapproval? She knew nothing of his reasons for being in the shop. Could a soldier not be in a woman's shop without censure? This lady's London notions had no place here.

Gabe stepped forwards.

Emmaline smiled, but averted her gaze. "I will be ready in a *minute.* I need to close up the shop."

"Tell me what to do and I'll assist you." Better for him to be occupied than merely watching her every move.

"Close the shutters on the windows, if you please?" She straightened the items on the tables.

When Gabe secured the shutters, the light in the shop turned dim, lit only by a small lamp in the back of the store. The white lace, so bright in the morning sun, now took on soft shades of lavender and grey. He watched Emmaline glide from table to table, refolding the items, and felt as if they were in a dream.

She worked her way to the shop door, taking a key from her pocket and turning it in the lock. *"C'est fait!"* she said. "I am finished. Come with me."

She led him to the back of the shop, picking up her cash box and tucking it under her arm. She lit a candle from the lamp before extinguishing it. "We go out the back door."

Gabe took the cash box from her. "I will carry it for you."

He followed her through the curtain to an area just as neat and orderly as the front of the shop.

Lifting the candle higher, she showed him a stairway. "*Ma tante*—my aunt—lives above the shop, but she is visiting. Some of the women who make the lace live in the country; my aunt visits them sometimes to buy the lace."

Gabe hoped her aunt would not become caught in the army's march into France. Any day now he expected the Allied Army to be given the order to march against Napoleon.

"Where is your son?" Gabe asked her. "Is he at school?" The boy could not be more than fifteen, if Gabe was recalling correctly, the proper age to still be away at school.

She bowed her head. *"Non."*

Whenever he mentioned her son her expression turned bleak.

Behind the shop was a small yard shared by the other shops and, within a few yards, another stone building, two storeys, with window boxes full of colourful flowers.

She unlocked the door. *"Ma maison."*

The contrast between this place and her home in Badajoz could not have been more extreme. The home in Badajoz had been marred by chaos and destruction. This home was pleasant and orderly and welcoming. As in Badajoz, Gabe stepped into one open room, but this one was neatly organised into an area for sitting and one for dining, with what appeared to be a small galley kitchen through a door at the far end.

Emmaline lit one lamp, then another, and the room seemed to come to life. A colourful carpet covered a polished wooden floor. A red upholstered sofa, flanked by two small tables and two adjacent chairs, faced a fireplace with a mantel painted white. All the tables were covered with white lace tablecloths and held vases of brightly hued flowers.

"Come in, Gabriel," she said. "I will open the windows."

Gabe closed the door behind him and took a few steps into the room.

It was even smaller than the tiny cottage his uncle lived in, but had the same warm, inviting feel. Uncle Will managed a hill farm in Lancashire and some of Gabe's happiest moments had been spent working beside his uncle, the least prosperous of the Deane family. Gabe was overcome with nostalgia for those days. And guilt. He'd not written to his uncle in years.

Emmaline turned away from the window to see him still glancing around the room. "It is small, but we did not need more."

It seemed...safe. After Badajoz, she deserved a safe place. "It is pleasant."

She lifted her shoulder as if taking his words as disapproval.

He wanted to explain that he liked the place too much, but that would be even more difficult to put into words.

She took the cash box from his hands and put it in a locking cabinet. "I regret so much that I do not have a meal sufficient for you. I do not cook much. It is only for me."

Meaning her son was not with her, he imagined. "No pardon necessary, *madame*." Besides, he had not accepted her invitation because of what food would be served.

"Then please sit and I will make it ready."

Gabe sat at the table, facing the kitchen so he could watch her.

She placed some glasses and a wine bottle on the table. "It is French wine. I hope you do not mind."

He glanced up at her. "The British pay smugglers a great deal for French wine. I dare say it is a luxury."

Her eyes widened. *"C'est vrai?* I did not know that. I think my wine may not be so fine."

She poured wine into the two glasses and went back to the kitchen to bring two plates, lace-edged linen napkins and cutlery. A moment later she brought a variety of cheeses on a wooden cutting board, a bowl of strawberries and another board with a loaf of bread.

"We may each cut our own, no?" She gestured for him to select his cheese while she cut herself a piece of bread.

For such simple fare, it tasted better than any meal he'd eaten in months. He asked her about her travel from Badajoz and was pleased that the trip seemed free of the terrible trauma she and her son had previously endured. She asked him about the battles he'd fought since Badajoz and what he'd done in the very brief peace.

The conversation flowed easily, adding to the comfortable feel of the surroundings. Gabe kept their wine glasses filled and soon felt as relaxed as if he'd always sat across the table from her for his evening meal.

When they'd eaten their fill, she took their plates to the kitchen area. Gabe rose to carry the other dishes, reaching around her to place them in the sink.

She turned and brushed against his arm. "Thank you, Gabriel."

Her accidental touch fired his senses. The scent of her hair filled his nostrils, the same lavender scent as in her shop. Her head tilted back to look into his face. She drew in a breath and her cheeks tinged pink.

Had she experienced the same awareness? That they were a man and a woman alone together?

Blood throbbed through his veins and he wanted to bend lower, closer, to taste those slightly parted lips.

She turned back to the sink and worked the pump to fill a kettle with water. "I will make coffee," she said in a determined tone, then immediately apologised. "I am sorry I do not have tea."

"Coffee will do nicely." Gabe stepped away, still pulsating with arousal. He watched her light a fire in a tiny stove and fill a coffee pot with water and coffee. She placed the pot on top of the stove.

"Shall we sit?" She gestured to the red sofa.

Would she sit with him on the sofa? He might not be able to resist taking her in his arms if she did.

The coffee eventually boiled. She poured it into cups and carried the tray to a table placed in front of the sofa. Instead of sitting beside him, she chose a small adjacent chair and asked him how he liked his coffee.

He could barely remember. "Milk and a little sugar."

While she stirred his coffee, he absently rubbed his finger on the lace cloth atop the table next to him. His fingers touched a miniature lying face down on the table. He turned it over. It was a portrait of a youth with her dark hair and blue eyes.

"Is this your son?" If so, he'd turned into a fine-looking young fellow, strong and defiant.

She handed him his cup. "Yes. It is Claude." Her eyes glistened and she blinked rapidly.

He felt her distress and lowered his voice to almost a whisper. "What happened to him, Emmaline? Where is he?"

She looked away and wiped her eyes with her fingers. "Nothing happened, you see, but everything…" Her voice trailed off.

He merely watched her.

She finally faced him again with a wan smile. "Claude was so young. He did not—does not—understand war, how men do bad things merely because it is war. Soldiers die in war, but Claude did not comprehend that his father died because he was a soldier—"

Gabe interrupted her. "Your husband died because our men were lost to all decency."

She held up a hand. "Because of the battle, no? It was a hard siege for the British, my husband said. Remy was killed because of the siege, because of the war."

He leaned forwards. "I must ask you. The man who tried to molest you—did he kill your husband?"

She lowered her head. "*Non.* The others killed my husband. That one stood aside, but his companions told him to violate me."

His gut twisted. "I am sorry, Emmaline. I am so sorry." He wanted even more than before to take her in his arms, this time to comfort her.

He reached out and touched her hand, but quickly withdrew.

"You rescued us, Gabriel," she said. "You gave us money. You must not be sorry. I do not think of it very much any more. And the dreams do not come as often."

He shook his head.

She picked up the miniature portrait of her son and gazed at it. "I told Claude it happened because of war and to try to forget it, but he will not. He blames the *Anglais,* the British. He hates the British. All of them. If he knew you were here, he would want to kill you."

Gabe could not blame Claude. He'd feel the same if he'd watched his family violently destroyed.

"Where is Claude?" he asked again.

A tear slid down her cheek. "He ran away. To join Napoleon. He is not yet sixteen." She looked Gabe directly in the face. "There is to be a big battle, is there not? You will fight in it." Her expression turned anguished. "You will be fighting my son."

Chapter Two

Emmaline's fingers clutched Claude's miniature as she fought tears.

"I did not mean to say that to you." The pain about her son was too sharp, too personal.

"Emmaline." Gabriel's voice turned caring.

She tried to ward off his concern. "I am merely afraid for him. It is a mother's place to worry, no?" She placed the small portrait on the table and picked up her cup. "Please, drink your coffee."

He lifted his cup, but she was aware of him watching her. She hoped she could fool him into thinking she was not distressed, that she would be able to pretend she was not shaken.

He put down his cup. "Most soldiers survive a battle," he told her in a reassuring voice. "And many are not even called to fight. In Badajoz your son showed himself to be an intelligent and brave boy. There is a good chance he will avoid harm."

She flinched with the memory. "In Badajoz he was foolish. He should have hidden himself. Instead, he was almost killed." Her anguish rose. "The soldiers will place him in the front ranks. When my husband was alive the men used to talk of it. They put the young ones, the ones with no experience, in the front."

He cast his eyes down. "Then I do not know what to say to comfort you."

That he even wished to comfort her brought back her tears. She blinked them away. "There is no comfort. I wait and worry and pray."

He rubbed his face and stood. "It is late and I should leave."

"Do not leave yet," she cried, then covered her mouth, shocked at herself for blurting this out.

He walked to the door. "I may be facing your son in battle, Emmaline. How can you bear my company?"

She rose and hurried to block his way. "I am sorry I spoke about Claude. I did not have the—the *intention* to tell you. Please do not leave me."

He gazed down at her. "Why do you wish me to stay?"

She covered her face with her hands, ashamed, but unable to stop. "I do not want to be alone!"

Strong arms engulfed her and she was pressed against him, enveloped in his warmth, comforted by the beating of his heart. Her tears flowed.

Claude had run off months ago and, as Brussels filled with British soldiers, the reality of his possible fate had eaten away at her. Her aunt and their small circle of friends cheered Claude's patriotism, but Emmaline knew it was revenge, not patriotism, that drove Claude. She'd kept her fears hidden until this moment.

How foolish it was to burden Gabriel with her woes. But his arms were so comforting. He demanded nothing, merely held her close while she wept for this terrible twist of fate.

Finally the tears slowed and she mustered the strength to pull away. He handed her a clean handkerchief from his pocket, warmed by his body.

She wiped her eyes. "I will launder this for you."

"It does not matter," he murmured.

She dared to glance up into his kind eyes and saw only concern shining in them.

"I am recovered," she assured him. New tears formed and she wiped them with his handkerchief. "Do not worry over me."

He stood very still and solid, as if she indeed could lean on him.

"I will stay if you wish me to," he said.

She took in a breath.

She ought to say no. She ought to brush him away and tell him she needed no one to be with her.

Instead, she whispered, "Please stay, Gabriel."

Something softened in his face and he reached out his hand to her. "I will help you with the dishes."

Her tension eased. He offered what she needed most at the moment: ordinary companionship.

They gathered the cups and coffee pot and carried them to the little sink. She filled the kettle with water and put it on the stove again. While it heated he took the tablecloth to the door to shake out. She dampened a cloth and wiped the table and the kitchen. When the water was hot, Gabriel removed his coat and pushed up his shirt sleeves. He washed and rinsed. She dried and put the dishes away.

What man had ever helped her do dishes? Not her husband, for certain. She'd not even required it of

Claude. But it somehow seemed fitting that Gabriel should help her.

When they finished, he wiped his hands on the towel and reached for his coat.

Her anxieties returned. "You will stay longer?"

He gazed at her. "Longer? Are you certain?"

Suddenly she knew precisely what she was asking of him and it was not merely to keep her from being alone. "I am certain."

She picked up a candle and took his hand in hers, leading him towards the stairway. There were two small rooms above stairs. She kept the door to Claude's bedroom closed so she would not feel its emptiness. She led Gabriel into the other room, her bedroom, her excitement building. She kicked off her shoes and climbed atop the bed.

He held back, gazing at her.

How much more permission did she need to give?

She'd vowed to have no more of men since her husband's death. Claude could be her only concern. He needed to release the past and see that he had his whole life ahead of him.

If Napoleon did not get him killed in the battle, that is.

Until Claude returned to her, she could do nothing, but if God saw fit to spare him in the battle, Emmaline had vowed to devote her life to restoring her son's happiness.

But Claude was not here now and Gabriel would not remain in Brussels for long. The British army would march away to face Napoleon; both Claude and Gabriel would be gone. What harm could there be in enjoying this man's company? In making love with him? Many widows had affairs. Why not enjoy the passion Gabriel's heated looks promised?

"Come, Gabriel," she whispered.

He walked to the edge of the bed and she met him on her knees, her face nearly level with his. He stroked her face with a gentle hand, his touch so tender it made her want to weep again.

"I did not expect this," he murmured.

"I did not, as well," she added. "But it—it feels *inévitable,* no?"

"Inevitable." His fingers moved to the sensitive skin of her neck, still as gentle as if she were as delicate as the finest lace.

She undid the buttons on his waistcoat and flattened her palms against his chest, sliding them up to his neck.

She pressed her fingers against his smooth cheek. "You shaved for dinner, *n'est-ce pas?*" Her hands moved to the back of his neck where his hair curled against her fingers.

He leaned closer to her and touched his lips to hers.

Her husband's kisses had been demanding and possessive. Gabriel offered his lips like a gift for her to open or refuse, as she wished.

She parted her lips and tasted him with her tongue.

He responded, giving her all that she could wish. She felt giddy with delight and pressed herself against him, feeling the bulge of his manhood through his trousers.

"Mon Dieu," she sighed when his lips left hers.

He stepped away. "Do you wish me to stop?"

"No!" she cried. "I wish you to commence."

He smiled. *"Très bien, madame."*

She peered at him. "You speak French now?"

"Un peu," he replied.

She laughed and it felt good. It had been so long

since she had laughed. "We shall make love together, Gabriel."

He grinned. *"Très bien."*

She unhooked the bodice of her dress and pulled the garment over her head. While Gabriel removed his boots and stockings, she made quick work of removing her corset, easily done because it fastened in the front. She tossed it aside. Now wearing only her chemise, she started removing the pins from her hair. As it tumbled down her back, she looked up.

He stood before her naked and aroused. His was a soldier's body, muscles hardened by campaign, skin scarred from battle.

Still kneeling on the bed, she reached out and touched a scar across his abdomen, caused by the slash of a sword, perhaps.

He held her hand against his skin. "It looks worse than it was."

"You have so many." Some were faint, others distinct.

He shrugged. "I have been in the army for over eighteen years."

Her husband would have been in longer, had he lived. He'd been rising steadily in rank; perhaps he would have been one of Napoleon's generals, preparing for this battle, had he lived.

She gave herself a mental shake for thinking of Remy, even though he'd been the only man with whom she'd ever shared her bed.

Until now.

A flush swept over her, as unexpected as it was intense. "Come to me, Gabriel," she rasped.

He joined her on the bed, kneeling in front of her and wrapping his arms around her, holding her close. His lips found hers once more.

He swept his hand through her hair. "So lovely." She felt the warmth of his breath against her lips.

His hand moved down, caressing her neck, her shoulders. Her breasts. She writhed with the pleasure of it and was impatient to be rid of her chemise. She pulled it up to her waist, but he took the fabric from her and lifted it the rest of the way over her head. With her chemise still bunched in his hands he stared at her, his gaze so intense that she sensed it as tangibly as his touch.

"You are beautiful," he said finally.

She smiled, pleased at his words, and lay against the pillows, eager for what would come next.

But if she expected him to take his pleasure quickly, she was mistaken. He knelt over her, looking as if he were memorising every part of her. His hands, still gentle and reverent, caressed her skin. When his palms grazed her nipples, the sensation shot straight to her most feminine place.

Slowly his hand travelled the same path, but stopped short of where her body now throbbed for him. Instead, he stroked the inside of her thighs, so teasingly near.

A sound, half-pleasure, half-frustration, escaped her lips.

Finally he touched her. His fingers explored her flesh, now moist for him. The miracle of sensation his fingers created built her need to an intensity she thought she could not bear a moment longer.

He bent down and kissed her lips again, his tongue freely tasting her now. Her legs parted, ready for him.

She braced for his thrust, a part of lovemaking always painful for her, but he did not force himself inside her. Wonder of wonders, he eased himself inside, a sweet torture of rhythmic stroking until gradually he filled her completely. The need inside her grew even stronger and she moved with him, trying to ease the torment.

More wonders, he seemed to be in complete unison with her, as if he sensed her growing need so he could meet it each step of the way. The sensation created by him was more intense than she had ever experienced. Soon nothing existed for her but her need and the man who would satisfy it.

The intensity still built, speeding her forwards, faster and faster, until suddenly she exploded with sensation inside. Pleasure washed through her, like waves on the shore. His grip on her tightened and he thrust with more force, convulsing as he spilled his seed inside her. For that intense moment, their bodies pressed together, shaking with the shared climax.

Gabe felt the pleasure ebb, making his body suddenly heavy, his mind again able to form coherent thought. He forced himself not to merely collapse on top of her and crush her with his weight. Instead, he eased himself off her to lie at her side.

As soon as he did so she flung her arms across her face. He gently lowered them.

She was weeping.

He felt panicked. "Emmaline, did I injure you?" He could not precisely recall how he might have done so, but during those last moments he'd been consumed by his own drive to completion.

She shook her head. "*Non*. I cannot speak—"

"Forgive me. I did not mean to distress you." He ought not to have made love to her. He'd taken advantage of her grief and worry. "I did not realise…"

She swiped at her eyes and turned on her side to face him. "You did not distress me. How do I say it?" He could feel her search for words. "I never felt *le plaisir* in this way before."

His spirits darkened. "It did not please you."

Tears filled her eyes again, making them sparkle in the candlelight. She cupped her palm against his cheek. "*Tu ne comprends pas.* You do not comprehend. It pleased me more than I can say to you."

Relief washed through him. "I thought I had hurt you." He wrapped his arms around her and held her against him, resting her head against his heart.

Gabe allowed himself to enjoy the comfort of her silky skin against his, their bodies warming each other as cool night air seeped through the window jamb.

She spoke and he felt her voice through his chest as well as hearing it with his ears. "It was not so with my husband. Not so…long. So…much *plaisir.*"

The image of a body in a French uniform flashed into Gabe's mind, the body they had been forced to abandon in Badajoz. Now he'd made love to that man's wife. It seemed unconscionable. "Has there been no other man since your husband?"

"No, Gabriel. Only you."

He drew in a breath, forcing himself to be reasonable. He'd had nothing to do with the Frenchman's death. And three years had passed.

He felt her muscles tense. "Do you have a wife?"

"No." Of that he could easily assure her. He'd never even considered it.

She relaxed again. "*C'est très bien.* I would not like it if you had a wife. I would feel *culpabilité.*"

He laughed inwardly. They were both concerned about feeling the *culpabilité,* the guilt.

They lay quiet again and he twirled a lock of her hair around his fingers.

"It feels agreeable to lie here with you," she said after a time.

Very agreeable, he thought, almost as if he belonged in her bed.

After a moment a thought occurred to him. "Do you need to take care of yourself?"

"Pardon?" She turned her face to him.

"To prevent a baby?" He had no wish to inflict an unwanted baby upon her.

Her expression turned pained. "I do not think I can have more babies. I was only *enceinte* one time. With Claude. Never again."

He held her closer, regretting he'd asked. "Did you wish for more children?"

She took a deep breath and lay her head against his chest again. "More babies would have been very difficult. To accompany my husband, you know."

What kind of fool had her husband been to bring his family to war? Gabe knew how rough it was for soldiers' wives to march long distances heavy with child, or to care for tiny children while a battle raged.

"Did you always follow the drum?" he asked.

She glanced at him. "The drum? I do not comprehend."

"Accompany your husband on campaign," he explained.

"Ah!" Her eyes brightened in understanding. "Not always did I go with him. Not until Claude was walking and talking. My husband did not wish to be parted from his son."

"From Claude?" Not from her?

Had her marriage not been a love match? Gabe could never see the point of marrying unless there was strong devotion between the man and woman, a devotion such as his parents possessed.

Emmaline continued. "My husband was very close to Claude. I think it is why Claude feels so hurt and angry that he died."

"Claude has a right to feel hurt and angry," Gabe insisted.

"But it does not help him, eh?" She trembled.

He held her closer. "Everyone has hardship in their lives to overcome. It will make him stronger."

She looked into his eyes. "What hardship have you had in your life?" She rubbed her hand over the scar on his abdomen. "Besides war?"

"None," he declared. "My father was prosperous, my family healthy."

She nestled against him again. "Tell me about your family."

There was not much to tell. "My father is a cloth merchant, prosperous enough to rear eight children."

"Eight? So many." She looked up at him again. "And are you the oldest? The youngest?"

"I am in the middle," he replied. "First there were four boys and then four girls. I am the last of the boys, but the only one to leave Manchester."

Her brow knitted. "I was like Claude, the only one. I do not know what it would be like to have so many brothers and sisters."

He could hardly remember. "It was noisy, actually. I used to escape whenever I could. I liked most to stay with my uncle. He managed a hill farm. I liked that better than my father's warehouse." His father had never needed him there, not with his older brothers to help out.

"A hill farm?" She looked puzzled.

"A farm with sheep and a few other animals," he explained.

She smiled at him. "You like sheep farming?"

"I did." He thought back to those days, out of doors in the fresh country air, long hours to daydream while watching the flocks graze, or, even better, days filled with hard work during shearing time or when the sheep were lambing.

"Why did you not become a farmer, then?" she asked.

At the time even the open spaces where the sheep grazed seemed too confining to him. "Nelson had just defeated Napoleon's fleet in Egypt. Lancashire seemed too tame a place compared to the likes of Egypt. I asked my father to purchase a commission for me and he did."

"And did you go to Egypt with the army?" Her head rested against his heart.

He shook his head. "No. I was sent to the West Indies."

He remembered the shock of that hellish place, where men died from fevers in great numbers, where he also had become ill and nearly did not recover. When not ill, all his regiment ever did was keep the slaves from revolting. Poor devils. All they'd wanted was to be free men.

He went on. "After that we came to Spain to fight Napoleon's army."

Her muscles tensed. "Napoleon. Bah!"

He moved so they were lying face to face. "You do not revere *L'Empereur?*"

"No." Her eyes narrowed. "He took the men and boys and too many were killed. Too many."

Her distress returned. Gabe changed the subject. "Now I have told you about my life. What of yours?"

She became very still, but held his gaze. "I grew up

in the Revolution. Everyone was afraid all the time, afraid to be on the wrong side, you know? Because you would go to *la guillotine*." She shuddered. "I saw a pretty lady go to the guillotine."

"You witnessed the guillotine?" He was aghast. "You must have been very young."

"*Oui.* My mother hated the Royals, but the pretty lady did not seem so bad to me. She cried for her children at the end."

"My God," he said.

Her gaze drifted and he knew she was seeing it all again.

Gabe felt angry on Emmaline's behalf, angry she should have to endure such a horror.

He lifted her chin with his finger. "You have seen too much."

Her lips trembled and his senses fired with arousal again. He moved closer.

Her breathing accelerated. "I am glad I am here with you."

He looked into her eyes, marvelling at the depth of emotion they conveyed, marvelling that she could remain open and loving in spite of all she'd experienced. A surge of protectiveness flashed through him. He wanted to wipe away all the pain she'd endured. He wanted her to never hurt again.

He placed his lips on hers, thinking he'd never tasted such sweetness. He ran his hand down her back, savouring the feel of her, the outline of her spine, the soft flesh of her buttocks. Parting from her kiss, he gazed upon her, drinking in her beauty with his eyes. The fullness of her breasts, the dusky pink of her nipples, the triangle of dark hair at her genitals.

He touched her neck, so long and slim, and slid his

hand to her breasts. She moaned. Placing her hands on the sides of his head, she guided his lips to where his fingers had been. He took her breast into his mouth and explored her nipple with his tongue, feeling it peak and harden.

Her fingernails scraped his back as he tasted one, then the other breast. She writhed beneath him. Soon he was unable to think of anything but Emmaline and how wonderful it felt to make love to her, how he wished the time would never end. Even if he had only this one night with her, he would be grateful. It was far more than he'd expected.

The need for her intensified and he positioned himself over her. She opened her legs and arched her back to him. His chest swelled with masculine pride that she wanted him, wanted him to fill her and bring her to climax.

He entered her easily and what had before been a slow, sublime climb to pleasure this time became a frenzied rush. She rose to meet him and clung to him as if to urge him not to slow down, not to stop.

As if he could. As if he ever wanted this to end, even knowing the ecstasy promised.

The air filled with their rapturous breathing as their exhilaration grew more fevered, more consuming. Gabe heard her cry, felt her convulse around him and then he was lost in his own shattering pleasure.

Afterwards they did not speak. He slid to her side and Emmaline fell asleep in his arms as the candle burned down to a sputtering nub. While it still cast enough light, he gazed upon her as she slept.

He did not know what the morning would bring. For all he knew she might send him away in regret for this night together. Or he might be called away to the regiment. Would the regiment be ordered to march, to meet Napoleon's forces?

Would he face her son in battle and take from her what she held most dear?

Chapter Three

Emmaline woke the next morning with joy in her heart. The man in her bed rolled over and smiled at her as if he, too, shared the happy mood that made her want to laugh and sing and dance about the room.

Instead he led her into a dance of a different sort, one that left her senses humming and her body a delicious mix of satiation and energy. She felt as if she could fly.

His brown eyes, warm as a cup of chocolate, rested on her as he again lay next to her. She held her breath as she gazed back at him, his hair rumpled, his face shadowed with beard.

This time she indulged her curiosity and ran her finger along his cheek, which felt like the coarsest sackcloth. "I do not have the razor for you, Gabriel."

He rubbed his chin. "I will shave later."

From the church seven bells rang.

"It is seven of the clock. I have slept late." She slipped out of the tangled covers and his warm arms, and searched for her shift. "I will bring you some water for washing *tout de suite*."

His brows creased. "Do not delay yourself further. I will fetch the water and take care of myself."

She blinked, uncertain he meant what he said. "Then I will dress and begin breakfast."

He sat up and ran his hands roughly through his hair. She stole a glance at his muscled chest gleaming in the light from the window. He also watched her as she dressed. How different this morning felt than when she'd awoken next to her husband. Remy would have scolded her for oversleeping and told her to hurry so he could have fresh water with which to wash and shave.

As she walked out of the room, she laughed to herself. Remy would also have boasted about how more skilled at lovemaking a Frenchman was over an Englishman. Well, this Englishman's skills at lovemaking far exceeded one Frenchman's.

She paused at the top of the stairs, somewhat ashamed at disparaging her husband. Remy had been no worse than many husbands. Certainly he had loved Claude.

Early in her marriage she'd thought herself lacking as a wife, harbouring a rebellious spirit even while trying to do as her much older husband wished. She'd believed her defiance meant she had remained more child than grown woman. When Remy dictated she and Claude would accompany him to war, she'd known it would not be good for their son. She had raged against the idea.

But only silently.

Perhaps her love for Remy would not have withered like a flower deprived of sun and water, if she'd done what she knew had been right and kept Claude in France.

Emmaline shook off the thoughts and hurried down

the stairs to the kitchen to begin breakfast, firing up her little stove to heat a pot of chocolate and to use the bits of cheese left over from the night before to make an omelette with the three eggs still in her larder. Gabriel came down in his shirtsleeves to fetch his fresh water and soon they were both seated at the table, eating what she'd prepared.

"You are feeding me well, Emmaline," he remarked, his words warming her.

She smiled at the compliment. "It is enjoyable to cook for someone else."

His eyes gazed at her with concern. "You have been lonely?"

She lowered her voice. "*Oui,* since Claude left." But she did not want the sadness to return, not when she had woken to such joy. "But I am not lonely today."

It suddenly occurred to her that he could walk out and she would never see him again. Her throat grew tight with anxiety.

She reached across the table and clasped his hand. "My night with you made me happy."

His expression turned wistful. "It made me happy, too." He glanced away and back, his brow now furrowed. "I have duties with the regiment today, but if you will allow me to return, I will come back when you close the shop."

"*Oui!* Yes." She covered her mouth with her hand. "Oh, I cannot, Gabriel. I have no food to cook and I have slept too late to go to the market." She flushed, remembering why she'd risen so late.

His eyes met hers. "I will bring the food."

Her heart pounded. "And will you stay with me again?"

Only his eyes conveyed emotion, reflecting the passion they'd both shared. "I will stay."

The joy burst forth again.

Gabe returned that evening and the next and the next. Each morning he left her bed and returned in the evening, bringing her food and wine and flowers. While she worked at the shop, he performed whatever regimental duties were required of him. It felt like he was merely marking time until he could see her again.

They never spoke of the future, even though his orders to march could come at any time and they would be forced to part. They talked only of present and past, Gabe sharing more with Emmaline than with anyone he'd ever known. He was never bored with her. He could listen for ever to her musical French accent, could watch for ever her face animated by her words.

May ended and June arrived, each day bringing longer hours of sunlight and warmth. The time passed in tranquillity, an illusion all Brussels seemed to share, even though everyone knew war was imminent. The Prussians were marching to join forces with the Allied Army under Wellington's command. The Russians were marching to join the effort as well, but no one expected they could reach France in time for the first clash with Napoleon.

In Brussels, however, leisure seemed the primary activity. The Parc de Brussels teemed with red-coated gentlemen walking with elegant ladies among the statues and fountains and flowers. A never-ending round of social events preoccupied the more well-connected officers and the aristocracy in residence. Gabe's very middle-class birth kept him off the invitation lists, but he was glad. It meant he could spend his time with Emmaline.

On Sundays when she closed the shop, Gabe walked with Emmaline in the Parc, or, even better, rode with her into the country with its farms thick with planting and hills dotted with sheep.

This day several of the officers were chatting about the Duchess of Richmond's ball to be held the following night, invitations to which were much coveted. Gabe was glad not to be included. It would have meant a night away from Emmaline.

His duties over for the day, Gabe made his way through Brussels to the food market. He shopped every day for the meals he shared with Emmaline and had become quite knowledgeable about Belgian food. His favourites were the *frites* that were to be found everywhere, thick slices of potato, fried to a crisp on the outside, soft and flavourful on the inside.

He'd even become proficient in bargaining in French. He haggled with the woman selling mussels, a food Emmaline especially liked. Mussels for dinner tonight and some of the tiny cabbages that were a Brussels staple. And, of course, the *frites*. He wandered through the market, filling his basket with other items that would please Emmaline: bread, eggs, cheese, cream, a bouquet of flowers. Before leaving the market, he quenched his thirst with a large mug of beer, another Belgian specialty.

Next stop was the wine shop, because Emmaline, true to her French birth, preferred wine over beer. After leaving there, he paused by a jewellery shop, its door open to the cooling breezes. Inside he glimpsed a red-coated officer holding up a glittering bracelet. "This is a perfect betrothal gift," the man said. He recognised the fellow, one of the Royal Scots. Buying a betrothal gift?

Gabe walked on, but the words repeated in his brain.

Betrothal gift.

Who was the man planning to marry? One of the English ladies in Brussels? A sweetheart back home? It made no sense to make such plans on the eve of a battle. No one knew what would happen. Even if the man survived, the regiment might battle Napoleon for ten more years. What kind of life would that be for a wife?

No, if this fellow wanted to marry, he ought to sell his commission and leave the army. If he had any intelligence at all he'd have taken some plunder at Vittoria, like most of the soldiers had done. Then he'd have enough money to live well.

Gabe halted as if striking a stone wall.

He might be talking about himself.

He could sell his commission. *He* had enough money.

He could marry.

He started walking again with the idea forming in his mind and taking over all other thought. He could marry Emmaline. His time with her need not end. He might share all his evenings with her. All his nights.

If she wished to stay in Brussels, that would be no hardship for him. He liked Brussels. He liked the countryside outside the city even better. Perhaps he could buy a farm, a hill farm like Stapleton Farm where his uncle worked. When Gabe had been a boy all he'd thought of was the excitement of being a soldier. Suddenly life on a hill farm beckoned like a paradise. Hard work. Loving nights. Peace.

With Emmaline.

He turned around and strode back to the jewellery shop.

The shop was now empty of customers. A tiny, white-haired man behind the counter greeted him with expectation, *"Monsieur?"*

"A betrothal gift," Gabe told him. "For a lady."

The man's pale blue eyes lit up. *"Les fiançailles?"* He held up two fingers. *"Vous êtes le deuxième homme d'aujourd'hui."* Gabe understood. He was the second man that day purchasing a betrothal gift.

The jeweller showed him a bracelet, sparkling with diamonds, similar to the one his fellow officer had held. Such a piece did not suit Emmaline at all. Gabe wanted something she would wear every day.

"No bracelet," Gabe told the shopkeeper. He pointed to his finger. "A ring."

The man nodded vigorously. *"Oui! L'anneau."*

Gabe selected a wide gold band engraved with flowers. It had one gem the width of the band, a blue sapphire that matched the colour of her eyes.

He smiled and pictured her wearing it as an acknowledgement of his promise to her. He thought of the day he could place the ring on the third finger of her left hand, speaking the words, "With this ring, I thee wed, with my body I thee worship…."

Gabe paid for the ring, and the shopkeeper placed it in a black-velvet box. Gabe stashed the box safely in a pocket inside his coat, next to his heart. When he walked out of the jewellery shop he felt even more certain that what he wanted in life was Emmaline.

He laughed as he hurried to her. These plans he was formulating would never have entered his mind a few weeks ago. He felt a sudden kinship with his brothers and sisters, unlike anything he'd ever felt before. With

Emmaline, Gabe would have a family, like his brothers and sisters had families. No matter she could not have children. She had Claude and Gabe would more than welcome Claude as a son.

As he turned the corner on to the street where her lace shop was located, he slowed his pace.

He still had a battle to fight, a life-and-death affair for both their countries. For Gabe and for Claude, as well. He could not be so dishonourable as to sell out when the battle was imminent, when Wellington needed every experienced soldier he could get.

If, God forbid, he should die in the battle, his widow would inherit his modest fortune.

No, he would not think of dying. If Emmaline would marry him before the battle, he would have the best reason to survive it.

With his future set in his mind, he opened the lace-shop door. Immediately he felt a tension that had not been present before. Emmaline stood at the far end of the store, conversing with an older lady who glanced over at his entrance and frowned. They continued to speak in rapid French as he crossed the shop.

"Emmaline?"

Her eyes were pained. "Gabriel, I must present you to my aunt." She turned to the woman. *"Tante Voletta, puis-je vous présenter le Capitaine Deane?"* She glanced back at Gabe and gestured towards her aunt. "Madame Laval."

Gabe bowed. *"Madame."*

Her aunt's eyes were the same shade of blue as Emmaline's, but shot daggers at him. She wore a cap over hair that had only a few streaks of grey through it. Slim but sturdy, her alert manner made Gabe suppose she missed nothing. She certainly examined him carefully before facing Emmaline again and rattling off more in French, too fast for him to catch.

Emmaline spoke back and the two women had another energetic exchange.

Emmaline turned to him. "My aunt is unhappy about our…friendship. I have tried to explain how you helped us in Badajoz. That you are a good man. But you are English, you see." She gave a very Gallic shrug.

He placed the basket on the counter and felt the impression of the velvet box in his pocket. "Would you prefer me to leave?"

"Non, non." She clasped his arm. "I want you to stay."

Her aunt huffed and crossed her arms over her chest. How was Gabe to stay when he knew his presence was so resented?

He made an attempt to engage the woman. *"Madame* arrived today?"

Emmaline translated.

The aunt flashed a dismissive hand. *"Pfft. Oui."*

"You must dine with us." He looked at Emmaline. "Do you agree? She will likely have nothing in her house for a meal."

Emmaline nodded and translated what he said.

Madame Laval gave an expression of displeasure. She responded in French.

Emmaline explained, "She says she is too tired for company."

He lifted the basket again. "Then she must select some food to eat. I purchased plenty." He showed her the contents. *"Pour vous, madame."*

Her eyes kindled with interest, even though her lips were pursed.

"Take what you like," he said.

"I will close the shop." Emmaline walked to the door.

Madame Laval found a smaller basket in the back of the store. Into it she placed a bottle of wine, the cream, some eggs, bread, cheese, four mussels and all of the *frites*.

"C'est assez," she muttered. She called to Emmaline. *"Bonne nuit, Emmaline. Demain, nous parlerons plus."*

Gabe understood that. Emmaline's aunt would have more to say to her tomorrow.

"Bonne nuit, madame." Gabe took the bouquet of flowers and handed them to her, bowing again.

"Hmmph!" She snatched the flowers from his hand and marched away with half their food and all his *frites*.

Emmaline walked over to him and leaned against him.

He put his arms around her. "I am sorry to cause you this trouble."

She sighed. "I wish her visit in the country had lasted longer."

He felt the velvet box press against his chest. "It is safer for her to be in the city."

She pulled away. "Why? Have you heard news?"

He kept an arm around her. "No, nothing more. There is to be a ball tomorrow night. There would not be a ball if Wellington was ready to march."

They walked out of the shop and across the court-yard to her little house. Once inside, Gabe removed his coat; as he did so he felt the ring box in its pocket and knew this was not the time to show it to her. Her aunt, unwittingly, had cast a pall on Gabe's excitement, his dreams for the future.

She busied herself in readying their meal. Their conversation was confined to the placement of dishes and who would carry what to the table.

When they sat at the table, she remarked, "It is a lovely meal, Gabriel. I like the mussels."

He smiled at her. "I know."

As they began to eat, she talked about her aunt. "Tante Voletta came to Brussels a long time ago. After her husband went to the guillotine—"

Gabe put down his fork. "Good God. He went to the guillotine?"

She waved a hand. "That was when they sent everyone to the guillotine. He was a tailor to some of the royals, you see. *Voilà!* That was enough. Tante Voletta came here, to be safe. She opened the shop."

"Why does she dislike me?" he asked. "The English were opposed to the Terror."

She smiled wanly. "Ah, but the English are an enemy of Napoleon. My aunt reveres Napoleon. He made France great again, you see." Her smile fled. "Of course, he killed many by making them soldiers."

What she feared for her son, he remembered.

He turned the subject back to her aunt. "I dislike causing you distress with your aunt. What can I do?"

She shrugged. "You can do nothing."

He gave her a direct look. "Would you prefer I not spend the night tonight?"

Her lips pressed together. "Stay with me. She will know we are lovers soon enough. Everyone around us knows it by now and will delight in telling her of all your coming and going."

He frowned. "Do I cause trouble for you with your neighbours, as well?"

She smiled again. "*Non,* Gabriel. Here a widow is allowed lovers. They might think I am wise to bed you. Most of my neighbours like the money the English bring. My aunt likes English money, too, but she would never say so."

They talked of inconsequentials through the rest of the meal and the cleaning up afterwards. The sky was not quite dark.

Emmaline wiped her hands on the towel. "I am tired tonight. Do you mind if we sleep early?"

"Whatever you wish, Emmaline." Gabe was not about to make anything more uncomfortable for her.

Their lovemaking that night was bittersweet, slow and filled with emotion, as if both of them realised how fragile it could be to love each other.

The words 'With my body I thee worship' repeated in Gabe's mind as his eyes drank in her beauty and his fingers memorised the feel of her. He wanted to erase the tension between them that her aunt's arrival had caused. He wanted to convince her with his body that he needed her in his life.

They reached the pinnacle of pleasure in a slow climb this night, but finally writhed together in its acute glory. No night-time sharing of confidences this time. They merely held each other in silence.

Perhaps in the morning, with the hope of dawn, he could make love to her again and bare his soul to her as they lay next to each other in tangled linens.

Gabe drifted off into disturbed dreams. He was a child again, cast out of doors, alone in a storm, no one near to hear his calls, no one to shelter him. Lightning flashed in his dream and its clap of thunder jarred him awake, his heart pounding.

The sound came again.

Emmaline sat up. The sound repeated. It was not thunder, but something hitting the window, which was open only a crack.

"Someone is out there." She scrambled out of the bed, a sheet wrapped around her.

She lifted the sash and looked out the window.

"Maman!" a voice called in a loud whisper. *"Maman!"*

"Mon Dieu," she cried. "It is Claude." She grabbed her nightdress and put it on. "My son is here."

Chapter Four

Emmaline dashed out, not even bothering to put on a robe. She ran down the stairs, threw open the front door and hugged her only child, who now stood a head taller than she.

He lifted her off her feet and crossed the threshold. *"Maman!"* He spoke in French. "I am here."

Her feet touched the floor again and she stepped back to look at him. In the unlit room she could see little more than a shadow, a shadow that looked so much like her late husband that it made her gasp.

"Let me light a candle so I can see you." She pulled him further into the room. "Why are you here? Have you come home to me?"

"No, *Maman*." It seemed as if his voice had deepened the few months he'd been away. "You must tell no one, but the army is nearby. Close enough for me to come see you. I cannot stay long. I must return before dawn."

She lit a taper from the dying coals in the kitchen stove and moved around the room lighting candles. "Do you need food? Something to drink?"

"Whatever is quickly prepared." He sank down on her sofa.

In the light she could see his hair, as dark as her own, pulled back in a queue. His face had matured a bit, even to the point of a thin moustache above his lip. He did, indeed, look as Remy must have looked in his youth. Claude wore the blue coat of his uniform with the gray overalls that the soldiers wore to keep their white trousers clean. He would have been able to slip through the streets unseen.

"Do not light too many candles," he told her. "No one must know I am here."

She blew out the one she'd just lit. "I'll bring you some wine." There was wine left in the bottle she and Gabriel had shared. She poured it into a glass for Claude and brought it to him.

Gabriel! She had forgotten. She hoped he did not show himself.

He drank half of it quickly. "Thank you, *Maman*."

She sat opposite him and reached out to touch his face. "I'll prepare your food, but please tell me first if you are well. Tell me why you are so close by."

He took another sip. "I cannot tell you why we are close by, but I am very well. They have allowed me to join the cavalry, Maman. I am a cuirassier. That is a great privilege."

Claude had loved horses from the time he could toddle across a room. When they had travelled with his father, Claude was happiest riding with his father on his horse. Poor Coco, the mare, had been lost to them after Badajoz, another heartbreak for Claude.

Here in Brussels, Emmaline could never afford to keep a horse, but Claude had befriended Mr Engles, who ran a stables nearby. Claude performed whatever chores the man would give him, anything to be with the horses. Eventually Mr Engles began to pay him and Claude saved every franc until he could purchase a horse of his own. Named Coco. Claude rode Coco away to Napoleon's army, and most likely having Coco was why Claude was allowed to join the cuirassiers.

"I am not surprised." She smiled at her son. "You probably ride better than most of them."

Would being in the cavalry keep him safer than the infantry? She prayed it was so.

He finished the wine. "They are veterans of the war and I have learned much from them."

Learned how to fight and kill, she thought. But had they taught him how to face men wanting to kill him?

She took his glass and stood. "I will bring you more. And some food."

He rose and followed her to the kitchen, but suddenly froze. "What is this, Maman?"

She glanced over her shoulder and saw him pointing to Gabriel's red coat, hanging over the chair.

"An *English soldier's* coat?" His voice cracked. He gaped at her in disbelief. After a moment his face flushed with colour. "You have an *English soldier* here?" He looked around, as if the man would step out from behind a curtain.

"Claude, I can explain—"

"Where is he? In your bed?" His voice squeaked again.

Before she could say another word, he dashed to the stairs and leaped up them four at a time.

She ran after him. "Claude. Wait!"

"Show yourself," Claude shouted in French. "Show yourself, you dog."

From the bottom of the stairs, Emmaline glimpsed

Gabriel in his shirt and trousers, standing in the doorway of her bedchamber. Claude charged him and they disappeared into the room. As she hurried up the stairs she heard something crash to the floor.

"I'll kill you!" Claude yelled.

Emmaline reached the doorway. From the light of a candle Gabriel must have lit, she could see Claude trying to strike him and Gabriel, larger and stronger, holding him off.

"I'll kill you!" Claude cried again, his arms flailing. He sounded like a wounded child.

"Stop it, Claude." She tried to pull him away from Gabriel. "Someone will hear you. They will discover you are here."

He immediately stopped, but glared at her, his chin trembling. "*He* knows I am here. *He* is the enemy."

"*Non, non,* Claude." Emmaline faced him. "Do you know who this is? Do you?"

He spat. "An Englishman in your bed. How could you do such a thing?" He took two breaths before charging Gabriel again. "Did you force her?"

Gabriel again held him off.

Emmaline jumped between them. "He did not force me, Claude. He is our rescuer. Do you not remember him?"

Claude backed away, looking puzzled.

"This is the captain who kept us safe in Badajoz." She tried to keep her voice down.

"Claude—" Gabriel started.

Claude leaned forwards, pointing his finger at him. "Do not say a word! There is nothing you can say to me, you English dog!"

Emmaline pushed him back. "Calm yourself, Claude. We will go downstairs and talk about this."

He looked as if he was about to cry. "This is traitorous, *Maman.*"

"I cannot be a traitor to Napoleon. I am not in his army. You are." She seized his arm and yanked him towards the door. "Come downstairs." She turned to Gabriel and spoke in English, "Will you come, too?"

Gabriel nodded.

He did not follow immediately, though. Emmaline took advantage and spoke to Claude. "You must remain calm and quiet. If someone hears you yelling and fighting, you will be discovered."

"Do not be a fool, *Maman,*" he countered. "*He* will turn me in. I am already lost."

"*He* is Gabriel Deane, a good man who will do what is right."

A part of her wanted Gabriel to take her son prisoner. At least Claude would stay alive, but she'd been a soldier's wife too long not to understand that Claude would find being a prisoner worse than death.

Claude sat down on the sofa and she sat down next to him, leaving the chair opposite the sofa for Gabriel.

He entered. "Shall I pour wine?"

"*Oui,* Gabriel. *Merci.*" She forgot to switch to English.

He brought the glasses and the wine and placed them on the table, pouring the first and handing it to Claude.

Claude kept his arms crossed over his chest.

"Take it, Claude," Emmaline said in French.

He rolled his eyes, but did as she said. Gabriel handed the next glass to Emmaline before pouring one for himself.

"Tell Claude I have no intention of hurting you in any way. That—that I have the highest esteem for you," Gabriel said.

Emmaline translated.

Claude closed his eyes as if he wished not to hear. "I cannot speak with him about you, *Maman*. Ask him what he will do with me."

She turned to Gabriel. "Claude believes you will take him prisoner, but I beg you will let him go."

His brow furrowed. "This is asking a great deal of me, Emmaline. My duty—"

Her throat tightened. "Please, Gabriel. Please allow him to leave."

He glanced away, as if thinking.

"What are you saying?" Claude asked her in French.

She gestured for him to be quiet. "Gabriel?"

He rubbed his face. "For you, Emmaline, but only if he swears he has not been gathering information for Napoleon."

She turned to Claude. "Have you come to Brussels for any other reason than to see me?"

He looked surprised. "*Non, Maman*. What other reason could there be?"

"To find out about the English?"

He gave her a withering glance. "I cannot learn anything in the dark. And I must return before light or be branded a deserter." His expression reminded her of when he'd been five years old. "I wanted to see you before—before the battle."

She grasped his hand. He averted his gaze.

She turned to Gabriel. "He only came to see me."

Gabriel nodded. "Very well. I'll do as you desire."

She squeezed Claude's hand. "Gabriel will allow you to go."

He blinked in surprise. "Then I must leave post-haste."

"I will pack you some food." She rose, shaking inside

at the thought of saying goodbye to her son, not knowing if he would ever return to her.

She wrapped bread and cheese in a cloth and, with tears pricking her eyes, brought it to him.

He took the package in his hand. "We must blow out the candles."

She blew out the nearest one and started to move to the others, but Gabriel said, "I'll do it."

Claude walked towards the door.

"Claude." Emmaline's throat was tight with emotion. Her son put his arms around her and held her close. "Please be careful," she said. "Come back to me."

"I will, *Maman*." His voice sounded raspy and very young. "Do not worry." He held her even tighter.

A moment later he was gone, fading into the night like a wisp of smoke.

She covered her face with her hands.

And felt strong arms embracing her again. She turned around and let Gabriel's embrace envelop her. "I am so afraid for him. So afraid I will lose him." She sobbed.

"I know," he murmured. "I know."

When her sobs turned to shudders, he picked her up in his arms and carried her upstairs, laying her on the bed and holding her against him.

When she quieted she said, "I fear I'll never see him again."

"I know," he murmured again.

Gabe rose with the first glimmer of dawn, but he'd hardly slept.

The ring remained hidden in his uniform pocket, along with all his hopes for the future. He'd lain awake most of the night, debating whether to ask her to marry him that morning. Was there any chance at all she'd say yes?

She'd defended him with her son, he'd realised, and with her aunt. That heartened him. He was certain he could convince Madame Laval that an Englishman could be as good for her niece as a Frenchman. And he could show Claude he was nothing like the men who'd killed his father and almost raped his mother.

If he had enough time.

But time was a commodity Gabe no longer possessed. Claude's visit meant the French were near and were not likely to be waiting for the Allied Army and the Prussians to meet them on French soil. If the French were marching into Belgium, the battle was imminent.

He pulled on his clothing and glanced at Emmaline, looking so beautiful in sleep it took his breath away.

He understood why soldiers married on the eve of battle. Merely gazing at her made him desire to pledge his fidelity for ever. For the first time, surviving a battle really meant something to him—he wanted to survive to be with her for ever. And if it was his lot to die in battle, as his wife she would receive all his worldly goods. Either way he could provide her with a secure life.

Gabe picked up his boots and carried them below stairs so his footsteps would not wake her. In the kitchen, he lit the stove and put the kettle on. He made some of the Belgian coffee that he'd become accustomed to. He brought the coffee pot to the dining table. After pouring a cup, he leaned back in the chair, against his coat that still hung there. He reached in to the inside pocket and removed the small velvet box. Opening it, he gazed at the ring, imagining it upon Emmaline's finger.

If he did not propose to her this morning, he might not get a second chance.

He closed his fingers around the velvet box and heard her step on the stairway. He stood and quickly shoved the box in his trouser pocket.

"You are awake already." She sounded weary and tense. "I will make you breakfast."

"No, sit." He pulled out her chair. "I will serve you today."

"*Non,* Gabriel, it is for a woman to do." She took his arm, as if to prevent him from entering the kitchen.

He faced her, placing his hands at her waist and leaning his forehead against hers. They stood silent that way, Gabriel savouring her scent, her heat, the softness of her skin.

"Today I will cook for you," he said again, easing her into her chair, stroking a stray lock of hair off her forehead.

He walked into the kitchen and cracked the eggs into the pan. He glanced back at her.

She sat with her elbows on the table, her face in her hands. Thinking of her son, he thought. Worrying over him. Missing him.

When Gabe had been a boy, returning from visiting his uncle on the farm, he'd sometimes wondered if his family had noticed he'd been gone. It often seemed as if they greeted him the same as they would if he'd been gone an hour.

He shook his head and attended to the eggs. This was time to think of Emmaline, not himself.

He poured her coffee and placed her eggs on a plate, adding bread, butter and jam. She looked up as he approached, putting a smile on her face. As he sat opposite her, he felt the ring in his pocket, reminding him of his decision.

Later, he would ask her, after she finished eating.

"This is very good." She looked at him and he could tell she was trying to be cheerful.

Their conversation was forced, all the ease between them these past weeks gone. They talked mostly of the food, as if they were two strangers seated together at a dinner party. When finished, Gabe gathered the dishes and carried them back into the kitchen.

Emmaline followed him, putting her palm on his back. "I will tend to the dishes. You have done enough." She glanced out of the window that looked over a narrow alley. "It is very light outside. I will have to open the shop soon."

Gabe thrust his hand in his pocket and closed his fingers around the velvet box. He released it and drew his hand out to touch her on her shoulders. "Come away for a moment." He led her to the sofa and sat down with her, clasping her hand in his. "I have something to ask you."

She met his gaze with interest, but only as much as if he were preparing to ask her what she would like him to purchase for their dinner.

He glanced down at her hand, imagining the ring on her long, graceful fingers.

"We have had a short time together," he began.

She nodded, her expression turning wary. "You are going to say goodbye to me."

He squeezed her hand. "I am going to propose that I never say goodbye to you."

Her brows rose.

"Emmaline, I am asking you to marry me. I want you—want to be with you for ever."

She paled. "Marry me?"

"I know the timing is ill. With Napoleon's army so near, there must be a battle soon. But maybe we can marry quickly. I will find out the rules, see if it is possible—"

She pulled her hand away. "We cannot marry!"

His heart was pounding fast. "Maybe not before the battle, but afterwards, then."

She jumped to her feet. "*Non,* Gabriel. How can I marry you? You are a British soldier."

"I can sell my commission. After the battle."

Her eyes flashed. "After the battle? Do you think that will make a difference?"

His face stung as if she'd slapped him. "Have I not shown you in every possible way the sort of man I am? Have we not been happy together?"

She looked away. "It is not the sort of happiness that can last."

"Has it not been, Emmaline?" Gabe rubbed his hand against the outside of his pocket, feeling the box through the cloth. "I have experienced enjoyment that is meant to be fleeting. I know the difference. You cannot pretend this was a mere diversion for you."

She could not meet his eye. "Of course I have enjoyed being with you, but I do not want to marry you."

He leaned towards her. "Why?"

She took a breath. "My son despises you—"

"He does not know me. When the war is over, there will be time—"

She lifted her hand for him to stop. "The war will never be over for Claude. Do you not see? It will never be settled in his heart. I have tried—" Her voice cracked with emotion. She looked into his eyes. "I am all Claude has. He has lost too much. He has endured too much. I cannot abandon him."

"I do not wish you to abandon him. He is a part of you. I want you both." Gabriel's insides felt as if they'd turned to stone. He knew even as he spoke the words that he'd lost her, that, if she believed she must choose between them, she must choose her son.

She lowered her gaze and her long lashes made shadows on her cheeks. "No, Gabriel. I cannot turn away from my son. Not even for you."

He felt as if he'd had the breath knocked out of him. His very reason to exist had simply vanished like smoke into thin air.

He turned away and retrieved his coat.

Emmaline's chest constricted as she watched him put on his coat, his back to her. Never had it occurred to her that he might want to marry her. How could he have thought of this time as anything but a brief affair? Soldiers were always having liaisons in whatever place they were billeted. She'd seen it herself and, of course, Remy had threatened her with it when she had balked at going to Spain with him.

But Gabriel had said the word *marriage,* and all she could see was the hurt and anger and betrayal in Claude's eyes from the night before.

She wanted more than anything to believe their days and nights could continue as they had done, full of passion and pleasure and companionship, but she knew better. He could promise her anything, but he could not promise to heal Claude's wounds. Once, long ago, she'd chosen a husband's wishes above what she'd known was best for her son. She would not do so again.

Or Claude might be lost for ever.

Gabriel, his back still to her, buttoned his coat, his scarlet uniform coat, the coat he would wear in the battle when the Allied forces met Napoleon's army, when this man who had given her so much happiness would face her son, who knew nothing of what it was to fight in a battle.

Men died in battle.

For the thousandth time she prayed that God would spare Claude's life. She prayed for Gabriel, as well.

Even though she would never see him again.

He walked to the door without looking at her. Her legs trembled and the room seemed to close in on her.

He opened the door, but turned to her. "Goodbye, Emmaline." His voice was so soft she could hardly hear him.

A moment later he was gone.

Wanting to sink to the floor in a miserable heap, Emmaline instead forced herself to square her shoulders, to tackle the chores that needed finishing before she opened the shop. She started for the kitchen to wash the dishes, but something on the dining table caught her eye.

A small black-velvet box.

Chapter Five

Gabe made his way back to his hotel as if wearing blinders, noticing no one and nothing, not even the weather. On previous mornings, he'd savoured this same walk, enjoying all the sights and sounds, savouring the fresh morning air. This morning his mind was as mechanical as an automaton, turning it over and over that Emmaline was lost to him.

Back in his room at the Hôtel de Flandre Gabe shaved and changed. He would regain control of his emotions, he told himself. There were plenty of women in the world besides Emmaline, women with whom to share brief moments of pleasure. It would be enough. No longer would he dream of a home, a wife, a family. He would remain in the army where he belonged.

Conjuring up visions of another life had been a momentary lapse of sanity.

As a soldier he had one duty now. For Emmaline he had compromised that duty, delaying the report that the French were near, but he would delay no longer.

Gabe went straight to the Allied Army headquarters.

As he entered the white-stone building, the two men he least desired to encounter walked towards him: Edwin Tranville, the man who'd tried to rape Emmaline, and his father, General Lord Tranville. The general had managed to inherit a title since Gabe had last seen him.

"What are you doing here, Deane?" the general barked. As a greeting, it was one of Tranville's most cordial. His son, whose face bore a scar from his temple to his mouth, created by Emmaline's knife, did not even bother to acknowledge him.

"Sir." Gabe bowed to the general, a respect the man did not deserve. "I need to see Wellington or one of his aides-de-camp."

"You?" Tranville's brows rose. "What reason could you possibly have to see the Duke or his aides?"

If Tranville had not been Gabe's superior officer, he would not have replied. "The French army has crossed into Belgium."

Tranville frowned. "How can you know that? What evidence do you have?"

"I encountered a French soldier in the city last night." This was wasting Gabe's time.

Tranville's eyes narrowed. "Encountered? Where?"

Gabe glanced from the general to his son, who was now leaning against the wall, as if needing it to keep him upright. How much did Edwin remember about that night in Badajoz? Gabe wondered. Had he told his father about it?

No matter what, Gabe refused to lead them to Emmaline. "I saw him on the street."

Tranville laughed. "On the street? Not having a casual stroll through the Parc? Do not be a damned fool. If you saw anything at all, it was probably a Dutch infantryman."

"I did not mistake the uniform. The man was not desiring to be seen and why would a Dutch infantryman be trying to hide?"

Why did he even bother arguing with Tranville? Gabe did not care if Tranville believed him or not. "In any event, I feel it is my duty to report it."

Tranville's nostrils flared. "Do not mention this to Wellington. Do not waste his Grace's time."

Gabe shrugged. "To one of his aides, then."

Tranville huffed. "You will say nothing. Am I making myself clear? Your duty has been discharged by making your report to me."

Gabe persisted. "And you will pass on this information?"

The general's voice rose. "As I am your superior officer, you will not question what I will or will not do. The Duchess of Richmond is giving a ball tonight, in case you did not know, and I will not have his Grace and other *gentlemen* distracted by this foolishness." He emphasized the word *gentlemen*.

When General Tranville became Gabe's superior officer, he had made certain that Gabe did not rise in rank past captain. The general did not believe in field promotions or those based on merit. Gabe had come from the merchant class and only true gentlemen advanced the proper way, by purchasing a higher rank. It was a matter of pride to Gabe that he did not advance through purchase, although his family, and now he, could have afforded it.

Tranville waved a dismissive hand. "Go see to your men or whatever nonsense you must attend to. You can have no further business here."

A string of invectives rushed to the tip of Gabe's tongue. He clamped his teeth together.

"Yes, sir!" he responded, bowing and performing a precise about-face.

Gabe walked away, keeping a slow pace so that Tranville would not suspect he'd been roused to anger.

As he reached the door to the outside, he heard Edwin drawl, "How very tiresome."

Later that evening Gabe learned his information had been accurate and that General Tranville had not passed it on. Wellington heard about Napoleon's march towards Brussels at the Duchess of Richmond's ball, a good twelve hours after Gabriel reported it to Tranville. Wellington was said to have remarked, "Napoleon has humbugged me, by God. He has gained twenty-four hours' march on me."

Gabe would have saved Wellington half that time.

The next day Gabe's regiment, the Royal Scots, joined other Allied forces at Quatre Bras where they met the French. How quickly it all came back, the pounding of cannon, the thundering of horses, battle cries and wounded screams, a terrible, familiar world, more real to Gabe than his idyll at Brussels. The fighting was hard, but almost comforting in its familiarity.

Musket volleys assaulted Gabe and his men. Six times steel-helmeted cuirassiers charged at them with slashing swords.

As Gabe yelled to his soldiers to stand fast, he scanned the French cavalry thundering towards them. Was Emmaline's Claude among them? Would Gabe see her son struck down? Would his own sword be forced to do the deed?

The weather turned foul. Black storm clouds rolled in and soon thunder and lightning competed with the roar of cannon. Late in the battle Gabe glimpsed the

cuirassiers charging upon the 69th Regiment, seiz-
ing their colours. Feeling traitorous, Gabe blew out
a relieved breath. If the French cuirassiers had been
vanquished, Claude would have had a greater chance
of being one of the casualties. Gabe prayed Claude had
survived.

For Emmaline's sake.

The battle ended in a great deal of mud, with neither side the victor, and both the Allies and the French
retreated.

The following day Gabe's regiment marched to a
location Wellington had chosen to next engage Napoleon, near a village called Waterloo.

That night the rain continued to fall in thick, unre-
lenting sheets, soaking the earth into mud. Gabe and
Allan Landon, now a captain like himself, were fortunate to share a reasonably dry billet with another officer.
After Badajoz, Gabe had become good friends with
Landon, although their temperaments and backgrounds
were often directly opposed to each other. Landon, with
his rigid sense of right and wrong, came from an aristocratic family and had, God help him, political ambi-
tions. Gabe would rather impale himself on his sword
than deal with politics.

Good thing he had never told Landon about partak-
ing of the spoils of war. At Vittoria, in Spain, Napoleon's brother, Joseph Bonaparte, had fled in panic,
abandoning his riches, which were scattered across a
field, tempting even the most honest of men. Gabe,
like countless other soldiers, had filled his pockets. Not
Landon, though. Landon had been appalled.

The shack's roof pounded with the rain. Gabe and

Landon huddled near their small fire that gave them little relief from the chill.

One of the junior officers, streams of water dripping off the capes of his cloak, appeared in their doorway of their shack. "General Tranville wants to see you, Captains."

Gabe groaned. "More nonsense. I'll make a wager with you."

Landon clapped him on the back. "You know I never gamble."

They wrapped themselves in their cloaks and dashed through the downpour to the peasant's hut that Tranville had made his billet.

"Mind your boots! Mind your boots!" Tranville shouted as they entered. Edwin, a sour look on his scarred face, manned the door.

They cleaned as much of the mud off as they could, the rain sneaking down the collars of their coats. After closing the door behind them, Edwin took a swig from a flask. Some sort of spirits, Gabe reckoned.

Tranville barked orders at them, nothing more than mere posturing, however.

He fixed the men with what he must have thought was a steely glare. "I'll have no laggardly behaviour, do you hear? You tell your men they are to hop to or they'll answer to me."

"Yes, sir!" chirped a young lieutenant.

Gabe put on his most bland expression. He could endure Tranville for this brief period, but only because it was warm and dry in the hut.

"Landon," Tranville went on, "I want you to find Picton tonight. See if he has any message for me."

General Picton was the commander of the 5th Division of which the Royal Scots were a part. Landon's task was to carry messages for Picton and Tranville during the battle, but it was ridiculous to send Landon out in this weather merely on the off chance Picton might have a message.

Landon must have had the same reaction. He glanced over to the small window, its wooden shutters clattering from the wind and rain. "Yes, sir."

"And stay available to me tomorrow. I may need you during the battle."

Landon knew that already, of course. "Yes, sir."

Tranville nodded in obvious approval. His gaze drifted to Gabe and his lips pursed, but luckily his glance continued to his son, who was sitting on a stool sneaking sips from his flask.

There was a knock on the door and Tranville signalled for Edwin to open it. With a desultory expression, Edwin complied.

"Oh, Good God," Edwin drawled, stepping aside.

Jack Vernon, the ensign—now lieutenant—who'd been with them in Badajoz, stood in the doorway.

Gabe poked Landon to call his attention to Vernon. He noticed that Tranville caught his gesture and quickly erased any expression from his face.

Vernon slanted a glance at Gabe and Landon before turning back to Tranville and handing him a message.

Tranville snatched the paper from Vernon's hand and snapped at him, "You will wait for my reply."

Gabe exchanged another glance with Landon. This was not the first time Vernon and Tranville had encountered each other, obviously. Whatever had transpired between them had left them acrimonious.

Tranville stretched his arm and seemed to be writing as slowly as he could. He dragged out this interaction with Vernon, presuming it would annoy the lieutenant, no doubt. Finally Tranville said, "Leave now."

Landon spoke up, "With your permission, I'll leave now, as well."

"Go." He waved him away.

Vernon left, Landon right behind him.

"Do you have further need of me?" asked Gabe.

"Of course not," snapped Tranville. "All of you go."

Once outside Tranville's billet, Landon and Gabe pulled Vernon aside. "Do you have time for some tea?" Landon asked.

Vernon nodded gratefully.

They led him through the rain to the shack and heated a kettle on the small fire. The third officer in the billet lay snoring in a corner.

When they finally warmed their hands on the tin mugs of tea, Vernon glanced to their sleeping mate and back to them. "I need to tell you. I broke my word about keeping silent about Badajoz. I was forced to tell General Tranville."

Gabe straightened. "Tranville!"

Vernon held up his hand. "It was not something I wished to do, but I had little choice. I showed him the drawings I made of the incident. Tranville threatened my family; the only way I could silence him was by threatening to expose Edwin. You are safe," he assured them. "I did not show enough to identify you, not even your uniforms."

"Did you show the woman's face? Or her son's?" Gabe asked, his chest tightening.

Vernon shook his head.

Relieved, Gabe rubbed his face. "Damned Tranville. I hope some Frenchman puts a ball through his head."

"Watch your tongue, Gabe," Landon cautioned, gesturing to their sleeping roommate.

Vernon rose. "I had better deliver my message."

Gabe shook his hand.

Before he walked out he turned to Gabe. "What of the woman, Captain? Do you think she found a safe place for herself and her son?"

"She did," Gabe answered. "In fact, she lives in Brussels. I saw her there."

Landon sat up straight. "You did not tell me that."

Gabe shrugged. There was no more he wanted to say.

"And the boy?" Vernon asked.

Gabe looked from one to the other. "In the army." Let them think he had joined a Belgian regiment.

After Vernon left, Landon turned to Gabe. "How did you come to know the woman was in Brussels?"

"I encountered her by chance." Which was almost the truth, if you didn't add that he deliberately pursued her all the way to her shop.

"I thought she was French," Landon said.

"She came to Belgium to live with a relative, she said." He did not wish to talk about her. "I do not know a great deal more."

Except everything she'd shared as they lay in each other's arms after making love. Except how her smile seemed to make colours brighter. How the warmth of her skin made him feel as if he'd come home at last.

Landon dropped the subject and soon left to find Picton. For the rest of the night Gabe tried to ignore the water dripping from the ceiling and the wind whistling through the cracks in the walls. Mostly he tried not to think of Emmaline, how comforting it felt to sleep next to her, how wrenching it felt to lose her.

He needed sleep before facing cannonade, charging cavalry and thousands of soldiers marching towards them to the sound of the *Pas de Charge*.

The next day the rain dwindled to a light drizzle, but did not cease until mid-morning when the sun was finally visible again. Everyone prepared for what they knew would be the main battle.

Gabe conferred with his lieutenants and saw to the readiness of his company, ensuring they had dry powder and plenty of ammunition. His uniform was damp from the incessant rain, but those of his men were soaked through. As the sun heated the air, clouds of vapor rose from their coats and from the ground, lending an eerie cast to the scene.

The two armies faced each other across a gently sloping valley at a right angle to the Brussels road. One farm, La Haye Sainte, fortified by the King's German Legion, was on one side of the valley. Hougoumont, another farm, occupied by the Coldstream Guards, was on the other. Gabe's Royal Scots, along with other regiments of British, Dutch, German and Belgian troops, were strung the length between the farms with the forest of Soignes to their backs. Wellington ordered these troops to remain on the back slope of the ridge, so for most of them the battle was heard and not seen. Gabe witnessed a bit more from horseback. He watched the first attack on Hougoumont a little before noon, the first action of the day. Two hours later it was the Royal Scots' turn. The formidable French column advanced into the valley. The ground trembled under their feet. Their drums pounded in the Allies' ears as they marched up the hill.

The Royal Scots and the other regiments were ready.

Hidden behind the crest, Gabe held his men back until Picton gave the order. All at once the British rose up in front of the French column and fired. Front ranks, standing shoulder to shoulder, fired on order, then dropped down to reload. Those behind them moved forwards and fired. Front ranks advanced again. Volley after non-stop volley poured into the French columns. Countless Frenchmen fell, only to be trampled on by the hoards of their comrades marching behind them.

Gabe rode along the line of his men, urging them to stand and keep firing, but, as devastating as their muskets were, there were simply too many enemy soldiers coming at them. In seconds they would be overpowered.

All was not lost. The British cavalry came in the nick of time, charging down the hill, routing the French infantry. Gabe cheered the French infantry's frantic retreat. He watched the cavalry cut a swathe through the fleeing men, slaughtering them as if scything grain.

The sight brought relief, but no pleasure, and soon turned to horror. The British cavalry were cut off by French cuirassiers. The tables were turned, and now it was the British on the run and the French cavalry on the slaughter.

Was Emmaline's Claude among them? Gabe wondered. Was he quenching his thirst for vengeance, or had he already fallen? Claude was too young and new to battle to hone the instinct for survival that became second nature to veteran soldiers, an instinct that had served Gabe well.

By four o'clock, fighting continued around Hougoumont and La Haye Sainte and Gabe prepared for another attack of infantry. Again the men were pulled back to the far side of the ridge. Gabe rode to the crest of the hill to see for himself what they would face next. Again the ground trembled, but this time with the pounding of horses' hooves. Like a huge, unstoppable wave thousands of French cavalry, line after line of them, charged directly towards them.

Wellington gave the order to form square, a battlefield formation where men stood three deep, a line presenting bayonets, a line to fire, a line to reload. Cavalry horses would not charge into the bayonets and the muskets could fire at will. The interior of the square sheltered the wounded, the artillerymen and the officers, whose job it was to make sure the men stood fast, kept shooting and closed any gap.

"Fire at the horses," Gabe shouted to his men. Without his horse, a cavalryman was helpless.

Gabe wound up in the same square as Landon, who, thank God, was unscathed. Gabe might have got his wish about General Tranville. He'd been seen falling from his horse during that first infantry charge and no one had seen him since. His son Edwin, coward that he was, had disappeared at the beginning of the battle. Gabe presumed he was hiding somewhere that cannon fire and musket balls could not reach.

"Fire at the horses," Gabe yelled again. "Stand fast."

Gabe's square held and, as far as he could tell, the other British squares held as well, even though the French charged again and again. Between charges Landon rode off to render assistance to Hougoumont, which was now on fire. Gabe stayed with his company, their numbers dwindling with each attack, the square becoming smaller and smaller.

The ground around them was littered with dead and dying horses and men, their screams melding with the boom of cannon and crack of musket fire. The air filled with smoke and it was difficult to see much further than ten to twelve feet.

Between cavalry attacks, Gabe worried that the French would train their artillery on the squares, or that more columns of infantry would join the charge. Neither happened. Just more cavalry. As the latest onslaught neared, a gap formed on one side of the square. Gabe rode to it. "Close the gap," he ordered.

A cuirassier on a dark bay horse rode directly for the opening, but Gabe's men fired on him as they closed ranks again. The rider jerked like a rag doll as several balls hit him. The horse was such a beauty, Gabe was glad his men had missed it. Its rider tumbled from the saddle as the horse ran on. The man rolled towards the square, landing about four feet from Gabe. His helmet came off and bounced into the body of a French comrade.

Facing Gabe was the youthful countenance of Claude Mableau. The boy struggled to rise. One of his men aimed his musket at him.

"Do not fire," Gabe cried, dismounting. "He's no threat." He ran out of the square and grabbed Claude by the collar, dragging him inside to where the other wounded lay.

"A Frenchie, Captain?" one of the man asked.

"Spare him," Gabe ordered, not caring if the man thought him soft on the French. "He's just a boy."

Emmaline's boy.

Chapter Six

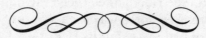

She'd heard the guns all day, the booming of cannon fire, like the thunder of the two previous days without the rain.

Everyone said this was the big battle, not the one two days before when the cannons were also heard. It seemed to Emmaline that plenty of wounded men came into Brussels after that one. If this were the big battle, it could only get worse.

Tante Voletta had insisted they close the shop and pack up all the lace to hide in the attic.

"Those English will use our lace for bandages, I am sure of it," her aunt had said. "They are gauche."

For two days they packed away lace. It helped make the time pass, but now that the task was done, nothing was left to distract her. Emmaline's heart seized with fear at each battle sound. Did that cannon ball strike Claude? Was he anywhere near it? Would he come back to her? Or had he died already, in that first battle? Had he been placed at the front of the charge so the musket balls would hit him first?

He was a soldier's son, she forced herself to remember. Perhaps he was born with a soldier's sense of self-preservation. Besides, she would know if he died. She was certain she would feel his life leave his body as profoundly as she felt when she gave birth to him.

Tante Voletta sent her out to purchase stores of food. Many of the English had fled to Antwerp, but still what shops were open had few supplies. Perhaps other shop-keepers had hidden their stock, as well.

The streets remained busy with wagons carrying supplies, people fleeing or wounded arriving. Rumours were everywhere. On one corner it was believed that Napoleon was at the city gates; on another corner the Allies had him in retreat. Either way the rumours went made Emmaline feel sick inside. There could be no possible victory for her in this battle.

A wagon of wounded British soldiers came into view. Emmaline ran alongside it. "What news of the battle?" she asked them.

"Bloody hard going," one of the soldiers answered, which told her nothing.

Their red coats reminded her of Gabriel. Perhaps they knew how he fared. "Are you Royal Scots?"

"No, ma'am," he answered.

The wagon rolled on.

Emmaline put her fingers on her chest, feeling for the beautiful ring she wore on a chain around her neck, hidden under her clothing. Somehow she did not believe a mere war could kill Gabriel Deane. He was too clever, too strong and too good a man to be lost to battle. She only wished they could have parted with loving words, not the harsh ones that had escaped her lips when she refused his proposal.

She closed her eyes and could still see the wounded

look on his face. Why had he not understood? It was impossible for her to marry Gabriel, a British soldier, when her son so vehemently hated him. Gabriel should have known that.

The sound of a hundred hooves thundered in her ears. She dropped her basket as an entire regiment of Hanoverian cavalry galloped past her. Emmaline froze, expecting to see Napoleon himself on the heels of these German horsemen.

No one came.

She bent down to retrieve her basket and was seized with a sharp anxiety, like shafts piercing her skin. No more shops—she just wanted to go home, to wait in solitude for some final word of who was winning and who was losing, who was alive and who had died. Whether Claude would return to her.

The towers of St Michael's Cathedral loomed above her. She glanced up at them and whispered a prayer that God would deliver Claude back to her.

She added a prayer for Gabriel. Not for him to return, but for him to live.

She crossed herself and hurried to the lace shop, walking around the back and entering the yard through the gate. After opening the rear door of the shop, she climbed the stairs to her aunt's rooms.

"This is all you could purchase?" Her aunt took the basket from Emmaline's hands and peered inside it.

She wrapped her arms around her still-shaking chest. "There was not much to buy."

A cannon boomed and they both turned towards the sound.

"I am weary of that!" her aunt exclaimed. She examined each item in the basket. "Did you hear any news of the battle?"

Emmaline shook her head. "No one knows the outcome."

"Pfft!" Tante Voletta waved a hand. "Napoleon will win."

Emmaline kept silent. She did not want the French to win. Claude would never leave the army if that happened. "Do you need my company? Because I would rather go to my own rooms."

"Go," her aunt said. "But come to me when you learn of the victory."

Emmaline, however, did not go out in search of news.

She spent the evening on her sofa, hugging her knees and repeating her prayers. She lay down and pressed her hand against the ring under her dress. As she felt its circle in her fingers, she watched the flame of a single candle. The cannonade stopped and as darkness fell she could hear the rumble of wagons passing through the streets. Her candle grew shorter and shorter and soon her eyes grew heavy. She fought to stay awake. How could she sleep while the fate of her son was in question?

The sounds in the street were rhythmic and lulling. Her eyes closed.

And flew open again.

A loud rapping at the door startled her awake. She sat up, heart pounding.

"Emmaline," she heard a man's voice. "Open the door."

Gabriel!

She flew to the door and pulled it open.

He was a mere shadow in the dark yard, but as he stepped inside, she could see he carried something over his shoulder.

Her eyes widened.

"I've brought your son."

"Claude!" Her hands clasped over her mouth. Was he dead? "Claude!"

"He's wounded." Without another word he carried him upstairs.

She grabbed the candle and followed. Claude's head lolled back and forth with each step Gabriel made.

Gabriel opened the door to Claude's room and placed him on the bed. Immediately he began to undress him.

Emmaline lit more candles, her hands trembling. "Where is he hurt?"

"His head." He ripped away Claude's bloody shirt. "His neck. And leg."

She stood by the bed, finally able to touch her son. She helped pull off his trousers, stained with his blood. He'd been shot in the thigh, but a quick examination showed that the musket ball had passed through. On his neck, right above his collarbone, was another wound. She placed a finger near the spot.

Claude flinched and moaned—signs of life, at least.

"Water." Gabriel's voice sounded forced. "Need to wash. See the wounds better."

She sprang to her feet. "I'll fetch some."

She returned with a stack of towels, a pitcher of water, a basin and cup. As she placed them on the bedside table, Gabriel swayed and looked as if he might collapse to the floor.

She hurried to him, helping him regain his balance. "Are you injured, Gabriel?"

He shook his head. "Tired."

"Sit in the chair." She eased him over to a wooden chair near the bed and ran to pour him a cup of the water.

He drank it greedily, but gestured for her to return to Claude.

Emmaline washed away blood and mud and bits of grass and cloth from her son's skin and from his hair. Beneath his matted hair was a long gash. A musket ball had scraped him, but had not penetrated. His thigh had a huge hole in it from which blood still oozed. His chest was riddled with round red spots, turning to bruises.

"His chest plate stopped some of the musket balls," Gabriel said. The cuirassiers wore steel chest plates, like the armour of medieval times.

The most worrisome wound was the one on his neck. The musket ball needed to come out.

She turned to Gabriel. "He needs a surgeon."

He rubbed his face. "Won't find one. There are thousands who need a surgeon. Most worse off." His gaze met hers. "Too many." A haunted expression came over his face.

Emmaline could not allow herself to think of what horrors he'd seen. She must think only of Claude, how to keep him alive.

She forced herself to remain calm. "I will remove the ball."

"Emmaline—" he began in a warning tone.

She set her jaw in resolve. "There is no other choice. I have seen it done before. I must try."

She ran from the room and gathered any items she could think of that would help her remove the ball: her knitting needles, a long embroidery hook, tweezers, scissors. The sky was turning light. At least she would be able to see better.

Back in Claude's room, she pushed the bed to the window and set her tools on the bed next to her son.

Gabriel rose from the chair. "I'll hold him still."

How he would have the strength to do so, she didn't know, but he stood on the opposite side of the bed and held Claude's shoulders. She carefully inserted the knitting needle into the wound to find the path of the musket ball. Claude's eyes opened and he cried out. Gabriel held him fast.

Swallowing against a sudden wave of nausea, Emmaline did not have to probe far. "It is not deep!"

Her tweezers were about five inches long, plenty of length to reach the ball. It took several tries to pull it out, all the while Claude writhing with the pain of it. He quickly lost consciousness and became limp. Finally she manoeuvred the ball to the opening and was able to hold it between her fingers. Gabriel released Claude and leaned against the wall.

"One more thing if you can stand it," she said to Gabriel. "I want to sew his head wound closed."

Gabriel's arms trembled as he held Claude's head while Emmaline put thread and needle through the skin, but Claude did not regain consciousness.

"Sit down now," she told Gabriel after she was done.

She bandaged the wounds and covered Claude with clean linens and a blanket. He again moaned, but it was a relief to hear him make any sound. Later, as she had done when he was ill as a child, she would spoon broth down his throat and wipe his brow with cool compresses if he became feverish. There was little else she could do.

She stepped back from his bed.

Gabriel rose. "I must leave."

She touched his arm. "Take some food first. Something to drink." She wanted to tell him not to leave her, to stay. With his steadying presence, she felt as if she could do anything to keep Claude alive. Without him, she was alone.

She walked downstairs with him and made him sit at the table where he'd sat so many happier times before.

"Just something to drink," he said.

She gave him wine and he drank it like water.

"Now I must go." He stood again and walked towards the door.

"Gabriel." She ran to him as he opened the door. "Who won the battle?"

He gave her a weary look. "The Allies."

She was relieved. When—*if*—Claude recovered, he would not return to the French army. There would be no need if the British had won. He could have a normal, peaceful life.

Gabriel put his hand on the doorknob again.

"Gabriel!" she called again.

He turned.

She swallowed against a threat of tears. "Thank you for my son."

He touched her face with a gentle hand and started to walk away.

She seized his arm. "Gabriel. How did you find him? You said there were so many…"

Again a bleak look crossed his face. "The cuirassiers attacked. I saw him fall near me."

"They let you save him?" Surely it would be difficult to protect a Frenchman when so many were in need.

His eyes turned hard. "No one could stop me." He crossed the threshold and made his way to the gate and out of her life.

Emmaline leaned against the door jamb, tears burning her eyes, a sob choking her throat. What had he risked for her?

To save her son.

Chapter Seven

London—June 1817

Two years after the battle of Waterloo, Gabe's life could not have been more altered. Waterloo had ended the war and Napoleon had been exiled to Saint Helena, far enough away in the south Atlantic to pose no further threat. For a time, Gabe's Royal Scots had been part of the Army of Occupation in France. Gabe wished they'd been sent somewhere more distant, not so close to Brussels, not so filled with reminders of what he most wanted to forget.

The orders finally came that the whole battalion would be shipped to Canterbury. Once there, however, Gabe's battalion was disbanded and he was placed on half-pay. In what seemed like an instant he had no regiment, no orders and literally nothing to do.

Now he was in London and, like other officers let loose in a non-military world, was haunting the Horse Guards hoping to discover a regiment looking for officers, or visiting the War Office to get the forms necessary to write to regimental agents for a commission to purchase. On this warm June afternoon Gabe strode into the War Office to pick up more copies of the form the office had run out of the week before. Gabe had performed this same errand the day before and the day before that, without success. He was not optimistic that this day would yield a different result.

Three other officers of his acquaintance were on their way out.

"Deane!" one of them cried, slapping him on the back. "Come for more forms, have you?" He spoke with a thick Irish accent that had earned him the nickname 'Irishman'.

"Indeed," Gabe responded without enthusiasm. "Are you going to tell me they have a new supply?"

Another man, Major Hanson, stepped up. "Not going to tell you that. Webberly even offered a bribe if the fellow would find him one copy, but apparently there are still none to be had today. Maybe tomorrow, the fellow said."

Webberly, the third of the trio, shook his head. "I was certain a bribe would work."

Gabe gave him an impassive look. "I'd be grateful for the opportunity to pay a bribe." What else was he to do with his money?

Hanson jostled him. "Do not speak so loud. The clerks will smell a profit."

The clerks already knew of Gabe's willingness to bribe them for more forms. He'd made the offer days ago.

Irishman laughed. "Now, Captain Deane, my dear fellow, are you so eager for a commission? It would mean leaving our company and the fine accommodations of the Stephen's Hotel."

They all had rooms in the Stephen's Hotel on Bond Street, a place popular with military men.

Gabe responded with sarcasm, "Not at all. I'm merely pining for the lost luxuries of army life."

"You are wasting your time today, Deane," Hanson told him. "Come with us. We plan to make great use of a tavern and deprive it of several pints of ale."

It was tempting to seek the oblivion that alcohol could bring. Most of the officers at Stephen's Hotel drank too much, but, after Brussels, Gabe had learned that whatever you wanted to drown with drink was still with you when morning came. Along with the devil of a headache.

"Not this time."

The men bid him goodbye, and Gabe proceeded to the clerk's desk anyway.

The clerk barely glanced at him. "No forms today. Maybe tomorrow."

Gabe tapped on the man's desk with a finger. "If the forms do arrive tomorrow, will you save me some?"

The clerk raised one brow. "For the amount we agreed upon?"

Gabe gave him a level stare. "Indeed."

The clerk grinned. "We have a wager going here as to who among you officers will be the first to break down and accept a commission to the West Indies."

The 1st battalion of the Royal Scots was stationed in the West Indies. There were always commissions open there, because so many officers caught fevers and died.

Gabe had survived that dreadful place once; he had no desire to chance it again, even if it would free him from the tedium of London.

Gabe had already travelled to Manchester, the home of his youth and where his family still resided, a place he'd not seen for at least ten years. It was nearly like going to a foreign land. Factories and warehouses had sprouted everywhere. Nieces and nephews had sprouted as well, too many for him to count. His mother and father had turned shockingly old and neither they nor his brothers or sisters seemed to know what to do with him.

He'd wound up spending most of his time with a twelve-year-old nephew who asked question after question about every battle on the Peninsula and every detail of Waterloo. The boy had reminded him of Emmaline's Claude, or, more accurately, what he imagined Claude might have been like if not for Badajoz.

After a few weeks of intense discomfort on all sides, Gabe made an excuse to leave. He suspected the family was relieved he was no longer there to distract them from the routines of running what was now a very prosperous drapery warehouse. With Manchester's new mills and a canal that improved the shipping of goods, the town seemed to have turned into a Garden of Eden for cloth merchants.

After Manchester, Gabe visited his uncle on the hill farm. Even that idyll was about to be lost. Stapleton Farm was up for sale and his uncle would soon be vying with younger men by the scores who were also seeking employment. Had matters turned out differently in Brussels, Gabe might have bought the place. He'd learned his lesson, though. He belonged in the army. No sense dreaming otherwise.

He'd returned to London and the tedious days of applying for a commission. What odds were offered that he would be the one to break down and go to the West Indies? Surely he'd be a safe bet.

"I'll be back tomorrow," he said to the clerk who'd

already turned his attention back to the papers on his desk.

"Undoubtedly," the man replied.

Gabe walked out of the office and back on to the street. He took a breath.

Lawd. He needed more to do. Exercising his horse in the morning and visiting the War Office or Horse Guards in the afternoon was simply not enough.

Most of his fellow officers attended society balls and other entertainments in the evenings, hoping to find a wealthy heiress to marry. Even that occupation was closed to Gabe. With the glut of younger sons in town, the son of a merchant was no matrimonial prize. Besides, marriage was not in the cards for him. He'd learned that lesson in Brussels.

Gabe walked slowly back to the hotel, ignoring the book shops, ironmongers, milliners and tea shops on Bond Street. Head down, he approached the entrance of Stephen's Hotel, hoping not to see anyone he knew. He was not in a humour for friendly discourse on the weather or any other subject. As he entered the hotel, he removed his shako and threw his gloves inside it. Holding it under his arm, he crossed the hall, making his way to the stairway.

"Captain!" The footman who attended the lobby called after him. "Captain!"

He'd almost made good his escape. Turning, he fixed his fiercest glare on the unfortunate fellow.

The man took a step back. "Ah, sir." He bowed. "You have a caller. Waiting in the front parlour." The footman gestured to the room and withdrew posthaste.

Gabe clenched his hand into a fist. Who did he know in London who would call upon him? Allan Landon, perhaps? He'd seen Allan a few weeks ago, but neither of them had shared their direction. He knew other officers, but they were all staying in this hotel. If they wished to waste his time, they would simply knock at his door.

He rubbed his forehead.

On the other hand, he had written countless letters trying to find a commission. Maybe his caller had an answer for him.

He entered the room, dropping his hat on a table inside the door.

The parlour looked empty at first, although the curtains were open and fresh flowers were in a vase on the mantel.

A sound came from the high-backed chair facing the fireplace. A swish of skirts and a peek of a bonnet.

A woman?

She stood before him. *"Bon jour, Gabriel."*

Emmaline.

She looked even more beautiful than the image of her that inhabited his dreams at night. Her lace-lined bonnet of natural straw perfectly framed her flawless face. The dark blue of her walking dress made her eyes even more vibrant.

Good God. After two years, she still had the power to affect him.

"What are you doing here?" His tone came out more sharply than he intended.

She clasped her white-gloved hands together. "I came to see you, Gabriel."

He shook his head. "I meant, why are you in London?"

She fingered the front of her dress. "To see you."

She had come to see him?

Gabe had laboured hard to bury the deep wound of

losing her, but now she was here. Was it possible she'd regretted sending him away? Enough to travel this long distance to find him? Enough to search for him, to discover where he lived?

Against his better judgement, a tiny seed of hope germinated.

He managed to disguise the fact. "How did you find me?"

"With luck." She smiled wanly. "A maid at my hotel said many officers stayed here."

He really did not care about how she had found him. Only one question truly burned inside him. "*Why* did you come to see me?"

Her lips trembled before she spoke. "Oh, Gabriel. I need you."

The hard earth he'd packed around his emotions began to crack.

She swallowed and went on, "I need your help."

He came to his senses. "Help with what?"

She met his eye. "I need you to find Claude."

"Claude." The son who'd driven a wedge between them.

Of course it would be for Claude that she would travel all this way, to a foreign country that had so recently been at war with her birthplace.

She stepped closer to him. "It is so terrible. He is here in England." Her gaze still managed to hold him in thrall. "Do you remember how he was so filled with hatred?"

Could he forget?

She took a breath. "He became a cuirassier to get revenge for—for what happened at Badajoz. What happened to his father. And to me. All these years Claude has not forgotten any of it. Fighting the English in the war was supposed to be the revenge, but, *alors,* you know what happened."

"Why come to England, then, if he hates it so?" Wouldn't Claude want to stay away and keep his mother away, as well?

She wrung her hands. "He remembers one name from that day—Edwin Tranville. He has come to England to kill him."

Edwin Tranville. Gabe pressed his fingers against his temple. Damned Edwin Tranville. "What has this to do with me, Emmaline?"

Her eyes pleaded. "I need you to find Claude and stop him."

What a fool he was. She'd come to England for her son, not for him.

He gave her a level look. "What makes you believe I would help you?"

She lowered her gaze so that her long dark lashes cast shadows on her cheeks. "Oh, Gabriel. Who else can help me? I cannot go to—to the *gendarmerie* and tell them my son wants to kill a man. I might as well send Claude to a guillotine. I came to you, because I do not know anyone else." Her voice cracked with emotion. "I know only you."

Her emotion shook him. He paced in front of her. "Well, I cannot help you." His response was firm. "I have my own life to attend to, Emmaline. I am waiting for a new commission. Word could come any day and, when it comes, I must be here or the position will go to someone else."

"You are not in the army any more?" Her gaze flicked over his uniform coat and her brow creased as if in confusion.

"My regiment was disbanded. I'm on half-pay."

"Half-pay? What is that?" Her eyes widened suddenly and her voice rose. "Do you need money, Gabriel? I can pay you money to help me."

"I do not need money," he snapped. What he needed she could not give him, not without forsaking her son. "The army pays half of a salary when a soldier is idled, but do not concern yourself. I have plenty of money."

"Even so…" she fingered the front of her dress "…I will pay for your help."

Did she think he would accept money for such a thing? It galled him that she would presume they could make some sort of business arrangement after what they'd had together.

What he thought they'd had.

"How old is Claude now?" he asked.

She looked puzzled. "He is now eighteen years."

"I was in the army, taking care of myself when I turned eighteen. Claude is his own man now. He must act on his own and accept the consequences."

She seized his arm. "You do not understand. He will be caught. He will hang for murder."

Her touch radiated through him. "That is his decision."

"*Non, non,* Gabriel," she cried. "You must stop him. He cannot hang. I cannot bear it."

Gabe felt himself weaken. Claude was her whole world, more important to her than anything or anyone else. Gabe had carried Claude off the Waterloo battlefield for that reason—for *her*—even while the cries of countless other wounded men had filled his ears. He did not regret doing so, but how many times was he expected to rescue Claude for her?

He closed his hands around her arms and lifted her

away from him. He must think of himself now. Not of Emmaline. "I cannot go looking for him."

She did not relent. "Then find Edwin Tranville. Warn him. Tell him to hide himself until I find Claude. I will send word to you when Claude returns to Brussels with me."

He blew out a breath. "I am not going to look for Edwin Tranville." He wanted nothing to do with Edwin Tranville. "No more discussion."

He walked to the door and opened it. If she did not leave soon, his rapidly eroding resolve might entirely wash away. "I bid you good day."

He pictured himself holding her in his arms, inhaling her essence, feeling her warm curves against his body.

She paused to face him. "I am staying at the Bristol Hotel, if you decide differently."

He closed the door behind her and immediately paced the room, angry at her for making this request, angrier at himself for hoping she'd come for *him*. He turned towards the windows and watched her step out of the building onto the pavement. She took a few steps, then stopped to look for something in her reticule. She pulled out a lace-edged handkerchief and dabbed at her eyes.

His insides twisted.

With one distraught glance toward the building she started to walk away.

But the three officers he'd run into at the War Office were approaching her, returning from the tavern, no doubt. They swayed with drink and talked so loudly he could almost hear their words. They exclaimed in pleasure when catching sight of her.

The three men circled her, doffing their hats and bowing, their greetings too exuberant, too ungentlemanly. She tried to push past them, but they blocked her path. She stiffened and tried again.

Three drunk men in red coats? It was like Badajoz.

Gabe sensed her panic as if he were inside her skin. He grabbed his shako and hurried out of the parlour, crossing the hall to the front door. As he opened it the three men were right there, about to step inside. Through them Gabe saw Emmaline rushing away.

Hanson put an arm around Gabe's shoulder. "Deane, my good friend. You just missed the most delectable creature. In fact, you might be able to catch up to her if you hurry." Contrary to his words, though, he pushed Gabe inside with them.

"She was a sight for sore eyes, that is to be sure," agreed Irishman. "A pity Webberly scared her off. Never did know how to approach a lady."

Webberly shoved him. "What *lady* would be walking out of Stephen's alone?" He laughed. "Shall we wager on whose room she was visiting?"

Gabe clenched a fist. "I saw the three of you through the window. You frightened her."

Hanson guffawed. "And you were rushing to her rescue? Great strategy, Deane! No better way to get a woman into bed than to come to her rescue."

Irishman staggered ahead. "I've a bottle in my room if you've a mind to wet your whistle before dinner is served."

"Come with us," Hanson said to Gabe.

"No, I have an errand." He drew back.

"Come to us when you are done." Irishman gestured for Hanson and Webberly to hurry. "We'll save you a drink."

"Four-to-one odds Deane is going after that fancy piece," Webberly cried.

The others laughed, but Gabe was already across the threshold. Once outside he ran out to Bond Street and managed to catch sight of Emmaline in the distance, walking alone.

He followed her, as he had that first day he'd glimpsed her in Brussels. Irishman, Hanson and Webberly were harmless enough, but that did not mean there were no other men out there who could pose a danger to her.

He stayed close enough to keep her in sight, all the while cursing himself for involving himself with her again, for even caring about her safety when she so obviously cared only for what assistance he could render her. As soon as she was safely back to her hotel, he'd wash his hands of her.

"It is none of my affair!" he said aloud, receiving a startled glance from a gentleman passing by.

Walking back to her hotel, Emmaline still trembled inside. The three officers had frightened her badly, bringing back the terror of Badajoz, but she'd collected her wits in time. Straightening to her full height, she had ordered them to leave her alone. They immediately backed off, apologising with exaggerated politeness. She was glad she'd not panicked and run away. Inside she still felt the fear, but she'd learned that, even when afraid, it was best to demand what she wanted.

She had not hidden her fears for Claude from Gabriel, however. She'd even mentioned the guillotine to him. She well knew that the British hanged men for murder, but her imagination kept showing Claude ascending steps to a guillotine. She again could hear the sound of the blade being raised, the excited rumblings of the crowd, the blade whizzing in its descent and the indescribable sound of it doing its work. It was as if she were still a girl standing in the Place de la Revolution holding her mother's hand.

She forced herself to concentrate on putting one foot in front of the other, making her way to her hotel on Cork Street. It was not a far walk from Gabriel.

Gabriel.

How she had missed him. A part of her had wanted to weep for the joy of gazing upon him again, hearing his voice, inhaling his essence. The pain of sending him away had settled into a dull, enduring ache, but now the wound had reopened and bled freely again.

He was still so angry with her.

She could not blame him. He'd offered her his name and his protection and she'd sent him away, knowing that if she chose him her son would be lost to her for ever and she would never have a chance to help Claude find a way to happiness and peace.

It would be impossible to make Gabriel understand. It was not him she had rejected so cruelly. She simply could not turn away from her son, not when it was her fault Claude was so vengeful.

She should have defied her husband all those years ago, run away with Claude so her husband could not take him away from her. She'd been cowardly.

C'est vrai, she would never have met Gabriel, then. She would never have known those brief weeks of bliss with him. She would never have hurt him so acutely, either. Now she had wounded him all over again by coming to see him and asking for his help.

Her head was reeling. How was she to find Claude on her own? No one in England would help her, not with her French accent and story of a son who planned to kill an Englishman. *Non,* she would be reported to the English *gendarmerie;* perhaps she and Claude both would climb up to the scaffold.

She needed Gabriel. Needed him. Gabriel had found Claude on a battlefield littered with thousands of dead and dying men; he would know how to find him in England. Gabriel would protect her, as well, keep her safe from Edwin Tranville, who still frightened her as much as he had the day he'd tried to rape her and kill Claude, the day he'd laughed when the other men killed her husband. Emmaline should have killed Edwin Tranville herself that day. Gabriel had stopped her.

Gabriel.

Did all her thoughts return to him? When she had risen from her chair in the parlour she thought her heart might stop at the sight of him. She'd forgotten how grand he was, how formidable, a man who could do anything, even come through a battle unscathed to return her son to her.

And here she was, asking him to do it again, to find Claude against nearly impossible odds, to again snatch him from the jaws of death. She had no doubt that Gabriel could do it.

If he would agree.

Emmaline entered her hotel and told the hall servant to send her dinner to her room. She'd procured the most inexpensive room available, trying to conserve her funds so that she could pay Gabriel all she possessed to help her find Claude. Instead he'd been insulted by her offer of money.

Emmaline climbed three sets of stairs to her room and immediately took off her bonnet and gloves. She undid the buttons of the blue spencer she'd sewn to match her blue muslin dress. She was still French enough to take pride in her appearance.

When Claude had been recuperating, he'd wanted to learn English. She'd had plenty of time to sew while drilling him in English words and phrases.

If she'd only known why he wanted to speak the language.

She had sewn clothes for him, because he had outgrown his old ones, and next for herself, using as inspiration the gowns of the most fashionable English ladies who came into the lace shop. She'd been glad to see her clothes were not out of place in London.

Had Gabriel admired her appearance? She wished for his admiration of her ensemble as strongly as she detested the attention it had brought from the three drunken soldiers.

She lay upon the bed and stared at the ceiling, but her mind's eye saw only Gabriel: his dark unruly hair; his chocolate brown eyes; the expressive mouth that had once pressed against her own lips.

She groaned.

She ached for him. Seeing Gabriel this day made her yearn for those glorious nights when he shared her bed. She'd been happy with him. Even with Claude in the army and Napoleon on the march again, those days with Gabriel had been the happiest she had ever known and she'd missed him every day thereafter. She pulled out the ring she still wore on a chain under her dress. This reminder of him rested always against her heart and kept him near to her, even after two years' absence.

Finding Gabriel when she came to London had been far easier than she expected. One of the hotel maids here had told her to ask for him at Stephen's Hotel.

"If he's an officer and he's in London, then he will be staying at the Stephen's Hotel. Mark my words," the girl had said.

She'd been correct. Emmaline arrived in London that morning and by afternoon she had found him. And lost him again.

Now what was she to do?

An idea occurred to her. If Gabriel was at the Stephen's Hotel, maybe Edwin Tranville was there, as well. *Non,* if that were so, surely Gabriel would have told her. Besides, if Tranville were so easy to find, Claude would have killed him already and her strong, handsome son might already have hung by the neck for it.

Claude had grown strong again, even though it had taken him two years to fully recover from his wounds at Waterloo. As his strength grew, so did his restlessness. He finally asked to travel to Paris to visit her parents. Emmaline had agreed, hoping a change in scene would be good for him.

But he had never arrived in Paris. Instead a letter came, explaining his true destination and his avowed intent.

That had been a month ago. Where was he now? And how would she find him?

She came back to Gabriel.

She must think of a way to make him agree, though why should he help her when she had rejected him so cruelly?

She flung an arm across her face, trying to hold off the despair that threatened to completely overwhelm her.

She'd give anything to keep her son from throwing his life away. Anything. But what did she possess that would entice Gabriel to help her?

Emmaline sat up.

She had said she would give *anything* to save Claude.

Well, she would do more. She would give Gabriel *everything*.

Everything.

He would not refuse.

Chapter Eight

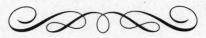

Gabe descended the stairway to the hotel's dining room, deciding he might as well distract himself and eat. Staying alone in his room had been no help. One minute he had surged with anger at Emmaline for coming back into his life and re-igniting his need for her, the next minute he knew he must help her. It would require no effort on his part, after all.

He knew where to find Edwin Tranville.

Mere weeks ago he'd been thrown into Edwin's company. He'd run into Allan Landon, his friend since Allan had been his lieutenant in Spain. Allan was no longer in the army, but was working for Lord Sidmouth and the Home Office, as was, astonishingly, Edwin Tranville. They were charged with combating seditious acts. Allan had learned that a group of soldiers planned to gather to protest against unemployment and high prices. He wanted to stop the protest before the soldiers risked arrest. Gabe had run into Allan when Allan was searching for Edwin, who knew where the gathering was to take place. Gabe helped him search. They found Edwin in a tavern, drunk as usual. Allan quickly left to stop the march and Gabe wound up playing nursemaid to Edwin.

No mention of the soldiers' march ever reached a newspaper, so Gabe surmised Allan must have been successful.

Luckily Edwin had apparently been too drunk to remember Gabe's interference. Gabe had no wish for Lord Tranville, Edwin's father, to learn he was in London seeking a new commission. Lord Tranville would certainly foil any chances Gabe possessed.

Gabe approached the door of the dining room. The Stephen's Hotel was a popular place to dine and almost like a club for officers who could not gain admittance to White's or Brooks's.

No sooner had Gabe entered the dining room than he was hailed by the three officers who accosted Emmaline. They waved him over to sit with them. Gabe shrugged. They'd done her no real harm, nothing any man with a little drink would not have done when encountering a beautiful, unaccompanied woman. Besides, it would be advantageous for him not to be alone with his own thoughts.

"We are making a wager," Irishman said, "with Webberly's timepiece—how many minutes until the fried soles are served? Are you in?"

"I never wager." Gabe lowered himself into a chair.

Hanson immediately poured Gabe a glass of wine. "There's the pity of it. We could have a game of whist after dinner if you were a gambling man."

Gabe scanned the room. "I trust someone here would accept."

Irishman drummed his fingers on the table. "We sat

down not more than ten minutes ago, and the servant brought the wine immediately—"

"And thereby earned my eternal gratitude," interrupted Webberly.

Irishman went on. "So, I estimate it should be another ten minutes at least,"

"I wagered another twenty minutes," Hanson said.

Webberly lifted a finger. "And I, fifteen."

Unimaginative lot, thought Gabe. They all bet in equal segments. Likely the food would come on some other point of the clock, like eight minutes or thirteen.

At that moment the soup arrived and they fell silent, except for some audible slurping. No sooner were they done with the soup than the fried sole was served.

Irishman jostled Webberly. "How much time? What does your timepiece say?"

Webberly picked up the gold watch from the table and pressed the button to open it. "What time did the wager start?"

His two friends looked at him blankly and all three burst into laughter.

Irishman lifted his glass of wine. "'The better the gambler, the worse the man!'" A quotation by Publius Syrus, Gabe recalled from his school days.

"Then we are the best of men." Webberly took a gulp from his wine glass.

Their dinner conversation drifted into more serious matters, such as who among their acquaintance had found commissions, who was still looking, and who might become desperate enough to accept a place in the West Indies.

The conversation was not enough to keep Gabe from being haunted by the memory of Emmaline's desolate expression when he sent her away. He pushed around slices of scalloped potatoes and finally jabbed at his fried sole.

There was only one way to exorcise himself of her image. Do as she wished. Find Edwin, warn him, and be done with it.

In the morning he'd visit the Home Office, perform this one more service for her, and maybe purge her from his mind for ever after.

The next morning Gabe set out early, planning to walk the distance to the Home Office because the weather was so fine and the exercise would calm him.

He turned on to Bond Street. And saw Emmaline.

She walked towards him with a determined, yet graceful step, and he disliked that her mere appearance affected him so strongly. This day she wore pale lavender and the mere hue of her clothing brought back to him the lavender scent from the lace shop, the scent that always wafted around her.

She, too, caught sight of him. As she drew nearer, her pace remained carefully even.

"Good morning, Gabriel," she murmured when they were in earshot. She looked directly into his eyes.

"I am surprised to see you, Emmaline." She appeared to be walking back to Stephen's Hotel to seek him out again.

Gabe had not expected or intended to lay eyes on her again. After warning Edwin, he'd planned to write her a letter and have it delivered to her hotel.

"I still have hopes to convince you to help me." She lowered her gaze. "May I have a moment of your time to speak to you?" She spoke so carefully, so hesitantly.

He paused. "Walk with me."

They walked in silence, crossing Piccadilly and making their way towards Green Park.

"I have a new proposal to present to you," she said to him, breathless from keeping up with his long strides. "Could we not stop so I may tell you of it?"

What would she offer now? More money? Or merely play upon his obvious regard for her? He did not wish to hear more from her.

Still, he seemed unable to refuse. "We will stop in the Park."

They could cross through Green Park to reach the Home Office. There would be benches there where they might sit, where she could catch her breath and spill out this new proposal he had no wish to hear.

The Park was fragrant with blooming flowers and the scent of leafy trees and sprouting grass. Warm breezes whispered through the shrubbery, and Gabe for a moment was transported back to the Parc de Brussels where he and Emmaline had strolled in happier days.

They came upon a bench and he gestured for her to sit. "Say what you need to say."

She lowered herself on to the bench and looked disconcerted when he remained standing. Her hand fluttered to her face. "How to begin…"

Gabe gazed through the trees, his insides seared by memories and false hopes.

She fingered the front of her dress. "You once seemed to have a regard for me, is that not so, Gabriel?"

"Once." He refused to admit more.

"We did well together, *non?*" She smiled, but her lips trembled.

He merely stared at her.

"You proposed marriage to me, *non?*"

He still did not speak, not knowing where she was leading, surmising it would cause him pain.

She took a breath. "I will marry you now, Gabriel." She waved a hand. "If—if you help me find Claude and stop him from doing this terrible act, I will marry you and go wherever you wish and do whatever you say." She made a quick, decisive nod, as if convincing herself that she could indeed perform such a distasteful task.

Gabe gaped at her. "Marry me? What of Claude, then? Will he cease to despise me if I stop him from what he wishes to do?"

A great sadness filled her eyes, but her chin lifted in determination. "He will probably hate you the more for it, but that cannot be as important as him being alive. It is better for Claude to live and have a chance for happiness, even if he chooses to exclude me from his life."

Her son's life. To save it, she'd agree to anything. Even to marry Gabe.

It felt as if she had now twisted the knife she'd plunged into his chest two years before. Did she think he wanted her to give up the most important part of her life for him?

When he'd proposed to her in Brussels, he'd meant their marriage to be a pledge of love and fidelity between them, not a contest between him and Claude. *You win, Gabriel. I'll marry you.* That had not been what Gabe meant about wanting to win her hand. Possession of her company was not the prize, winning her away from her son was not victory. Spending his days and nights with her, sharing their dreams together, that was the prize, much more valuable. Gabe wanted to grow old with Emmaline, but not at the expense of her attachment to her son. What kind of man did she think he was?

She gazed back into his eyes, her expression tense. "Well, do you agree? Will you help me?" Her voice wobbled.

This offer of hers—this *sacrifice*—stung worse than her initial rejection, which, even though he did not like it, he'd understood. God help him, he had even envied the devotion she bestowed on her son. He'd never been that important to his own mother, not with all his brothers and sisters needing her more, but this was not about his needs. It was about Emmaline. She needed her son like she needed air to breathe. As painful as it was, Gabe would never take away her life's breath. He refused to be the sacrifice she must make, the price of saving Claude from his own folly.

"Gabriel?" she asked anxiously.

He could at least force her to explain. "I thought you did not want to marry a man your son would despise."

Panic flickered in her eyes. She glanced away. "I never despised you, though. We—we were good friends, were we not?"

Good friends. Such a far cry from being her life's breath.

She went on, "It will be enough to know Claude is alive. I...I will even—how did you say it?—follow the drum with you when you return to the army."

"You will marry me and travel with me as a soldier's wife?" She'd hated such a life when her husband had demanded it of her. More sacrifice she was willing to make, for the sake of her son.

She blinked. "If you are able to prevent Claude from murdering, yes, then I will marry you." She looked up again. "I will gladly marry you."

"What a compliment to me," he murmured.

"Qu'est-ce que tu as dit?" She shook her head. "I mean, what did you say?"

"It is of no consequence." He gestured to the path. "Shall we be on our way?"

She rose and clutched his arm. "You did not answer me."

There was no more than an inch separating them. The sun lit her anxious face and the lavender scent he'd imagined became real. At the Parc de Brussels they'd stood together just like this, sheltered from view by a large allegorical statue. He'd leaned down and tasted her lips that day and held her in his arms.

The urge to kiss her and hold her again was unabated even though *he* was the sacrifice she would make to save her son from a hanging. He leaned closer and she rose on tiptoe, so close their breath mingled.

"Your answer?" she whispered.

He stepped back. He ought to let her think he'd go along with making her choose him over her son. It would serve her right for thinking so little of him.

He was no card player, but he could bluff like one. "Very well, Emmaline. I will hold you to your promise. I will prevent Claude from murdering Edwin Tranville and you will marry me."

Her lips trembled again, but she nodded, her hand pressed against her chest.

He started to walk and she skipped to catch up to him. "Where are you going?"

"I am headed to the Home Office," he said.

"The Home Office?"

He set a fast pace. "The place where Edwin Tranville is employed."

She strained to keep up with him. "You know where he is?"

"I always knew where he was."

She sounded angry. "You were going to warn him? Even before I spoke today?"

He stopped and faced her. "That is correct, Emmaline. I was planning to do that much for you, but you made a new bargain. After I speak to Edwin today, I'll proceed to where I might obtain a special licence so you and I can be married right away."

She gazed straight ahead. "Do not forget you must ensure that Claude does not kill this man. Then I will marry you."

He gave her a sardonic smile. "That is our bargain."

They did not speak until the buildings on Whitehall came into view.

"We are near," Gabe said.

When they approached the Home Office building, Emmaline shrank back. "Must I see him?"

"See who?"

"Edwin Tranville." Her voice turned low and shaky.

He'd forgotten. She did not know Edwin as a drunken coward, but as a dangerous man who'd tried to rape her and kill her son.

He put his hand over hers. "Do not fear," he murmured. "He cannot hurt you."

She looked up into his eyes and he could almost think that the connection he'd believed they had in Brussels had returned and was real.

He led her through the hallways to the rooms housing the Home Office. She shrank back as he opened the door.

A clerk sat behind a desk, looking very much like the clerk who sat behind the desk in the War Office. The man raised his eyes. "Yes?"

Emmaline stood behind Gabe. He could feel the stiffening of her muscles. She was bracing herself to see Edwin again.

Gabe inclined his head. "Edwin Tranville, please."

The clerk glanced down again. "Edwin Tranville is not here."

"When might we expect him?" Gabe asked.

"Never," the clerk said. "He will not be back."

Emmaline moved forwards. "Did something happen to him?"

"No." The man regarded her with a puzzled but admiring expression. He glanced down again and restacked the papers in front of him. "Lord Sidmouth gave him the sack."

Emmaline looked at Gabe. "What does this mean, 'gave him the sack'?"

"Terminated his employment," the clerk answered. "Mr Tranville failed to fulfil his responsibilities."

Somehow this was not a surprise. It was more bewildering that Sidmouth had hired Edwin in the first place.

"Is Mr Landon here, then?" Perhaps Allan would know where to find Edwin.

The clerk laughed drily. "Not since he married an heiress and no longer needs to work."

Allan married? And to an heiress? Lucky woman. He was the best of men and would make the best of husbands.

"Do you know where I might find Tranville?" Gabe asked. "Does he reside with his father, Lord Tranville?"

The man shrugged. "He lives at the Albany."

"Thank you." Gabe nodded to the man.

When they walked out the door, Emmaline seized his arm. "Gabriel, is Edwin Tranville's father a lord?"

"He is."

She whispered, "This makes it worse for Claude."

Always Claude. Anger twisted inside Gabe and he hated feeling it. He did not wish to feel a rivalry with her son.

"Will we go to this Albany?" she asked.

He shrugged. "It is a logical next step." And not too much more exertion on Gabe's part, before he could end this charade.

Their walk to the Albany on Piccadilly reminded Gabe of their strolls through Brussels' streets, but only in contrast. Gone was the ease between them, the pleasure of merely walking at her side. Still, he was struck with the odd feeling of how right it seemed that they walked together again.

He must take care. It was startling how easily his fantasies about her grew. He must not forget that her sole purpose was to save her son and she would do anything to rescue him from his folly.

Even marry.

Gabe tried to keep that thought in his head. It helped ward off fanciful musings.

The Albany was a popular bachelor residence for the aristocracy, so it stood to reason top-lofty Edwin would live there.

When they reached Piccadilly, Emmaline remarked, "There are many shops here."

Gabe made a sarcastic smile. "Did not your Napoleon call England a nation of shopkeepers?"

"He is not my Napoleon," she snapped. Her voice turned low. "Never *my* Napoleon."

The Albany was set back from the street, a three-storey house flanked on two sides of a courtyard by wings two storeys high. They crossed the courtyard, Emmaline receiving curious and appreciative glances from the young gentlemen they passed. Gabe disliked their open admiration.

He led her through the main doorway and found a servant attending the hall.

"Is Edwin Tranville here?" Gabe asked the man.

"Cannot say," he answered. "I do not know of all the comings and goings. Shall I send someone to his room?"

"Please," Gabe answered.

The man made a vague gesture towards the wall. "You may wait here."

Gabe endured Emmaline receiving more leering glances by men who passed by. She nervously fingered the front of her dress, which did nothing to keep him from thinking about how pleasurable it had once been to undress her.

"I do not wish to see him," she murmured.

Gabe's compassion was sparked again. "If you like, I can escort you back to your hotel and return here later."

She shook her head. "I do not wish to delay."

Two men crossed the hall and this time their glances at Emmaline were plainly lascivious. Gabe nearly stepped forwards to defend her.

He controlled the impulse. It would help nothing to engage impertinent young men in fisticuffs.

Finally the servant returned, another man accompanying him.

This man approached them. "You asked for Mr Tranville?"

Gabe nodded. "We did."

"Mr Tranville is not here. I am his man. May I ask the reason you are calling upon him?"

Gabe responded, "I served with him in the Royal Scots."

The valet looked at Emmaline and raised his brows.

Good God. Even a valet was being insulting. Gabe glared at him. "My betrothed accompanies me at my request. Do you have some objection?"

The valet's cheeks turned bright red. "I beg your pardon, Captain."

"When will Mr Tranville return?" Gabe demanded.

The valet pulled on his collar. "I do not know precisely. He has travelled out of town. I am awaiting instructions from him whether he wishes me to follow him."

Gabe frowned. He should have known Edwin would make this complicated. "Where is he?"

"I do not know precisely," the valet answered. "I am awaiting his direction."

"Non!" Emmaline exclaimed.

Gabe spoke quickly. "Someone must know where Tranville went. Is there anyone here who might know?"

The valet shook his head. "I do not know if he is acquainted with anyone here."

"But we must find him!" cried Emmaline.

Gabe put a stilling hand on her arm. "Is his father in London at present?"

"I do not believe so," the valet answered. "I believe he is at his estate."

Gabe turned to Emmaline. "It is no use."

She looked stricken, but there was nothing more they could do here now. She held back, but finally nodded. She took his arm and they started to walk towards the door.

The valet called after them, "Mr Tranville's cousin resides in London. Perhaps she knows where he is."

Emmaline's fingers squeezed Gabe's arm. Her expression turned hopeful.

"Where may we find her?"

The valet gave them her direction on Bryanston Street. "Her name is Miss Pallant."

Gabe and Emmaline walked out of the Albany and back to Piccadilly Street.

"May we call upon this Miss Pallant?" Emmaline asked him.

He felt as if in a snare, but one he'd chosen to walk into. "We may go there as soon as you wish."

"Now, Gabriel?" Her eyes pleaded.

"Now, Emmaline."

Chapter Nine

Emmaline leaned back against the worn leather of the hackney coach, grateful to Gabriel for hiring it. Her feet hurt from trying to keep pace with him when they walked. When they'd strolled through Brussels he'd never walked so fast.

She supposed she ought not to repine too much about Brussels and how rapturous her time with him had been. Matters were so altered between them now.

His reaction to her bargain to become his wife had not been at all what she had expected. She thought she was offering him what he desired, but it only seemed to make him angrier at her. Did he not know that if it were not for Claude, she would have married him long ago?

She touched the ring she wore beneath her dress, the one that reminded her daily of how important to her he had been.

And still was.

Sitting next to him in the carriage was difficult. She could feel the heat of his body, inhale his scent, feel every breath he took, every flexing of muscle. Being so close reminded her of tangled sheets and naked skin and the glorious nights she'd spent enfolded in his arms.

Now he avoided touching her and the space between them on the carriage seat seemed to crackle with unpleasant emotions.

The coach stopped and he glanced out the window. "We are here."

He opened the door and climbed out, turning to offer her his hand. She felt a shock of awareness when his glove touched hers. Her senses came alive to him and she wished they were still in Brussels, closing the lace shop, crossing the yard to her little house and climbing the steps to her bed chamber.

Instead, he led her to the door of a townhouse, the residence of this Miss Pallant who was Edwin Tranville's *cousine.* The town house was built of dark-grey brick with a red-brick fan design above windows with white sashes. What would an English house look like inside? What would the mistress of such a house think of a Frenchwoman whose son planned to kill her cousin?

She shuddered.

Gabriel sounded the knocker and after a few minutes it was opened by a large man who looked more like a soldier than a servant.

Before the man could speak Gabriel cried, "Good God. Reilly?"

A wide smile lit the man's face. "Captain Deane!"

The two men shook hands like long-lost brothers.

"Come in. Come in." Reilly stepped aside. "It is a pleasure to see you, sir."

"What the devil are you doing here?" Gabriel ushered her inside.

Reilly laughed. "I'm the butler here, if you can believe that."

"The butler?" Gabriel shook his head.

"My lady found me when I was as low as a man can get. No job. No food. Thinking of turning to thievery, I was." He paused. "But never mind that. I expect you are here to see—"

At that moment another man, more finely dressed, entered the hall. "Who's come, Reilly? I heard voices."

"Allan?" Gabriel sounded shocked.

"Gabe!" This man rushed forwards and embraced Gabriel. "Thought I'd lost track of you. But you found me. I'm so pleased."

"Indeed."

This appeared to be a joyful reunion, so Emmaline was happy for Gabriel. She just hoped it would also mean they would find the cousin who could lead them to Edwin Tranville.

Gabriel's friend glanced at her with a curious expression and Gabriel seemed to belatedly remember her presence.

He took her arm and presented her. "Allan, this is Madame Mableau."

Allan looked even more curious. *"Madame."* He bowed.

"Do you not recognise her?" Gabriel asked.

Emmaline's brows rose. Was she supposed to know this man?

Allan shook his head.

Gabriel darted a glance towards the butler before turning back to his friend and speaking in a low voice. "She is the woman from Badajoz." He turned to her. "Emmaline, this is Captain Allan Landon. He was there."

She gasped. In Badajoz. He must have been the one who carried Edwin Tranville away. "Captain Landon."

The Captain's eyes widened. "*Madame!* My God. I hope you are well—" He examined her again. "But you must be well. You look so lovely. Why are you here?"

"I fear we are in the wrong house." She wanted to find Edwin Tranville's cousin, but Gabriel was so happy to see his friend. If she knew the correct house, she would call upon the cousin alone.

Gabriel explained. "We thought this the residence of Miss Marian Pallant."

Landon looked even more puzzled. "It is, but—" He tapped his forehead. "Forgive me. Let us sit. Have refreshment."

"I'll tend to it, Captain," Reilly said.

Landon offered Emmaline his arm and led them to a drawing room, a comfortable room, with upholstered sofas and chairs of the best brocade. Porcelain figurines, a matched set of a shepherd and shepherdess, decorated the mantelpiece. They might have come from the finest china shop in Brussels.

"Please sit," Landon said, leading her to a sofa. Gabriel remained standing.

She did not want to sit or have refreshment. "Please. Is Miss Pallant here? It is urgent that we speak to her."

"Urgent?" Landon frowned. "What is this about?"

She turned to Gabriel. "How much may we tell him?"

Landon stiffened. "By God, you will tell me all of it if it involves my wife."

"Your wife?" Gabriel blinked.

Landon fixed his gaze on him. "I am married to Marian Pallant."

"The heiress." Gabriel nodded. "Yes. They said at the Home Office you had married an heiress."

Landon folded his arms across his chest. "Why were you at the Home Office and why was my wife being discussed there?"

"Do not tell him." Emmaline rose. "Perhaps we cannot trust him."

Gabriel put his hand on her arm. "Allan, we are looking for Edwin. His valet sent us here."

Landon's eyes narrowed, his expression angry. "Edwin." He looked at Emmaline. "Why do you wish to see Edwin? After what he did—"

Gabriel answered, "We are attempting to prevent a wrong. Emmaline's son has vowed to revenge himself on Edwin and we are trying to intervene."

Emmaline held her breath, carefully examining Landon's expression to see if he would act as friend or foe.

"God knows Edwin deserves it." Allan expelled a breath. "I presume you spoke to his valet at the Albany. Edwin was not there?"

"Out of town, apparently," Gabriel responded. "We were hoping his cousin—" he smiled "—*your* wife would know where he had gone."

"Is she here?" Emmaline broke in. "May we speak to her?"

Landon looked at her with kindness. "She is not here."

Emmaline averted her gaze, disappointed tears stinging her eyes.

"Madame." Landon's voice was soothing. "She will return later this day."

There was a knock on the parlour door and the butler entered with a tray with a carafe, glasses and tea things. "Brought both, Captain," Reilly said. He bowed out.

"Sit, now," Landon said. "Gabe, I suspect you would rather have the brandy."

"Indeed."

Landon told them about meeting his wife during the battle of Waterloo and again when the war was over. They'd been married only a few weeks. "I cannot say if Marian knows Edwin's whereabouts or not."

They all fell into silence; Emmaline sipped her tea while the men drank brandy.

Alan drained his glass and set it on the table. "I have an idea, but I need time to work on it. You both must come for dinner tonight at eight."

"Your wife will not mind?" Emmaline asked.

"Not at all." His expression turned proud. "She is an exceptional woman. She will assist you if she can." He smiled. "And she will enjoy having you as our guests for dinner."

Enjoy it? Emmaline could not imagine that a lord's niece who owned such grand things would enjoy dining with a shop girl. There was no *égalité* in England, it was said. But, then, the English did not use the guillotine; that was to their credit.

The rope, however, could be equally as lethal.

When she and Gabriel left and were seated in another hackney coach, she asked him, "Are you certain I should attend the dinner?"

He looked puzzled. "Why would you not?"

"I work in a lace shop."

He shrugged. "What does that matter? This is about locating Edwin's whereabouts."

She sighed. He did not understand.

He walked her to the door of her hotel. "I will have a coach here at seven-thirty." He bowed and walked away.

* * *

Emmaline descended the stairs and entered the hall of her hotel just as the clock sounded quarter past seven. If she had stayed one more minute in her room, she'd have perished from nerves. Once more she looked down at her dress and smoothed the skirt. Ladies dressed formally for dinner, she'd heard, but she had nothing like that to wear. Except for the dress she'd worn while travelling, Emmaline only had one more dress that Gabriel had not seen, a rather plain walking dress, but it was a pretty deep-rose colour. She'd quickly embellished the neckline with a lace ruff and added a peek of lace at the cuffs. She hoped it would be enough.

Gabriel was already waiting and stared at her as she crossed the hall to meet him at the door.

"Is my dress acceptable?" she asked him.

"Yes." His gaze flicked over her again. "It is acceptable." His voice was rough.

His reaction did not much relieve her mind.

A hackney coach waited on the street and Gabriel escorted her to it. The sky was still light and the evening as fine as ones they had shared in Brussels, but his company, much as she desired it, lowered her spirits.

As he assisted her into the coach, she set her chin. She must accept these difficult and confusing feelings about Gabriel for Claude's sake. And she must remain hopeful. This night she would meet Edwin Tranville's cousin and they would discover where to find him. Once Tranville was warned, they could work on finding Claude.

Claude would give up this foolish plan of vengeance for her. He must!

Her thoughts filled the time it took the coach to take

them back to Bryanston Street, which was a good thing, because Gabriel did not speak to her.

He looked very handsome in his uniform, with dress trousers and shoes instead of boots. He was freshly shaved and, sitting so close, she could see some pink scrapes on his cheek. She wished she could soothe them with her fingers.

She sighed.

"What is it?" Gabriel asked her.

She nearly jumped. "I did not speak."

"You sighed." His voice was low. "Were you thinking of Claude?"

"No."

He gave her answer no heed. "I suspect Mrs Landon will know how to locate Edwin, if that is what concerns you."

It was her turn to be silent. What would he think if he knew what had inspired her sigh?

The coach stopped at Bryanston Street and, as he had done earlier that day, Gabriel took her hand to help her out. Their gazes caught and held for a moment. Emmaline's heart quickened.

"Let us go." He made it sound as if she'd deliberately delayed them by gazing into his eyes.

The same soldier-butler opened the door and escorted them to the drawing room. Emmaline heard voices and spied Allan through the doorway.

He strode towards them, gesturing for them to enter. "Gabe! Come in. Come in."

Once they were in the parlour Emmaline's attention was immediately drawn to the two ladies present, both elegantly dressed.

One was exceptionally beautiful, with shining auburn hair and a face that might belong to a portrait at Versailles. The other, a confident, smiling blonde, was already assessing her. Which was Edwin Tranville's cousin? she wondered.

"Look who is here." Allan extended his arm.

A second gentleman stood. "Hello, Captain."

"Vernon?" Gabriel walked up to him, and the two men shook hands. "I am astonished you are here."

Landon grinned. "He is my surprise."

Emmaline knew this man. He also had been at Badajoz. He had drawn pictures of horses to amuse Claude. He turned to her. "*Madame,* do you remember me?"

She clasped his hand. "I do. You are Ensign Vernon."

He covered her hand with his own. "Now I am Mr Vernon. I sold my commission two years ago."

"Come meet our wives," Allan said.

The auburn-haired beauty was Vernon's wife, who insisted she be called by her given name, Ariana. The blonde, then, must be the cousin.

She did not wait for Emmaline to be presented. "I am Marian Landon." She gave her husband a quick glance. "I am Edwin's cousin."

Emmaline curtsied. "Have you learned why we are here, *madame?*"

The lovely lady looked stricken. "Allan told me. He told me what my cousin did to you and to your son. And that he was with men who killed your husband. I am so sorry."

"Thank you, *madame.*" Emmaline had not been certain she would be received so kindly.

Mrs Landon reached out and touched Emmaline's hand. "Please do call me Marian."

Her husband walked over to a table with a decanter and glasses. "Let us not talk about that now. Dinner will be ready soon. In the meantime, some refreshment." He lifted the decanter. "Claret, everyone?"

They drank claret and the men talked of the army and other officers they had known. The ladies talked of the theatre and the arts, things Emmaline knew little of, but she was not surprised to learn that Madame Vernon was an actress. How ironic that she'd thought the woman as beautiful as a painting, because her husband, the man who'd drawn pictures for Claude, now painted portraits.

At dinner Emmaline learned that Jack Vernon had a portrait of his wife in an important exhibition.

"I need to tell you," Vernon said, "my mother and her husband are in town. They came only a few days ago, for the end of the Season and for the exhibition. But you must know..." He swallowed "You must know that my mother's husband is General Lord Tranville." He looked at Emmaline. "Edwin's father. I might as well add that my mother, before she married Tranville, was in his keeping."

Landon gaped. "No. I do not believe it."

Emmaline turned to Gabriel. "What is this 'in his keeping'?"

He paused a moment before answering. "She was his mistress."

She lifted a shoulder. What was the fuss? In France such would be considered a trivial piece of information. In fact, she had been Gabriel's mistress.

So briefly.

"Is that why you were forced to tell Tranville about Badajoz?" Gabriel asked.

Vernon glanced at his wife. "In part—"

Ariana interrupted. "And in part due to me, I'm afraid."

Gabriel took a sip of the wine and seemed lost in thought.

"We will call upon the father of Edwin tomorrow, will we not, Gabriel?" Emmaline asked him.

"Not you, Emmaline." His voice was firm.

"Why not?" she cried.

"Tranville must not know who you are." The look on his face alarmed her.

"He is right," Vernon agreed. He turned to Emmaline. "I was forced to tell Tranville what his son tried to do to you and your boy. He and I have a mutual agreement not to speak of it. He has good reason not to retaliate against me, but he would feel no such restraint in lashing out against you or your son, if he thought *his* son would be disgraced."

Emmaline's eyes widened. They acted as if this father was to be more feared than the son.

Gabriel set down his wine glass. "I will go alone tomorrow."

"I'll go with you, if you like," Allan offered.

"No." Vernon leaned forwards. "None of you can go. Tranville is shrewd. If he connects you to the incident with Edwin, he'll find some way to silence you. I will go."

Ariana shook her head. "Jack, he will never tell you what you want to know. He never speaks with you unless he cannot avoid it."

Her husband shrugged. "My mother will convince him."

She laughed. "She is more likely to side with him."

"That is true, I'm afraid." He crossed his arms over his chest.

"I should go." Marian straightened. "I am perfect for the task. Uncle Tranville will not question why I am asking about Edwin. I am the only one in existence who might care where Edwin is."

"I shall go with you," Allan said. "We owe your uncle and Vernon's mother a call. It would be the most natural thing in the world for us to do so."

Marian turned to Emmaline and Gabriel. "Come tomorrow for dinner. We will know something then and can decide what to do next."

The ladies retired to the drawing room and Allan, Gabe and Vernon remained in the dining room, drinking brandy.

Gabe absently ran his finger along the rim of his glass, while Vernon and Allan continued to discuss the impending visit to Tranville.

Ever since Emmaline had walked into his life again, Gabe's emotions had been in a muddle. It was best he stay out of Tranville's sights; the man had the power to ruin his chances for a new commission, after all. At the same time, he was having difficulty sharing the task of helping Emmaline, even with his friends.

Vernon pointed a finger at Allan. "Take care you don't even hint why you ask about Edwin."

"We will be careful." Allan smiled. "I'm afraid both Marian and I are well practised in keeping secrets." He turned to Gabe. "What is between you and Madame Mableau?"

Gabe felt his face burn. "There is nothing between us."

Allan persisted. "But she sought you out."

"Who else? She does not know anyone in England." He tried to sound matter of fact.

"I cannot forget those days in Badajoz," Vernon

said in a low voice. "It is difficult to blame her son for remembering it with such hatred."

Gabe stared into his drink. "A lot of bad things happened during the war. We must leave it behind us." At least that was what he aspired to do.

Vernon slid cautious glances at them both. "Did any of it ever come back to you?" His tone was hushed. "I had moments when I actually thought I was back there."

"I have had nightmares about it," Allan admitted.

Gabe dreamt of Badajoz as well, but the dreams always were about Emmaline.

How odd it was that one event in Badajoz bound him with Allan and Vernon and that none of them could escape being affected by it still. Even more ironic, they were all connected to Edwin Tranville. At least Gabe did not have to count Edwin among his family. Theoretically, he could walk away from all this and never think of it again.

Theoretically.

He could have refused to help Emmaline. He had no reason to be involved. None of them did, except that they had witnessed Edwin's despicable behaviour and Gabe had learned precisely how acutely it had affected Emmaline and her son.

She had looked more beautiful than ever this night, a worthy rival even for Jack Vernon's wife. The lace on her dress reminded him of the lace shop, of her busy fingers smoothing the delicate creations, folding them or presenting them for display. He imagined her selecting the lace for her collar and cuffs from the strips of lace hanging over rods in the shop. He could see her pleating it and sewing it to her dress, her eyes concentrating on her work, her lips pressed into a line, her fingers as graceful as a ballet dancer as she pulled the needle through. Those same fingers had stroked his naked skin, those lips had showered him with kisses, and her eyes, until that morning when he had proposed marriage, had looked upon him with desire.

"Are you thinking of that night, Gabe?" Allan asked.

He glanced up and realised he'd missed some of the conversation.

"The night in Badajoz?" Not the nights he'd made love to Emmaline in her bed.

Allan's brow creased. "Yes—what were you thinking of?"

Gabe stared into his drink. "I was thinking that we should have killed Edwin that night."

"Gabe!" Allan looked shocked.

Gabe went on. "No one would have known. We would have done the world and ourselves a good turn."

Vernon lifted his glass to his lips. "I'm inclined to agree."

Allan shook his head. "You are speaking nonsense. I know you, Gabe. You would not take a man's life without cause."

"It seems to me we had good cause," Gabe retorted. "This revenge of Claude's, this quest of his mother's, none of it would be necessary had we rid the world of him that night."

How different might it have been if they had put a period to Edwin's existence. Perhaps even Brussels would have been different.

Chapter Ten

The next night they again gathered in Marian and Allan's drawing room, connected by one event, one person, the person Gabe was now duty-bound to find. He glanced at Emmaline as Allan poured glasses of claret and passed them around. She had chosen a chair, not wanting Gabe to sit next to her, he supposed. He envied Jack and Ariana, so comfortable together on the small sofa. But Emmaline did not appear to take heed of them or of Gabe. Her gaze darted from Allan to Marian. Gabe could feel her impatience for them to speak.

Allan's grave expression showed that there would not be a celebratory toast. Gabe sipped his wine and waited.

Allan finally took a seat next to his wife on the other sofa. "I won't tease you any longer. We do have news of Edwin…"

"He is no longer in London," Marian finished for him. "I'm so sorry."

"We do know where he is, however," Allan continued. "He's gone to Bath."

"My uncle sent him there," Marian explained in their seamless joint narrative. "You see, my uncle made a quick trip to town about the same time as the soldiers' march, and he was furious to learn how abysmally Edwin failed in his duties to Lord Sidmouth, so he banished Edwin to Bath, to the house that was my aunt's." She turned to Jack. "You remember the house, do you not?"

Jack nodded. "About a mile off the Wells Road."

"That is it." She turned back to Gabe and Emmaline. "Uncle Tranville told Edwin to stay there and not show his face in town until his shameful behaviour was forgotten." She made a wry smile. "That is nearly an exact quote. Minus the malediction."

Allan turned back to Emmaline with a reassuring look. "Bath is not far. A day's journey by coach on good roads."

"Then I will travel there tomorrow." Emmaline darted a glance at Gabriel as if unsure that he would accompany her.

"Will you escort her there, Gabe?" Allan asked. It was more like an order than a question.

Did he think Gabe would leave this task to her alone? She was wrong to have asked it of him and insulting to offer herself in marriage as payment, but Gabe was not without honour and compassion. He'd seen how frightened she was at the prospect of coming face to face with Edwin.

Gabe met Allan's gaze. "I will take her."

"Tomorrow, Gabriel?" Emmaline still looked tense.

He stood. "Tomorrow. But I need time to make arrangements, so I'll not stay to dinner."

Emmaline rose.

He barely looked at her. "You may remain, Emmaline.

Jack and Ariana can see you back to your hotel." He glanced at Jack.

"Our pleasure." Jack stood and shook his hand.

Emmaline took a step towards him. "I want to come with you."

He shook his head. "Your company will make it more difficult." Her mere presence made everything more difficult, arousing sensations and emotions that were best buried in the past.

Their gazes caught for a moment, but Gabe quickly turned away.

"The coaches leave very early. Be ready at four in the morning. I will come to pick you up." He bowed to the others. "Good night."

Allan walked him to the door. "Is there any way we can help?"

"You've already helped." Gabe collected his hat and gloves.

Reilly appeared in the hall and opened the door for him.

Allan walked him to it. "Maybe some day we can all put Badajoz to rest. After this, perhaps."

Gabe shook his hand. "Perhaps."

Gabe stepped out into the night and headed towards Oxford Street in search of a hackney coach to carry him to the Strand and the Angel Inn where passage on a fast coach to Bath could be procured.

At four the next morning, Emmaline waited in the hall of her hotel, her portmanteau, packed with all her possessions, at her feet. As she watched out of the window, she twisted the drawstring of her reticule, fighting an attack of nerves.

She feared encountering Edwin Tranville almost as

much as she feared they would find him too late. As if it were yesterday she could feel his hands on her, forcing her to the cobbles, lifting her skirts. She could smell the stink of spirits on his breath, the smell of her husband's blood spilled nearby.

Emmaline shuddered with the memory, enraged tears stinging her eyes. She remembered the knife in her hand, remembered its point piercing Edwin's face, slicing his cheek like a piece of raw meat. If only Gabe had not stopped her. She would have pushed that knife into Edwin's body, stabbed him like the others had stabbed Remy, killed Edwin like the others had killed Remy.

If only Gabriel had not stopped her.

Non. She must not regret Gabriel. He'd hidden her and Claude. He'd protected them, given them money.

And when he'd returned to her in Brussels, he'd shown her a happiness unlike any she'd ever hoped to experience. She let her thoughts turn to the pleasure of being held by Gabriel, of his kisses and caresses, of the intense joy of joining her body to his.

The sound of horses' hooves broke into her reverie. A hackney coach appeared out of the darkness and approached the front of the hotel.

She turned to the hall servant, a young man dozing in a nearby chair. "My coach is here."

He roused himself to unlock the door and open it for her.

As she stepped out into the pre-dawn air, Emmaline saw Gabriel approaching, like an apparition formed from out of the departing night.

She gripped the handle of her portmanteau and met him halfway.

With only a nod for a greeting he took her bag, brushing her hand with his, rousing her body's yearnings, the memories of which had soothed her from more painful ones.

She followed him to the coach. He touched her again to help her inside and she fought the impulse to bury herself in his arms, to press her face against his chest and the strong rhythm of his heartbeat.

Instead she was greeted by Jack and Ariana Vernon.

"We decided to accompany you," Ariana said in her musical voice. "Jack contacted Gabe after we left you last night. It seemed the logical thing to do."

"I grew up in Bath," her husband explained. "And I know Edwin. I am in a good position to help."

Ariana smiled. "And I would not allow him to leave me behind."

Emmaline could not have been more surprised that these mere acquaintances were willing to help a Frenchwoman, someone they could just as easily perceive as their enemy.

Gabriel climbed in and sat next to her, of necessity brushing her shoulder with his own.

"We managed to get seats for all of us in the same coach," Jack went on. "That was a stroke of good luck."

"Do we ride to Bath in this coach?" Emmaline asked, fearful at how much it cost to hire such a vehicle. Her funds were limited.

Gabriel replied, "This takes us to the inn where the Bath stage departs."

The hackney began to roll. Emmaline lost track of where they were headed, but the coach soon pulled up to a busy coaching inn, its sign displaying a picture of an angel. Even at this early hour, the place was a bustle of activity.

They climbed out of the coach. Gabriel took Emmaline's arm and escorted her to a place out of the way of horses' hooves and carriage wheels and men carrying huge bundles on their shoulders.

She managed to ask him, "How much money do I give you for the fare?"

He set down her portmanteau and his travelling bag. "Do not speak to me of money. I can easily afford the cost of this trip for us both."

His tone puzzled her. Why was he so generous to her when he so obviously resented making the trip?

Jack and Ariana joined her; Ariana put a comforting hand on Emmaline's arm. "By tonight we shall be in Bath, and tomorrow Jack and Gabe will find Edwin and all will be set to rights."

Except that Emmaline must still find Claude and convince him to abandon this dangerous vengeance. "Do you know Edwin Tranville?" she asked.

Ariana shrugged. "I have met him, but I can claim no real acquaintance with him. I remember him as a disagreeable man who drinks too much wine." She gave Emmaline a sympathetic look. "Jack told me something of your encounter with Edwin. It was terrible, but I doubt Edwin poses a threat to anyone now."

"Except to my son," Emmaline murmured.

Gabriel returned, and he and Jack picked up their baggage.

"This way," Gabriel said.

Soon they were seated inside a large coach with two other passengers. Gabriel again sat next to her, giving her the window seat, and the Vernons sat across from them. A woman next to Jack carried a large basket smelling of sausage. A man dressed in a shabby brown coat and knee breeches sat opposite her.

With the bleat of a horn and much shouting, the coach

lurched forwards, and soon they were on a road headed out of the city.

The sky lightened with each mile of the journey, although a steady drizzle of rain hid the sun. Ariana soon snuggled against her husband and fell asleep. Emmaline wished she could lean against Gabriel in a like manner, to feel him hold her like Jack held Ariana. With the two strangers in the carriage, there was little any of them could say to the purpose of their travel to Bath, so Gabriel and Jack conversed about army matters and other mundane topics. Gabriel said nothing to Emmaline.

At the first stop to change horses, he finally spoke to her. "Stretch your legs while you can."

She did not need to be urged.

She and Ariana used the necessary while Gabe and Jack purchased some food ready-packed for travellers; within ten minutes they were back in the carriage and on the road.

By mid-day, the clouds had cleared and the carriage passed rolling green fields dotted with white sheep and picturesque villages. England was a tidy place, Emmaline thought, watching these pretty scenes pass by. How fortunate these villages were to have escaped the very untidy Revolution.

Ariana, awake now, read a book and Jack busied himself sketching in a small notebook he'd taken from his coat pocket. Emmaline remembered him drawing horses for Claude in Badajoz.

"What do you sketch, Monsieur Vernon?" Emmaline asked.

He smiled at her. "Call me Jack." He handed her his notebook.

On the page was an image of a posting inn complete with carriages and post boys and travellers.

"It is where we last stopped," Emmaline exclaimed. "It looks just like it."

Ariana gave a proud glance over the top of her book.

Emmaline showed it to Gabriel. "Does it not look like the last inn?"

"Very like." His voice was curt, as if he disliked her forcing him to speak to her.

She handed the notebook back to Jack and wondered if she and Gabriel would ever talk easily again, as they had in Brussels.

"May I draw you, *madame?*" Jack asked.

"Moi?" She shrugged. "I suppose. If you desire it."

"Remain still," he said.

It was a curious feeling to have a man look at her so intently. She supposed Gabriel had done so in Brussels, but Jack merely concerned himself with her image. Gabriel's gaze had reached directly into her soul.

Ariana peeked at the sketch and grinned in appreciation. "You've got her!"

Jack continued moving his pencil here and there before he handed the notebook to Emmaline.

She gazed at it in surprise.

Surely he'd made her prettier than she really was. The woman in the drawing gazed with large, expressive eyes fringed with thick lashes. Dark tendrils peeked out of her bonnet and her lips looked full and moist.

"Do I look like that?" she murmured.

Gabriel touched her hand, tilting the book so he could see. "He almost does you justice."

Emmaline's breath caught at his words.

Jack laughed. "That's praise, indeed!"

Her hand trembled as she handed the notebook back to Jack.

He tore the page out and handed it back to her. "For you."

"Merci," she whispered. She held the drawing, trying to think of a place she could put it without wrinkling it.

As if reading her mind, Gabriel reached for it. "Shall I put it in my coat pocket? It will stay safe there."

She released it to him and watched him place it carefully in an inside pocket, directly against his heart.

At the fourth change of horses, the woman with the sausage departed and an eager, fresh-faced youth bounded in. After about ten minutes on the road, the boy seemed unable to contain his chatter. He talked non-stop, asking questions, disclosing the private matters of his family and friends, remarking upon everything he saw out the window. "I see sheep." "Those are mulberry bushes." "The road sign pointed to Bath." After nine hours of travel his fellow travellers were less than appreciative of his commentary, but the lad was too enthusiastic about everything to notice.

He reminded Emmaline of Claude at the cusp of adolescence, in the fresh tone of his complexion and the constant fidgeting of hands and feet. Claude, though, would have been silent and unsmiling, keeping his thoughts to himself.

Emmaline's throat tightened with grief for the life her son had been forced to lead. Not wanting the others to notice, she clamped her eyes shut. Soon the boy's voice lulled her and she finally fell asleep.

When Emmaline woke her cheek was pressed against Gabriel's chest and his arm was around her shoulders.

"Come. We have arrived," he whispered.

For one brief moment she thought she was back in Brussels, back in Gabriel's arms. She blinked the illusion away and allowed him to assist her from the carriage. He and Jack collected the baggage and they all entered the inn.

"I've stayed at the White Lion before," Ariana said to her while Gabriel and Jack spoke to the innkeeper. "It is not a bad place."

Jack walked over to them. "We've procured a set of rooms with a private sitting room. Gabe is having dinner sent up."

A maid came to show them to their rooms and a manservant followed with the baggage. Emmaline's bedchamber was a little room with just a bed and a chest of drawers holding a mirror, bowl and pitcher. A towel hung on a peg on the wall.

At the meal Gabriel shared his plan. In the morning he and Jack would walk to the house off Wells Road and call upon Edwin Tranville. Ariana and Emmaline would remain at the inn.

Ariana protested, "We will not stay cooped up in the White Lion. I shall take Emmaline on a tour of Bath and we will wait for you in the Pump Room."

A pump room seemed a very odd place for a rendezvous. Why would anyone wish to meet in a place where water was pumped? Emmaline merely nodded, however, too exhausted to question anything.

"Emmaline—" Gabriel's voice turned deep "—you must go to bed."

Her heart raced at his words.

"Yes," Ariana agreed. "You look as if you will collapse in a heap at any moment." She stood and put her arm around Emmaline, as if she would need help rising from the chair. "Come. I will help you undress."

Emmaline glanced back to see Gabriel's eyes upon her, his expression unfathomable.

Emmaline woke to a knock on the door. A maid entered, a girl of no more than sixteen with a riot of blonde curls that refused to be tamed beneath a cap.

"Good morning, ma'am," the girl said cheerfully. "I've brought you fresh water and am here to help you dress."

"How kind," Emmaline mumbled.

The maid laughed. "Kind, it wasn't. The officer paid me well for it."

"The officer?" But she knew who the girl meant.

"The one in your party." With that matter-of-fact statement, she emptied the dirty water from the bowl into the chamberpot and placed the jug of fresh water on the chest. "You can wash while I take this out." She lifted the chamberpot. "I'll be right back."

A few minutes later, Emmaline was dressed and the maid, still talkative, was pinning up her hair. "You are French, aren't you, ma'am? I can always tell, because you talk in that French way."

"*En réalité,* I live in Brussels." Emmaline preferred not to think of herself as French anymore.

"*En réalité,*" the girl repeated. "That sounds like French talk."

"Many people speak French in Belgium."

The girl paused. "I never knew that."

Emmaline glanced away. "Did—did you ever hear of a young man speaking in the French way who came to Bath recently?"

"We get lots of them now the war is over," the girl replied.

"He would be just a little older than you and very enamoured of horses."

The girl stuck in another hairpin. "I'll ask my brother. He works in the stables. He might remember if a fellow talked of horses."

She decided to add, "The Frenchman, he might be asking for Edwin Tranville."

"The baron's son?" The girl put in more pins. "Nobody likes him, I've heard, but I don't know why. It was big news when General Tranville became a baron, I remember that from when I was little. People used to talk about that family a lot." She patted Emmaline's hair, signifying she was finished. "There you are. I'm to brush your travelling clothes as well, but is there anything else for me to do? The officer told me to ask."

"Non," Emmaline responded. "Thank you."

The girl smiled and curtsied and opened the door.

"Do not forget to ask your brother," Emmaline added.

"I'll do it, ma'am."

As the maid left, Ariana appeared in the doorway. "I've been waiting for you. Jack and Gabe left a half-hour ago. Come. We shall breakfast on Lunn's buns and you will see something of Bath."

"What is Lunn's bun?" Emmaline asked.

"You shall see!" Ariana said cheerfully.

A few minutes later they were on the street and Emmaline had her first glimpse of Bath.

"Oh, my," she exclaimed.

The buildings were all made of honey-hued stones. They passed one after the other until coming upon a huge church that towered over everything and looked as if it belonged in France. The church was built of the same golden stone as the other buildings. The pavement was paved with flagstone so their shoes and their hems stayed clean. People were already up and about. Young men laughing and ogling young ladies as they passed. Old men in white wigs leaning on canes. Grey-haired dames swathed in shawls and carried about in sedan chairs.

Emmaline kept her eyes peeled for a blond-haired man with a scar on his face. Or for Claude.

They entered a building with a cheerful bow window and sat at a small table. Ariana ordered them both Lunn's buns and coffee.

The buns were round-shaped bread, each filling a small plate. They were still warm from the oven.

"It is a *brioche!*" Emmaline exclaimed.

Ariana frowned at her. "A Lunn's bun is only made in Bath."

Emmaline added clotted cream and jam and took a bite. "It is a very good *brioche.*"

Ariana smiled again. "We shall take a walk after this."

"But when will Gabriel and Jack return? Perhaps we should go directly to this pump room."

"We have time," Ariana said as she nibbled on her bun. "Time enough to talk of you and Gabe."

Emmaline did not know how to talk of her and Gabriel, even if she wished to do so. "I do not comprehend."

Ariana tilted her head pensively. "There must be an attachment, surely."

"Attachement?" Gabriel certainly did not seem to wish for one, although he had accepted her bargain of marriage.

"Emmaline, he looks upon you like a lover might, but there is such a distance between the two of you. What happened?"

Emmaline took another bite of her bun. How long had it been since she'd had a friend with whom to share confidences? Growing up, she'd learned never to share private matters; one never knew what might be construed as treason. She could never share her views about France with her zealous family and her husband had never been interested in what she thought or felt.

Only with Gabriel had she been able to bare her soul.

"I cannot speak of Gabriel." She met Ariana's gaze. "It is for him to tell you, not for me. He must decide."

Ariana shook her head in frustration. "Men will speak of nothing, do you not realise that? They will hold things in until they are destroyed from the inside. I have seen it in Jack, although he manages to release his emotions in paint. He will not even tell me exactly what Edwin did to you and your son, not really."

"I will tell you that much." Emmaline's voice rose. "Edwin laughed when his compatriots stabbed my husband to death in front of my son. He tried to violate me and when my son tried to defend me, Edwin tried to kill him, too. That is the scene your Jack came upon in Badajoz."

Ariana reached across the table and took Emmaline's hand. "No wonder your Claude feels as he does. Jack and Gabe will warn Edwin, for Claude's sake. And for yours." She smiled in kindness. "Let us finish our Lunn's buns and then I will show you the beauty of Bath."

Emmaline's appetite failed her, but she forced herself to eat most of the meal.

Afterward, true to her word, Ariana refrained from asking more about Gabriel or Edwin Tranville. She led Emmaline through the hilly streets of Bath, promising to show her a grand sight. Emmaline pretended to enjoy the walk, even though her shoes pinched her feet and she worried the whole time that they would not reach the pumps in time to meet Gabriel.

"What is it you wish to show me?" Emmaline asked again, although Ariana had already told her she must wait and be surprised.

Finally they came upon a row of buildings that formed a huge circle, all built with the honey-coloured stone. They walked to the centre of the paved courtyard that the buildings surrounded. Emmaline twirled all the way around to see them.

"This is the circus," Ariana said. "But come."

"There is more?" Truly, she just wanted to go to the room where the pumps were, even if they arrived early.

They crossed the courtyard and came on to a more ordinary street, but, as they continued, another marvellous sight appeared before them.

"Oh!" Emmaline exclaimed. The view was majestic.

"The Royal Crescent!" cried Ariana. "Bath is famous for it. I wonder you have never heard of it."

"We never heard much of England," Emmaline explained.

This time the golden buildings were curved in a crescent and faced a fine park. The sight of them was like nothing Emmaline had seen before, both unexpected and interesting. Even so, she could admire them only so long before she felt impatient to be off.

Finally her guide said, "Let us go to the Pump Room."

Emmaline expected them to proceed to the river where a pump would likely be placed, but instead they entered a building near the big church and walked into a very elegant room with several people standing about.

"Do you see them?" Ariana craned her neck and surveyed the room.

"This is the Pump Room?" It looked more like a very elegant assembly room.

Ariana still searched the room. "Yes. You can take the waters if you like." She pointed to a counter where capped maids handed small glasses to the people flocked around it.

"Take the waters?" This was making no sense.

"From the springs," Ariana explained in an incredulous voice. "Do not tell me you have not heard of the therapeutic waters of Bath?"

"Ah." She finally understood. They pumped therapeutic waters into this room. "It is like *Les Eaux-Chaudes* in France." The waters of *Les Eaux-Chaudes* were supposed to be healthy to bathe in and to drink.

Ariana was no longer listening. "I see someone."

"Edwin?" Emmaline's heart beat faster.

"No, but someone who might know him." Ariana pushed through the crowd and, before Emmaline could follow, disappeared.

Emmaline's knees shook. Suppose she encountered Edwin Tranville all alone? If only Gabriel were with her, she would not be afraid. She stood on tiptoe and scanned the throngs of people in the room, looking for him. Gabriel would be taller than most of them, more easily seen.

Some people shifted and she saw Ariana, not far away, speaking to an older gentleman. Relieved, she turned towards the door so she might see Gabriel when he walked in.

She caught a glimpse of red. Gabriel's coat. He stood near the doorway, sweeping his gaze around the room. He searched for her, she knew. Her heart raced again, but not in fear. It was the excitement of merely seeing him.

She hurried to him through the crowd. "Gabriel!"

Gabe turned at the sound of her voice.

She advanced towards him, hands extended. "Did you find him?"

The hopeful expression on her face touched at his guilt. His failure.

He stepped back and averted his gaze, not wanting to witness her disappointment. "Edwin has left Bath. We have not yet learned where he went."

She lowered her head and he resisted the urge to touch and comfort her. "I am sorry."

Ariana walked up to them. "What news?" she asked him. "Where is Jack?"

Gabe turned to her. "Edwin has left Bath. Jack is asking among old acquaintances for news of his whereabouts."

Ariana made an exasperated sound. "I will wager Jack discovers Edwin has been gone a week. I've spoken with Lord Ullman. I knew he was acquainted with Edwin." She touched Emmaline's arm. "Lord Ullman is the older gentleman with whom I was speaking just now. He saw Edwin a week ago, but not since. Edwin was in the company of other men. One of them was named Nicholas Frye, the other, a Mr Stewel. Lord Ullman has not seen any of them for a week and believes they left Bath together."

The two beautiful women were drawing curious glances from people standing near them. Gabe did not like it. "Let us return to the inn. Jack will meet us there. With any luck he will know where Edwin has gone this time."

Once outside, Ariana halted. "Let me visit the the-atre. I still know people there and perhaps they have heard something." She shooed them forth. "You go on. I'll come to the inn afterwards."

Emmaline did not take Gabe's arm as they walked back to the inn. She avoided touching him or speaking to him. Gabe suspected she was bitterly disappointed that he had again failed to find Edwin.

When she had reached for him in the Pump Room, he'd again felt that bond between them, the one cre-ated from endless conversations and passionate love-making. The moment passed as swiftly as it had come and must have been illusion. Gabe gritted his teeth. He must remember that his importance to Emmaline was connected to the successful rescue of her son. Nothing more.

But could he find Edwin fast enough to warn him before Claude made good his vow of vengeance? With each step the task became more difficult, more impos-sible.

Gabe could not blame Emmaline for losing faith in him. He felt it in the increased tension in her muscles, the worried set of her mouth, the despairing expression in her eyes.

He glanced away from her, hating his acute aware-ness of her every breath, of every twinge of her anxiety. He knew she was thinking of Claude, fearful that he had reached Edwin, fearful that he'd already murdered him.

Gabe thrust aside his own concerns and tried to reas-sure her. "Just because we have not found Edwin does not mean Claude has found him."

She merely glanced at him, her eyes wide and in pain.

He tried again. "It should be easier for us to find

Edwin than for Claude to do so. Claude has no contacts, no friends here in England."

She gazed up at him. "But he has been looking for much longer."

They reached the inn and climbed the stairs to their set of rooms. In the hallway, the maid with the unruly blonde hair broke into a grin when she saw them approach.

"Good day to you, sir," she said brightly. "And to you, ma'am."

He and Emmaline murmured a greeting and passed her.

"Oh," she called to them, "I talked to my brother."

Emmaline seized his arm so he would stop. She turned. "What did your brother say?"

Even a clod could not miss her intense interest.

The maid glanced first at him, then smiled at her. "You were very right. There was a Frenchman asking about Edwin Tranville in the stables. My brother remembered him because he knew a great deal about horses."

Emmaline tightened her grip on Gabe's arm. "What else?"

The girl shrugged. "That was all, ma'am."

"When did this man speak with your brother?" Gabe asked.

She became more animated. "It happened about a week ago, my brother said."

Gabe fished in his pocket and found a coin. He handed it to the maid, who grinned and curtsied. "Thank you, sir!"

Emmaline walked to the door and waited there until he joined her and unlocked it. He could feel her distress escalating even higher.

Once inside he gave in to his desire and reached for her. She collapsed against him. "Oh, Gabriel," she cried. "Claude is ahead of us. He is ahead of us in finding Edwin Tranville."

Footsteps sounded in the hallway and the doorknob turned. Gabriel released Emmaline and she stepped away from him.

Jack entered the room. "I have discovered where Edwin has gone!" He paused a moment to catch his breath. "To Blackburn for the cock-fighting."

Chapter Eleven

One brightly plumed cock lunged at another, drawing blood with his sharp beak. Feathers flew, and the other bird, a black-breasted red, lashed out with silver spurs affixed to its clawed feet.

"That's the way!" one man yelled while he stared down into the pit. "Kill the bloody fowl!"

Another man shoved him. "My bird's not done for yet."

The brightly plumed cock shrieked and lashed back, wings flapping, dust rising. More blood splattered on the dirt beneath their feet.

A roar broke out in the crowd, and several red-faced, sweaty men threw down bets.

"Kill him! Attack!" The shouting continued.

Claude Mableau stood at the edge of the crowd, heedless of the sound and caring nothing about the two cocks locked into a battle to the death. Claude's attention was consumed by only one man.

Edwin Tranville.

Claude watched Tranville's eyes flash with excitement

as he devoured the violence in front of him and swigged from a leather-sheathed flask. His shrill laughter rang in Claude's ears.

Claude had seen that same expression on Tranville's face once before, heard that same macabre laughter. It had been years ago at Badajoz when Tranville watched Claude's father being stabbed to death. Like the cocks now jabbing with beaks, two English soldiers had plunged knives into Claude's father until he fell to the cobblestones and his blood pooled around him.

The scent of burning wood and gunpowder and fear again filled Claude's nostrils, scents belonging to that earlier time, that other place of violence and death.

He'd been a boy then, too afraid to come to his father's aid. He was no boy now. He stood inches taller and weighed a good two stone heavier than the scar-faced man who'd invaded his thoughts so vividly throughout the years.

The other two men were a blur in his memory. That night they'd been shrouded by shadows, but Claude had seen Tranville so clearly the man's image was etched on his brain.

Claude had been searching for weeks, and finally he was close to Tranville, the man who'd celebrated Claude's father's death by trying to rape his mother.

Claude took a deep breath and the knife hidden under his coat pressed against his chest. He slipped his hand inside and curled his fingers around its hilt. The handle fit Claude's hand to perfection. Its blade was thin and sharp. All Claude needed to do was sidle up to his enemy, slip the blade from under his coat and jab it into Tranville in any number of lethal spots that would guarantee his death. Claude could slink away before the cock-wild crowd would even notice.

He tasted the prospect of success and moved closer, reaching a spot behind Tranville, so close he could smell Tranville's unwashed hair and the brandy on his breath.

Claude's fingers closed around the knife's handle.

One of Tranville's friends, the one called George, pushed his way between them. "Come on, Edwin. Out now." George pulled Tranville off the wooden bench and dragged him towards the door.

Claude's heart pounded. He froze for a moment, thinking the friend had guessed what Claude had been about to do, but the man took no notice of him.

Bitterly disappointed at being even unwittingly thwarted, Claude followed Tranville and his companion out of the building and into the drizzle of the early evening. Keeping to the edge of the path, Claude bent his head low to look as if he were paying Tranville and his friend no heed.

"I wanted to see the end!" Tranville protested. "It promised to be a battle to the death."

"Did you have money on it?" George asked.

"No," Tranville admitted.

"Never mind, then." George waved to Tranville's other two companions, Harry, with blond hair so light it looked white, and Nicholas, whose red hair and spindly legs made him resemble the cocks in the pit.

These *messieurs élégants* had never been soldiers, Claude was certain of that. In fact, if Claude had not recognised Tranville's scarred face, he would never have guessed Tranville to be a soldier.

Claude ducked into the shrubbery so he could make his way close enough to the men to hear what they said to each other.

Harry called to Tranville as he approached, "We need

your blunt. The innkeeper is demanding his money for the rooms and the damages."

"Damages?" Tranville looked puzzled.

Nicholas clapped him on the shoulder and laughed. "You were too deep in your cups to remember. We sported a bit with his daughter; it is not our fault that some of the furniture and crockery was broken. The damned man says he'll go to the magistrate unless we pay."

Tranville fished in his pockets and drew out a purse. "I have a little left."

"The rest of us are all done up," George said. "We'll have to rusticate at my family's estate for a while. I sent a message for the coachman to pick us up tomorrow."

"Sounds like a dead bore," Tranville said.

They walked towards the inn and their voices faded, but Claude had heard enough. He would discover more at the inn's public rooms that evening and the stable in the morning. Wherever he went he befriended stable workers, who always could tell him what he needed to know in order to track Tranville.

Perhaps it was for the best he had not killed Tranville this day. Better to confront Tranville and compel him to disclose the names of the two men who'd actually killed his father. Claude liked the idea of facing Tranville, eye to eye. He wanted Tranville to know who murdered him and why.

Claude took a breath and reached into his coat and again felt the warm metal of the stiletto.

If no opportunity afforded him to kill Tranville tonight, he'd follow him to the next destination. No matter what, Claude was certain to eventually devise a way to confront Tranville alone.

And finally avenge his father's murder.

* * *

The next day Gabe and Emmaline set off for Blackburn while Jack and Ariana returned to London.

It took Gabe and Emmaline three days to reach Blackburn from Bath, in Gabe's mind a journey more difficult than a fortnight's march through the hills of Spain. Indeed, Gabe would have preferred a hard ride on horseback instead of this cushioned coach, sitting next to Emmaline. He was forced to remember how it had felt to hold her, to make love to her.

How had he come to spend so much time in her company, to be so constantly reminded of the past, so frequently tempted? He felt trapped in a vortex, spinning deeper and deeper. True, he could escape her at any time, merely by refusing her request to find Edwin and save her son. He ought to do that very thing: return to London and continue the search for a commission.

But that would mean abandoning her. He could no more abandon her than he could require her to for ever be separated from her son.

He ought to be wishing she'd never come back to turn his emotions into complete disorder, but even in this misery of confusion, he relished her company.

Once being seated beside her had seemed like a joyous gift. Now each turnstile they crossed, each village they passed, merely intensified the unease between them. They spoke as little as possible to each other. Even when others were not present and they could talk freely of their search, there was little new to be said.

To make matters worse, the journey turned into a familiar one. The Bath coach eventually travelled to Manchester and they were required to wait several hours in the inn there until the stage to Blackburn arrived. All the while they remained in Manchester Gabe worried he might happen upon someone who knew him.

There was little reason to think he'd be recognised. His appearance was so altered by his years in the army that his only real danger was if a member of his family happened to come into the coaching inn. To limit that slim possibility Gabe secured a private dining room so that he and Emmaline could wait out the time alone.

That came with its own dangers. To be alone with her, just the two of them, intensified memories of the intimacy they'd once shared.

After what seemed an eternity, they climbed in the coach to Blackburn. Gabe breathed another sigh of relief that none of his brothers were also making the journey. In his childhood, frequent trips to the then-new textile mills in Blackburn were a part of his father's business. As a boy, he'd sometimes accompany his father and brothers, but he was needed only to carry bolts of cloth. Gabe mostly felt in their way.

Sometimes, if lucky, he'd been able to go off on his own and explore Blackburn as much as he wished.

When the stagecoach finally reached the outskirts of Blackburn, the afternoon was well advanced. Luckily the posting inn was close to Miller's blacksmith shop where Jack had learned Edwin and his companions were bound. Miller was well-known for his cock fights. Gabe had even sneaked into Miller's on some of his boyhood expeditions.

After securing their lodging, Gabe asked the innkeeper whether Edwin was a guest. Why not? Maybe their luck would change. Maybe they would find Edwin this day and Gabe's duty to Emmaline could be discharged and he would part from her once more.

The innkeeper slid his finger up and down the pages of his register book. "What name again?" the man asked.

"Edwin Tranville."

Emmaline stood behind Gabe and he sensed her tension, as if her nerves were connected to his own.

The innkeeper turned back another page. "There have been several comings and goings." He glanced up. "The cock fights, you know."

"If he did not sign the book, perhaps you will see the name of one of his companions, Frye or Stewel."

The innkeeper's brows shot up. "I remember those two. Frye and Stewel. Troublemakers. I tossed them out—good riddance to them!"

Gabe frowned. "They are no longer here?"

"Gone several days already." He tapped on his book.

Emmaline made a small cry. Clutching Gabe's arm, she asked, "Did Edwin Tranville stay?"

The innkeeper pointed to names on the page. "I cannot read the names. There were two others with that lot, though, come to think of it. Can't say if the fellow you are seeking was one of them."

Gabe peeked at the page. The signatures indeed looked like scribbles.

Emmaline spoke up. "He would have a scar."

The man raised a finger. "Ah, yes! Scar on his face from here to here?" He pointed from his temple to his mouth.

"That is the one," Gabe responded. "What can you tell us of him?"

The innkeeper laughed. "I can tell you he depleted my stores of brandy. More than that I do not know. He and his friends left the same day, thank the Lord." He shook his head. "You could ask in the stable. One of the workers might know more."

"We will do that." Gabe gestured to their baggage. "Can someone take our things up to the rooms? We'll go to the stables now."

The innkeeper called to a boy in the other room and told him where to take the luggage. Gabe gave them both coins in exchange for their assistance. He and Emmaline hurried to the stable.

"I recall them," one of the stablemen said. "They left in a private carriage. It came and fetched the lot of them and carried them away after the horses rested."

Another man spoke up. "There was a crest on the side of it. With a bird, I think."

"Do you know where they went?" Gabe asked.

The first man scratched his head. "Can't say I do. The coachman waited inside the inn. Did not pass the time with anyone here." The other shrugged in agreement.

"*Pardon,* sir," Emmaline broke in. "Was there a young Frenchman here at that time? He would have been a *connoisseur* of the horses."

"Mableau?" He grinned. "Nice fellow. Not French, though. Said he was from Brussels. He left about the same time as that other lot, come to think of it, but I did not see him go."

The other worker also shook his head.

"Thank you." Gabe tipped both stable workers. "We are staying at the inn. I would be grateful if you would come and tell me if anyone else knows more."

As they walked out Emmaline grabbed Gabe's arm. She needed steadying. "What do we do now, Gabriel?"

What, indeed? Gabe had no notion of how to look for a group of young men who had left in a private carriage. They could be anywhere.

"We go back to the inn." What else could they do?

She stepped in front of him and clutched at the lapels of his uniform coat. "We cannot give up! Claude has followed them. We must find him before it is too late!"

He dug his fingers into her shoulders, not knowing whether to push her away or to enfold her in his arms and comfort her.

He released her, now pulsing with desire and resentment. It was madness to feel attached and distant at the same time.

By all rights he should abandon this charade. He needed to return to London, to be present if word came of a commission. If an opportunity presented itself, he had to pounce on it or lose it to one of the countless other men eager to return to full military service.

He opened his hands as if telling himself he would not touch her again. "We will walk back to the inn where you will stay. I will go to the cock fights and ask among the spectators. Perhaps someone will know where they were bound."

Her eyes met his and roused his tenderness again. "I want to go with you."

He turned away and started walking. "Not to a cock fight."

She said nothing else to him as he escorted her back to the inn and arranged for a meal to be sent up to her room.

Gabe spent a good two hours watching birds attack each other so men could bet on them. When a boy, watching the fights held all the excitement of the forbidden, but now it disgusted him. He'd seen too much bloodshed during the war. Watching birds jab and slash each other held no amusement.

He did manage to engage a few men in conversation. Some recalled seeing Edwin but only now noticed he and his friends were gone. Gabe found no one who knew where they might have travelled next.

"They lost a great deal of money," one man said, patting his coat pocket. "I know because I profited nicely from it."

Where would spoiled young gentlemen go if low on funds? Gabe had no idea. He checked in a few nearby taverns before making his way back to the inn. These Blackburn streets were both familiar and strange. Like his home town, Manchester, Blackburn, too, had changed. The mills had multiplied. A canal had been built. More people crowded its streets. Dusk had fallen and Gabe imagined they were bound for their homes and families. He fancied they'd settled into a life where they could predict what would happen one day to the next. He did not know whether to envy or pity them.

With the inn in sight, Gabe stopped. All he had to offer Emmaline this night was more disappointment. How long could he continue to search, especially with no clues at all of where to look next?

He must eventually face the fact that he could not help her.

Gabe pressed his fingers against his forehead. He needed a drink. Or two. Or three. He turned around and went back to the tavern he'd just left.

Seating himself in a dark corner, he signalled the serving maid. "Brandy," he ordered.

"Open the door, Frenchie!" The man's voice was slurred and Emmaline heard one of his companions laugh, as if those words were very droll.

He pounded on the door again and the wood bent with the force.

Emmaline jumped back and hurriedly dragged a wooden ladderback chair to wedge under the doorknob. Remy had taught her the trick many years before. It was her husband's version of protecting her when he marched them into places of danger.

"Let us in!" the man growled. "You know you want us."

That brought more laughter.

She feared no one would hear them. Her room was a considerable distance from the stairway, at the end of a long hall and around a corner from Gabriel's.

Gabriel.

Where was he? He'd been gone for hours. Had something happened to him?

"Open, woman! No more teasing." The door bowed again under the man's fist.

Emmaline dug into her portmanteau for her sewing scissors, securing it in her hand so that its point made a weapon. If the men broke in, she would scream. She would fight. She would stab.

She'd done it before, the day Gabriel had encountered her in Badajoz and prevented her from killing Edwin Tranville.

Where was Gabriel?

"Frenchie!" the man called again.

Suddenly a new voice roared, "Stay away or you'll answer to me!"

Gabriel!

Through the door Emmaline heard sounds of a scuffle. Gabriel was only one man against three. She must try to help him. Still gripping her scissors, she pulled the chair away and flung open the door.

Two of the men were already fleeing down the hall. Gabriel lifted the remaining one by the collar and tossed him after them like a sack of flour. The man scrambled to his feet and scampered away.

Gabriel turned to her, his eyes still flashing with violence. He breathed hard as he took one step towards her. "Are you injured?" His voice was rough and it frightened her.

"Non," she managed.

He advanced closer and she backed into her room.

"You will wish to know what happened," she said quickly. She'd been foolish and had not heeded his orders. He would be angry at her. "I did not stay in my room. I went below to ask about Claude in the public rooms. Those men followed me back here."

His gaze bore into her, too much like a jealous Remy when he thought another man had taken notice of her.

She raised her palm and continued to back away. "I did nothing to entice them. I did not even speak to them. They would not leave me alone. I left when their attentions became unseemly."

He leaned closer to her. "I told you to stay in your room."

Emmaline felt transported back in time. How many times had she played a scene like this with Remy? Next she would admit her mistake, promise never to defy him again, beg his forgiveness.

She stopped herself. This was Gabriel, not her husband. She could speak her mind to Gabriel.

She lifted her chin. "How many hours were you gone, Gabriel? I thought something bad had happened to you." He smelled of spirits. "I did not guess you would spend the hours in a tavern."

He glanced down for a moment before raising his

eyes to her again. "No matter. You should not have left your room." A line creased his forehead. "What if I had not come upon them when I did?"

She lifted her hand, still holding the scissors. "I armed myself."

He stared from her hand to her face and his angry expression dissolved. Bracing himself against the bed-post, he swept his arm toward her portmanteau. "Pack your scissors and other things. You will stay in my room tonight."

A thrill rushed through her.

He had never shared a room with her, not since Brussels. At every inn along the road he'd secured separate rooms. When her room was next to his, she would be so lonely for him she would press her ear against the wall and listen to him moving about. When his bed creaked beneath him, she longed to be lying beside him, returning to those nights of lovemaking they'd once so happily shared. Alone in her bed, she'd yearned for his arms to comfort and protect her when she woke in terror from the nightmare, the one that placed her back in Badajoz, Edwin laughing at her husband's death, Edwin forcing himself on her, the stench of spirits on his breath.

Emmaline packed swiftly, aroused that his gaze followed her every move. Closing the buckle on her portmanteau, she said, "I am ready."

He reached for the bag, brushing against her, her skin delighting in the contact. It was all she could do not to skip down the hall after him.

They turned the corner and stopped at the door to his room. He fumbled with the key, but finally gained them entry. The room was nearly identical to hers in its furnishings and space. The bed was as small, but she did not mind that. It meant sleeping close to him.

Maybe if they shared lovemaking again, he would talk to her again instead of merely barking instructions. Maybe if she joined her body with his, they would both rediscover a piece of the bliss they'd shared at Brussels.

He placed her bag on a stool near the window and turned to her, his eyes raking her from her head to her toes.

Her breath quickened and she waited.

He crossed the room to her, stopping inches from her. He took her hand and lifted it.

And placed a key in her palm. "Lock the door behind me."

She gaped at him. "You are leaving?"

He gazed down at her and her senses filled with him, making her ache for wanting him. He leaned closer, his lips nearing hers.

He straightened. "I will sleep in your room."

He turned to pick up his own bag.

Emmaline's voice trembled. "Do not leave me alone."

With a resolute look, he headed towards the door.

She felt sick inside, bereft that he did not wish to be with her, that he no longer desired her as she desired him. It made her despondent at what this boded for their bargain, their eventual marriage.

He placed his hand on the doorknob.

"Gabriel!" she pleaded.

He turned back to her.

Chapter Twelve

Gabe knew he should not have turned back. Her face was flushed, her breathing rapid, her eyes pleading with him to stay. *Do not leave me alone,* she'd begged.

How heartless could he be? She'd nearly been attacked by drunken men. She'd endured that horror before at Badajoz.

But how could he convince her that at the moment *he* was not safe, not when the blood was surging through his veins from tossing those men away from her door, not when the sight of her now aroused him into a fevered state.

"No harm will come to you here," he forced himself to say. "If those men dare return, they will find me in your room, not you."

Her hand trembled. "I want you to stay. I do not want to be alone."

He still gripped the doorknob. "I have been drinking, Emmaline. So much that I cannot trust myself with you."

She walked towards him. "But I trust you, Gabriel."

He held up a hand for her to stop. "I am as dangerous to you right now as those men."

She came closer. "What would you do to me, Gabriel, that I would so dislike?"

He stiffened while desire coursed through him. He longed to tear the clothes from her body, to feel her bare skin beneath his fingertips. He longed to taste of her dark-rose nipples, to bury himself inside her.

She extended her hand to him. "Stay."

He dropped his bag and seized her by the shoulders. "Emmaline—"

She winced and he loosened his grip. He had not meant to cause pain. The brandy had eroded his control—could she not see? It muddled his thinking. "You want this?" he rasped.

She nodded and her eyes flared with a desire that seemed to equal his own.

His body reacted as if she really wished to bed him, but why would she do so now? She was with him out of desperation, not choice. And she would marry him out of that same desperation.

"It is what I want." Her voice was husky, unhesitant. She turned away and pulled a chain over her head, a necklace he'd not realised she'd worn. She set it aside and turned back to him, raising her arms and running her fingers through his hair.

His hand slid to the smooth column of her neck. His fingertips felt the rapid beating of her pulse. She responded to his touch by tilting her head like a cat wanting to be petted.

"I do most certainly want this," she whispered, her voice like a fleeting summer breeze.

She twined her arms around him and pulled his head down until he could no longer resist tasting her lips again. He crushed her mouth against his, a man starving for want of tasting her. She tasted of heaven, of warm nights and peaceful days. This was what he'd lost, what he would lose again. Losing her the first time had almost crushed his very soul—what would happen when he lost her again?

Pain be damned. She was here now, willing to let him love her again—no, *wanting* him to make love to her again. She wanted that pleasure again. The brandy he'd consumed had not addled his thinking to that degree. She *wanted* this.

So, why shouldn't he? Men made love to willing women all the time. He'd done it. Many times. Why the devil stop now?

Still kissing him, Emmaline began to work the buttons on his coat. He quickly shrugged it off and tossed it aside. She stepped back to unfasten her dress and his fingers flexed with the impulse to rip the fabric away.

Her dress dropped to the floor and she backed him towards the bed, kicking off her shoes. "I will remove your boots."

He sat upon the bed while she pulled off his boots, then he drew her close so he could untie the lacings of her corset. His hands shook with impatience as he worked the knot.

When he finally freed her from the garment, she unfastened the fold of his trousers. He pulled off his shirt.

They'd undressed like this in her Brussels bedroom many times, only this felt different to him, more urgent. But then the brandy made everything seem more than it was. The brandy made him hurry. The brandy made him willing to think only of this moment and nothing more.

Soon they tumbled together on the bed, freed of

clothing and restraint, skin against skin. He'd forgotten how beautiful she was, how narrow her waist, how flawless her skin, how full her breasts.

No, he'd really not forgotten; he would never forget anything about her. He'd merely tried to force her from his mind. But now she was with him again, in the flesh. In the warm, smooth, erotic flesh. He inhaled her fragrance, linen and lavender, so familiar, as if she for ever carried the scent of the lace shop with her. Even the sound of her breathing was familiar. He hated to admit he felt more at home at this moment than he'd felt when visiting the house of his birth, the family who shared his blood.

Rational thought tried to poke through his reverie, but he pushed it away. He did not care that she wanted his hands on her merely out of carnal desire. His carnal needs drove him, as well. He did not care if she did this merely to keep him from abandoning the search for Claude—

He pulled away.

"*Qu'est-ce que c'est?*" she asked, then shook her head. "I mean, what is it? What is wrong?"

He could no more accept her lovemaking as payment than he could accept marriage.

"I need to know if you want this, Emmaline." His voice came out too loud, too rough. "Do you want this?"

Her breath accelerated. "You must ask this again? I have never stopped wanting this."

She reached for him and he rose over her, convinced that her fever was running as hot as his own. Her legs parted for him and he thrust himself inside her, rushing in spite of himself, as if he could lose everything if he did not seize this moment.

Miraculously, she did not cry out in pain, but in

passion, and immediately she moved with him, as fast as he moved, as forcefully as he pushed. He felt everything in the moment. All his longing for her, all the delight in joining with her again, but that was not the total. He also felt the agony of her sending him away, the rage at her bargain with him, the cold realisation that he would part from her again.

His body chased emotion and thought away, replacing them with a pure physical need, the need nature supplied every creature, the need that promised man indescribable pleasure. Every muscle, every nerve, every part of him embraced the pleasure, and every part of him raced to the culmination, the climax.

She stayed with him on this frenzied journey, as if her every muscle, nerve and limb were as much a part of him as his own. They even breathed in unison.

The moment came.

Together they cried out. Together they convulsed with pleasure. Together they suspended time. All that existed was here, now and each other.

Their lassitude came in unison, as well. Gabe relaxed beside her, holding her close as if otherwise she might evaporate like dew on morning grass. She snuggled next to him, entangling her legs with his so that even now he felt connected to her.

"I have missed that," she murmured.

He was surprised he had lived without it.

As the sensation ebbed, he wondered how long it had been since she'd lain with a man. It was inconceivable to him so passionate a woman could deny such needs, especially when her beauty no doubt attracted many willing men. Who could blame her? After all, he'd not been celibate since Brussels.

Although, if he were honest with himself, any release

he'd found among the willing Parisian courtesans had meant nothing to him.

He firmed his resolve. This must mean nothing as well, mere physical release.

She rose on one elbow and looked down at him. "What is it, Gabriel?"

He had not even moved. "What? Nothing."

"Something upset you suddenly."

Her hair was all a-tumble, distracting him with its sensual beauty.

"A stray thought, nothing more." He brushed her locks away from her face. "We forgot to take down your hair."

She sat up and felt for her hairpins, pulling them out so that her hair fell over her shoulders and down her back.

Gabe combed the tresses with his fingers. "Still as lovely," he whispered.

She leaned down and placed her lips on his, her hair tickling his chest, her kiss arousing him once more.

To the devil with the past and the future. What did a soldier care for such things? Reach for what was within grasp.

She broke off the kiss and climbed atop him, speaking the words that were in his mind. "I want you again," she murmured.

When dawn flooded the room with light, Gabe made love to her again, as aggressively as the night before, lest daylight change everything. Nothing gentle between them, they grabbed at the pleasure, demanded it of each other and built it to an explosive force.

Afterward, as she lay in his embrace, he sensed the

moment her lassitude turned to tension again. "What do we do now, Gabriel?"

To find Edwin and stop Claude, she meant.

He should tell her now that it was no use. There was nowhere to search, no clue to explore. He must return to London.

He composed the words in his mind and pictured himself telling her. He imagined her face when he dealt the crushing blow. It pained him as much as if he were inside her skin, enduring her disappointment and fear. Could he truly wound her in the way that would hurt her the most, by saying there was no way to save her son now?

He could not.

"I was thinking," he began, stating a plan that would sound as if he'd deliberated on it all night long instead of making it up as he spoke. "We should rent a horse and carriage, something I could drive myself. We can head out in some direction and ask about Edwin at the posting inns. If one direction fails to find someone who has seen them, then we'll backtrack and start in another direction."

"You will do this, Gabriel?" She sat up and her smile rivaled the sunshine. "*Très bon.* We will find someone who remembers seeing them. I know we will!"

She lowered herself to kiss him again, a kiss filled with relief and gratitude for a decision he might very well regret later.

Reluctantly he broke off the kiss. "Let me dress and go out now to see what I can arrange."

It took some time to track down an available carriage. After asking at several posting inns, Gabe finally found someone willing to rent him a gig. The one-horse vehicle was not as fast as a curricle with two horses, but it would have to do. He had no wish to search for something better all day and lose the time on the road.

When he returned, Emmaline had their bags all packed.

"Let us eat breakfast, enough to last us most of the day," he told her. After a hearty breakfast they would leave on this next, probably hopeless, leg of their journey.

Soon they sat in the public room, drinking mugs of hot coffee and eating slices of ham, cheese and bread. Their table was located in the path most patrons needed to pass to be seated, so their conversation was frequently interrupted. Not that there was much conversation between them. What was he to say to Emmaline after their impassioned night together?

As they ate, a man bumped into Gabe's chair. He looked to see who it was.

"Beg pardon," the man said.

Gabe spoke to Emmaline after the man passed. "Are you concerned that the men who accosted you will show up here?"

She shook her head. "Not at all. They will see you first and avoid you, I am certain."

Another man walked by, nodding a greeting. Gabe recognised him as one of the men he had questioned during the cock fight.

He glanced back at Emmaline and their gazes caught. Something had changed between them, he had to admit.

They were carnally aware of each other once again.

Emmaline blinked, and her expression turned to worry. "Where do we begin to look?"

Gabe shrugged. Perhaps it was only he who was

preoccupied by their lovemaking. Her son consumed her thoughts. As always.

"We can toss a coin," he suggested.

"Toss a coin?" Her brows knit in confusion.

He waved a hand. "We can go in any direction. One gives us as much a chance of succeeding as another."

He took a sip of coffee, glancing up as yet another man walked by.

The man stopped. "Gabe?"

Gabe felt the blood drain from his face. It was his brother Paul.

His brother made a surprised sound. "Gabe! By God, it is you!"

Gabe rose and his brother enveloped him in a rough hug. "It is prodigious good to see you, but what the devil are you doing here?"

What spate of ill luck brought Paul here at the exact moment Gabe was sitting with Emmaline?

Without waiting for Gabe's answer, Paul looked from Emmaline to Gabe, a question in his eyes.

Gabe moved closer to her. "Emmaline, may I present my brother, Mr Paul Deane. Paul, Madame Mableau."

Emmaline extended her hand. "It is a pleasure to meet you, sir."

Paul clasped it. "You are French!" His eyes widened and he slid a very curious glance towards Gabe.

"Belgian," she said.

Two other men had to squeeze by, and the serving girl stood with a tray full of food. "Your breakfast, sir," she said to Gabe's brother.

Gabe pulled out a chair. "Join us, will you?"

He signalled the tavern girl to put the food on the table.

His brother sat, but looked from Gabe to Emmaline

instead of at his food. "What are you doing in Black-burn, Gabe? Are you billeted here?"

"No," he replied. "I am still awaiting a commission."

Paul did not even seem to hear him. His brow was creased and he looked at Emmaline, trying to puzzle out who she was and why she was sharing breakfast with Gabe.

Suddenly Paul's eyes widened as if understanding dawned at last. His face immediately flushed red.

"What goes here?" he whispered to Gabe, inclining his head towards Emmaline.

She was witnessing all this, of course.

Paul's disapproving expression looked so much like their father's that Gabe was taken aback. Paul always had been a strait-laced prig. No doubt he'd concluded that Gabe and Emmaline had shared a bed as well as breakfast. He acted as if Gabe were seventeen and caught in a peccadillo, instead of a man in his mid-thirties who damned well could bed whomever he wished and didn't need an older brother to pass judgement on him.

Or on her. It was unspeakably ill mannered of Paul to gesture and whisper and eye Emmaline so blatantly. He might as well point to her and yell, "Harlot!"

Emmaline had already blushed. Gabe was certainly not going to embarrass her more by giving his brother what for.

He made his voice mild. "To answer your questions." Both the spoken one and the unspoken one. "Madame Mableau and I are in Blackburn on business, a private family matter that will not concern you—"

Paul's brows rose as if waiting for more.

"I will lay your suppositions at rest and tell you what I intended to keep private a while longer—"

Paul's expression turned smug. Emmaline stared down at her plate.

Gabe reached across the table and covered her hand with his own. He'd be damned if he let Paul shame her one second longer.

"Emmaline and I are betrothed."

Chapter Thirteen

Emmaline's gaze flew to his face. "Gabriel," she mouthed.

His brother Paul released a laugh and rose to clap Gabriel on the shoulder. He took her hand from Gabe's and shook it again. "That's the stuff. Delighted for you. Can't see all the secrecy—"

"None the less, you will respect our wishes," Gabriel intoned.

She had felt such humiliation when Gabriel's brother so obviously disapproved of her. These English were such *moralistes* about such matters.

She did not wish to feel shame for bedding Gabriel. She had never experienced such desire for him as she had the previous night. Never, not even during their happy nights in Brussels. It was as if all her anxieties for Claude, her fear of the drunken men and Gabe's battling with them had transformed into passion. Even now her senses flared with the memory of its intensity.

Gabriel's brother returned to his seat. "When are you planning to tell our mother this happy news? Are you returning to London after this? You should stop in Manchester on the way. Introduce her to the family."

"We are not returning to London," Gabe answered him.

"No? Where are you headed?" His brother slapped his forehead. "Of course. To our uncle's. You are planning to pay him a visit."

In Brussels Gabe had spoken of an uncle who lived on a sheep farm, but she did not know if this was the uncle his brother meant.

"Yes," Gabe responded so quickly it took her aback. "We intend to call upon Uncle Will."

Emmaline gaped at him. Did he mean that? What about Claude? Tranville? "Gabriel, you said—"

"Never mind what I said." He silenced her with a firm gesture and a stern look. "We are visiting my uncle and announcing our betrothal to him."

Not searching for Tranville? Not stopping Claude? Emmaline's insides twisted into a knot.

She'd felt hopeful for a moment. She'd begun to believe in Gabriel, that their marriage might not be so grim, not with nights filled with lovemaking like they'd so recently shared. And then he abruptly changed what he'd promised to do.

How quickly her disquiet returned.

Gabriel behaved as Remy would have done, making plans and pronouncements without a word to her, without a moment's consideration of her wishes. By the time Remy thought to tell her of where they would march or where they would live, it was a *fait accompli,* as autocratic as Gabriel with this visit to the uncle.

She trembled with anger. "Why not ask your brother to accompany us to this uncle?"

Gabriel shot her a surprised look.

Paul seemed to notice nothing amiss, however. He patted her hand. "Cannot do it. I'm off today. Taking the canal to Liverpool. I'm riding the barge with the goods we purchased here. It is a slow trip, you know, but pleasant."

"*Quel dommage.* What a pity," she responded with false emotion.

Paul rubbed his lip. "Dashed if I don't feel guilty now. Uncle Will is so close; I ought to have called on him." He dived into his plate of eggs. "Too late now."

"What news of the family?" Gabriel asked. Apparently he'd dismissed her chagrin. That was like Remy, as well.

But she was acting like Remy's wife, not speaking directly, relying on sarcasm that men seemed too obtuse to realise. *Alors,* this behaviour was exactly how she'd put Claude in danger all those years ago, when she hadn't refused to follow her husband to Spain. She had not learned the lesson, had she? To confront, to defy, to demand.

Emmaline tried to act as if she were listening politely while the two brothers spoke of their large family, people she did not know. She must explain to Gabriel that she had no wealth of family. She had only Claude to be precious to her. Surely stopping Claude from committing murder was more important than visiting an uncle?

She shuddered, remembering the stable worker had said that Claude had left Blackburn the same day as Edwin.

She pressed her hand against her stomach. What if Claude had already found Edwin? What if he was lying in wait, ready to strike Edwin dead? What if a delay to visit this uncle kept them from finding Claude and stopping him in time?

The hand holding her fork began to shake.

Louisa Finch strode out of Rappard Hall, glad to escape its walls and breathe in the fresh morning air. On a routine day she savoured the singular pleasure of a morning's ride. It gave her some respite from the duties she'd assumed at the Hall. On horseback she could forget she was a poor relation, lucky to have a roof over her head, food to eat and clothing on her back. Lady Rappard was her late mother's cousin and Louisa's closest living relative. Louisa was glad to show her gratitude to Lady Rappard by assuming the running of the house in her absence and by taking over the housekeeper's duties. Poor Mrs Dart. Louisa supposed when Lord and Lady Rappard finally noticed the poor lady was too feeble and forgetful to complete her duties, they would pension her off to a cosy retirement. Then would Louisa become the housekeeper? To slip irrevocably into servant status was what she most dreaded.

She tried to shake off that thought.

It would be fortunate for her to have such respectable employment, but, at seventeen, daughter of an aristocratic family, she yearned for more than being buried on a country estate.

Louisa laughed out loud at herself. She was happy enough at Rappard Hall. The servants were like family to her, and she had Pomona, her lovely horse. Lord Rappard had allowed her to keep her horse, an expense she certainly could not bear on her own. Riding in the morning, useful work in the day, leisure in the evening. It *was* enough.

Her disquiet must be due to her cousin George and

his friends descending upon the house. They were noisy and dirty and rude, and that Nicholas Frye was forever uttering suggestive remarks and giving her leering stares. He made her exceedingly anxious, especially because she must be constantly vigilant lest Nicholas and the other two guests bothered the maids in such a manner. George certainly was turning a blind eye to his friends' antics.

She reached the stable and entered its wide doors, greeted by the scent of hay and leather and horse.

Mr Sellars, the stablemaster, walked up to her, wiping his hands. "Good morning to you, Miss Finch. You are here to ride today, eh?"

She smiled. "As always, Mr Sellars, if it is not too much trouble. I hope you are in good health today."

"Fit as a filly. Thank you for asking," the man responded. "I'll get someone to saddle Pomona for you." He gesture to a nearby groom. "Saddle Pomona for Miss Finch, lad."

The young man turned and nodded.

"Is that your new worker?" she asked Mr Sellars. "How is he faring?"

"Never saw a lad so good with horses," Mr Sellars responded with a satisfied look. "I tell you, it was a stroke of luck your cousin allowed John Coachman to give that lad a ride, else I would never have found him for hiring. He's a hard worker. Takes the filthiest job without complaint."

Mucking out the stables, she presumed. She glanced at the new worker curiously. He was lean and only a few inches taller than herself. She could not see his features clearly, but he looked to be around her age.

Mr Sellars went on. "I believe I'll let him accompany you."

She pursed her lips at him. "Now you know I feel perfectly comfortable riding alone. There's no need to take a worker away from you."

He shook his head. "Won't hear of such nonsense. Would never forgive myself if something happened to you out there alone." He turned and raised his voice. "Saddle a horse for yourself, lad. You'll be riding with Miss Finch." He gave Louisa a conspiratorial wink. "Mark my words. He'll choose the horse that most needs a long ride."

A few minutes later, the young man led a saddled Pomona and a spirited black gelding named Apollo, who indeed looked as if he were champing at the bit for a good run.

Louisa liked the looks of this new groom. He had dark hair in need of a trim poking out from under his cap. His face was clear and his large eyes were a vibrant blue, framed by dark thick brows. What's more, there was a touch of sadness in those eyes and a melancholy turn to his full lips. Perhaps that was why she felt an inexplicable kinship.

Mr Sellars nodded and walked away without introductions. The young man held out a hand to assist her on to the mounting block.

She looked into those blue eyes as his strong hand gripped hers. "You are the new groom. Welcome. I am Louisa Finch."

He released her and glanced away as she finished mounting. When she was in the saddle, his eyes met hers again.

He removed his hat and bowed his head. "I am Claude Mableau."

Chapter Fourteen

Claude mounted the fine black horse that so reminded him of his own lost Coco, although this steed was undoubtedly of a finer pedigree. He could not help feeling excited to be riding such a horse, even if riding with this young lady unsettled him.

She looked to be a girl in the first bloom of womanhood, perhaps no more than two years younger than his eighteen years. Her cheeks were creased by dimples, created by a smile that seemed to bring sunshine into the stable with her.

Merely to glance at her made it hard for him to breathe.

Who was she? He'd heard of Lord and Lady Rappard, now summering at Brighton, and knew of their son, George, one of Tranville's friends. No one had spoken of a girl living at Rappard Hall. Was she a member of the family or a servant?

Her riding habit did not look as fine as some ladies' dresses he had seen since being in England. Perhaps she could be a servant. But what servant would have permission to ride such a fine horse as Pomona?

English people were such a puzzle.

She spoke, her voice as light and carefree as a summer breeze. "I hope you do not mind riding with me."

Mind? To be on horseback? To be near her for a time? It would be a joy.

"I do not mind," he responded.

They rode out of the stable and into the bright sunshine.

"You are French!" She sounded as if she was pleased by the notion.

Still, he'd learned it was not prudent to admit to his true nationality. "I am from Brussels."

"How exciting that is." She led them behind the stables where the paddocks were. The few other workers toiling there seemed to take little notice of them.

"Where do you wish to ride, miss?" he asked as they faced empty fields.

She laughed again, this time a throaty sound that made his male parts stir. "As far as we can go!"

She urged her horse into a gallop. It took him a stunned moment to follow. They whipped through thick green grass towards hills dotted with white sheep. Pomona ran with relish. Apollo galloped as if set free from a long confinement.

Claude felt almost happy.

When they approached a low hedge, he started to shout a warning to her, but Miss Finch jumped it with ease. He laughed aloud as Apollo sailed over behind her.

Miss Finch called to him as they charged on, "Glorious, is it not?"

It was not good for the horses to run full out for too long. He sensed it was time to slow down and was about to tell her so, when she pulled on her reins.

She signalled Pomona to walk. "We should rest the horses. There is a stream nearby. They can drink."

The stream was a short distance away, nestled between lush green-leafed trees shading each bank. When they came closer, Claude heard the tinkling of the water running over rocks. It was like music. On the other side of the stream's banks, black-faced sheep gazed at them curiously from their green pasture.

"Is this not a pretty place?" Miss Finch exclaimed.

He did not wish to admit that any place in England was pretty, even if this spot seemed as idyllic as if appearing in a dream.

Without answering, he hurried to assist her to dismount and led the horses to a spot where they could easily dip their muzzles into the water.

Miss Finch lowered herself gracefully to a grassy spot. "Come sit with me, Claude."

He hesitated. What was proper in England for a stable worker to do?

What did he care? He was French and equal to any man...or woman.

He sat next to her.

She smiled over at him. "Tell me about Brussels and why you left your home to come here."

He shrugged. "I wanted to travel."

"I would love to travel!" She laughed softly. "Although I am not certain I would pick Lancashire to visit. I cannot imagine what attracted you to this place."

One man attracted him to this place, but he could

not explain that to this pretty girl. "Is Lancashire your home, miss?"

She averted her face, but not before he saw her expression turn solemn. "I grew up in Sudbury." She turned back to him. "It is not far from Newmarket."

"I have heard of Newmarket." Newmarket was a place for horse breeding and racing, too. Claude knew of such places.

"But I have lived here at Rappard Hall for two years," she went on, her expression composed now. "I am what we English call an impoverished relation. Lady Rappard, my mother's cousin, was kind enough to give me a home."

His brows knit. She was a member of the family.

She lifted her chin. "Oh, but you must not feel sorry for me. I am quite fortunate. Besides, Lady Rappard needs me. Mrs Dart, the housekeeper, is so old that she requires my help to properly run the house."

"You are the housekeeper?" he asked, confused again.

She shook her head. "It is merely how I repay Lord and Lady Rappard for my livelihood."

He did not know what to say. It seemed she was neither family nor servant, but something in between. He still did not know if he risked being sent packing for talking to her.

"It is not a bad thing!" Her cheerful tone seemed forced. "Of course, with my cousin George and his companions in residence, there is quite a bit more to do."

Cousin George. His companions included Edwin Tranville. The man Claude had come to murder.

A cloud covered the sun and the stream no longer sparkled. Claude reminded himself he was not here to become enamoured of an English girl, no matter how prettily she smiled at him.

"I rode atop their coach, but that is all I've seen of the young gentlemen," he said.

There was much more he wished to know about them, however. Such as, what time did they retire at night? Which bedchamber was Tranville's?

She frowned, then glanced up at the clouds and stood. "Perhaps we should head back."

He hurried to bring her horse to her and to help her mount. This time his thoughts were not consumed with how delicate she felt or how his fingers tingled from merely touching her. Tranville had intruded into his thoughts and his mind was filled with how he might find him alone.

They took a slow pace back to Rappard Hall, a pace that gave Claude more time to think about his quest for revenge. He lagged half a length behind her, and they did not speak. Still, he admired her confident handling of the horse, her comfort in the sidesaddle.

When Rappard Hall came into view Claude looked upon it with disdain. A *château,* it would be called in France, although certainly a French *château* would be grander. The house was large enough, but boxy in shape and constructed of red sandstone over which ivy and moss had grown. It had one large tower perched on top of its three storeys, as if it had been stacked there like a child's set of blocks. The windows, however, were what most interested Claude. Which one would reveal Tranville?

"I will ride you to the door and take Pomona back to the stables for you."

She smiled at his offer, as if it had been an unselfish one. "That would be so kind, Claude."

He was not kind. He was a miserable dog. His intent was solely to more closely examine the house, to see where he might enter it, to discover where he might finally confront Tranville.

And kill him.

Gabe stowed the luggage in the gig and glanced at Emmaline. She stood stiffly, her face averted. He could almost feel the tension inside her. He'd been acutely aware of it ever since his brother had joined them at breakfast.

Cursed luck. What were the odds that a member of his family would visit Manchester at the same time, stay in the same inn and walk into the public rooms at the precise hour he sat there with Emmaline? Now it was almost noon. Paul's appearance had delayed their departure. Half the day was nearly gone.

Even worse, Paul had gaped at Emmaline as if she were merely some doxy with whom Gabe was trifling. Gabe had seethed at the knowing look Paul had given him and at the tone of disapproval in Paul's voice.

He frowned with the memory and raised the hood of the carriage so Emmaline would be shaded from the sun and protected from any sudden shower. He turned to help her into the seat.

Emmaline stepped back. "How could you do this to me, Gabriel?"

How was he to answer? His brother's presumptions about her were rude, but not entirely incorrect. He and Emmaline were lovers, after all. The previous night proved that.

"My brother's appearance was unfortunate—" he began.

She waved a hand. "Do you think I care about that? You broke your word to me! That is what I care about. You dictate a visit to this uncle when you know all I want to do is find Claude and stop him."

He was shocked. "You think I broke my word?"

Was her opinion of him so low that she thought he would forget their purpose of being together or the promise he'd made to her about continuing the search?

"What else can I believe when I heard you with my own ears?" She crossed her arms over her chest. "I do not wish to visit this uncle, Gabriel. I will not go with you."

The horse shuffled, as if impatient to be moving. So was Gabe. His bargain with her was to prevent her son from murdering Edwin Tranville, and, even though his chances of success were now exceedingly slim, he intended to try every means he could think of to accomplish that feat.

He looked directly into her eyes. "We search for Claude, Emmaline. What I spoke to my brother was fiction. What I said to you was truth." He paused. "Unless you would have preferred I explain to him we merely shared a bed during our quest to keep your son from murdering a baron's son?"

She looked down at her feet. "I did not realise."

He extended his hand and this time she allowed him to lift her up to the gig's seat. He climbed up beside her and signalled the horse to begin moving. Though he could not remember when he'd last driven a carriage, the skill came back readily and he eased the horse into the traffic on the road.

She was silent, but subdued. How easily she had misjudged his character.

And his feelings towards her.

As he drove he spoke, "My uncle is to the northwest. We will head south. Towards London. London or Brighton seems their most likely destination."

The horse faltered as other carriages, wagons and riders clogged the road out of Blackburn. Gabe pulled on the ribbons to keep the horse steady.

"I am sorry, Gabriel," she murmured.

Her wounding words still stung, no matter her apology.

She turned to him and he caught her earnest expression. "Why did you tell your brother we were betrothed?"

She did not understand? He gritted his teeth. He gave her a scathing look. "I had the frivolous notion to protect your reputation."

"Oh," she murmured.

"I did not forget the terms of your bargain, if that is what you presumed." Being considered the sacrifice she would make in return for her son's life was hardly something that would slip his mind.

Gabe admitted to himself a fledgling hope that sharing a bed with her might have altered matters between them. He would not make that mistake again. Oh, he would make love to her again, if she wished it. He'd be a fool to deny himself such pleasure. From now on, though, he would not forget that what they shared in bed could never equal her bond with her son.

Gabe manoeuvred the gig on to the London road.

They rode in silence for a couple of hours until Gabe sighted a posting inn in the distance.

"We'll stop here. The horse can rest and refresh herself while we enquire about Edwin or Claude."

They enquired if anyone had seen, in recent days, four young gentlemen in a private carriage with a crest on the side, a crest with a bird.

No one remembered seeing such a vehicle, nor did they recall a young Frenchman travelling alone.

They stopped at every posting inn on the road, asking the same questions, receiving the same answers. Gabe and Emmaline travelled almost as far as Manchester before Gabe turned around, taking a different route back towards Blackburn and checking at different inns. The answers were still the same. No hint of Edwin Tranville or Claude.

With each mile Gabe felt Emmaline's distress grow. He could not help but be affected by her growing despair.

The last inn where they made enquiries was nearly back to Blackburn and the sky was turning dark.

"We should stay the night here," Gabe told her. "Tomorrow we'll try in a different direction."

She nodded, looking exhausted and defeated.

That night they shared a room and a bed and Gabriel made love to her again, not quite as impersonally as he'd vowed. Their passion was fuelled by the tension of the day and by Gabe's need to comfort her against her fear that perhaps they were already too late.

Before they roused from the bed the next morning Gabe made love to her again. As they were preparing to head out, he bought a newspaper and searched its columns for news of a murder having already occurred. No news item was found.

This time Gabe drove the gig east towards the Irish Sea, passing through Preston and Leyland and Chorley, attempting to cover any road Edwin and his friends might have taken.

To no avail.

Two more days passed like this as they headed north, then west. Gabe could not ease Emmaline's despair.

"We will try again tomorrow," Gabriel said to her, as he held her in his arms once again. In spite of all it meant to him, the ultimate loss of her, his own heart ached at the pain she endured on behalf of her son.

She pressed her face against the skin of his chest and stifled a sob. "What if we are too late?" she asked him. "What if we are too late?"

Claude swept the floor near the stable doors, keeping busy while anticipation throbbed through his every vein, the anticipation of seeing Louisa Finch. She came to the stable to ride every morning at this time, and Claude made certain he was the groom available to ride with her.

No, not Louisa Finch. He must not make her important to him. It was the prospect of riding a fine horse like Apollo that appealed to him, he told himself. It was the chance to gallop over fields and hills, the air whipping at his clothing and filling his lungs. The pleasure of it almost drove thoughts of revenge out of his mind.

Almost.

At night he'd left his bed to creep up to the house. Already he'd discovered what doors were left unlocked, allowing him entry. He'd managed to glimpse Tranville, but still did not know where he slept. When he discovered Tranville's bedchamber, Claude's plan was to confront him there, make him divulge the names of the two soldiers who'd killed his father, and plunge the stiletto into Tranville's heart.

By morning, when Tranville's body was discovered, Claude would be far away.

The only part that bothered him was that Louisa would know he'd killed Tranville. She would never understand why he must commit murder. She'd hate him for it.

A sound made him glance up from his work.

Louisa walked towards him.

As she'd done the last three days, she would ask to ride Pomona and he would ride with her.

His pulse quickened at the prospect of her bright, daring eyes, her rose-tinged cheeks, her expressive pink lips.

"Good morning, Claude. Will you ride with me today?" This morning her smile seemed forced; her tone, sad.

What had happened? She always appeared happy when she came to ride, as if she, like he, grasped freedom only on the back of a horse.

"Yes, miss." He doffed his cap and banked his initial enthusiasm. "Do I saddle Pomona for you as before?"

"Yes, indeed." She seemed to be making an effort to sound cheerful.

While he saddled Pomona and Apollo she was uncharacteristically silent.

"What is troubling you, miss?" he could not help but ask.

"Troubling me?" She made a pretence of a smile, but

her voice cracked. "Why, nothing." She paused. "An attack of the blue devils, I suppose. It will pass."

He did not know what blue devils were, but something had changed her usual sunny manner.

He helped her onto her horse and his senses flared as before, but he felt as if he'd committed some offence by feeling his excitement so viscerally.

When they rode out of the stable, all of the young gentlemen—Tranville included—were walking towards them. Claude was careful to keep his eyes downcast.

"So this is where you disappear to, Cousin?" George Rappard said.

"I like to ride in the morning," she responded in a tight voice.

None of the young men seemed to give Claude any notice, but he was acutely aware of Tranville, his scarred face looking sallow in the morning light.

"Where is the gamekeeper?" her cousin went on. "We have a notion to go fishing and need poles and tackle."

"I have no idea where he is," she responded. "You should find the poles in his shed."

Claude could volunteer to find the poles and tackle for the young men. Perhaps he would be ordered along to assist them as he'd been ordered to ride with Louisa. This might be his opportunity to lure Tranville away from the others, to confront him and to exact his revenge.

All Claude needed to do was speak up.

And leave Louisa.

She moved her horse forwards, her spine rigid in the saddle. "Good day, Cousin. Gentlemen."

Claude followed her.

When they were out of earshot of the young men, she turned to him. "Let us not gallop today," she said.

"As you wish, miss," he responded.

She continued, her voice as strained as it had been speaking with her cousin. "I thought we might ride to the abbey."

There was an abbey nearby? Claude did not know the English had abbeys.

She went on, "George and his friends will not go there. I—I would not wish to disturb their fishing at the stream."

She led him on a path they had not ridden along before. Claude followed, but the brief sight of Tranville again filled Claude's nostrils with the scent of Badajoz. His father's blood. Tranville's drunken stench. Claude shook his head to dispel the memory.

He hated thoughts of Tranville to intrude during these brief interludes with Louisa. Usually when he rode with her the grass seemed greener, the sky bluer, the wildflowers more fragrant.

But today her mood—and his—was like a black cloud rumbling across the sky. He lowered his head and felt the darkness surround him.

They reached the crest of a hill and below them was the abbey.

"This is it?" Claude looked down on what was nothing more than piles of rubble, marking what must once have been walls. One tower still stood. Although it was open to the sky, it gave a hint to what grandeur once must have existed in this small valley.

"Is it not lovely?" she exclaimed, some of her usual liveliness returning.

To Claude it was a dreadful sight. What must have been a huge, thriving place was now nothing at all.

Louisa started down a path. She looked over at Claude. "Come. Shall we explore?"

When they reached the pile of stones, they dismounted. The horses wandered to a steam nearby to quench their thirst. Claude supposed it must connect to the same stream in which he and Louisa usually watered the horses, the same stream in which Tranville and his friends would fish, but here it was no more than a thin strip of water easily crossed with one giant step.

Claude followed Louisa through an arched entrance. All the walls or their remnants were red sandstone, the same as Rappard Hall.

Louisa stared up at a majestically high wall that must have once contained windows of coloured glass. "This place makes me feel peaceful."

Claude frowned. "It is rubble. What happened to it?"

She glanced around. "Centuries ago, King Henry VIII seized all the abbeys and Cromwell sold the land to important men. That is how Lord Rappard's ancestors came here. It has been their property ever since."

Claude had heard of that English king who abolished the Roman Catholic religion so he could divorce one wife and marry another.

"They allowed it to fall down?"

The magnificent Notre-Dame had been preserved for the people as a Temple of Reason. These buildings had been left to crumble and decay.

"I suspect eventually the family wished for a modern house. In fact, many of the stones from the abbey were used to build Rappard Hall and its buildings."

That explained why some walls had all but disappeared, their presence only marked by those remaining in the ground, like paving stones.

She sat on the sill of what once had been a window

and gazed around. "Ghosts gather here at night, spirits of the slain monks. A lady in white has also been seen, wandering through the rooms. It is said she is waiting for her lover to return from the sea. Poor thing," she added sombrely. "She cannot escape this place."

She dropped her head into her hands and burst into tears.

Shocked, Claude rushed to her side and, without thinking, put his arm around her. "Miss? What distresses you? Why do you weep?"

She straightened, but did not move away. He handed her a folded handkerchief from his pocket, glad that it was clean. She wiped her eyes with it. "It is silly of me. I am not usually such a watering pot."

It took him a moment to comprehend the meaning of *watering pot*.

She shook her head. "My life here is happy enough. I do not complain, but my—my cousin and his companions are so unpleasant. They yell and shout and run around. They are draining Lord Rappard's wine stores and waste so much food. They have already broken some porcelain that Lady Rappard held dear." She wiped her eyes again. "It is too awful. They talk like—like ruffians. Even in my presence. And I must keep the young maids away from them... I hate it all so dreadfully!" More tears poured from her eyes.

Something hardened in Claude at the mention of her cousin and his friends. His comfort turned to an effort to gain information. "Surely they will leave soon, will they not?"

"George whines that they are stuck here for a month until he receives his next quarterly portion."

A month? Claude did not intend a whole month to go by before he performed his sworn duty. Although a month of working in the stable and riding with Louisa all day would be very pleasant.

"Where do they spend their time? Perhaps you can avoid them." Where might he encounter Tranville? he meant.

She waved an exasperated hand. "They intrude everywhere. My only escape is to ride with you."

Claude should have felt gratified that this young and pretty girl, who was perfection in his eyes, liked the time she spent with him and treated him like a friend, not a servant. Instead he felt annoyed that she told him nothing of use.

"Oh, Claude!" She threw herself into his arms and wept against his chest. He had no choice but to hold her. Her clean scent and her soft curves finally drove out his thoughts of vengeance.

When she broke away, her smile turned more genuine. "I feel better. Sometimes all it takes is a good cry. Shall we ride some more?"

He merely nodded, too overwhelmed with the pleasure of having held her in his arms to speak. They walked over to the horses. When he lifted her in the saddle, she smiled down at him and his body responded to her.

He quickly turned away so she would not see. In some discomfort, he mounted Apollo, and he had some time to recover as she led them up the hill on the other side of the valley from whence they had come. Claude looked down on some pretty farm buildings, smaller than those at Rappard Hall.

"This is the farm that borders the Rappard property," she explained. "There is a road at the bottom of the hill. We can follow it back to our stables."

She seemed more relaxed on the way back. Claude,

on the other hand, was stirred up in many ways. By her. By seeing Tranville. By his purpose for being at Rappard Hall.

They rode into the stable. In the relative darkness, he helped her dismount and she gave him a quick hug before turning away and hurrying back to her dismal life.

That night in the room Claude shared with the other grooms, he tossed and turned on his cot. It was not their snoring that kept him awake this night, but rather thoughts of Louisa, the first girl who had ever stirred his senses.

How ironic that it was an English girl who so enraptured him. Even if there were *égalité* between them, as there would be in France, he would never court an English girl.

Alors. This was foolish thinking. He sat up in bed and rubbed his face. This was no time for romantic reverie. He had more important considerations.

Claude pulled on a shirt and trousers and carried his shoes out of the room, to put on before leaving the building. When he stepped out into the night, stars sparkled in the sky and the almost-full moon turned the grass to silver.

Lights shone from upper-floor windows at the Hall. As if he were a moth to those flames, he headed directly to the house, choosing a spot where he had a good view of the lighted windows, but could not be seen spying.

He waited, his limbs stiffening from the cool, damp air and from fatigue. His lids grew heavy and he struggled not to doze on his feet.

A silhouette appeared in the window, a man raising

a bottle to his mouth and drinking from it. Tranville? Claude held his breath and waited to be sure.

The man disappeared for a moment then carried a candle to the window. For a brief moment the candle illuminated the man's face.

It was indeed Tranville, jagged scar and all.

And now Claude knew exactly which room was his.

Chapter Fifteen

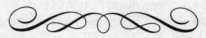

Gabe awoke in yet another posting inn. He blinked his eyes and struggled to remember exactly where they were.

Clitheroe.

They'd been headed north towards Lancaster to see if Edwin and his friends were bound for the Lake District, but it had soon been clear the route was again wrong. Next Gabe chose for them to go west, deciding to circle back to Blackburn on different roads, ones that were far less travelled. It was no real surprise that the young gentlemen had not been seen by anyone Gabe and Emmaline encountered.

Where the devil had they gone?

It was as if they'd fallen off the edge of the world. Of course, it was entirely possible that Gabe had just missed the certain road, certain inn, or one person who would have remembered seeing them.

He rolled over in the lumpy bed and gazed at Emmaline. God help him, she looked worried and fretful even in sleep. Tendrils of hair had escaped her plait and he fought the urge to brush them away from her face.

His heart twisted. How he had utterly failed her!

His bones ached from countless bumps in the road and he pined to stretch his weary muscles. He might wake her by doing so. The least he could do was allow her to sleep.

What a contrast these last three days had been from their lazy days in Brussels, where being together had been so easy, so full of peace and pleasure. Now each hour in his company merely increased the tension he sensed inside her. When they'd first lain next to each other in this bed, she'd been like cracked crystal. Gabe feared a mere touch would shatter her.

She'd wept in her despair for her son; Gabe had held her so close he could feel her damp lashes on his skin. There had been no words he could speak to console her. No such words existed. He'd merely held her until she'd fallen into exhausted sleep.

How confident she'd been of his ability to find Edwin and stop Claude from murdering him. He remembered her earnest entreaty in London, her surety that he alone could succeed in saving her son. Again. She'd staked her whole future on it.

Well, at least if he failed she would no longer feel obligated to marry him. Perhaps that thought consoled her.

Gabe grimaced. How churlish to even think of it. The pain of her misguided promise to marry him seemed inconsequential in comparison to the pain he sensed inside her.

At his failure.

He'd missed something, Gabe was convinced. Some piece of information that should have told him where to search. Something. Again he went over everything they'd learned, every place they searched, trying to find that missing piece of information.

If only he knew what it was.

No longer able to lie still, Gabe slipped out of the bed and stretched to finally ease his stiff muscles. As quietly as he could, he walked over to the bureau and poured some water from the pitcher into the basin. He dampened a cloth and wiped his skin, letting the bracing morning air dry him. Making lather from a piece of soap, he scraped his razor along his cheek. In the mirror, he glanced back at Emmaline. She raised herself on one elbow, before sitting up and rubbing her eyes.

Their gazes caught in the mirror, a silent communication of hopelessness.

He finished shaving and emptied his soapy water so the basin would be clean for her. As he began to dress, she padded across the room, naked. They'd slept together naked, as they had each of these nights, nights spent in passionate oblivion.

Except this past night. They'd not made love this past night.

If she had wanted it, he would have willingly complied. Anything she wanted he would have done for her. Anything to give her solace. If she gave any sign this morning of needing the scant comfort of his body, he would offer it. All he desired was to ease the pain he sensed inside her, the sheer despair that her son was lost.

And Gabe had done nothing to save him.

But she asked nothing of him. What he saw reflected in the mirror was her anguish.

She turned away again. Even in her despair her movement was graceful, so perfectly womanly his senses were aroused. He drank in her flawless skin, her pleasing curves and narrow waist. He knew from memory how it felt to trace his fingers down the length of her spine, how warm and willing she was to his touch.

It would be difficult to part from her. Again.

Gabe's anger at her had been erased by her misery and his failure to ease it. What did his vanity matter when she was so thoroughly unhappy? He could not detest her for loving her son, for wanting to do anything to save her son's life.

He tried to imagine his own mother feeling that way about him.

Impossible.

His mother had many children and grandchildren to fill any small place in her heart she might have once reserved for him. Emmaline had only Claude.

Or, rather, she so filled her heart with love for Claude that there was no room in it to spare for anyone else. Not even for Gabe.

That was reality, not something for self-pity. Gabe had known about her love for her son from the moment he'd looked into her eyes at Badajoz. He'd made the decision to love her for it then; he could not stop now.

He finished dressing.

Emmaline slipped on her shift and undid the plait in her hair. With long graceful strokes she brushed out the tangles as if trying at the same time to soothe herself.

Gabe put on his boots. "Shall I see if there is a newspaper to be found?"

She flinched as if struck by a rod. "Can it wait a little?"

"Of course." He stood. "I could arrange for breakfast, then. Would you like to eat it in the room here?"

She shook her head. "Will you wait for me? I will dress quickly."

He crossed the room to her and stood behind her. Gently he turned her around and held her against his chest. "Whatever you wish, Emmaline."

She melted into him. "What do we do now? We've searched everywhere."

"Make our way back to London." He held her tightly. "Start all over again."

Futile though it would be.

When they were on the road again Emmaline tried to cheer herself. They'd not found any news of Edwin's murder in the papers, after all, and it was another fine day. She should be grateful for good weather. Their travel would have been slower and more miserable if it had rained.

She ought to be grateful to Gabriel, as well, for his tenacity, his willingness to drive all over the countryside, asking at inn after inn, for not giving up, not losing hope. In her heart, though, she knew all hope was gone.

Somewhere in England, Claude was near Edwin, planning Edwin's murder. Or had already accomplished the deed and was arrested, awaiting hanging. Perhaps if a newspaper carried an account of the murder, she could still reach Claude in time to say goodbye.

Emmaline shook away that horrible thought and forced herself to gaze at the rolling hills of pasture and farmland that they passed. She let the steady pace of their intrepid horse lull her and ward off total despondency.

The land reminded her of Belgium, rolling grassy hills dotted with peacefully grazing sheep. She and

Gabriel had once driven out into the Belgian country-side to similar scenes.

"This must be sheep-farming land," she commented, to rid herself of the contrast between her happiness then and her misery now.

Gabriel shifted, as if surprised that she spoke. Their conversation had heretofore been less than perfunctory.

"It is." He paused before adding, "I tended sheep on these very hills."

It was her turn to be surprised. "Here?"

"The hill farm where my uncle is employed is close by." His tone was matter-of-fact. "These pastures are part of it."

"C'est vrai?" She glanced at the land again. "Truly? Is this the uncle you told your brother we would visit?"

"Yes."

He'd said when they started out this morning that they were not far from Blackburn. His plan was to return the horse and gig there and secure passage back to London for the morrow.

She set aside her own worries for a moment. "Gabriel, is this the uncle you told me about in Brussels, the one with whom you spent happy days?"

"It is," he responded, his voice remaining even.

"We should call upon him, should we not? We are so close and you told your brother you would." What did an extra hour or two matter? They would still have time to reach Blackburn. There was no real need to hurry now. Claude was lost.

He looked at her carefully. "Are you certain?"

She nodded. "He is your *family*." Her throat tightened at the word family and she turned away in case tears would burst from her eyes.

They quickly came upon an even narrower road

leading up a gentle hill. He turned the gig on to it and, as they reached the crest, the farm and all its buildings could be seen in the valley below. A white-stucco farmhouse, three storeys high, with a shingled roof, was framed by large trees and a flower garden. Fanning out from the house was a series of outbuildings and beyond them half-a-dozen tiny cottages.

On their search for Claude they had passed many prosperous country estates with magnificent mansions and numerous farm buildings nearly as grand. This property was much more modest and, because of that, its appeal was greater. Emmaline could imagine a family running this farm, living happily in such a comfortable place.

As they descended into the valley Emmaline could see that the garden was tangled with weeds and the house was tightly shuttered. A dog crossed the path from one barn to another, followed by scampering chickens, the only signs of life. It made her sad. Why was such a lovely place neglected?

As if reading her thoughts, Gabriel said, "The farm is for sale, and the farmhouse is vacant. There are only enough workers left to tend to the sheep."

"It is for sale? What happens to your uncle if it sells?" Would he be out of a job? Gabriel had told her that unemployment plagued the whole country.

"My uncle ought to have been pensioned off, but he stays on to keep the farm running. I do not know what will happen to him." He paused and added. "I once considered purchasing it."

"You have so much money?" She was surprised. "Why did you not purchase it?"

He looked sad. "I lost my reason to. Besides, I am a soldier, not a farmer."

She did not have a chance to ask him what he meant by losing his reason to purchase the farm. An old man emerged from what looked like a stable. He stopped and gazed at them for a moment, then hurried to greet their carriage.

"Gabe! It is you!" The man laughed with delight. "What a surprise."

Gabriel jumped from the gig and embraced the man. "Uncle."

Emmaline's eyes stung with tears at the reunion. She wanted so much for such a reunion with Claude.

"We were nearby," Gabriel explained. With his arm around his uncle, Gabriel's tall frame dwarfed the wiry, grey-haired man. He walked his uncle over to her. "Emmaline, this is my uncle, Mr William Deane."

"I am enchanted to meet you, Mr Deane," she said.

The man shuffled, looking shy.

Gabriel seemed to struggle for words. "This is... Madame Mableau, Uncle. We are travelling together."

Emmaline's brows rose. This time he did not tell his relation they were betrothed.

His uncle seemed to accept Gabriel's explanation. "Well, I am glad you came to visit. I was about to go to the cottage for tea. Young Johnny is in the stable. He can tend to your horse."

He shouted for the stable boy and Gabriel helped Emmaline from the gig. She was silent while she walked next to Gabriel on the path to a pretty thatched cottage. The dog bounded after them.

The cottage reminded her a little of her house in Brussels. It opened to a sitting room with a kitchen in the back. Stairs led to a second floor, but it was spare of colour and decoration. No lace in sight.

Gabriel's uncle swept off the seat of a chair with his hand. "Sit, miss...*madame*...ma'am."

She smiled at him. "Call me Emmaline. But you and Gabriel must do the sitting to share your news." She removed her hat and gloves and set them on a side table near the door. "Show me the kitchen and I will make the tea."

It felt almost normal to be heating water in a kettle and brewing tea. Uncle Will's kitchen was easy to negotiate, as spare as the other room. Hearing Gabriel's voice talking to his uncle gave her an ease almost like they had once shared together.

She brought the tea pot and cups to the small dining table.

"What news of the sale of the farm?" Gabriel asked.

"No one offering as far as I am told." Gabriel's uncle took the cup from Emmaline's hands. "There was some talk of his lordship acquiring the land, but they say he and her ladyship are off to Brighton, so we won't know until hunting season. His lordship will be back then."

Gabriel turned to Emmaline. "He means the earl whose property borders this one." He sipped his tea.

His uncle laughed. "News in the village is that his son and some friends have come to hide from creditors. His lordship will not like that when he hears of it."

Gabriel's tone changed. "His son is there?"

"That he is," his uncle responded, apparently not noticing Gabriel's heightened interest. "Came about a week ago. Mr Appleton—you remember him, Gabe? The blacksmith—Appleton has it from Connor, he's one of the footmen at the Hall—that they have been emptying the wine cellar and causing havoc."

Gabriel stared at him. "How many of them?"

"How many?" His uncle looked puzzled.

"How many of the son's friends came with him?"

His uncle shook his head. "I don't know. More than two, I think, from what was said."

Gabriel shot to his feet. "I am going there."

Emmaline stood, as well. "Is it—?"

"It must be," he said, reaching for his hat.

"Then I am going with you," she insisted.

His uncle rose with more difficulty. "What the devil is going on?"

Gabriel turned to him. "I cannot explain now, Uncle. We have been searching for someone, and I believe he is among young Rappard's party."

"But—"

Emmaline grabbed her hat and gloves, but did not bother to don them. They left his uncle standing in the doorway as they ran back to the stable. Gabriel reached the stable first and was already hitching the resigned-looking horse back to the gig, aided by a puzzled stable boy.

"Stay here, Emmaline," Gabriel told her, quickly double-checking the harness.

"Non." She climbed on to the gig herself and quickly tied her bonnet and pulled on her gloves. "Claude may be nearby."

He climbed up beside her and drove the gig out at a faster pace than heretofore.

Emmaline held on as they raced down dirt-packed roads. The same scenery she'd admired before whizzed by, a blur, while she prayed that Gabe's intuition was correct, that Edwin Tranville would indeed be there. Alive.

A red-stone mansion came into view and Gabriel drove directly to its door. The sides of their stalwart horse were heaving when Gabriel jumped down and turned to assist her. They rushed to the door and Gabriel pounded on it. He glanced at her and Emmaline saw her own anxiety mirrored in his eyes.

If Edwin was not here… If they were too late…

After what seemed a remarkably long time to wait, the door was opened by a liveried footman.

Gabriel did not wait for the man to speak. "Is Mr Edwin Tranville a guest here?"

The footman looked surprised. "May I tell Mr Tranville who is calling?"

Edwin was here! Emmaline took a breath and attempted to calm herself. They'd come in time.

Gabriel spoke in a calmer voice. "I am Captain Deane from Tranville's old company. I have been looking for him to give him news of some importance."

The footman stepped aside to allow them entry. "Come in."

They entered a hall with polished wooden floors and wainscoted walls. A huge painting of a man wearing armour was on one wall. On the opposite wall hung armaments in a symmetrical design surrounding a shield on which was the family crest. In the centre of the crest was a falcon, its wings outspread.

A crest with a bird on it.

Emmaline exchanged a glance with Gabriel. He nodded. He'd seen it, too.

The footman said, "You may wait in the drawing room. I will see if Mr Tranville is receiving callers."

Gabriel handed him his hat and gloves. "Is there someone who can attend to my horse?"

"I will send someone for your horse." The man placed Gabe's things on the hall table and led them to the drawing room.

The drawing room had a carved marble fireplace with a huge mirror above it. There were several sofas and chairs upon which to sit. Gabriel and Emmaline remained standing.

The footman bowed and left them.

"He is here." Emmaline whispered to Gabriel after the man was gone.

"Thank God." Gabriel paced the floor.

Emmaline stared at the door. Her knees shook and she suddenly felt as if she could not breathe. "I have not seen him since that day."

Gabriel came to her and held her arms in his strong hands. "He cannot hurt you."

She nodded, only partly consoled.

They waited for what seemed like eternity. Each minute marked by the mantel clock made Emmaline's heart pound harder.

Why was it taking so long for Edwin Tranville to appear?

Chapter Sixteen

Footsteps finally approached the drawing-room door.

In a moment Emmaline would face him, the man who had inhabited her nightmares for so many years, the man who had thought it a lark to watch her husband slain, who had tried to rape her and kill Claude.

The man whose life she needed to save.

She forced herself to turn towards the door.

It opened.

The creature who stood there was almost unrecognisable, slightly stooped, abdomen as round as a woman with child. He swept limp straw-coloured hair off his forehead and swayed slightly as he crossed the threshold. Surely she had never encountered this man before.

Except his yellow-tinged face was marked with a jagged scar from the corner of his eye to his chin, the scar she'd cut into him.

Edwin Tranville's gaze passed over her without much interest and riveted on Gabriel. "Lawd. What the devil brings you here, Deane? Last time I had the dubious pleasure, you caused me the loss of my employment."

Gabriel straightened his spine. "I lost you your employment? You were insensible from drink. Sidmouth sacked you for it."

Edwin waved him off and slumped into a chair. "No matter. It is dashed early in the day for a social call, is it not? I had to be roused from my bed."

Emmaline glanced at the clock. "It approaches noon."

Edwin directed his gaze at her and raised his brows. "If we have been introduced, ma'am, it has totally slipped my mind."

She gasped. His face was burned in her memory, yet he had forgotten hers.

Gabriel came to her side. "Do not be insulting."

Edwin smirked. "Why? Do not tell me she is your wife."

Gabriel's hands curled into fists and Emmaline could feel the anger rising in him. With a sudden movement, he seized Edwin by his coat lapels and hauled him back into a standing position.

"This is not a social call," Gabriel snarled.

Edwin's expression changed to shock and fear.

Gabriel shook him. "Cease your nonsense and listen to me."

Edwin nodded.

"This is the woman you tried to rape and kill in Badajoz."

Emmaline's knees trembled. Gabriel's sudden violence frightened even her.

Edwin tried to pull away. "I never—"

"Do not deny it," Gabriel went on, his voice deep and rumbling. "I was there. Others were there. We saw you." He released Edwin as suddenly as he'd seized him. "She cut your face."

Edwin's hand flew to his scar. He staggered back,

hatred flashing through his eyes. Emmaline's fingers twitched and she remembered the feel of the knife as it had sliced through Edwin's skin.

Edwin pointed a finger at Gabriel and laughed. "You are inventing this, Deane. I can tell." He shifted to a sing-song voice. "I have no need of your attempt at humour, which cannot be your purpose for calling. Even I cannot believe you would come all this way—" He stopped himself and peered at Gabriel. "How the devil did you know I was here? I've not written to anyone of my whereabouts."

Gabriel glared at him. "We have been searching the countryside for you."

Emmaline's thoughts raced throughout this exchange. Could it be Edwin truly did not remember what had happened in Badajoz? Surely he was lying about it.

"Searching for me?" Edwin laughed again. "Whatever for? To tell me I'd done something I never did?"

Emmaline spoke up, surprising herself. "You tried to kill my son. Do you not remember? Do you not remember the blade of my knife cutting into your face to stop you?"

Again his fingers flew to his scar, and his eyes darted as if searching for the memory. "I—I was wounded in the siege."

Gabriel shoved him back into the chair. "You hid from the siege, but when it was over, you were eager to take part in the plunder of the city. I do not know what else you did that day, but I know what you tried to do to this lady and her son."

Edwin wrapped his arms around his abdomen and winced as if in pain. "So what is this about? Did you chase me down to extort money from me or some such thing? Are you in that much need of funds, Deane?"

Gabriel stiffened. "I need nothing from you. If you would cease your babbling, I will tell you why we are here."

Edwin made a show of keeping his mouth closed.

Emmaline dreaded Gabriel's explanation. Could a baron's son have Claude arrested for planning to murder him? It seemed a likely possibility.

Gabriel paced several steps before beginning to speak. "We came here to save your life."

Edwin laughed.

"It is true!" Emmaline cried.

Gabriel leaned down to him. "Believe me. Your life is of no consequence to me, but we have knowledge of someone who wants to kill you for what you did at Badajoz. Our concern is for him, that he not commit such a crime, even against the likes of you."

"This is nonsense." Edwin's trembling hands belied his words. "I did nothing. Nobody wants to kill me."

"But he does," Emmaline cried. "He may be nearby even now. You must allow Gabriel to protect you."

"He may be lying in wait for you," Gabriel said.

Edwin shrank in the chair. "No! There is no one lying in wait for me."

Emmaline felt sick inside. How could they convince him?

Gabriel went on. "Listen to me. You were with two other soldiers, men who killed this woman's husband. You tried to rape her, until her young son attempted to stop you. You tried to kill him and this woman battled with you, cutting your face. Another soldier chased off the others, but I also arrived at this time. You were drunk. You were carried back to your billet—at considerable risk, I might add."

"Landon," Edwin whispered. "But he carried me

away from the city walls, not from the city. I'd fallen trying to scale the walls."

Gabriel shook his head. "Your father invented that story. I assure you, I would not wish to set eyes on you again if not to prevent this person from killing you and risking a hanging for it."

Edwin glanced away, and it was clear his mind was turning. After a moment, his eyes narrowed and he pointed to Emmaline. "You are in league with him. If not for money, then to ruin me! Deane has always hated me. Is he paying you to go along with this story?"

Emmaline felt outrage. "We speak the truth."

Edwin's voice went up in pitch. "It is not the truth. I would not do such a common thing." He pointed to Emmaline. "I received this scar because of the siege. I remember that." He glanced away and his voice dropped. "I think I remember that."

Gabriel spoke. "We want you to come with us now. I will take you to a place of safety. Some place where you can be protected. Your father's house, perhaps…"

Edwin rolled his eyes.

Gabriel appeared to ignore him. "When we know you are safe, we'll send word."

"Put my life in your hands?" Edwin's laugh was mocking this time. "No, thank you, indeed. I would not do so even if what you say is true. I will stay right here and not listen to your nonsense. It is a trick."

Gabriel shouted, "It is not a trick!"

"It is the truth," Emmaline repeated. What more could they say to convince him?

Edwin shook his head. "I'm too clever to fall for that. Goes with breeding, you know. You've always resented me for my rank, Deane."

Gabriel responded, "I outrank you. I made Captain well before you."

Edwin gave him a scornful look. "I meant my rank as a *gentleman*. You stink of trade and you always have."

Emmaline watched Gabriel flush with anger. With fists clenched he leaned towards Edwin, but somehow kept his temper.

Gabe spoke in a firm, low voice. "I am trying to save your life."

"Fustian!" Edwin stood, almost losing his balance. "You are starting to bore me. Leave me now or give me the great pleasure of having you tossed out."

They could not leave, could they? Emmaline refused to believe they had come so far, with such difficulty, only to be forced to walk away.

"Then we can do no more than warn you," Gabriel said. "Check your back and take care."

"Please, listen to us," Emmaline implored. A warning was not enough.

But Edwin merely made a dismissive gesture and sauntered to the door.

He paused, holding on to the doorknob, and turned back to them. "Now if you will excuse me. I have an attack of the runs."

Emmaline uttered a cry of frustration as he ambled out.

Claude pulled Apollo back as he and Louisa approached Rappard Hall. It would not do to let anyone see them riding side by side like equals.

Louisa sighed. "I wish we could simply ride away to some distant land."

It had been as perfect a morning as Claude was capable of imagining. Louisa had talked to him as a friend, as if none of England's notions about class separated them.

"You know," she went on, speaking loud enough for him to hear her, "I feel as if I have poured out my heart to you, but you say little about yourself."

"It is not my place," he responded. What could he wish her to know? That he was French? That he detested her country and its emphasis on class and status? That he'd sworn to kill for revenge?

She turned around and he was touched by the melancholy look on her face. "We cannot really be friends, can we?"

"Non." For all those reasons.

What would she think of him if she knew he now had a plan to confront and kill Tranville under the very roof where she slept?

He must carry out this plan soon.

After this halcyon morning spent with Louisa, he realised he should not remain at Rappard Hall many more days. He did not know how much longer he could resist asking even more of Louisa. The attachment between them grew stronger with every hour they shared.

Would she despise him after he killed Tranville?

How could she not? That thought pained him as surely as if it were he who felt the stiletto's sharp point.

Louisa glanced back to the vista below, Rappard Hall and its farm buildings.

"I dread returning," she said.

"Your cousin. His guests. I wish I could make them be civil to you." It offended his manhood that they should say things to her that a respectable young woman should not hear. He had no power, however, as a mere stable worker, to come to her defence.

"I will avoid them." She glanced back at him with a smile. "They cannot be rude to me if I stay out of their way."

As they descended the hill, they could see a small carriage drawn by one horse at the door of Rappard Hall.

Louisa shaded her eyes with her hand. "I wonder who that is. It looks like a man in uniform."

A man walked around the carriage. He wore a British officer's red coat and sash.

Claude's nerves went on alert. What was a British officer doing out here?

Louisa laughed. "I hope he has come to chase my cousin and his friends away."

Claude squinted into the sun. The officer climbed into a small carriage and disappeared behind the carriage's hood. He could see no more than the man's hands holding the ribbons. The carriage started off.

"He is leaving!" Louisa cried in a worried tone. "I should have been there to receive him. One never knows how George will deal with matters of importance."

Claude's brow furrowed. The officer could not be looking for him, could he? *Non,* it was impossible. No one in England knew of him. His mother was the only one who knew his plans and certainly she would reveal them to no one.

Even so, the red-coated officer felt like a bad omen, a sign he must no longer tarry.

As they entered the paddocks behind the stable, Claude gazed at Louisa, memorising this image of her, seated so expertly upon her horse. Her back was straight, her waist narrow, and a peek of brown curls were visible beneath her hat.

She turned to glance at him and smiled once more.

Perhaps that was what he would remember the best. Her lovely lips curved into a smile that lit up her eyes and put dimples in her cheeks. Perhaps on lonely nights he would remember that once a lovely English girl had smiled when she looked upon him.

He averted his gaze, following instead the small carriage that made its way down the path to the road. He scanned the farm, thinking how well tended it was, how kind Mr Sellars and the other grooms had been to him, how thrilled he was to have cared for and ridden such beautiful horses.

He patted Apollo on the neck and the horse bobbed his head in pleasure.

Apollo would be the third horse he'd come to love and the third horse he'd endure losing. His father's horse. His own Coco. Now Apollo.

But even that paled in comparison to losing Louisa.

Gabe turned the gig on to the road back to the hill farm.

"What a stupid man," Emmaline exclaimed. "Vile and stupid and stinking of spirits."

"Indeed." Gabe wondered something else, as well. Edwin looked more ill than drunk.

Emmaline shifted in her seat. "He should not have said those awful things to you about gentlemen. *He* is not a gentleman!"

He turned to her. "He was never a man of good character. If he had been, he would never have done what he did to you and Claude."

"Ha!" She pulled at her gloves. "I did worse to him. Every day in the mirror he must look at what I did to him."

Her anger was much more welcome to Gabe than

her despair. Soon the fact that he'd failed her would again plunge her into desolation. Finding Edwin had accomplished nothing, after all.

Except they might discover that Claude was near. If they could find Claude and reason with him, Emmaline's wish might come true at last.

She put her hand on his arm. "Do you think he tells the truth that he does not recall what happened?"

He frowned. "He was very drunk that day, much worse than usual. It is possible he has no memory of it."

"It is unfair." She gazed out at the road ahead. "Claude and I must always remember it."

And I must remember as well, thought Gabe.

She grew silent and he knew her mind was filled with thoughts of her son.

He cleared his throat. "Let us stay the night with my uncle. Tomorrow you must rest. I will go to the nearby villages and enquire about Claude. If he is close, someone will know it. Someone will remember him."

She wrapped her arm through his and leaned against him. "I will go with you."

He glanced at her beautiful face. "We'll see."

Gabe turned his attention to the familiar land around him, land whose seasons had remained the same as the days of his boyhood. The scent of the grass, the baying of distant sheep, the warmth of the sun on his face, brought back memories of peaceful days. This land refreshed one's spirits, restored one's hopes.

Perhaps it would work its magic on her.

"What if we do not find Claude?" she asked, her voice taut with tension. "How can we stop him if Edwin will not let us near?"

"We try to find him first."

"I feel Claude near, Gabriel," she murmured. "I feel the danger."

Gabe felt the danger, too, as well as a sudden unshakeable sense of doom.

In spite of the worry, they spent a bucolic evening at Uncle Will's house. Emmaline cooked the dinner, roasting a chicken and making *frites,* the potatoes Gabe had not tasted since their shared dinners in Brussels. Uncle Will ate with such relish he barely spoke, except to say, over and over, "This is delicious."

After dinner Emmaline insisted Gabe sit with his uncle while she washed dishes. Afterwards, she picked up some of Uncle Will's mending, needing to keep busy, Gabe understood. By the time darkness fell, she sat by the lamp pushing a needle through the cloth and Gabe had nothing left to talk about with his uncle.

They sat in silence for several moments, until his uncle leaned back. "So tell me why you were so fired up to find that fellow at Rappard Hall."

Gabe should have known his uncle would get around to asking. It was very apparent that Gabe and Emmaline had remained troubled since their return.

"I cannot speak of it," Gabe said, glancing towards Emmaline.

He made it Emmaline's decision what, if anything, to say to his uncle. Gabe knew Uncle Will would not press the matter, but he also knew his uncle would worry about what distressed his nephew.

Emmaline returned Gabe's gaze with a resigned expression. "Tell your uncle all of it, Gabriel. I want him to know."

He was surprised at her decision, but he faced his uncle and began the story at Badajoz. It was the only way to make Uncle Will understand Claude's need for revenge. Gabe told his uncle how he and Emmaline had searched England for Edwin, knowing Claude might also be near. They'd hoped warning Edwin would be enough to keep him safe until they could locate Claude and convince him to abandon his dangerous plan. Gabe explained Edwin's reaction to their warning.

Uncle Will listened intently, his hands folded in front of his lips. When Gabe came to the end, his uncle slowly opened his hands and rubbed his face. He gazed off in the distance. "A French fellow... Seems to me I heard of a French fellow—"

Emmaline dropped her mending. "Where?"

He tapped his lips before going on. "Appleton—the blacksmith—seems to me he spoke of a Frenchman. Sellars—do you remember him?" he asked Gabe. "Sellars runs the Rappard stable. He hired a new fellow, Appleton said. A French fellow. Good with horses."

Emmaline rose to her feet. "He is hired to work at the Rappard stables?"

He'd been within easy reach when they'd called upon Edwin at Rappard Hall.

Uncle Will nodded. "Best worker Sellars ever had, he told the smithy."

It was like placing the wolf among the sheep.

Gabe shot to his feet. "It must be Claude!"

Emmaline rushed over to him. "We must go now! It cannot wait until tomorrow. Tomorrow might be too late."

"I will go." Gabe turned to his uncle. "Do you have a fast horse I might ride?"

"There's only one horse fit for riding," his uncle replied. "The riding horses were sold. Stapleton's heir sold all he could. All that's left are work horses."

"Let us saddle him now," Gabe said.

Emmaline grabbed her hat and gloves from a table near the door. "I will go with you. I must!"

He grasped Emmaline's shoulders. "I can go faster if I ride alone."

She clung to him. "You must let me go with you!"

He shook his head. "Time is of the essence. Trust me to do this."

She nodded, but tears filled her eyes as she looked up at him. "I have this terrible feeling—"

He gave her a swift embrace and did not tell her he shared her worst fears.

Chapter Seventeen

Claude entered the house through an open door that led to the still room and the kitchen. A glow from embers in the oven gave the only light, but he'd seen and memorised enough of this level to grope his way to the stairway.

He was in luck. He easily discovered the servants' staircase. As he climbed in the darkness, he kept an image of the house in his mind. He needed to find the right room on the right hallway.

On the second floor, he opened the door to the corridor. To his surprise it was lit by a sconce on the wall, making it easier for him to see, but also easier to be discovered. Heart pounding, he closed his eyes to visualize the house again. He was in the correct wing. Now he must choose the correct door. Opening his eyes, he counted. One. Two. Three.

Would he find his enemy there? From outside he'd watched him readying for bed, saw him extinguish his candle. Had Tranville remained in the room?

The rest of the house seemed quiet and dark, except

for the flickering candle in the sconce. Holding his breath, Claude stepped out into the hallway and crept quietly to the third door. From somewhere he heard voices, muffled and distant. Dare he go on?

He'd come too far to stop now.

He reached the door and tried the knob. It turned. He opened the door only wide enough to slip through. Enough moonlight streamed through the curtains to reveal the shape of the bed and other furniture in the room. Gradually more details revealed themselves. The shape of bottles on a table. Clothing thrown over a chair.

The whole room smelled foul.

A loud snore startled him. He expelled an excited breath. Tranville was here.

Claude moved slowly towards the bed, reaching inside his coat to slip the stiletto from its sheath. As he got closer, the stench worsened and he recoiled. It was the stink of Tranville, even stronger than before.

He covered his nose and mouth with his hand until he reached the bedside and placed the point of the stiletto against Tranville's throat.

"Wake up, you villain!" he spoke in a loud whisper.

Tranville woke with a start. The tip of the stiletto pierced his flesh. A drop of blood appeared. "What?"

"Silence or I'll stick this all the way through your throat!" Claude pressed the point against Tranville's skin again for emphasis.

"Who—who are you?" The whites of Tranville's eyes seemed to glow in the dark. "You are French? You are the Frenchman? They said—I did not believe them."

"Be quiet!" Claude growled. "I was once the boy whose mother you tried to violate. In Badajoz. Remember? You laughed when the others killed my father. I want their names. I'll kill you if I do not have their names." He would kill Tranville no matter what.

"I do not know their names. I wasn't there, I tell you. You have the wrong man." Tranville retched and the point pierced him again. More blood trickled from the wound. "Don't kill me!"

Claude moved the point away slightly. "I have the right man. I heard your name. My mother sliced your face."

Tranville's hand touched his cheek. "I'm going to be sick." He turned his head and retched.

"Answer my question!" Claude cut him again.

"I cannot!" A gurgle sounded in Tranville's throat and he spat on to the bed linens.

Claude averted his face in disgust.

The man sat up and clutched at his abdomen. "This is a hoax. I told Deane so. He has gone too far."

Claude whipped the stiletto against Tranville's chest.

Deane had been the name of his mother's English lover.

He put pressure on the stiletto. "Why do you mention Deane?"

Had Deane been the British soldier he and Louisa had seen earlier?

"Come, now. He is your partner, is he not? You are all in this together." He sneered. "You made it too coincidental. Not well done at all. They come today; you come tonight. I'm too clever not to figure this out."

"They?" Had there been another person in the small carriage? He'd been unable to seen anything more than a glimpse of a soldier.

Tranville's expression turned defiant. "The French woman who said she cut my face. Did you not say that was your mother? Have you forgotten your lines in this little farce?"

His mother? Here? With Deane?

Claude pushed the stiletto against Tranville's chest and drew more blood.

"I'm bleeding!" Tranville cried, raising his voice. "No!"

"Quiet!" demanded Claude.

He needed to end this. The risk of discovery was becoming too great. Deane was near. With his *mother*. He must finish this now and make his escape.

Claude gripped the stiletto and pushed the point in further.

Tranville cried aloud.

A vision of Louisa flashed through Claude's mind. What if she woke from Tranville's cry? What if she discovered him over Tranville's lifeless body?

He moved the knife away.

Another cry rang out, this time a woman's scream. Louisa?

The sound came from somewhere in the house. Nearby.

"Help me!" It was Louisa's voice. "Help!"

What was happening to her?

Claude could never ignore such a cry. With a frustrated growl he pulled himself away from Tranville's bed and ran out of the room into the hallway, thinking only of Louisa.

"Someone help me!" she cried.

Shoving the stiletto in its sheath inside his coat, he followed the sound of her voice, turning down another corridor on this same floor. A sliver of light shone under a doorway. He made his way to that door and pressed his ear against it.

"Let me go, Nicholas. Go away," he heard. "Someone will come to help me."

A man laughed. "No one can hear you. Edwin is the only one on this floor and he's probably passed out from drink. Stop acting the tease. You want this as much as I do."

Claude opened the door. On the bed Nicholas Frye straddled Louisa, holding her by the wrists. She struggled to free herself.

Hot with rage, Claude crossed the room and seized Nicholas by the collar, jerking him away. *"Ne pas la toucher!"* Do not touch her!

Nicholas rolled to the floor, but quickly found his feet again. Claude punched him in the stomach. A whoosh of air escaped the man's lungs and he staggered back. Claude charged him, pushing him against a dressing table. It shattered and its bottles and pots broke on the floor, making a great noise and filling the room with the flowery scent of Louisa's perfume.

"Help me!" Nicholas shouted, his voice booming much louder than Louisa's. "George! Harry!"

Claude heard the pounding of feet, but he continued his attack, striking Nicholas with his fists in a frenzy of violence.

He heard Nicholas's friends enter the room and one seized him from behind, pulling him off Nicholas and effectively restraining him.

"Now you will get your just deserts," Nicholas cried.

Claude's cheek exploded with pain as Nicholas's fist struck him and struck him again. Blood poured from his nose while Nicholas pounded on his chest and stomach. Claude tried to kick him, but Nicholas easily dodged away.

"Stop! You are hurting him!" Louisa, her hair

tumbling loose over her shoulders, scrambled off the bed and grabbed Nicholas's hair in her fingers, trying to pull him away.

Her cousin George seized her. "Louisa, stay out of it!"

Tranville appeared at the door. "Oh, good," he drawled. "Finish him off. He tried to kill me."

"He attacked you, as well?" Nicholas's face turned ugly.

Claude watched the man's fist aim directly for his eye. Ears ringing with pain, he forced his eyes open to see Louisa straining against her cousin's grasp. Another fist hit him and she cried out.

Tranville leaned against the doorjamb, blood trickling down his neck and staining his white nightshirt.

Nicholas was breathing hard when he abruptly stopped the onslaught. Claude fell to his knees. His head throbbed and his vision dimmed.

He'd failed to kill Tranville. He'd failed to rescue Louisa. He'd failed.

Just like at Badajoz.

In that instant he felt transported back to that flame-engulfed Spanish city. Again he watched red-coated men striking his father and plunging a knife into his father's chest.

Claude shook off the vision. He managed to reach inside his coat for his stiletto. He pulled it out.

Harry shouted, "He has a knife!"

"The one he stabbed me with," Tranville said.

Nicholas knocked the stiletto from Claude's hand. Both Claude and Nicholas lunged for it as it clattered to the floor. Nicholas seized it. With a grin he unsheathed it and stepped towards Claude.

Claude glanced up, the taste of his own blood in his

mouth, the pounding of pain ringing in his ears. His eyes riveted on the stiletto and he prepared to die.

Like his father.

Gabe approached Rappard Hall, his horse's sides heaving. Through a window he could see a scuffle, a man being beaten.

"Good God!" he exclaimed aloud. Was he too late?

He dismounted at the front door and ran up to pound on it.

It opened immediately. A wide-eyed elderly footman pointed to the stairway. "They are fighting!"

Gabe bounded up two flights of stairs and spied Edwin standing at one of the doors.

"Lawd!" exclaimed Edwin, jumping aside as Gabe ran past him and burst into the room.

A man turned in surprise. He held a knife and looked as if he was about to plunge it into Claude's chest.

"Oh, no, you don't." In one swift motion Gabe seized the man's wrist and twisted it until the knife fell to the floor.

Two other men rushed at him, but Gabe swung the first man around and used him as a battering ram, shoving them all across the room against a wall. They tumbled to the floor like a set of skittles.

Gabe snatched the knife, a thin, lethal stiletto, and was ready for them when they made it back to their feet.

"Get back!" Gabe ordered, whipping the stiletto under their noses like a sword.

The three men retreated until they stood flat against the wall.

From the corner of his eye Gabe saw a young woman run to Claude and wrap her arms around him. Claude's face looked battered. His nose bled as did a cut above his eye. His clothes were ripped and dishevelled.

Gabe swallowed. He'd almost been too late. He'd almost cost Emmaline her son.

He shook the thought away and aimed the knife at Edwin's friends. The scent of perfume filled the room. Gabe quickly glanced around. This must be the young woman's room, not Edwin's, but Edwin had blood on his shirt. What exactly had happened here?

He asked the young woman, "Miss, are you harmed?"

"No," she responded, still holding on to Claude. "But—but this man received a terrible beating."

Claude looked up at him. "Captain Deane," he said in a raspy and pained voice.

"He is an intruder!" cried the man who'd wielded the stiletto. "He attacked our friend and this lady. What did you expect us to do?"

"Claude did not attack me! He came to my aid." The young woman snatched a robe from the foot of the bed and wrapped it around herself. She pointed to the man who'd wielded the stiletto. "Mr Frye accosted me and Claude stopped him."

Edwin entered the room and leaned against the wall next to the door. He gestured to the blood on his night-shirt. "Come now, Deane. You sent this fellow. He tried to kill me."

"Stubble it, Edwin!" Gabe shouted. "You brought trouble on yourself. Unless you want more of it, shut your damned mouth."

Edwin scoffed. "Who could possibly cause me more trouble than you have?"

Gabe glared at him. "Your father. He's seen proof of what happened in Badajoz."

Edwin's eyes flashed with surprise. "Proof?"

"Proof of what?" Frye asked.

Gabe advanced on him and put the point of the sti-letto under his chin. "Keep silent." He turned a steely gaze on the other two men. "And you lot? Who are you and what have you to say?"

One replied. "Ha-Harry Stewel, sir. I only saw this stranger fighting with Nicholas. I did not know Nicholas attacked Miss Finch."

Gabe nodded and pointed the stiletto at the last man. "And you?"

This one straightened his spine. "I am George Rap-pard. This is my house." He pointed to Claude. "This fellow is an intruder! As are you, sir!"

Gabe ignored his accusation. "Is Miss Finch a guest in your house?" he asked, staring him down.

Rappard looked confused. "Guest? No, she's a cousin. She lives here."

Gabe leaned in close so that mere inches separated his face from Rappard's. "You should be less concerned about intruders and more about protecting your cousin from your friend."

Rappard's eyes widened.

Gabe stepped back again and looked at each man in turn. "You are a disgrace to your names." He turned to Frye. "You and Edwin most of all."

George Rappard, looking disturbed, turned to his cousin. "Did Nicholas really accost you?"

Her eyes shone with tears. "Yes."

Frye's voice rose in protest. "She enticed me. It is all her fault."

Claude struggled to his feet. "You cannot blame her!"

"No. No. No." Rappard waved his hand at Frye. "You've been bothering her the whole visit. I did not credit it until now." He faced Gabe. "I would like to end this with as little fuss as possible. I certainly would not like it to become known to the magistrate. Or my parents." He peered at Gabe sheepishly. "May—may I know who you are, sir?"

"Captain Deane, lately of the Royal Scots." Gabe offered little more explanation. "I have been searching for Edwin. I called upon him here earlier today."

Rappard made a mollifying gesture. "I will not ask why, nor what possessed you to return at this hour. I am only grateful that you did." He took a step towards Miss Finch. "Forgive me, Louisa."

Miss Finch nodded.

The young man sounded sensible and the situation was calming. Perhaps Gabe could get Claude safely back to his mother after all.

"I will be content to leave now," Gabe said. "I'll take Claude with me, but you must assure me that this young lady will be safe under your protection."

"You have my word on it." Rappard turned to Edwin. "I do not know what trouble you caused, Edwin, but I think you should leave." He glared at Frye. "I demand you leave, Nicholas. There is a coach passing though the village tomorrow. You both will be on it. You are no longer welcome here." To Gabe, he said. "You may go anytime."

"We leave now, Claude." Gabe retrieved the stiletto's sheath from the floor and put the knife inside his coat. "No argument."

Claude did not argue. He did not speak at all, but merely limped towards the door, one hand pressing his ribs. He looked Edwin directly in the eye as he passed. Edwin shrank back.

In the hallway, Gabe offered Claude an arm, but Claude pushed him away.

"Wait!" cried Miss Finch. "I will walk you out." She ran to Claude and lent him her shoulder for support. Claude accepted her help.

Gabe shrugged and followed them to the stairs.

The servants were clustered at the bottom of the stairway in the hall.

"Miss Louisa," the elderly footman asked, "what happened?"

"I will explain later," she said as they descended the stairs. "All is well now."

She, Claude and Gabe walked out of the door.

As soon as they were outside, Miss Finch embraced Claude. "How can I ever thank you for saving me!"

He shook his head, but held her in return. "Do not make me so good, Louisa. I am not."

Gabe watched them, his hands on his hips. Obviously more than a chance rescue connected these two.

She pulled away and put both palms to his cheeks, making him look at her. "Do not say more. To me you will always be my hero and my good friend."

Claude looked down on her. "I am afraid for you to stay in this house."

She gave a wan smile. "My cousin is in earnest, I believe. But I will also stay the night in the housekeeper's room and remain with the servants until Nicholas and Edwin leave."

He held her close again. "Goodbye, Louisa."

"Make haste, Claude." Gabe spoke gently.

Claude broke away from her. "I must retrieve my satchel."

"I will get it. Where is it?" Gabe asked.

"Around the back of the house behind the large tree." His gaze did not leave Louisa's.

Gabe found the satchel and led the horse to Claude,

who still stood with Louisa. She held on to him as if she could not bear for him to leave.

"You ride." Gabe offered an arm to help Claude mount.

Claude ignored it and mounted on his own, uttering a pained cry as he did so.

His Louisa blew him a kiss as Gabe led the horse away.

When they reached the road, Claude, sounding very defeated and in pain, asked, "Where are you taking me?"

Gabe turned. "To your mother."

Chapter Eighteen

Gabe led the horse well past the Rappard gate before Claude spoke. "Why did you bring my mother to this place? I demand you tell me. Why did you bring her here?"

Of all Claude might have said, these words were not what Gabe expected. He stopped the horse and stepped closer. "Do you wish to make me the villain in this escapade?"

Claude's eyes flashed back at him, filled with resentment and accusation.

Gabe schooled his emotions. "Your mother is in England because of you. She journeyed from Brussels to seek me out for the sole purpose of asking my help to find you and stop you from killing Edwin Tranville."

Claude's spine stiffened, but the action seemed to cause him a spasm of pain. "The honour of my family demanded it."

Gabe kept his gaze steady and his voice firm. "Was it honourable to sneak away, to hide your intentions from your mother? You knew she would not approve. Instead of facing up to her, you lied about your whereabouts and informed her in a letter."

Claude lowered his head.

At least Claude showed some guilt for what he'd done to Emmaline. Gabe intended to make it even clearer. "Your mother was frantic for you. She was terrified she would lose you."

Claude's voice turned defensive. "She merely presumed I would fail."

Gabe shot back, "No. She feared you would succeed and be caught and hanged for murder."

In the moonlight Claude's eyes now filled with misery. "I did not succeed, did I? I failed to kill Tranville." The young man turned his face away. "I failed again, like before."

"Before?" How many attempts had Claude made?

"In Badajoz."

Ah! Gabe was beginning to understand. Claude's need for vengeance was fuelled by anger at himself. "When you were merely a boy?"

Claude's nod was almost imperceptible. "They killed my father and I could not stop them. Edwin Tranville tried to rape my mother and I could not stop him." He wrapped his arms around his ribcage and took in a laboured breath.

A memory returned. Young Claude flung over his father's body, crying, *"Papa! Papa!"* Gabe felt a wave of pity.

"You were a boy. They were men. Not only men, they were soldiers. You were helpless against them."

Curse that Frenchman. Mableau had dragged his wife and son into war. He had caused the horror in their lives. Perhaps Emmaline and Claude would have found happiness had they stayed in France, had they never seen Badajoz.

Had they never had reason to meet Gabe.

"It does not matter now." Claude sounded like a bitter child. "Because you have prevented me from killing your friend."

So Gabe was back to being the villain? He laughed. "Edwin is no friend of mine. I stopped you from killing him only for your mother's sake."

Gabe held on to the horse's bridle and signalled the animal to start walking again. Claude winced in pain with each step the horse took. It was no wonder. The young man was bruised all over, in body and in spirit.

Gabe took his time before speaking again, because he suspected Claude would not credit anything he had to say.

Still, the young man deserved an explanation. "Your father was a soldier, Claude. Soldiers die in war. Your father died in the ugliest part of war, when men riot and plunder, but it was still war." Emmaline had given this same explanation their first night together in Brussels. "Three thousand of our men were killed in Badajoz that day. I don't condone what came after, but perhaps none of those men would have acted so barbarically had they not endured such hard fighting. You never had a chance to learn how a battle can affect a man. You were injured too quickly—"

Claude interrupted him. "How do you know I was injured quickly?"

Gabe had assumed Emmaline had told Claude. "You charged my square at Waterloo. I saw you fall and dragged you into the square for safety."

"It is true?" Claude gaped down at him. "You carried me to Brussels, to my mother?"

Gabe glanced away, the pain of that parting with her still raw. "It was the least I could do for her."

Claude looked so distressed that Gabe decided to leave him to his thoughts.

They travelled on in silence until Gabe spied the gate of the hill farm ahead of them.

There was one more matter he must address before returning Claude to Emmaline once again.

He slowed their pace. "I want you to tell me what happened tonight. The whole of it."

Claude's head lifted. An obstinate expression was quickly replaced with a resigned one. "I went to Tranville's room to kill him. I tried to push the knife into his heart, but I could not make myself do it. You may call me a coward if you like."

"Were you afraid to kill him?" Gabe asked.

"I was not afraid!" Claude responded quickly. He paused as if reluctant to go on. Finally he said, "I thought of how it would be for someone to discover him dead. To see all the blood. I did not wish that experience on—on anyone."

Gabe would wager it had been Miss Finch he'd thought of.

Claude went on. "Then I heard Louisa's cry and I tried to rescue her, but the others ran into the room and overpowered me."

It was not lost on Gabe that Claude, a mere groom, addressed her by her given name.

Claude made a strangled sound in his throat. "I failed at saving her as well."

"She seemed to think you saved her," Gabe said, trying to help the young man salvage some measure of self-respect.

Claude shook his head determinedly. "All I did was nearly get myself killed. You were the rescuer. Not me."

They reached the farm gate, and Gabe stopped again. "I need your word that you will no longer attempt to kill Tranville."

Claude peered at him. "I thought you said he was no friend."

Gabe explained again, "He isn't. I wish I'd killed him myself that day in Badajoz. He's caused nothing but trouble for people I do care about."

"Like my mother?" Claude's resentment re-emerged.

Gabe spoke quietly. "You have already put her through enough grief and worry. She does not deserve more. I need your word that you will not cause her further distress."

Again Claude lowered his head. The young man cared about his mother's feelings; that was one thing to his credit.

He raised his head again and gave Gabe a direct look. "I give you my word. I failed to kill Tranville once; I will never try again."

Gabe merely nodded.

He led the horse through the gate towards the farm buildings, large dark shapes against night sky.

"We are here," he announced, but felt no pleasure in it. "I'll take you directly to your mother."

Emmaline heard the horse approach and hurried out the cottage door. The agony of waiting was over, but what now?

Gabe's uncle, having spent the last two hours pacing outside, grabbed a lantern and was already halfway down the path to the stable. She ran after him.

The indistinct outline of a man leading a horse came

into view, but she could not see enough until Gabe's uncle reached them. Then the lantern light shone on Gabe's imposing figure and revealed another man on the horse's back.

Her heart raced. Could it be?

She could not make herself move, as Gabe and his uncle led the horse and rider towards her. When they were about ten feet away, she finally saw him.

"Claude! Claude!" She ran to him.

"Maman." His voice sounded old and in pain. Even in the darkness she could see his face was bloody.

"You are hurt!" she cried.

"We'll take him to the cottage," Gabriel told her.

She walked at her son's side, looking up at him, impatient to examine his wounds, to feel her arms around him.

When they reached the cottage, Gabriel offered a hand to help Claude dismount. Claude pushed it away and dismounted on his own. He almost lost his footing.

Gabriel caught him and held him until Emmaline took her son into her arms.

"Claude." Tears sprang to her eyes. *"Mon fils. Mon cher fils."* Her dear son had been returned to her.

Gabriel had brought him to her one more time.

She kissed Claude's cheeks and hugged him until he uttered a pained sound.

He spoke in French. "My ribs are sore."

Alarmed, she released him, but wiped at the blood on his face. *"Mon Dieu!* We must get you inside." She glanced back to Gabriel and asked in English, "What of Edwin Tranville?"

"Unharmed."

"Dieu merci," she murmured as she helped her son through the doorway.

Uncle Will said, "I'll tend to the horse. And I'm set to bunk with the stable lads, so the cottage is yours."

Mr Deane had told Emmaline earlier that he would leave the cottage for the night. She'd appreciated the kindness, and the privacy for herself and her son. There was so much to say to him, so much to explain.

"Come in and sit, Claude," she said in French, leading him to a sofa. "I'll see to your wounds. Are you hungry?"

"No, Maman. Not hungry." His reply was curt.

"You must be thirsty, then. I'll bring you some tea."

Gabriel stepped through the doorway, carrying Claude's satchel. Emmaline's gaze turned to him and she searched for words to express all that filled her heart. None were sufficient.

Instead, she said, "I need some towels and bandages."

"I'll get them for you." He started up the stairs and she followed him.

He glanced at her in surprise, then placed Claude's satchel in the smaller room. "Claude can sleep in here," he said. "You may use the other room."

She nodded. "Where will you be?"

"I'll sleep on the sofa." He walked over to a chest of drawers and removed a stack of towels and two rolls of cotton cloth.

As he handed them to her, she grasped his arm. "Gabriel." She looked directly into his eyes. "*Merci*, Gabriel. *Merci*. For my son. For everything." The words were not enough, but it was all she could say.

He drew away, inclining his head to the stairs. "He needs you."

As they descended the stairs together, Claude turned and looked daggers at them.

At the bottom of the stairs, Gabriel said, "I will leave you alone."

Her lip trembled. Her son was still so angry. Did he not understand? Gabriel had done everything for him. He'd done everything for her.

Without looking back, Gabriel parted from her and walked out the cottage door.

Emmaline watched him leave before bringing the towels and bandages to Claude.

"I need to get some water." She went into the kitchen and returned with a basin of water.

She knelt in front of Claude and bathed his face. There was a cut above his eye and dried blood beneath his nose. His cheeks were swollen and already bruises were starting to form.

"After I clean you up, I want you to tell me what happened."

Claude nodded wearily.

She demanded nothing of him while she tended his wounds. After she bound his chest with the bandages, she brought him tea.

His hand shook as he lifted the cup to his lips.

His eyes met hers. "Why are you with him, *Maman?*"

His words took her aback. After what Claude put her through, he should be explaining to her, not the other way around.

She sat next to him on the sofa. "You ask me such a question? I am with Gabriel because of you, because of what you came to England to do. How could you, Claude? How could you think to commit such a sin?"

Claude's hands balled into fists. "I wanted to avenge my father. And you."

She put a hand on his knee and made him look at her. "You would have hanged for it. And then you would be gone to me. You must promise me to give up this revenge. You must promise to forget all about killing Edwin Tranville."

He crossed his arms over his chest. "Your captain has made me give my word."

Gabriel saw even to that. "Oh, Claude. I am so glad." She leaned back. "But what happened? How did you get hurt?"

He told her of trying to kill Edwin Tranville, but stopping short of it. He said Edwin's friends had caught him and beat him, until Gabriel arrived and put a stop to it.

She said another prayer of thanks for Gabriel.

Claude's explanation was choppy and disjointed and left her with many questions. Perhaps Gabriel would answer them for her.

She brushed a hand through her son's hair. "I am glad you did not kill."

He turned away.

She added, "I could not bear being left all alone."

"Alone?" His eyes flashed. "What of your English lover? You do not need a French son."

She gripped his hand. "Do not speak of him in such a tone! After all he has done for you—"

Claude lifted his chin. "Spare me the list of how many times he has come to my aid."

She leaned back on the sofa and pressed her fingers against her temple. Claude remained bitter, as caught up in that long-ago time in Badajoz as ever.

Perhaps Claude could never come back to her as he'd been in his boyhood days, before his father was killed in front of him. She covered her mouth, grieving again at what her only child had endured and again feeling the guilt of her part in it.

Claude would never give up his hatred for the nameless men who had killed his father, or for Edwin Tranville. It was a hatred so strong it encompassed even Gabriel.

She spoke softly to him. "You should know I am going to marry him."

Claude went pale. *"Non."*

She fingered the ring beneath her dress. "He asked me to marry him in Brussels before the battle, but I said no. I will marry him now, however."

He winced in pain. "Why?"

Why? Because she had promised to marry him if he found her son. No, that was not it. Perhaps it was because she was grateful to him for saving Claude's life yet again?

No. It was because she could not imagine spending a day without him near her, to wake in the morning with him not at her side. She could not bear to tumble into bed alone without the comfort of his arms.

Emmaline blinked in awe. She realised suddenly that, even if he were sent to Brazil or Egypt or China, she would still choose to be with him. She belonged with him.

Claude's eyes narrowed. "It is because of me, is it not? You feel you must accept him because he saved my life. You think it is paying him back somehow."

That had once been the bargain she'd made with Gabriel when they began this journey to find Claude. It was no longer the reason.

She loved Gabriel, needed him, knew he would never fail her. She wanted a chance, a lifetime, to show Gabriel that she, too, would never fail him.

I love you, Gabriel, she said to herself, joy filling her heart.

She met Claude's gaze and unconsciously slipped into English. "I want to marry Gabriel. How could I not after all he has done?"

Claude shot to his feet and responded in French. "You even abandon our language for your captain? I cannot speak to you any longer. I want to go to bed."

His anger made her want to weep. "You are tired," she said, fighting tears and hoping he would see more clearly in the morning. "We are all very tired. There is a bed for you above stairs. You will find your satchel in the room where you are to sleep."

He grasped his ribs and walked painfully to the stairs. "I presume you sleep with him in another room?"

She ached for him. "Not tonight."

He gripped the banister as he climbed the stairs.

"Claude!" she cried.

He stopped, reluctantly turning to her.

"You will not leave me again?" Her voice rose an octave. "You will be here in the morning and not do anything foolish?"

He answered in a low voice. "I will not leave and I will do nothing foolish." He continued up the stairs, but paused again. "I wish you would make me the same promise."

From outside Gabe watched Emmaline minister to her son. He saw her bathe Claude's battered face and cleanse his wounds. Gabe remained in the shadows, near enough to the open window to see her, to hear them talk together. It was not eavesdropping, because he could understand only bits of the French. He simply needed to watch her. Hear her voice.

She and Claude argued. About him, no doubt. Perhaps she'd told him of the bargain she'd made with Gabe. He'd fulfilled his part of it.

Gabe heard her switch to English. "I want to marry Gabriel," she said. "How could I not after all he has done?"

After all he has done.

She intended to keep her part of the bargain. To marry him out of gratitude. Out of obligation.

Now, even more than when she had first proposed it, he knew he could never hold her to it. Now his love for her had again flourished, but in a way that meant he could not bear hurting her. If he wished to be selfish, he could marry her and for ever separate her from her son.

But Gabe could never be the sacrifice she must make for her son's life. He loved her too much to deprive her of what she held most dear.

Her son.

Through the window he watched her climb the stairs. He waited longer, alone in the darkness, making certain both she and Claude would be asleep before he re-entered the cottage.

When all remained silent, Gabe opened the door and entered as quietly as he could. He pulled off his boots and padded across the room to the sofa. Removing his coat, he rolled it into a pillow for his head. The sofa was too short, so he positioned a chair on which to prop his legs.

And tried to will himself to sleep.

It was no use.

The loneliness kept him awake, a loneliness that seemed to return from the distant time of his boyhood days.

He made a frustrated sound and rose from the sofa.

Padding across the room in his bare feet, he stood at the open window. A breeze wafted the curtains and cooled his face.

It almost soothed him.

He parted the curtain and gazed out into the moon-filled view. The outbuildings. The path leading to the stable. The distant hills.

The silence and neglect made the farm a sad place, echoing his own sadness. It pained him to see the farm's deterioration from something beautiful to something neglected and forlorn. If he closed his eyes he could imagine it as it had been. Bustling. Its buildings repaired. The parks and gardens tidy and flourishing.

He turned and surveyed his uncle's sitting room. He thought of Emmaline in his uncle's kitchen or seated in that chair, mending his uncle's shirt. She would look so perfect in the big house, overseeing the meals and running the household. He could imagine her seated across from him at the other end of a long dinner table, sharing the news of the day. He could envision encountering her in one of the rooms, filling a vase with flowers or opening curtains. He could see her in the garden, her face shaded by a wide-brimmed straw hat, looking as fresh and beautiful as the blooms that once had grown in abundance there.

He'd dreamed of living with her on a farm like this one, sharing hard work and happy times.

And peace.

He ran a hand roughly through his hair.

What did a soldier know of peace? A soldier belonged some place where men fought each other over matters other men considered worth their lives.

He turned back to the window for another glance at the moonlight-filled view, then returned to the sofa and the imposing quiet of the cottage. He again forced his eyes closed.

At least he could pretend he would fall asleep. He could pretend he was not leaving something that might have once been beautiful and now would never be.

But all his mind's eye could see was Emmaline. *Emmaline.*

He heard a swish of skirts and opened his eyes to see her moving towards him like some angelic apparition. In the dim light from the window, he could see her hair loose upon her shoulders and the skirt of her nightdress flowing around her.

She came closer. "Gabriel? Are you awake?"

He reached for her, and she settled beside him, curling against him on the sofa, her body fitting perfectly against his. Her scent comforted him. Her warmth soothed him.

"Is anything amiss?" he managed.

"No." She touched his face and with her fingers brushed the hair off his forehead. "I needed to be with you."

He found her lips and she returned his kiss with eagerness, opening her mouth and touching her tongue to his. His senses burst into flames as she urged him on top of her, unfastening his trousers. He ran his hand up her bare leg to her waist, raising her nightdress as he did so. Heedless of being still half-clothed, he entered her and felt the enveloping heat of her connecting them as only a man can connect with a woman.

The loneliness he'd felt a moment ago vanished.

In so many shared beds in inns throughout the countryside they'd reacquainted themselves to the pleasures of their lovemaking. Gabe had long stopped trying to convince himself he was merely using her for pleasure.

Making love to her was like breathing air. Necessary for life.

She alone could fill the void within him, he realised. She alone completed him.

He touched her, kissed her, savoured her and brought her desire to the same fevered pitch as his own. When he drove her to her peak, he relished the completeness, the connection, the mounting pleasure this lovemaking gave him.

As his seed spilled inside her, joy flooded through him, then softly mellowed into languor, leaving him with one oppressive thought.

This would be the last time he made love to her.

This would be goodbye.

Chapter Nineteen

Emmaline could not coax Gabriel into bed with her in the chamber above. She knew he would never sleep if she remained with him on the sofa, so she reluctantly left him and climbed the stairs alone. A peek into Claude's room showed him motionless. His even breathing suggested he slept. Suddenly very tired herself she went into the other room and crawled into bed.

The next morning sunlight burst through the window like an abundance of cheer. Emmaline sat up and stretched and thought surely this day was full of promise. Claude was safe, with her and Gabriel. Perhaps, here on this quiet farm, Claude could talk to Gabriel and begin to appreciate what a fine a man he was, even if he was English and an army officer.

She hugged herself. How could Claude not learn to value Gabriel? Gabriel was a marvellous man, steadfast and strong, a performer of great feats. Like returning her son to her.

The ring she wore around her neck swung on its chain as she flung off the bedcovers and rose. She dressed hurriedly. The men would need breakfast and it delighted her to be able to cook the meal for them, as Gabriel had once cooked breakfast for her.

She checked in the other room. Claude still slept, the *cher enfant*. Sleep would help heal his wounds, she hoped, both the visible ones and the ones he hid inside.

She skipped down the stairs, but slowed as she reached the last steps.

The sofa was empty and the sitting room tidy. Gabriel had risen already and was not in the room.

His uncle appeared in the kitchen doorway, wiping his hands on a cloth. He froze when he saw her.

"Good morning, Mr Deane," she said brightly. "I hope that you have not eaten. I wanted to cook your breakfast for you."

He placed the cloth back in the kitchen and his forehead furrowed. He inclined his head towards the table. "There is a note for you."

A prickle of trepidation crawled up her spine, but she ignored it and smiled. "Is it from Gabriel?"

He nodded, but his expression was grim.

She breezed over and picked up the letter, an unsealed, folded piece of paper with *Emmaline* written across the outside in a strong, sure hand.

She unfolded it and read:

Dearest Emmaline,
In my uncle's possession is a sum of money suf-
ficient to take you and Claude back to Brussels.
I plan to send you a hired carriage tomorrow to
carry you both to Hull, where you can get pas-
sage to Belgium. Within a very few days you will
be back home.
    You must know that I never meant to make you

marry me. I'm meant for the army, not marriage, and even your gratitude is not reason enough to drag you into a soldier's life. Nothing is. Please forgive me for making you believe I would require that of you, you who have given me such happiness. You deserve an easier life than the one I have chosen.

I also would never separate you from your son and deprive you of the person who has always been first in your heart. It is enough for me to know he has been restored to you.

Return to Brussels and be happy, dearest Emmaline. I will think of you there, strolling in the Parc or toiling in the shop surrounded by white lace. Time and distance will never dim my memories of you.
With undying affection,
Gabriel

"Non!" She held the letter against her chest. Gabriel's ring pressed into her flesh. She looked up at his uncle. "He has gone?"

The old man's face melted into sympathy. "At dawn. Said he'd take the gig back to Blackburn."

"And then?" Her throat twisted in pain.

He glanced down. "He did not say."

He had simply left? She could not believe it to be true.

"He must have said something," she insisted. "What did he tell you?"

His uncle shrugged. "He told me to make certain you took the purse he left with me."

What did she want with money? She wanted Gabriel. She swung away.

His uncle walked over and put a comforting hand on her shoulder. "Now, do not fret, *madame*. There is nothing to do. I think Gabe wanted to spare you. He said you meant to marry him in gratitude for finding your son, but that he wouldn't—"

"Non!" She shook her head. "Not for gratitude."

Was his leaving her fault? She had never told him of her change of heart. She'd been too wrapped up in Claude. She'd never told Gabriel that she wanted to be with him no matter what, no matter where the army sent him.

His uncle nervously took his hand away. "He said the army was no place for a woman."

Had his uncle read her mind? "He is going back to London to find some regiment to join." And she would never know where he was, nor would she ever see him again. It was unbearable.

"I suppose you are right." His uncle rubbed his chin and nodded decisively, as if he'd just that moment been convinced.

She unfolded the letter and read it again. He did not want her to endure the hardships of a soldier's life. He did not want to separate her from her son.

She squeezed her eyes shut.

So unlike Remy. So unlike the husband who she'd been afraid to defy, whose selfishness had irreparably hurt them all. It was so clear now that Gabriel loved her in a way that Remy never could. Gabriel would not think of himself, but of her. And of Claude.

She refolded the paper and put it carefully in the pocket of her dress.

Footsteps sounded on the stairs and she and Gabe's uncle turned towards the sound. Claude paused on the stairs, gripping the banister. His eyes were ringed with dark bruises and the gash above his eye resembled a slash of red paint.

Emmaline took a breath and spoke to her son in French. "I was about to make breakfast." To Gabriel's uncle she said in English, "Mr Deane, may I cook for you as well?"

"I ate." He stepped towards the door. "I'm late in seeing to the sheep." Pausing at the doorway, he bowed. "If you will pardon me." He glanced up at Claude. "Make yourself at home, young fellow."

Claude inclined his head and waited until the older man had walked out of the door.

He continued down the steps. "Where is your captain?" His tone sounded bitter. Sleep had not mellowed him.

Emmaline averted her gaze and wrapped her arms around the ache inside her. "He is gone."

"When will he return?"

She tried to breathe normally. "He will not return."

His voice rose in surprise. "I do not comprehend."

She turned back to him and snapped, "He has left and will not be back." She started towards the kitchen. She could not speak to Claude about this, not when her feelings were so raw. She felt as if someone had scraped all the flesh from her body. "Sit, Claude. I will cook you breakfast."

Gabriel could still feel Emmaline beside him in the gig as he drove the small carriage they'd shared for so many days. He remembered her tension when she sat beside him. Her worry. Her need to lean on him some of the way.

At least now her worries were over. He'd given her back the chance for happiness by restoring her son to her and sending them both back to Brussels. Gabe felt good about that. It had been a worthy deed.

Even if it had sunk him into gloom.

He glanced around him. The green hills dotted with peaceful sheep were a stark contrast. What a peaceful life the scene represented, another stark contrast to the world he best knew. The army. Battle. Death.

That was all a soldier was good for, fighting battles and vanquishing enemies. Much of the life was grim, but there was an excitement to it as well. Fighting a battle, surrounded by the enemy, pitting man against man—there was nothing like it, nothing like the exhilaration of facing men bent on killing you, but cutting them down instead.

He closed his eyes for a minute and remembered the sounds of battle, the smells, the expressions of despairing shock in the eyes of men when his sword fatally struck them. In the throes of fighting, Gabe had experienced the power of life and death, the thrill of survival.

He opened his eyes to the clear blue sky, where white clouds mirrored the sheep grazing on the green hills. The air smelled of life, of grass and wildflowers and horse. The only sounds in his ears were of the breeze rustling the leaves of trees, the rhythmic pace of the horse's hooves, an occasional bleating from the sheep on the hill. The sounds of peace.

His memories of battle sickened him. What was war compared to a day like this?

Gabe shocked himself. What had happened to that boy who had looked upon such a fine day with boredom, pining for the thrill of the army? What had happened to that soldier?

Emmaline.

Meeting Emmaline had changed him. She'd made

him yearn again to belong to someone, to want a family, a home.

How cruel Fate could be! To give him Emmaline, then whip her away. He'd done the right thing by leaving her, he told himself again. She belonged with her son, not with him. He would not be the cause of splitting them up.

He'd return to the army, a place where home and family did not exist.

He laughed aloud, startling some birds who must have thought themselves safe in the shrubbery. Their wings flapped as they took to the air. Fleeing, as he was fleeing.

He did not know if he could return to the army. He still was without a commission. There were still few captaincies to be had. He had no more connections to snag one of them than he'd had before Emmaline had walked back into his life.

Gabe flicked the ribbons, quickening the pace of the horse. In two or three hours he'd reach Blackburn. He'd return the horse and carriage and book passage to London. In a few days he could again visit the War Office. If no other commissions had come through in his absence, at least the Royal Scots would still have a place for him in the West Indies. He could easily return to that oppressive heat and damp, those incessant insects and fevers, and the abhorrent duty of stamping out rebellion among slaves who merely wished to be free.

Good God.

Was that what Fate had in store for him? Was that where he belonged?

Only four days after Gabriel had left her, Emmaline and her son stood on the deck of a packet bound for the Continent.

"I swear I will earn the money to pay him back," Claude said, still fuming about the fact that Gabriel's money had paid for their passage. "Every last *penny.*" He spat out the English word as if it were rancid meat.

Emmaline stared at the bank of the River Hull, at the English land she was leaving behind. "It was Gabriel's gift to us."

He made a disparaging sound.

These last few days with Claude had been difficult. His anger was still so palpable, she'd feared he would run off again at any moment to go in search of Edwin. She'd had to be so careful not to upset him any more than he was upset already.

When he was back in Brussels perhaps he could begin to leave the past behind and look to his future. Perhaps his future was in France. It might be best if he did visit her parents in France and not lie about it as he had done before.

It was so much easier to think of what Claude should do, where Claude should go, than think of her own future. To Emmaline, her future loomed empty and lonely, even though her aunt would expect her back at the lace shop.

Without Gabriel at her side, everything seemed empty and lonely.

She glanced at Claude. He'd removed his cap and the river breeze tousled his dark curls, so much like her own. When she blinked her eyes, he looked one moment like the boy he'd once been, another moment, like a man.

The boy reminded her of another voyage for which Gabriel had paid, the one that had got them out of Spain and back to France. The memory stabbed at her heart.

"I am glad to be leaving England," Claude said,

although his tone seemed to contain some regret. Regret for not killing Edwin?

She had the sense there was more to it than that, but she took a deep breath. "I am glad you are leaving England, as well."

He glanced at her. "What of you, *Maman?* You do not say you are glad to leave."

She returned his gaze, but did not answer.

He frowned. "You are still pining for Captain Deane, even after he abandoned you."

Smaller boats crowded the river. Ahead of them, Emmaline could see the North Sea. When they reached it, she would truly be leaving England—and Gabriel—behind.

Her throat tightened. "Leave me to my feelings, Claude. I cannot speak of them."

His brows knit in an expression of disapproval that reminded her too much of his father.

She took a breath. "He didn't abandon me, Claude. He left because he thought it was best for me."

"He decided what was best for you?" He sniffed in disdain.

Claude's father had also decided what was best for her and she'd feared defying him. After all she and Gabriel had been through, though, she could never fear him, no matter what.

She watched the land slowly slipping past. "Why do you want to make Gabriel a villain, Claude? He has done only good for you."

He rubbed the wood of the boat's railing and murmured, "He asked the same thing."

"The same thing?" Her brows rose.

"About why I made him the villain." He leaned on the railing. "I do not know why, *Maman,*" he answered with defiance. "I have to credit him with saving me and saving Lou—Miss Finch." He paused. "But his red coat reminds me he is a British soldier and then I remember the red coats who killed Papa."

"But Gabriel had no part of that. He took us to safety. Do you not remember?"

He pushed away from the railing. "I remember. I remember all of it." He paused. "Except about him rescuing me at Waterloo. I thought you made up a story about that, but I now believe it was true. Deane has rescued me countless times." His eyes flashed with emotion. "But that is it, do you not see? He succeeded where my father failed. Where I failed. Time and time again. I know it makes little sense, even to me now, after my time at Rappard Hall." His eyes took on a faraway look for a moment, before filling with pain again. "I only know I cannot forgive him."

He stalked away from her.

Emmaline did not move from the deck until the last glimpse of England faded from her sight. Even then, she did not turn towards the Continent, towards Antwerp where the packet would dock, or towards Brussels, a place she had once called home.

Chapter Twenty

Gabe walked back to Stephen's Hotel, not even seeing the book shops, ironmongers, milliners and tea shops on Bond Street. He'd just come from signing his name to papers that set the course of his future; his brain was still mulling over whether or not he'd made the right decision.

No use in that. His signature made matters final.

He shrugged. He had many regrets in his life. If he regretted what he'd done this day, he could merely add it to the list.

Emmaline was not one of his regrets, however. She had not been far from his thoughts when he had put pen to paper today. How different it would have been if Emmaline could have been at his side. Still, he was not sorry he'd left her. He'd done right by her by leaving. What he did regret was that circumstances made it impossible for him to be with her. That would always be number one on his list of regrets.

Gabe lifted his gaze from the pavement and was surprised to see how near he was to the hotel. He quick-ened his step.

When he reached the entrance, he prayed the hall would be empty. A few of the men who were here before had found commissions, and others had managed to make advantageous marriages, but there were plenty of men left who would chew his ear off. Bored with their inactivity, they would insist upon knowing all the tedium of his life, and he had no wish to have to dodge questions. He wanted to keep his recent activity to him-self.

Gabe entered the hotel and removed his shako and gloves. He threw his gloves inside his hat, as he always did. At least the hall looked empty. Glad of that piece of luck, he started across its length to the stairway.

The footman who attended the lobby suddenly appeared. He dashed to the stairway, pausing when he saw Gabe. "Oh, Captain," the man cried, out of breath. "Someone to see you. Waiting in the front parlour." He continued past Gabe up the stairs. "Forgive me. Have to run."

"Who is it?" Gabe cried, but the man merely waved a frantic hand and pounded up the steps.

Gabe tapped on the banister. So much for his wish to escape any company. He turned and made his way to the parlour door.

Perhaps Allan Landon or Jack Vernon had called. That would be tolerable. He'd sent word to them of his return and had already met with them to fill them in on what had happened with Edwin.

And Emmaline.

As he turned the knob of the parlour door, he had the sensation of being pulled back in time. Entering, he dropped his hat on a table and thought of the day Emmaline had surprised him in this very room.

Just as it had that day, the parlour looked empty. Fresh flowers adorned the mantel and the sound of a swishing skirt came from the high-backed chair facing the fireplace.

Gabe froze.

Emmaline stood before him. "*Bon jour,* Gabriel."

"Emmaline?" His voice was no more than a whisper.

He'd never thought to see her beautiful face again, her fair skin and blue eyes and the lips he'd dreamed of kissing when sleep eluded him at night.

He recovered himself. There was only one reason she would return here. "Is it Claude?"

She blinked, as if confused, then met his gaze again. "*Non. Non.* Claude has not run away again. That is not why I am here."

"Why, then?" Whatever it was, he would help her again, he immediately resolved. He knew now that no other choice was possible for him. Let her ask a thousand times. He would always come to her aid.

She glided towards him with that familiar grace. As she neared, the scent of lavender reached him. "I came to speak to you."

He cocked his head, more puzzled than ever. She did not seem as tense as she had been when she had stood in this same place before. Neither did she seem at ease.

She glanced up at him. "A long time ago, I did not speak up when I should have. I had not the courage. It was a terrible mistake I made then. I made another one when we were together last, by not saying what I needed to say soon enough. You were gone before—" Her voice broke.

She was troubled and he felt the pain of that as if it

were his own pain. "What do you mean? Tell me. I will help you in any way I can."

She smiled and raised her hand to caress his cheek. "My *cher capitaine*."

He seized her hand, lifting it in a silent question about the gold band with its glittering sapphire that adorned her finger.

"I used to wear it on a chain beneath my dress, Gabriel," she whispered. "There has never been a day I did not wear your ring."

He dropped her hand, still puzzled.

She lowered her hand and stepped back, but then looked as if she were steeling herself for combat. "I said I would marry you. I came to tell you that is what I want. I want to marry you."

His spirits dipped. This smacked of her self-sacrificing bargain again. "Emmaline, I already freed you of that obligation. I do not know how to make it clearer to you. I do not require you to marry me."

Her eyes widened. "You do not comprehend. I *want* to marry you, if—if you also desire it. That is what I travelled here to tell you. I do not want to be apart from you. I will follow you to wherever the army sends you. I do not care where it is as long as I can be with you." She gripped his arm. "I came to say this to you. To make sure you know that I say this because I love you. I have loved you since Badajoz when you were so kind to us. I loved you in Brussels, but I was afraid. I am still afraid, but it frightens me more to be without you."

Gabe felt himself go warm all over, but he dampened his burgeoning hopes. "What of Claude? Surely he will not accept you marrying me."

Her eyes filled with sadness. "No, he will not. Claude

said to me that he will never see me again as long as I am with you."

Gabe shook his head. "Then, it is no use. I will not be the cause of you losing your son."

Her fingers tightened on his arm. "You are not the cause. Nor am I. It is Claude who chooses it."

He looked down at her, seeing her suffering at her son's declaration. He also saw something else.

Her resolve.

She went on, "You said yourself that Claude is a man now. He must make his decisions and live with them." A ghost of a smile flitted across her face. "Besides, he said he would still write to me, so that is something. As long as I know he is well and seeking his own happiness instead of revenge, I am content. And who can say? Perhaps he will change his mind after a time."

Gabe's hopes glimmered again. Dare he indulge them? "Are you certain, Emmaline? Are you certain you want to marry me?"

"Mais oui," she murmured. "More than anything."

He gathered her in his arms and held her close to him as if he feared loosening his grip would make her flutter away and he would lose her once again. "Emmaline. My love."

Her voice filled with emotion as he held her. "Gabriel, there is so much I cannot give to you. I cannot give you children. I have no dowry, nothing to bring to a marriage, except my promise to devote myself to you—"

"It does not matter," he reassured her. "We can be a family, just you and me. And I certainly do not need your money. I need you."

"Then I will go anywhere with you, Gabriel." Her voice was firm. "Have you found a commission yet? Tell me where we will go next."

He released her and held her at arm's length so he could look into her eyes. He laughed aloud. "I have no commission! Oh, Emmaline. I am not even in the army any more. I sold out completely. Do you mind returning to Lancashire? I have just today purchased the hill farm, the one my uncle manages. We will own the farm. I can take care of my uncle and all the other people whose livelihoods depended on it. We will make it prosper again. Together."

He drew her to him again, this time lowering his lips on to hers for a kiss that burst forth from the joy in his heart. Beneath the kiss she laughed with happiness, before pressing her lips to his as if never to release them.

When they finally took a breath, Gabe twirled her around, laughing again. When he stopped he gazed at her as if to convince himself that she was real and that this was a dream come true.

He remembered his first glimpse of her amidst the horror of Badajoz, when he'd been alone and her family had been violently torn apart. Something had changed in him that day at the mere sight of her. He was changed still.

But now he understood. She was where he belonged, where he would always belong. He knew it deep in his soul.

He belonged with Emmaline.

He embraced her once more.

They were both home at last.

Epilogue

London—November 1817

It was a celebration dinner, but a quiet one. The recent death of Princess Charlotte in childbirth had the whole country in mourning, and London society remained swathed in black. Emmaline and Gabriel had just returned to London for a brief visit.

Even the tragic death of the English princess could not mar the happiness that had built between them over the past two months. After a quiet and private wedding, Gabriel had taken Emmaline for a tour of the Lake District and then to Manchester to meet his parents, brothers, sisters and countless nieces and nephews. It seemed to Emmaline that she was accepted into Gabriel's family as merely one of the crowd, which delighted her. After that visit, she and Gabriel had spent a few weeks at their new home, the hill farm which had been busy with the breeding season and Gabriel's efforts to return it to its former productivity.

Back in London for Gabriel to complete some

business related to the farm, Allan and Marian Landon had insisted upon hosting a dinner to celebrate their marriage. Included as guests were Jack and Ariana Vernon.

Both the Landons and Vernons greeted them as old friends, and Allan opened a bottle of French champagne and poured for everyone.

He offered a toast. "To your happiness!"

"To us all," Gabriel had countered, looking so handsome in his black coat, white linen and cream breeches that he took Emmaline's breath away.

As they all drank, Emmaline glanced around, remembering her anxiety the last time she had been in this room and her wonder at the willingness of these good people to help her find Claude, her surprise that they had all been connected by Badajoz.

"Tell us about your wedding and your trip!" Ariana insisted. The actress looked even more beautiful than usual. Her August performance in David Garrick's *Katharine and Petruchio* had been a great success, but now she was working on a different sort of production. Her second child.

Emmaline allowed Gabriel to describe the wedding and the trip, adding only a few details he'd omitted. Like some of the wonderful things he'd done for her while they travelled.

The Landons' butler, a huge former soldier, appeared at the door. "Beg pardon," he said.

"What is it, Reilly?" Marian asked.

He looked from Marian to her husband. "Lady Tranville is here. She wishes a moment to speak to you."

Lady Tranville? She was married to Edwin Tranville's father. She was also Jack's mother.

"Have her come in." Allan waved a welcoming hand.

"She may meet our guests and say hello to her son and daughter-in-law."

Reilly's expression turned firm. "You had best speak with her first."

With anxious looks, Allan and Marian excused themselves; Ariana attempted to dispel the aura of worry that had suddenly filled the room. "Proceed, please! Tell us all about your farm."

A few minutes later, a grim-faced Allan and a red-eyed Marian returned, accompanied by an older woman Emmaline presumed was Lady Tranville. Gabriel and Jack rose to their feet and Jack crossed the room. It was clear Lady Tranville had delivered some sort of dreadful news.

"Hello, Mother." He kissed her on the cheek and put an arm around her. "What has happened? Is it Lord Tranville?"

She shook her head. "Edwin."

Emmaline's heart rose into her throat.

Allan quickly made introductions. "I told Lady Tranville that everyone here would wish to hear this news." He held fast to his wife's hand and looked from one to the other, his gaze resting on Emmaline. "Edwin Tranville is dead."

"Dead!" Gabriel cried.

Emmaline felt afraid to breathe. "How?"

Lady Tranville answered, "From a liver ailment. He has been ill for many weeks." She patted her son's arm and looked sympathetically at Marian, who had been Edwin's cousin. "I did not wish to send a messenger. It is only a short walk." She backed to the door. "But I really need to return to my husband. He is shattered, as you might imagine." She glanced away. "He is sick with regrets."

After she left, Ariana crossed the room to Marian and embraced her. "How hard this must be for you."

Marian's eyes filled with tears. "I did care about him. In spite of all the bad things he did to us and to everyone here." She directed her gaze at Emmaline. "I knew him as a very sad little boy."

Allan guided Marian to a sofa. He sat beside her and she leaned against him.

Jack surveyed them all, as if memorising the scene they presented. "He died of drink. That is what a liver ailment means, does it not?"

They all seemed lost in their own thoughts.

Gabriel glanced away. "He connected us. He and his father. We would not be here, together, if not for what Edwin did to Emmaline." He shook his head and faced Allan and Marian. "Perhaps we should go."

Emmaline immediately stood. Emotions swirled inside her, none of them the sort of sadness one ought to feel at a man's death. She was relieved that Edwin was dead. She was grateful that Claude had not killed him. Most of all she was still angry at all the suffering he'd caused. "Yes, we intrude."

Marian straightened. "No, do not leave. I will recover in a moment. Gabe is right. Edwin did connect us all, in a strange way. I want us to be together."

So they stayed and had a more subdued dinner than originally planned, even though they quickly changed the subject from Edwin and the past to all their plans for the future.

It looked bright for all of them. Jack's reputation and fortune as an artist was growing all the time, as was Ariana's fame in the theatre. Allan and Marian were determined that Allan would win a seat in Parliament, and none of them doubted that he would indeed be successful. And there was Gabriel's hill farm. His plan might be more modest, but it was dearest to her heart.

Later, when Emmaline lay with Gabriel in the bed they shared in Grillon's Hotel, Gabriel mentioned Edwin again. "Hearing of Edwin's death must have affected you. Has it upset you?"

She thought before answering. "I am not unaffected. I do not have any grief for him," she admitted. "But if he died of drink, he killed himself, did he not? That seems a sort of justice. He destroyed himself as he tried to destroy us."

He nodded in understanding.

She nestled beside him. "We are all of us alive and happy. The Landons. The Vernons. You and me. Maybe some day even Claude. We survived and Edwin did not."

Gabriel held her tighter. "One thing I know is he can no longer hurt you or Claude or anyone else. We can look to the future and know he will never appear in it."

She kissed him. "I treasure our future, Gabriel. I feel very lucky."

He returned her kiss and cradled her next to him. Warmed by his bare skin, she soon heard him slipping into sleep. As she also drifted off, Edwin appeared in her dream, fading like a fog when the sun begins to shine. Into the sunlight appeared Gabriel, smiling at her.

Yes, she thought, waking again. She had found happiness. She was very, very lucky.

* * * * *

A Not So Respectable Gentleman?

DIANE GASTON

Prologue

Spring 1826

*F*lames.

White hot, blinding red and orange and blue. Flames roaring like a dragon, weaving through the stable, crawling up the walls, devouring everything in its path.

Leo Fitzmanning still saw the flames, felt their heat, heard the screams of his horses, as he entered the mahogany-shelved library of a London town house. The scent of smoke lingered in his nostrils and his muscles ached from battling the fire for nearly two days.

One moment of inattention, one second of carelessness, had cost him his stable and two outbuildings. He'd failed to notice the peg holding the lantern had become loose. The lantern fell, spreading flames in an instant.

He blinked the vision away and faced the man he'd waited nearly a month to see.

Mr Cecil Covendale rose from the chair and extended his hand across the paper-cluttered desk. 'Good day, Fitzmanning.' His manner seemed affable. That was a good sign. 'How are you faring since the fire? You appear uninjured.'

News apparently travelled swiftly the ten miles be-tween Welbourne Manor, on the outskirts of Richmond, and Mayfair.

'Only minor burns, sir.' He accepted the older man's handshake.

The stables, his horses and two outbuildings would cost a great deal to replace, a fact of which Covendale was, no doubt, aware.

'Word is you almost lost the house.' Covendale's ex-pression showed only concern, not the disdain Leo ex-pected in response to his failed enterprise. 'What a pity that would have been.'

Not for those who would rejoice at seeing Welbourne Manor destroyed. *Recompense for its scandalous past,* they would say, although Leo aspired to revise its repu-tation. To Leo and his siblings, Welbourne Manor was a beloved place. He would never have forgiven himself if he'd lost their safe haven, the house where they spent their unconventional childhood.

'The house is untouched.' Leo shrugged. 'The rest can be rebuilt.'

If one had the money, that is. Would Covendale guess nearly all Leo's funds had been invested in the stud farm, now nothing but ashes?

His mind reeled with all the tasks he'd left undone by keeping this appointment. Finding stables for the few surviving horses. Making arrangements for his stable workers, who had suddenly lost the roof over their heads and all their worldly possessions. He'd left them at the Manor, raking through the ashes, making certain that no glowing embers hid beneath the debris, hungry for more destruction. He ought to be working beside them, preparing to rebuild.

But nothing would have kept him from this appointment with Covendale. The man had already put him off for weeks. Some matters were even more important than Welbourne Manor.

'I presume you know why I wished to speak with you,' Leo began.

The smile faded from Covendale's face. 'I do indeed.'

Hairs rose on the back of Leo's neck. Why the change in expression? 'Your daughter told you?'

'She did.' Covendale lowered himself into his chair. He did not ask Leo to sit.

Leo's muscles stiffened. 'Then you know I have come to ask your permission to marry her.'

'I do.' Covendale sighed and shook his head as if in dismay. 'How do I proceed?'

Leo heard the fire's roar again. 'I assure you, the loss of my stable is only a minor setback. Your daughter will want for nothing.'

Leo would recoup his losses, he vowed. He'd borrow the money from his brother if he had to. Rebuild his stables to be grander. Make his stud farm even more prosperous, more respected.

'Perhaps.' Covendale winced. 'But—'

Leo cut him off. 'Are you concerned about her inheritance? I have no need of her inheritance.'

Mariel's great-aunt had bequeathed her a considerable fortune, to be bestowed upon her at age twenty-five if she remained unmarried, sooner if she married with her father's approval. If her marriage did not meet her father's approval, however, the fortune would be forfeited to some obscure and frivolous charity.

Leo pressed on. 'I ask your approval of our marriage only because I will not have Mariel give up her money for me.'

Leo and Mariel had discussed this. She'd insisted

her father would never approve of Leo. They'd considered running off to Scotland, but even though Mariel did not care about the money she stood to lose by eloping, she did care about the scandal it would cause her family, especially her younger sisters. Leo also had no wish for scandal. He planned to gain society's respect by producing the finest horses in England, even finer than his brother Stephen's horses. Furthermore, Leo would not take a penny of Mariel's money. It would always remain under her control.

He gave Covendale a steady look. 'I assure you, the money will remain in Mariel's hands. I will sign papers to that effect. We can make the arrangement before the marriage, if you like.'

Covendale raised a hand. 'Enough, Fitzmanning. This matter between you and my daughter has come as a complete surprise to me. I knew nothing of this—this—courtship before Mariel informed me why you sought an appointment.'

Leo had no defence for the secrecy, except that Mariel had desired it. 'Mariel and I have known each other since childhood, as you well know. She and my sisters have remained friends. We became reacquainted while she visited with them.'

In January, amidst Charlotte's wailing children and her barking pugs, Leo had found Mariel again. No longer was she the annoying girl with plaited hair who'd joined his sisters in trailing after him. Mariel had transformed into a woman so lovely that, for that first moment of glimpsing her again, he'd forgotten how to breathe. They met again at Charlotte's house and eventually contrived further meetings in secret. No one knew of their attachment, of the strong bond that quickly grew between them. No one knew that Mariel was the reason Leo left his brother's employ to establish his own stud farm. To make a loving, respectable home for her at Welbourne Manor.

Covendale waved a hand. 'Never mind that. When did you last speak with my daughter?'

It had been the day they'd discussed setting up this meeting. 'About a month ago.'

Since then there had been no opportunity to contact her. He'd thrown himself into setting up his farm to keep from missing her and to make the time fly.

Covendale glanced away, seeming to mull over something. He rubbed his face and turned back to Leo. 'A month can be a long time. Much can happen.'

Leo sprang towards the desk and came within inches of Covendale's nose. 'Has something happened to Mariel? I demand you tell me. Is she ill? Is she hurt?'

'Neither!' The man recoiled. 'She is betrothed!'

Leo stepped back. His brow knit in confusion. 'Betrothed? Yes. She is betrothed to me.'

'Not to you.' Covendale glanced away. 'She is betrothed to Lord Ashworth.'

Ashworth?

Edward Ashworth?

Ashworth had been a schoolmate of Leo's, an affable boy who'd grown into a decent man. He was titled, wealthy and well liked by everyone, the epitome of an ideal husband.

Covendale handed Leo a sheet of paper. 'It is all arranged. Here is the special licence. I could show you the marriage settlement papers....'

Mariel's and Ashworth's names were written legibly on the sheet of paper that allowed couples to marry elsewhere than a church and which waived the reading of the banns. The paper was signed by the Archbishop.

Leo shoved the paper back to Covendale. 'Does Mariel know of this?'

Covendale coughed. 'Of course she knows of it.'

'I would speak with her, sir. Send for her.' Mariel would never do this. Not without telling him.

'She is not here.' Her father raised his shoulders. 'She and her mother are in Herefordshire at Ashworth's estate.'

At Ashworth's estate?

Leo forced himself to meet and hold Covendale's gaze. Inside, his emotions flamed like the stable's burning rafters.

Why would she go there, if not…?

Covendale went on. 'Ashworth is a fine man, from a decent family. His is an old title. Mariel is not a foolish girl. She knows this is an excellent match for her. A real step up.' He made a mollifying gesture. 'You must look at this situation from my point of view. Do I approve your suit or the suit of a young man who possesses a title? Who will be better for my daughter?'

Leo glared at him. 'You cannot force Mariel to marry. She is of age.'

'I am not forcing her,' the man insisted. 'Her age is of issue, of course. That cannot be ignored. At twenty-one she's practically on the shelf. Her mother and I despaired of her ever making a good match. I believe she herself was becoming somewhat desperate—but, then, perhaps that is why she considered marrying you.'

Leo ignored that put-down. 'No. We pledged our devotion to each other.' Mariel's love was genuine. He would wager everything he possessed upon it.

Although most of what he possessed was now mere ashes.

Covendale clucked. 'Devotion? My poor, poor fellow. Devotion is fleeting. Whatever pretty words passed between you and my daughter are no match for what really matters.'

'And that is?' The fire again roared in Leo's ears.

Covendale shifted in his chair. 'A good name. Connections. Status in society.' He leaned closer. 'That is what my daughter desires and deserves. She will not have that if she marries you.'

So that was it? Good name? Status? Leo intended to build those things for himself. And he was not without connections. His father and King George had been fast friends, for God's sake.

Covendale smiled. 'Like all young women, she wishes to marry respectably.'

Leo's fists tightened. 'Have I ever conducted myself in any way that was not respectable?'

'Not that I've heard.' The man wagged his finger at Leo. 'With the exception of courting my daughter in secret.'

Leo burned as if the flames continued to surround him.

Covendale made another mollifying gesture. 'You must look at this situation rationally. Given a choice, Mariel cannot debase herself with—with a man of your birth.'

A bastard, he meant.

'Your father, for all his titles and high friends, flouted the manners of proper society. What is more, he and your equally scandalous mother reared you in a most amoral atmosphere....'

Was this explanation necessary? Leo had always lived with knowledge of his origins.

His father, the Duke of Manning, left his wife to set up housekeeping at Welbourne Manor with the equally married Countess of Linwall. They lived together for twenty years in unmarried, free-spirited bliss, producing Leo and his two sisters from their unsanctified union. His father's two legitimate sons, Nicholas, now the duke, and Stephen, a successful horse-breeder, spent nearly as much of their childhood at Welbourne Manor as Leo did. Also reared there was Justine, Leo's half-sister by a French woman his father bedded before meeting his mother.

Society called the lot of them The Fitzmanning Miscellany. But not to Leo's face, not if they wished to avoid broken bones.

Leo's hand curled into a fist. 'My brothers were reared at Welbourne Manor.' Except Brenner, his mother's legitimate son, the current Earl of Linwall. Leo and his siblings had not known Brenner until after their parents died. 'Do you consider them scandalous?'

'Of course I do!' Covendale exclaimed. 'But they are legitimate. Society accepts them for that reason alone. You, however, would not be accepted anywhere if not for the fact that your father was a duke. It was the only reason I ever allowed Mariel to befriend your sisters.'

Leo damned well knew society merely tolerated him. And his sisters. The difference between being the legitimate son and being the bastard had always been made crystal clear to him.

Truth be told, even his brothers treated him differently, albeit out of love for him. Nicholas and Stephen were forever trying to shield him from the consequences of his birth, to make it up to him for the shabby treatment by others. Their efforts were almost as painful as the barbs he'd endured as a schoolboy. Or the cuts, as an adult.

Society expected him to become a libertine like his

father, but he was determined to prove society wrong. From the time he'd been a mere lad, he'd made certain his behaviour was unblemished.

A man should be judged by his own character. And by his achievements. Leo intended to reach the pinnacle in both.

Mariel understood that. She'd supported him. Admired his drive. It had never mattered to her that his father had not been married to his mother. She'd loved *him*.

Leo faced Covendale and looked directly into his eyes. 'I do not believe any of this. This daughter you speak of is not the Mariel I know. She would not marry merely for a title. It is impossible.'

The older man pursed his lips. 'Well, there is also your financial situation. A stud farm is nothing to Ashworth's fortune. And now, with the fire, you have several buildings to replace, not to mention livestock. Even if we could ignore the vast inequality between your birth and that of Ashworth, you presently have nothing to offer my daughter.'

The fire. For all Leo's grand thoughts about achieving the pinnacle of respect, the ashes of his former dream revealed his failure.

Covendale turned all sympathy. 'I realise this is difficult for you. It is difficult for me that she left it to me to inform you, but I assure you, Ashworth came courting her and it has resulted in this.' He picked up the special licence.

Leo shook his head. 'She would have contacted me. Told me herself if her sentiments had changed.'

Her father held up a finger. 'It almost slipped my mind. Mariel did leave word for you. She wrote you a note.' Covendale opened a drawer and withdrew a sealed, folded sheet.

Leo took the paper from the man's hand and broke the seal.

It read:

> *Dear Leo,*
> *No time to write a proper note. I meant to be there*
> *in person, but Father will explain it all.*
> *Wishing nothing but good to you,*
> *Mariel*

It was written in her hand. The paper even smelled of her.

He crushed it in his fist. *Father will explain it all.*

'I'm sorry, boy,' Covendale said quietly.

The fire roared inside him again and flames filled his vision.

The special licence. Mariel's absence. Her note.

His failure.

There was no more denying it. She'd chosen respectability over him. A legitimate husband over a bastard one. And, without knowing, a wealthy man over a failure.

'I do not know what else to say to you,' Covendale said.

Leo barely heard him.

He thought about losing his horses, his stable. Losing Mariel was a thousand times worse. The pain was so intense he had to fight to remain upright. It was as if his insides were consumed by flames and what was left was ashes, a void that never could be refilled.

Respectability be damned. Stud farm be damned.

What had all his conscientious behaviour and hard work brought him? A pile of cinders.

Being jilted by Mariel.

He forced himself to rise to his full height. 'You are correct, sir. There is nothing more to say.' He nodded to Covendale. 'Good day.'

Leo turned and strode out of Covendale's library, out of the town house, into the grey afternoon drizzle.

And the emptiness that was now his life.

Chapter One

June, 1828—two years later

Loud pounding forced Leo from a dead sleep.

He opened his eyes and was stabbed by a sliver of sunlight, harbinger of a fine spring London day. He clapped his hands to his head.

Too much brandy. Now he was paying the price.

More pounding. A caller at his door.

Why the devil did Walker not send them away?

Walker was Leo's valet, but likely not out of bed himself. He and Leo had engaged in a bout of celebratory drinking after Leo returned from the card tables the previous night.

Walker might act as Leo's valet, but he looked nothing like a gentleman's gentleman. He'd been a ruffian from the Rookerie, caught by circumstance in Paris and hungry for a new life. Leo encountered him by accident and they had become more than gentleman and gentleman's man. They'd become friends...and now business partners.

The pounding resumed and Leo could just make out the voice of a man demanding to be admitted.

He groaned and roused himself from the bed, searching around the room for the clothes he'd shed the night before. The sound stopped and he sat back on the bed. Excellent. Walker would deal with it. Send the caller away.

Once, Leo would have been up and out to his stables at dawn. He'd have done a half day's work by this hour. He rubbed his face. That had been an age ago. A different lifetime. Being in London brought back the memory, but he'd carved out a new life for himself—from very rough rock, he might add—but it was a life that suited him surprisingly well.

Walker knocked and entered his bedchamber. 'Your family calls.'

His family? 'Which ones?'

'All of them.'

All six? His brothers *and* his sisters? 'What the devil do they want?'

'They would not tell me,' Walker replied.

Leo ran his hand through his hair. 'Why didn't you make some excuse? Say I was out?' It did Leo no credit that he'd avoided them for the fortnight he'd been in town, but he'd been busy. Besides, they'd never understand the direction his life had taken while he'd been away.

Walker cocked an eyebrow. 'I thought it unwise to engage in fisticuffs with a duke, an earl and one tiny, growling dog.'

Good God. His sister Charlotte brought one of her pugs.

'Very well. I will see them.' He pulled his shirt over his head. Walker brushed off his coat with his hand.

Leo's siblings had, no doubt, come with help to offer and would scold him for his behaviour, which had taken a downward path since last he'd been in London, although he trusted they'd never know the half of it. Let them believe the stories about him, that Leo was as much a libertine as his father had once been, but they would not know that Leo had faced situations their father would never have imagined facing.

He shoved his arms into the sleeves of the coat and pulled on his boots. 'I have the feeling I will not enjoy this.'

He left the bedchamber and entered the sitting room.

His brothers and sisters immediately turned to him. They stood in a circle. In fact, they'd even rearranged his seating into a circle.

'Leo!' Nicholas spoke first. As duke, he was head of the family. 'Good morning.'

Charlotte's pug yapped from under her arm.

Justine rushed over to him, clasping both his hands. 'Leo, how good it is to see you. You look dreadful.' She touched his cheek and spoke with some surprise.

'Indeed.' Brenner joined her.

He must look a sight. Unshaven. Rumpled clothes. Bloodshot eyes.

Brenner searched his face. 'Are you unwell?'

'Not at all,' Leo replied. 'Late night.'

Brenner and Justine comprised the most complex of his unusual sibling relations. She was his half-sister by his father, and Brenner, now Lord Linwall, was his half-brother by his mother. They were married to each other. Their love affair happened right after Leo's parents died.

Brenner flashed him one more worried look before wrapping his arms around Leo in a brotherly hug. The others swarmed around him. Charlotte burst into tears and wept against his chest. Nicholas and Stephen slapped him on the back. Even the pug raced around his feet and tried to jump up his legs. Only Annalise held back, but that was typical of her. She was observing the scene and would probably make a painting of it and call it *The Return of the Prodigal Son*.

Only he had no intention of returning to the well-meaning bosom of his family. He was just passing through, literally waiting for his ship to come in.

'What are you doing here?' he managed to ask.

Nicholas clapped his hands. 'Come. Let us all sit and we will tell you.'

One of the chairs was set just a little inside the circle. That was the one they left for him.

Nicholas leaned forwards. 'We are here out of concern for you.'

Of course they were. 'Concern?' They intended to fix things for him. Take care of him as they'd always done.

'We are so afraid for you, Leo!' Ever the dramatist, Charlotte punctuated this with a sob. 'What will become of you?' Her dog jumped onto her lap and licked her face.

This was all nonsense. 'What the devil are you talking about?'

Nicholas spoke. 'You are spending your time drinking, womanising and gambling.'

He certainly looked the part this morning.

'It won't do,' Nicholas went on. 'It is time you found some direction in your life.'

'Some useful occupation,' Stephen explained.

'Before it is too late,' Charlotte added.

It appeared that rumours of his rakish living had preceded him. To be sure, he often stayed up all night playing cards, but he womanised hardly at all and actually drank very little.

Except for this morning.

They could not know of his more clandestine dealings, one that nearly got him killed, and others that skirted the law and earned him a great deal of wealth.

Leo started to rise from his seat. 'I assure you, I am well able to handle myself.'

Brenner, who was seated next to him, put a hand on his shoulder and silently implored him to stay in the chair.

He sat back down. 'Do not trouble yourselves about me.'

'But we do,' whispered Annalise. 'I mean, we *must* trouble ourselves.'

Brenner took on a tone of reasonableness. 'We understood your need to get away, to travel. It was good for you to see something of the world, but now—'

'Now you are just drinking and gaming,' Justine broke in. 'You avoid the family. You avoid healthy pursuits.'

How easily they believed the worst of him. And how readily they assumed it was their job to fix him.

'You cannot know my pursuits.' He gritted his teeth.

'Oh, yes, we can.' Nicholas levelled his gaze at him. 'We have ways of finding out everything.'

Not everything, Leo thought. They obviously knew nothing about his investments. He'd wager a pony that they had never heard of what he and Walker had been through. And they'd never known the real reason he had fled England, why he still had no use for London society.

One after the other they begged him to change his life, to abandon his pursuit of pleasure. They implored him to *care* about something again, to invest his hopes and dreams in something.

He ought to tell them, but the shipment of goods he

was expecting was not precisely done to the letter of the law. Not that it would hurt anyone.

'The thing is…' Nicholas glanced towards Brenner, who nodded approval. 'We have a surprise for you.'

Stephen moved to the edge of his seat. 'We've rebuilt the stable at Welbourne Manor! And the outbuildings. Bigger and better than before. It is all ready for you. Complete with a fine breeding pair from my stables, already in residence at the Manor. Say the word—today, if you like—and I'll take you to Tattersall's to buy more horses. If you need money—'

Leo felt the blood rush to his face. 'No.'

Charlotte piped up. 'Nothing has changed at Welbourne Manor. Even the servants are the same. Halton, Signore Napoli, Thomas—'

'It is waiting for you,' Justine added. 'What do you say, Leo?'

Leo regarded each of them in turn. 'I sold Welbourne Manor to all of you. It is not mine any more. I no longer wish to breed horses. And I am not staying.'

'Leo—' Brenner began.

'No.' He spoke firmly. 'I do not need help. And I especially do not need for you to tell me what to do.'

'We are not…' Brenner protested.

It was no use to explain to them. He did not need them to help him. He did not need anyone. He'd proven it to himself. He had left the country after losing everything, and, almost out of nothing, built a solid fortune. Without a good name. Without top-lofty connections. What's more, he no longer sought the good opinion of the *ton*. He'd discovered self-reliance was more valuable than what society thought of him.

'I refuse to discuss this further.' Leo kept his voice firm. 'If you continue, I will walk out the door.' He softened. 'Tell me about yourselves. How are you faring? How many nieces and nephews do I have? I confess to have lost count.'

He only half listened as they proudly filled him in on their children, their lives. When they spoke, their faces glowed with contentment and deep satisfaction. They were happy and that gladdened him.

But their visit brought back memories. Of his dreams for Welbourne Manor, and a similar happiness that had almost been within his reach.

Late that night Leo again sat at a card table at a May-fair gaming hell. Tucked among discreet buildings off St James's Street, the place buzzed with men's voices and women's laughter. Smoke from cheroots filled the air. Disquieting. Smoke always disquieted him.

Leo held excellent cards. Perhaps a run of luck would settle the restlessness that had plagued him ever since his siblings' visits.

'Did you hear about Kellford?' the man on his right at the whist table asked as he rearranged his cards.

Leo lifted his eyes from his own hand without any great interest in Baron Kellford. He'd known Kellford in Vienna. 'Your turn, sir.'

But the man clearly would not throw down his card before disgorging his precious *on dit*. Did he have a trump card or not?

Leo's opponent rearranged his hand. Again. 'The news is quite amusing.' Pressing his cards against his chest, the fellow looked from Leo to the other two men at the table. 'Kellford is soon to be flush in the pocket.' He leaned back, waiting for one of them to ask for more.

Leo's whist partner took the bait. 'Did he engage some unbreeched pup in a game of piquet?'

That would be like Kellford. Take advantage of some green lad in London for the first time.

'Oh, he did not win a hand at cards, but he will win a hand.' The man chuckled at his clever wordplay and finally threw down a card of the leading suit.

Leo trumped it.

Seemingly unconcerned with the loss, the man grinned. 'Kellford is betrothed. He's marrying an heiress.'

Poor woman. Leo collected the markers he'd won.

His partner shuffled for the next deal. 'I'm the one who needs an heiress. Who did Kellford find? Some squint-eyed daughter of a wealthy cit?'

'Not at all,' the man said. 'He's marrying Miss Covendale.'

Leo froze.

No. Mariel married Ashworth. Hadn't she? Leo spent two years on the Continent, travelling as far as he could to keep from hearing news of her marriage to Ashworth. On his first day in London, who did he glimpse on Oxford Street? Ashworth. He'd half expected to see Mariel at the man's side. What had happened?

More to the point, why marry Kellford?

The noise and smoke-filled rowdiness of the gaming hell receded, and in his mind's eye Leo saw Kellford, whip in hand, about to strike a cowering tavern maid from the hotel where they both happened to be staying. Leo had pulled the whip from the baron's hand and forced Kellford out of the hotel.

'Come now. I hired her!' Kellford had protested. 'I would have paid her well.'

Leo closed his eyes and saw Mariel's face instead of that nameless girl.

'Mariel Covendale?' Leo's partner leaned back. 'Men

have been trying to win her fortune for years. How the devil did Kellford manage such a coup?'

How indeed.

'I do not know.' The gossipmonger shook his head. 'But the first banns have been read. I wager before the knot is tied, I'll learn how he did it.'

The fourth man at the table piped up. 'I wager a pony you will not.'

As the three men placed bets with each other, Leo stood and scooped up his share of the winnings.

'What are you doing?' his partner cried. 'The set is unfinished.'

'I must leave.' Leo did not explain.

He hurried out to the street. The night was damp after a day of steady rain. The cobbles glistened under the lamplight and the sound of horses' hooves rang like bells.

Leo walked, hoping the night air would cool emotions he thought had vanished long ago.

Kellford had once boasted of being a devotee of the Marquis de Sade, the French debaucher so depraved even Napoleon had banned his books. 'The man was a genius,' Kellford had said of de Sade. 'A connoisseur of pleasure. Why should I not have pleasure if I wish it?'

Now all Leo could picture was Kellford engaging in pleasure with Mariel.

A coachman shouted a warning to Leo as he dashed across Piccadilly. He found himself wandering towards Grosvenor Square within blocks of Covendale's London town house. From an open window in one of the mansions, an orchestra played 'Bonnie Highland Laddie,' a Scottish reel. It was near the end of the Season and some member of the *ton* was undoubtedly hosting a ball.

Did Mariel attend? Leo wondered. *Was she dancing with Kellford?*

He turned away from the sound and swung back towards Grosvenor Square, staring past the buildings there as if looking directly into her house on Hereford Street.

Had her father approved this marriage? Surely Covendale had heard talk of Kellford's particular habits.

Or perhaps not. One disadvantage of living a respectable life was being unaware of how low deeply depraved men could sink.

Leo flexed his hand into a fist.

He'd vowed to have nothing more to do with Covendale or his daughter, but could he live with himself if he said nothing? If he'd save a Viennese tavern maid from Kellford's cruelty, surely he must save Mariel from it.

He turned around and headed back to his rooms.

No brandy this night. He wanted a clear head when he called upon Covendale first thing in the morning.

Chapter Two

'Do not walk so fast, Penny.' Mariel Covendale came to an exasperated halt on the pavement.

'Sorry, miss.' Her maid returned to her with head bowed.

Mariel sighed. 'No, I am sorry. I did not mean to snap at you. It is merely that I am in no great rush to return home.'

Penny, a petite but sturdy blonde, so pretty she would have been prime prey in any household with young sons about, looked at her softheartedly. 'Whatever you wish, miss.'

The maid deliberately slowed her steps. After a few minutes, she commented, 'You did not find anything to purchase. Not even fabric for your bridal clothes.' Penny sounded more disappointed than Mariel felt.

Mariel smiled. 'That is of no consequence.'

In truth, she'd not cared enough to make a purchase. She'd merely wished to escape the house and her parents for time alone. Time to think. So she'd risen early and taken Penny with her to the shops. They'd browsed for hours.

Penny's brow furrowed. 'I cannot help but worry for you, miss, the wedding so close and everything.'

Too close, Mariel thought.

They crossed Green Street and Penny pulled ahead again, but caught herself, turning back to Mariel with an apologetic glance.

The girl was really a dear and so devoted that Mariel had been tempted to make her a confidante.

Better to say nothing, though. Why burden her poor maid?

Instead she gazed up at the sky, unusually blue and cloudless this fine spring day. Yesterday's rains had washed the grey from London's skies. Weather always improved if one merely has patience.

Unfortunately Mariel saw only grey skies ahead for her. And she had no time for patience.

For Penny's sake, though, she forced her mood to brighten. 'It is a lovely day, I must admit. That is reason enough to dally.'

Penny gave her a quizzical look. 'If you do not mind me saying, miss, you are so very at ease about everything, but it is only three weeks until your wedding, and you have no bridal dress or new clothes or anything.'

So very at ease? That was amusing. Mariel must be a master of disguise if Penny thought her at ease. 'I have many dresses. I'm sure to have enough to wear.' She wanted no special bridal clothes. 'If you like, tomorrow we can search for lace and trim to make one of my gowns more suitable for the ceremony.'

It was as good an excuse as any to be out and about again and Penny was a creative seamstress.

'We could do that, miss,' the maid agreed.

Coming from the shops on New Bond Street, they

had meandered through Mayfair, passing by Grosvenor Square and the Rhedarium Gardens, but now they were within a short walk of the town house she shared with her parents.

If this wedding were not looming over her, she'd be happily anticipating summer months in their country house in Twickenham. She missed her younger sisters, although it was good they had not been old enough for the London Season and all the pressures it brought. At twenty-three, Mariel had seen many Seasons, had many proposals of marriage.

Only one mattered, though, but that proposal occurred when she'd been two years younger and foolish enough to believe in a man's promises.

Foolish enough for a broken heart.

Luckily her powers of disguise had hidden the effect of that episode well enough. No one but her father ever knew about her secret betrothal. Or her heartbreak. She'd even trained herself not to think of it.

Mariel's throat constricted as they reached the corner of Hereford Street. She dreaded entering the house, facing her mother's unabashed joy at her impending marriage and her father's palpable relief.

Her spirits sank lower and lower as she and Penny neared the end of the street.

When they were within steps of the town house, its door opened and a man emerged.

He turned towards them and the sun illuminated his face. 'Mariel?'

She froze.

This man was the one person she thought never to see again, never *wished* to see again. He was the man to whom she'd been secretly betrothed, the man who had just inhabited her thoughts.

The man who had deserted her.

Leo Fitzmanning.

He was as tall as ever, his hair as dark, his eyes that same enthralling hazel. His face had become leaner these last two years, more angular with tiny lines creasing the corners of his eyes.

She straightened, hoping her ability to mask her emotions held strong.

'Leo.' She made her tone flat. 'What a surprise.'

His thick dark brows knitted. 'I—I have come from your father. I called upon him.'

'My father?' Her voice rose in pitch. 'Why on earth would you wish to see my father?' She had not even known Leo was in London.

He paused before closing the distance between them and his hazel eyes pleaded. 'Will you walk with me?'

She glanced over at Penny, who was raptly attending this encounter. Mariel forced herself to face him again. 'I can think of no reason why I should.'

He reached out and almost touched her. Even though his hand made no contact, she felt its heat. 'Please, Mariel. Your father would not listen. I must speak with you. Not for my sake, but for yours.'

For her sake?

She ought to refuse. She ought to send him packing with a proper set-down. She ought to turn on her heel and walk into her house and leave him gaping in her wake.

Instead she said, 'Very well. But be brief.'

He offered her his arm, but rather than accept it, she turned to Penny. 'You must follow.'

Leo frowned. 'I need to speak with you alone.'

Mariel lifted her chin. 'Then speak softly so she does

not hear, but do not ask me to go with you unchaper-oned.'

He nodded.

They crossed Park Lane and entered Hyde Park through the Cumberland gate. The park was in its full glory, lush with greenery and flowers and chirping birds.

He led her to one of the footpaths. It was too early in the afternoon for London society to gather in carriages and on horseback for the fashionable hour. The footpath was empty. Once Mariel would have relished finding a quiet place where they could be private for a few moments. She would have pretended that nothing existed in the world but the two of them. This day, however, it made her feel vulnerable. She was glad Penny walked a few steps behind them.

Off the path was a bench, situated in an alcove surrounded by shrubbery, making it more secluded than the path itself.

Leo gestured to the bench. 'Please, sit.'

'No.' Mariel checked to make certain Penny remained nearby. 'Speak to me here and be done with it.'

He was so close she could smell the scent that was uniquely his, the scent that brought back too many memories. Of happy days when she'd contrived to meet Leo in this park. They'd strolled through its gardens and kindled their romance.

He faced her again and she became acutely aware of the rhythm of his breathing and of the tension in his muscles as he stood before her. 'I will be blunt, because I have not time to speak with more delicacy.'

His tone surprised her.

'Please do be blunt,' she responded sarcastically.

She wanted to remain cold to him. She wanted not to care about anything he wished to say to her.

It was impossible.

Amidst the grass and shrubs and trees, his eyes turned green as he looked down on her. 'You must not marry Lord Kellford.'

She was taken aback. 'I am astonished you even know of my betrothal, let alone assume the right to speak of it.'

He averted his gaze for a moment. 'I know I have no right. I tried to explain to your father, but he failed to appreciate the seriousness of the situation.'

She made a scornful laugh. 'I assure you, my father takes this impending marriage very seriously. He is delighted at the match. Who would not be? Kellford is such a charming man.'

His eyes flashed. 'Kellford's charm is illusory.'

She lifted her chin. 'Is it? Still, he meets my father's approval.'

He riveted her with his gaze again. 'I tried to tell him the man Kellford is. Your father would not listen, but you must.'

A *frisson* of anxiety prickled her spine. With difficulty, she remained steady. 'If you have something to tell me about Kellford, say it now and be done with it.'

He glanced away. 'Believe me. I never would have chosen to speak this to you—'

His words cut like a sabre. He preferred to avoid her? As if she'd not realised that already. He'd avoided her for two years.

She folded her arms across her chest and pretended she did not feel like weeping. 'Tell me, so you do not have to stay a moment longer than is tolerable.'

His eyes darted back and flared with a heat she did not understand. 'I will make it brief.'

Mariel's patience wore thin. 'Please do.'

His eyes pinned her once more. 'What do you know of the Marquis de Sade?'

Was he changing the subject? 'I do not know the Marquis de Sade. What has he to do with Kellford?'

He shifted. 'You would not *know* him. And I suppose no gently bred young woman would have heard of him....'

'Then why mention him?' Why this roundaboutation? 'Do you have a point to this?'

'I dislike having to speak of it,' he snapped.

Enough. She turned to walk away.

He caught her by the arm and pulled her back. Their gazes met and Mariel felt as if every nerve in her body had been set afire. She saw in his eyes that he, too, was affected by the touch.

He released her immediately. 'The Marquis de Sade wrote many...books, which detailed scandalous acts, acts he is said to have engaged in himself.'

'Scandalous acts?' Where was this leading?

He nodded. 'Between...between men and women.' His eyes remained steady. 'De Sade derived carnal pleasure from inflicting pain on women. It was his way of satisfying manly desires.'

Mariel's cheeks burned. No man—not even Leo— had spoken to her of such matters before. 'I do not understand.'

He went on. 'For some men the pleasure that should come...in the normal way...only comes if they cause the woman pain.'

She'd heard that lovemaking—at least the first time—

could be painful, but he didn't seem to be talking about that. 'What pain?'

He did not waver. 'Some men use whips. Some burn with hot pokers. Others merely use their fists.' His cheek twitched. 'Sometimes the woman is bound by ropes or chains. Sometimes she is deprived of food or water.'

Her stomach roiled. 'Why do you say this to me?'

His features twisted in pain. 'Because Lord Kellford has boasted of such predilections. Because I have heard accounts about him. I have seen him use a whip—'

An icy wind swept through her. 'That is the information you needed to give me?'

'Yes.' His voice deepened. 'That is it.'

She glanced over at Penny, whose expression reflected the horror Mariel felt inside. Penny had heard it all.

Mariel had known Kellford to be a greedy, calculating man hiding behind a veneer of charm. Now she discovered he was depraved as well and that he would likely torture her. Hers would not merely be a wretched marriage, it would be a nightmare.

She turned from Leo and started to walk away.

Again he seized her, this time holding her with both his hands, making her face him, leaning down so he was inches from her face. 'You cannot marry him, Mariel. You cannot!'

He released her and she backed away from him, shaking her head, anger rising inside her like molten lava.

It was easier to be angry, much easier than feeling terror and despair. She fed the anger, like one fed a funeral pyre.

Why had Leo saddled her with this appalling information? Did he think it a kind gesture? A worthy errand? Would he depart from this lovely park feeling all self-righteous and noble? Might he even pretend this atoned for disappearing from her life and breaking her heart?

He had walked away from her without a word, as if she'd been nothing to him, and now he burdened her with this?

She felt ready to explode.

'Do you think you have helped me?' Her voice shook.

He seemed taken aback. 'Yes, of course. You can cry off. It is not too late.'

She gave him a scornful laugh. 'I can cry off.' Suddenly she advanced on him, coming so close she felt his breath on her face. 'You understand nothing, Leo.' Let him feel the impact of her wrath. 'I *have* to marry Kellford. Do you hear me? I have no choice.'

She swung around and strode off.

'What do you mean you have no choice?' he called after her. 'Mariel!'

She did not answer. She did not stop. She did not look back. She did not even look back to see if Penny followed. She rushed down the path and out of the park. Hurrying across Park Lane, she did not stop until she reached the door to her town house.

Out of breath, she leaned her forehead against the door and waited for Penny to catch up.

To herself she said, 'I have no choice, Leo. No choice at all.'

Chapter Three

Leo watched Mariel flee from him. Seeing her had shaken him more than he cared to admit. Her ginger-coloured eyes fascinated him as much as they'd done two years before. His fingers still itched to touch the chestnut hair, peeking from beneath her bonnet. And her lips? It had been all he could do to not taste of them once again.

He thought he'd banished her image from his mind, but the full glory of her flooded back to him. Her eyes sparkling with delight. Her smile lighting up his very soul. Had that all been illusion? She certainly seemed to find his presence distasteful to her now. Had she merely been pretending all that time ago?

It was a question that had once kept him awake at night and consumed his days. Finally he'd pushed it aside so well he'd thought he'd forgotten. One glimpse of her brought everything back.

But his emotions were not at issue here. No matter her feelings towards him, she must not marry Kellford.

Her words still rang in his ears. *I have to marry Kellford. Do you hear me? I have no choice.*

What did she mean *no choice?* Had Kellford compromised her? Good God, had the man already forced himself on her?

All manner of circumstances came to Leo's mind as he finally walked out of the park. He'd supposed this task relatively simple to discharge. Unpleasant, but simple. Merely call upon her father and warn him about Kellford and that would be the end of it. Cecil Covendale had not been pleased to see him; in fact, he'd been surly, as if he'd wished he could toss Leo out on his ear. Leo had minced no words. He'd explained precisely what Mariel faced if marrying Kellford. Covendale accused him of spreading falsehoods, ordered him to leave and never return.

Mariel had not assumed they were falsehoods, though. She'd believed him and still declared she must marry Kellford.

He must speak with her again, learn why she felt compelled to marry at all. She was only two years away from inheriting her fortune outright. It was madness for her to marry, let alone marry Kellford.

He crossed over to Hereford Street and glanced at Mariel's town house as he passed. Perhaps he should knock on the door again and insist she see him right now.

No. Her father would forbid him admittance. Leo needed to find some place where he might catch her alone and off guard.

The problem was, she did not attend the sorts of places that he frequented of late. Gaming hells. Taverns. Dank and dismal rooms in the Rookerie with Walker and the shipping partners. Mariel attended society functions, called upon society friends. With his newly acquired reputation, Leo was on no one's invitation list and would be an even more unwelcome caller.

He knew precisely how to rectify that problem, although it was a step he detested making. His brother Nicholas could get him invited anywhere. Who would refuse such a request of a duke? Nicholas would agree. As always, Nicholas would be delighted to help his bastard brother.

Leo walked the short distance to the ducal residence on Park Street. His knock was answered by a footman whom he did not recognise. The man's brows rose.

'Please tell his Grace his brother Leo desires a few moments of his time.' Leo handed the man his hat and gloves.

'I will see if his Grace is available.' The footman gestured to the drawing room off the hall. 'If you would care to wait...'

Leo strode into the drawing room, a room transformed from the gold-gilt furniture and rich brocades of his childhood into something warmer and more welcoming. The new duchess's influence, no doubt. Too fired up to sit, he wandered the room, noticing that the clock and some of the porcelain figurines were relics from his childhood.

As children they had not stayed in the Mayfair residence often, so it always had been a special treat. It had also been a place Leo had not felt at ease. He used to think about all the dukes and duchesses who'd once graced these rooms, including Nicholas and Stephen's mother. He wondered how she must have felt, knowing this house was sometimes occupied by her rival, Leo's mother, and her illegitimate children.

The footman appeared in the doorway. 'His Grace will see you now.'

Leo followed the man up the marble staircase to another more private drawing room, one where the girls had been allowed to practise the piano and where they all played at skittles.

Nicholas and his wife approached Leo as he entered the room.

'Leo! I hope this means you have had a change of heart.' Nicholas's tone, as always, was welcoming.

Nicholas's wife reached Leo first. It was evident she was expecting another child, news probably given to him the day before but not recalled.

'It is so wonderful to see you!' she cried, clasping his hands.

He leaned down to kiss her on the cheek. 'Emily. You look as beautiful as ever.' He glanced at her. 'I hope you are feeling well.'

'Very well, thank you.' She smiled.

Nicholas's expression turned serious. 'Are you in any trouble? You know I will help you in any way I can.'

Leo resented the assumption. 'No trouble. And if I were in trouble, I would not come running to my brothers.'

'No, you never did,' admitted Nicholas. 'But we always found out, did we not? And were there to help.'

Nicholas would never know what Leo had faced in the last two years and how well he'd managed on his own, but he gave his brother a grudging nod.

Nicholas clapped his hands. 'Then you have reconsidered our gift? Welbourne Manor is yours again for the asking. We can easily help you get back on your feet. Begin stocking your stables.'

Leo clamped his mouth shut lest he say something that would only lead to a shouting match.

Emily stepped in. 'Nicholas, enough!' She pulled at her husband's arm. 'Let us all sit down before you speak business.' She turned to Leo. 'We have tea. Let me pour you a cup.'

He lifted a hand. 'Thank you, no tea for me.'

She carefully lowered herself on a sofa and Nicholas sat beside her. Leo chose a chair adjacent to them.

Nicholas started. 'Why did you react to our plan as you did, Leo? You must know we are concerned about you. We would do anything for you.'

Leo stiffened. 'Your concern is unfounded.'

'But you disappeared for two years,' Nicholas went on.

'I wrote letters,' Leo protested. 'I kept you advised as to where I was.'

Nicholas shook his head. 'You told us nothing about what you were doing, you must admit. Then stories of your activities reached us, increasing our worry for you—'

Leo held up a hand. 'Those stories were greatly exaggerated, I am sure.'

He could agree that he had gone through a brief period of very heavy drinking, placing himself in dangerous situations from which he often had to resort to fisticuffs to escape. That period had been short-lived and he did not credit his heavy gambling as scandalous. All the other activities they could not know about.

Nicholas leaned forwards, worry lines appearing between his brows. 'I know that much can happen when you travel to new lands.' His duchess touched him and a look of understanding passed between them. 'You can tell me if anything happened to distress you.'

Nicholas was speaking about himself, Leo realised. Was he harbouring secrets of his own? 'Nicholas, believe me. Nothing of consequence happened to me.'

Meeting Walker had been important, of course, but

the crucial event in his life had happened before his travels. He'd never spoken of his secret betrothal to his siblings and, if Mariel had disclosed it, surely his siblings would have smothered him with their commiserations and battered him with their advice.

Which would still be the case today if he shared the truth of why he'd come to beg a favour of his brother, the duke.

Both Nicholas and Emily continued to gaze at him with sympathetic disbelief.

Leo lifted a hand. 'Stop looking at me like that! I did very well on my travels. It was a great adventure having no responsibilities. Quite freeing, in fact.'

Nicholas frowned. 'But you cannot live your life that way. You must let us help you secure your future. The plan for Welbourne Manor is a good one, is it not?'

Leo scraped a frustrated hand through his hair. 'Nick, I no longer wish to breed horses. I do not know how to convince you all of that fact.' That dream had been too connected to Mariel for him to pursue it now, and too connected to his misguided wish for society's acceptance.

'I cannot believe it,' Nicholas protested. 'You've loved horses since you were out of leading strings.'

'I still love horses.' Leo shrugged. 'I merely have no wish to breed them.' There were better ways to gain wealth and success, he'd discovered. More exciting ways.

'But—' Nicholas started.

Leo held up a hand. 'There is something I do need from you—'

His brother's demeanour changed. 'Anything, Leo. Anything.'

'I want to re-enter society.' How was he to put this?

'I will eventually wish to mix with members of the *ton* and I want to counteract the gossip that apparently has preceded me.' A bold-faced lie, of course.

This was a story Nicholas would believe, however.

'Of course. Of course.' Nicholas said. 'What can we do?'

'Take me along to society functions.' Ones that Mariel would also attend, he meant. 'I know I may not be welcome everywhere, but those where you think my presence would not be objectionable.'

Nicholas's eyes flashed. 'You are my brother. I dare say you'd better be accepted at any affair I condescend to attend.'

Nicholas would never accept the truth of Leo's situation. Or that it no longer mattered to Leo whether society accepted him or not. Leo wanted nothing to do with people who judged others by birth alone. If it weren't for needing access to Mariel, Leo would tell them all to go to the devil.

'I would be grateful, Nick.'

Emily brightened. 'Leo could accompany you to the ball tonight.'

'Indeed!' Nicholas clapped his hands. 'Come here at nine and we will go together.'

'Nine. I will be here.' He rose. 'I'll take my leave of you now, however.'

'No!' cried Emily. 'You have only just arrived. You must stay for dinner.'

Too many hours away. 'I cannot, but I appreciate the invitation.'

Nicholas helped Emily to her feet and she embraced Leo. 'Please know you are welcome in our house any time.'

Her sincerity touched him deeply. 'Thank you.'

Nicholas clapped him on the back. 'I will walk you to the door.'

It seemed an odd thing for a duke to do.

As they descended the staircase, Nicholas said, 'I am delighted that you asked for my help. I am very glad to give it.'

Leo felt a pang of guilt for so resenting what was offered him out of such brotherly affection.

'Do you have suitable clothes?' Nicholas asked. 'I'm sure I can fix it if you do not.'

If only such loving offerings were not so insulting. 'I have formal clothing,' he managed through gritted teeth. 'Where is this ball tonight, may I ask?'

'Lord Ashworth's,' Nicholas responded. 'Do you remember him?'

Ashworth's. Why did that irony not amuse him?

'I remember him.'

That evening as Leo and Nicholas stepped up to the doorway of the Ashworth ballroom, waiting to be announced, Leo immediately scanned the crowd, looking for Mariel.

Nicholas whispered to the Ashworth butler, who then announced, 'The Duke of Manning and Mr Leo Fitzmanning.'

The buzz of conversation ceased for a moment and all eyes turned their way. Leo supposed the silence was not merely the deference due a duke, but the shock at seeing the duke's bastard brother at his side.

Ashworth, whose girth had thickened since his youth, immediately stepped forwards from where he'd been standing to receive guests. 'Your Grace, how delightful you were able to come.'

A pretty young woman who'd been standing next

to Ashworth also approached Nicholas. 'I do hope the duchess is well, your Grace.'

'Very well, Lady Ashworth,' Nicholas replied. 'Simply not up to the rigours of a ball.'

Ashworth had married someone else, obviously.

Nicholas turned as if to present Leo, but Ashworth had already seized his hand. 'Leo! How delighted I am to see you!' The man pumped his arm enthusiastically. 'It has been an age and you have been abroad!'

Before Leo could form a response, Ashworth put an arm around his shoulder and brought him over to his wife. 'Pamela! Here is my dear friend!' It was kind of Ashworth to characterise him as such. 'May I present to you Leo Fitzmanning.'

Leo bowed. 'I am very pleased to meet you, Lady Ashworth.'

This woman, who might have been Mariel had events transpired as Leo thought they would, was a pretty doll-like creature who appeared as soft and affable as Ashworth himself.

'Mr Fitzmanning. How nice you could come.' Her words seemed as genuine as her husband's and in her expression there was no hint of censure for attending without an invitation.

At that moment other guests were announced and Leo left his host and hostess to their greeting tasks. Nicholas had been commandeered by some gentlemen now surrounding him, so Leo felt free to search for Mariel.

He moved through the crush of guests, nodding to those people who acknowledged him, noticing those who avoided looking his way. Though no one dared risk offending his brother by giving Leo the cut direct, he was aware of whispers about him in his wake.

The room was ablaze with candles and decorated with huge jardinières of flowers. Richly upholstered sofas and chairs were set against the walls and grouped for conversation. It had been a long time since he'd wandered through a Mayfair ballroom. Nothing had changed.

Except him.

In his travels he'd wandered through the worst parts of cities, the poorest parts, and often found people living with more dignity than some of these glittering guests, so quick to judge and disdain.

He heard a squeal. A rush of pink silk caught the corner of his eye.

His sister Charlotte advanced on him. 'Leo! You are here! I could not believe my eyes.' She seized his arm and dragged him with her. 'Come say hello to Drew. Justine and Brenner are here, too. Isn't it lovely?'

He had to admit it felt gratifying to be greeted with even more enthusiasm than Ashworth had shown. He received a brotherly embrace from Charlotte's husband, Drew, whom he'd known practically their whole lives, and answered Drew's many questions regarding his health, when he'd arrived, where he'd travelled from, why they had not seen him sooner.

Charlotte interrupted. 'Oh! Here is someone else you know, Leo. You must say hello.' She tugged him away from her husband.

And brought him face to face with Mariel.

Her dress was a deep-rose silk and a dark blue sash was tied at her waist. Matching blue ribbons adorned her hair, which was swept atop her head with curls framing her face. She was so lovely she seemed unreal.

She was obviously not delighted to see him, but even less delighted was the man at her side.

Lord Kellford.

Leo bowed. 'Miss Covendale.'

'Miss Covendale?' Charlotte cried. 'Since when do you call Mariel *Miss Covendale?*'

He shot Charlotte what he hoped was a dampening look. 'Since I am at a formal ball.' He turned back to Kellford and gave him a curt nod. 'Kellford.'

Kellford responded in kind. 'Fitzmanning.'

Mariel's eyes pleaded with him, as if she feared he would blurt out their long-held secrets. Did she think he would retaliate for her having spurned him? In any event, he was fairly certain she would not willingly speak to him privately, even if he could manage it.

Making matters worse, Mariel's father approached and on a flimsy pretext hustled her away. Leo turned back to Drew, asking him how his sister and nephew fared and about their estate, and pretending the brief exchange with Mariel meant nothing to him. A few moments later, Justine and Brenner appeared and were delighted to see him. He was soon enveloped by family, who remained near him the entire night, an armour he did not need. He could stand on his own anywhere, especially in the superficial gaiety of a Mayfair ballroom.

Kellford rarely left Mariel's side; Leo was beginning to despair of ever catching her alone.

Watching her altered something inside him, Leo had to admit. It would take some effort to turn his emotions to stone again. Still, he would never allow himself to be vulnerable to her smiles and promises. He must question, though, why he cared so much to discover why she must marry Kellford. And why he felt determined to prevent it.

He no longer believed he was merely playing the Good Samaritan.

Finally he spied her saying something to Kellford. She managed to walk away and leave the ballroom alone. Leo made an excuse to his family and followed her, taking care not to look obvious. He guessed she was bound for the ladies' retiring room, otherwise why would Kellford have let her go?

Catching a glimpse of her entering the room as another lady left, Leo retreated to a discreet corner where no one would notice him.

It seemed a great deal of time passed before she emerged again. Had she delayed on purpose to enjoy being free of her constant escort?

Leo quickly stepped from the shadows and seized her arm, pulling her out of sight of prying eyes.

'Leo! Let me go,' she whispered, trying to twist away.

He released her, but blocked her way back to the ballroom. 'Give me a moment.'

Her eyes darted. 'Someone will see us.'

'A moment,' he implored. 'Tell me the reason you feel you must marry. I'll fix it for you. Let me help you.'

Her face flushed with anger. 'You will fix it? Do not make me laugh, Leo. You have no right to even speak to me now.'

'I have no right?' he answered hotly. 'Because of the choice you made two years ago?'

'A choice I made?' Her brows knit in confusion.

'To marry Ashworth…' Leo had not wanted to pursue this matter.

'Marry Ashworth?' She gave a scornful laugh. 'Well, I obviously did not marry Ashworth. If I had, I would not be in this fix.'

It brought him back to the task at hand. 'Never mind. Tell me why you must marry Kellford.'

She stood so near his arms ached to hold her again.

He leaned closer, suddenly helpless against the need to taste her lips and recapture some of the youthful joy they'd shared.

Her eyes rose to his and her pupils widened. For a moment she did not move. He leaned closer.

'Leo,' she whispered, then pushed him aside. 'What does it matter? Move away. I must return to my charade.'

Her charade. She did not wish to marry Kellford, that was clear. And, like it or not, Leo had made the choice to help her. He'd not back out now.

At the moment, though, he could only watch her hurry back to the ballroom.

At the end of the evening as Leo rode back to the ducal town house with Nicholas, he asked, 'What event will everyone attend tomorrow night?'

'A party at Vauxhall Gardens hosted by Lord and Lady Elkins.' His brother stifled a yawn. 'But I will not attend. I prefer to stay home with Emily.' He glanced at Leo. 'Would you like to go in my stead? I can arrange that.'

'I would indeed.'

Anything was possible at Vauxhall Gardens.

Chapter Four

'Vauxhall Gardens?' Walker's brows rose.

'That is correct.' Leo opened a cabinet in his sitting room and pulled out a decanter of brandy. He poured himself a glass. 'I'll need a domino and a mask. Do you know where you might get one?'

The valet shrugged. 'I will find one, but what is this? A card game at Vauxhall Gardens?'

Leo lifted an empty glass in an invitation to pour some for Walker. 'Not precisely. It is a society event.'

Walker shook his head. 'Another society event? This is a change for you. May I ask why?'

Leo frowned, an image of Mariel flying into his mind, as well as one of Kellford brandishing a whip.

Walker's expression turned to one of concern. 'What is it, Fitz?'

Walker only acted the role of valet, which accounted for his plain speaking and familiar address. Few gentlemen—or servants, for that matter—would understand the sense of equality between the two men, born of mutual respect and one life-changing experience. Leo had fed Walker's thirst to better himself, teaching Walker to read and to speak like an educated man. Walker had shown Leo the skills he'd acquired to survive the Rookerie and provided the contacts that would make their present venture profitable. There was little they did not know about each other's lives.

Still, Leo had never told Walker about Mariel. His feelings for Mariel were a secret locked so deep inside him he did not know if he could ever dislodge them.

Walker's brows knit. 'Is this what your family asked of you? That you must rejoin society and attend its entertainments? And you are doing it?'

'No.' Leo lifted the glass of brandy to his lips. 'Although no doubt my family would be delighted by it. You know my opinion of society.' On the Continent he had learned that he needed only his wits and his courage to make money.

'Then what is this?' Walker circled with his finger. 'Why this visage of life and death, then? It must be more than some new scheme. If you are in trouble, you should let me in on it, you know.'

Leo smiled inside at the way the word *visage* dropped so easily off Walker's tongue. As did Walker's willingness to help, somewhat reminiscent of Nicholas's.

Leo took a sip of his brandy. He needed Walker's help, he was certain of that, and Walker was not as easy to fool as Nick. He was also not one to follow orders without an explanation. Walker had freed himself from blind adherence to orders.

Leo must stick close to the truth, but he had no intention of exposing what was still painfully raw.

'Do you recall Lord Kellford?' he finally asked.

Walker made a disgusted sound. 'The lout with the whip?'

'Precisely.' Leo lowered himself into one of the chairs. 'He is set to marry an…old family friend and I am determined to stop it. There is a masquerade party at Vauxhall tonight which I suspect he will attend. As will the lady.'

Walker stared at him and Leo had the distinct feeling the man was trying to decipher what Leo left unsaid. 'Does the lady know what he is?'

'I told her.' Leo tried to appear dispassionate. 'She insists she must marry him. I would like to discover why, what hold he has over her and then stop him.' Beneath his prosaic tone was a swirl of painful emotions. He took another sip of brandy. 'I shall see what I can discover as a guest at this Vauxhall affair. My brother will arrange my invitation.'

Walker sat in an adjacent chair. 'Then perhaps I can discover something from a different end. Shall I try to befriend some of his servants? See what they know?'

This was why Leo valued his valet-friend so much. Walker did not wait to be ordered about; he just acted.

'An excellent idea.' Leo smiled. 'After you find me a domino, that is.'

The music from Vauxhall reached Leo's ears just as the pleasure garden's entrance came into sight. Nicholas had insisted on providing the ducal carriage, and, if anyone witnessed it, Leo supposed arriving in such style could do nothing but help his acceptance as his brother's substitute.

As he moved through the garden's entrance, his domino billowed in the night's breeze and gathered between his legs, impeding his gait.

There could not be a sillier garment for a man, lots of black fabric fashioned into a hooded cloak, the accepted male costume for a masquerade. Once Leo put on his mask, the costume had advantages. No one would know who he was. He would be able to remain near Mariel without anyone suspecting his identity.

He knew she would attend. Before walking to his brother's house and donning his domino, he'd concealed himself near the Covendale town house and watched as Mariel and her parents climbed into Kellford's carriage. The evening remained light enough that Leo was able to clearly see her costume. Her dark green dress clung to her figure from neckline to hips. Gold-braid trim adorned the low square neckline and the long trumpet sleeves. Over the gown, she wore a matching hooded cape. How ironic she would dress as a medieval maiden, the quintessential damsel in distress.

Kellford, on the other hand, had exerted as much imagination as Leo. He, too, wore a black domino.

Leo hurried down the South Walk. Tall, stately elms shaded the area with its booths and the supper boxes. Ahead of him at some distance, Leo spied three triumphal arches and a painting of the Ruins of Palmyra so realistic it fooled many people into believing it was real. The three supper boxes reserved for the party hosted by Lord and Lady Elkins were located just before the arches.

His domino caught between his legs again and he slowed his pace, taking more notice of the gardens which seemed to show some tarnish since he'd last seen them. Or perhaps it was he who was tarnished.

He remembered his first look at Vauxhall, when still a schoolboy, the night his father and mother hosted a masquerade. He and his brothers had been allowed to attend until darkness fell and the drinking and carousing began in earnest.

A wave of grief washed over him. His parents had been blissfully happy, as scandalous as their liaison had been. They'd looked magnificent that night, costumed in powdered hair and shiny, colourful brocades, the fashionable dress of the last century. Surrounded by their equally scandalous friends and those few respectable ones who were loyal no matter what, they had been in their element. No one had enjoyed the pleasures and entertainments life had to offer better than his mother and father.

Perhaps they had enjoyed a masquerade in Venice before contracting the fever that killed them.

As Leo neared the supper boxes, so close to the ones his parents had secured that night, he stopped to put on his mask. He presented his invitation to the footman at the entrance. Because it was a masquerade, no guests were announced and Leo could slip into the crowd in perfect anonymity.

Almost immediately he found his sister Charlotte, dressed as a shepherdess, but he did not reveal himself to her. No, this night he'd take advantage of his disguise. He walked through the crush of people, searching for Mariel.

Finally the crowd parted, revealing her, as if gates had opened to display a treasure. Her hood and cape hung behind her shoulders. Her headdress was a roll of gold cloth, worn like a crown. She looked like a queen from a bygone age. He savoured the sight of her before moving closer.

He had no difficulty spotting Kellford or Mariel's parents, or the fact that Mariel was edging away from them. He stepped forwards to help her, deliberately pushing his way between her and Kellford and remaining in Kellford's way.

His ploy worked. She hurried away from them and let the crowd swallow her. Leo waited a moment before following her, confident he could find her no matter how many people obscured his view.

He was correct.

Darkness was falling fast, but he was able to glimpse her making her way out of the supper box. She covered her head with her hood and hurried towards the large gazebo in the centre of the gardens. The orchestra was still playing on its balcony, high above the area where guests danced to the music.

He continued, walking quickly, puzzled at what she was about. It was not safe for her to leave the protection of the supper boxes. In addition to revellers, Vauxhall Gardens attracted pickpockets and other rogues and miscreants who combed the gardens searching for easy prey.

She weaved her way around the dancers until she was on the other side of the gardens near the Grand Walk. She made her way to one of the trees that bordered the area and leaned against it.

He slowed his pace and stopped a few feet from her. 'Mariel?'

She started and then gave him a careful look. 'Leo.' Her tone was flat. Obviously his mask had not disguised him from her.

He came closer. 'It is not safe to walk alone here.'

'Indeed?' She lifted one shoulder. 'Do you not think walking alone is preferable to remaining on Kellford's arm? I confess, I do.'

He scowled. 'Is that why you ran off? To get away from him?'

She made a disparaging sound. 'Were you watching me, Leo?'

'I came in hopes of speaking with you,' he admitted.

She turned away to face the dancers twirling and

gliding like fairies in a dream. 'We can have nothing to say to each other.'

'I need to know—'

She stopped him from speaking, putting her hand on his arm and moving to the other side of the tree.

'What is it?' He glanced around.

She gestured with her chin. 'Kellford is looking for me.'

Leo caught sight of him, perusing the crowd, moving closer to where they stood.

He grasped her arm. 'Let us make you more difficult to spot.' He pulled her into the crowd of dancers.

The orchestra played a French waltz and the dancers had formed two circles, one inside the other. Leo led Mariel to the inner circle. He placed his hands on her waist; her hands rested on his shoulders. Their eyes met and locked together as they twirled with the circle of dancers. The sky grew darker by the minute and everything and everyone surrounding them blurred.

Leo only saw Mariel.

Her face remained sombre, as did his own, he imagined. Did she feel the same emotions that were coursing through him? Savouring. Yearning. Regretting.

How different their lives would have been had his parents been respectably married. Had there been no fire. They would have married. Had children. Built a prosperous stud farm together. Had a lovely life.

What foolish fancy. He'd learned early that it was no use to wish for what one could not change.

The orchestra stopped playing and a violinist began playing a solo. Some of the dancers stopped to listen; the others made their way back to their boxes or to the booths selling food and wine.

Mariel averted her gaze. 'Thank you for coming

to my rescue, Leo. Another good deed you have performed.'

She sounded despairing and he ached for her.

He searched for Kellford and no longer saw him. 'Walk with me.' He extended his hand.

Mariel hesitated. She should never have danced with him, even if it meant being discovered by Kellford.

Oh, she was full of foolishness this night. She'd so abhorred Kellford's presence being forced on her in this beautiful place of fantasy and romance that she'd impulsively run from him.

Perhaps she had sensed Leo nearby, because she was not entirely surprised when he appeared in front of her. It has been foolish indeed to dance with him, to swirl to the sensual melody, to lose herself in Leo's warm hazel eyes, his gaze more piercing framed by his mask.

No, she should not walk with him. She must be sensible.

But his fingers beckoned. 'Please, Mariel?'

She glanced around, wondering what would happen if Kellford found her, especially with another man. Mariel had sensed the falseness of Kellford's gallantry even before Leo told her of the man's perversions. His actions towards her might speak to others of a solicitous lover, but Mariel had known all along that all he wanted was her money. His solicitousness was merely a means to control her every move.

She'd been clever enough to escape him this night. She'd find some excuse to offer him for disappearing from his side.

If only she could think of some way to rid herself of him entirely.

She stared at Leo's extended hand, temptation itself.

Before she knew it, she'd placed her hand in his and felt his warmth and strength through her glove. 'Do not take me back to the supper box.'

He nodded.

They stepped onto the gravel of the Grand Walk and, like so many other couples, strolled to the fountain. Beyond the fountain the paths led through trees as thick as a forest. The Dark Walk, they called it, a place where lovers could disappear and indulge in intimacies forbidden in the light.

They entered the Dark Walk and walked past the illusionist making cards appear and disappear at will. They continued and soon the darkness of a moonless night surrounded them. Then, all at once, the thousands of gas lamps strung throughout in the trees were lit and the night blazed with light.

Mariel gasped. It was as if they'd been lifted to the stars. She glanced at Leo and saw the wonder of the sight reflected in his eyes, as well. It had always been like this between them. An instant understanding. Conversing without needing to use words.

To be so close to him again made it seem as if no time had passed, as if they were still young and full of optimism, eager to lose themselves in the Dark Walk. In those days he would have pulled her into the privacy of the trees. He would have placed his lips on hers and she would have soared to the stars with happiness.

She shook herself. They were no longer young and full of optimism. They were no longer in love.

They came upon an area almost as private as in her imagination, a bench set in among the shrubbery, almost completely concealed from the path itself.

'Shall we sit a moment?' he asked.

She should resist the temptation of him, not succumb to old fantasies. She'd grown out of them. He'd forced her out of them.

Still, she sat.

They removed their masks, but did not speak.

Finally he broke their silence. 'Tell me now why you must marry Kellford.'

She stiffened. Why did he persist in asking her this? She could not confide in him.

'Because I will help you.' He seemed to answer her very thoughts. 'But I must know the problem.'

She turned away from him, not wanting to believe in him again. How could she?

But he persisted. 'What hold does Kellford have over you? Has he compromised you?'

She swung back. 'Compromised me!' The thought was appalling.

'Has he forced himself on you? Is that why?' He blanched. 'Good God. Has he gotten you—?'

'No!' She held up a hand. 'Do not insult me. Do you think I would tolerate his touch?'

His expression turned grim. 'I think him quite capable of forcing himself on you. If it is not that, then tell me what it is. You said you *must* marry him. Tell me the reason.'

Her anger flared. 'I cannot tell you, Leo. You know I cannot.'

'Whatever it is, I can help you.' His gaze remained steady. 'I have ways.'

This was so much like the Leo she once knew, the young man who believed they could create a bright future together. She wanted to shake her head lest he be an apparition.

But she could not let him hurt her again. Trust in

him? Impossible. 'You once made promises to me, Leo. We both know what happened to those promises.'

He was opening the old wounds, wounds she'd been able to ignore even if they'd never healed.

'Mariel.' His voice turned tight. 'You broke those promises.'

'*I* broke them?' It had been devastation when she'd heard nothing from him. 'You left me!'

'What did you expect? You were marrying Ashworth. You chose a title over a bastard. What happened to that plan, by the way?'

'Ashworth again. Why do you persist in saying I would marry Ashworth? I was betrothed to you.' She felt as if she were bleeding inside once again.

'Your father—' he began, but did not finish.

The blood drained from her face. Had her father sent Leo away? 'Do you mean you spoke to my father?'

'You know I did. You set the appointment.' He clenched his jaw. 'Surely you have not forgotten that we planned for me to speak with your father. He told me you had chosen Ashworth.'

'No.' She shook her head. 'You never kept that appointment. I assumed it was because of the fire. My father said you didn't keep it.'

'Your father said that?' A look of realisation came over his face.

Her father. She felt the blood drain from her. Her father had been manipulating her even then. 'Tell me what my father said to you.'

'That you chose Ashworth over me, because I was a bastard with nothing to offer you. Since my stables had just burned down, he was essentially correct.' His eyes narrowed. 'Were you at Ashworth's estate that day?'

'At Ashworth's estate?' She felt cold inside. 'No. I

was in Bath. With my mother. She wanted to take the waters.'

They sat close to each other, so close their faces were inches apart. She could see the shadow of a beard on his chin, the lines at the corners of his eyes, the shadows within him that spoke of his own pain.

'He told me you chose Ashworth because of his title,' he went on, speaking as much to himself as to her. 'Because he was respectable.'

She almost weakened, almost transferred her anger to her father, who owned plenty of it already. But Leo was not wholly innocent in this.

She lifted her chin. 'You believed those things mattered to me? Titles and such? Is that what you thought of me? Why did you not speak with me yourself, Leo? You left without a word. Without a word. At first I thought it was because of the fire, but even then it shocked me that you would not come to me so we could plan what to do together. It took me months and months to realise that you had no intention of returning to me.' She felt as if she were bleeding inside.

His face turned stony, but she sensed turbulent emotions inside him. 'I was convinced you did not want me.'

'You were *easily* convinced, apparently. Did you think so little of me, Leo?' She slid away from him and crossed her arms over her chest as if this would protect her heart. 'Even if you thought all that nonsense about Ashworth was true, you did not try to fight for me, did you? Or try to make me change my mind? You never gave me a chance. You just took it upon yourself to run off.'

Her words wounded him, she could tell by his face, but they were true.

He spoke quietly. 'I am not running away now. I want to help you.'

She desperately wanted help, but not from him. The pain of his leaving her still hurt too much.

Her own father had manoeuvred the situation, true—she must deal with that later—but it was Leo who'd chosen to leave.

She stood and tied her mask back on. 'I want to go back.'

He rose and donned his mask, as well.

They entered the crosswalk that led back to the other side of the gardens. She took long deep breaths, trying to calm herself lest tears dampen her mask and give away her emotions. The closer they came to the supper boxes, the more she cringed at having to return to Kellford's side and to pretend to her father that he had not set about the destruction of her happiness two years before this. At the moment, though, it was worse to be with Leo. She was enraged at him—and perilously close to falling into his arms.

He'd held her many times when they'd discussed marrying, when they declared their love, said they would overcome all obstacles together.

She remembered when she'd learned his stables had burned down and most of his horses were lost. She'd read it in the newspapers. When her father told her Leo never showed up for his appointment, she'd imagined it had been because of the fire. She waited and waited until days stretched into weeks and weeks into months. She waited even after learning Leo had left the country. He would send for her, she'd thought.

But he never did.

He'd promised he would marry her, and now he promised he would find a way to prevent her marriage.

It was too late to believe in him. It hurt too much to be wrong.

She walked at his side, not touching him, her cape wrapped around her like a shield against him.

One good thing about his sudden appearance in her life was she now felt roused to battle harder against this forced marriage. She did not need him for it. All she needed was to remain single for two more years and her inheritance would be hers, free and clear. No man could use it to rule her life. No man could keep her from protecting her mother and sisters.

Her father told her he owed Kellford a large gambling debt, one so large that their family would be ruined if he did not pay. Apparently Mariel was payment of the debt. Or rather, her fortune was. How much of that was a lie, like the lies he told her about Leo? She wanted the truth.

Then she would know what to do.

It was a start. A plan. And her time was better spent dwelling on how to escape this dreadful marriage than on fantasies and regrets about Leo Fitzmanning.

They reached the arches; the supper boxes were just on the other side.

'Do not remain with me,' she demanded of Leo.

He seized her arm before she could leave him. 'I cannot let you go until you tell me what hold Kellford has over you.'

This was becoming tedious. Why not tell him? Perhaps he would leave her alone if she did.

She turned so she could look directly into his eyes. 'Kellford threatens my family. He has the power to ruin my father, my mother, my sisters.' She spoke the words slowly so he would not miss their importance.

'Mariel—' he began.

'No more promises!' She pulled out of his grip. 'Do not stop me again, Leo. This time I am the one who is leaving. Right now.'

Chapter Five

Once again Leo watched Mariel walk away, her dark green cape billowing behind her as she hurried back to the supper boxes. Once again she'd shaken him.

By God, he'd been thoroughly duped by her father. What an elaborate ruse the man had created, complete with a special licence, a story about Mariel's absence and Mariel's cryptic note. Enough to convince the bastard suitor he'd been thrown over for a man with a title. Leo had fallen for it, without a single question.

The realisation was like a dagger in the gut.

He deserved Mariel's anger. He'd not believed in her. He'd run away without a fight, so ready to believe her father's lies.

The dagger twisted. He might have gained happiness. She would have been spared pain. If only he had not been so easily misled, so abominably weak.

He straightened his spine. Never would he show such weakness again.

The truth sliced into him. He was responsible for her suffering. If he had done the right thing two years ago, she would not be betrothed to Kellford now. By God, he vowed he'd fix that. Even though such amends would not bring back what he'd lost. What he'd foolishly tossed away.

He slowly walked towards the supper box.

What was it that Kellford held over Mariel's family? The key was her father, Leo guessed. The bloody liar. What had Covendale done this time for which his daughter must pay?

Leo would find out. He'd begin a search for the answer this very night. Judicious questions posed in certain gaming hells should yield answers. Few secrets were safe in gaming hells, where men made it their business to discover what others were hiding. Leo's secret, his once-betrothal to Mariel, had, thankfully, never seen the light.

Leo re-entered the supper box, where the masked and costumed guests continued to laugh and flirt and imbibe too much wine. He distinctly heard his sister Charlotte's laugh above the others. Dear Charlotte. She'd certainly inherited their parents' capacity for enjoyment.

Keeping his distance lest his sister recognise him, Leo watched Mariel sidle through the crowd and pick up a glass of wine from a liveried servant carrying a tray. She made her way to the table of food and positioned herself in a nearby corner. Leo found a spot where he could keep her in view without being too obvious. She'd noticed him, though, tossing him one annoyed glance before pointedly ignoring him.

Not more than two minutes passed before Kellford bustled his way to the food table and placed paper-thin slices of ham on his plate.

Mariel marched up to him. 'There you are!' she snapped. 'If you insist upon being my escort, you might at least have remained by my side.'

Kellford nearly dropped his plate. 'Miss Covendale.'

He made a curt bow. 'I have been searching the Gardens for you.'

She laughed. 'Searching the Gardens? Do you think me such a fool that I would leave the party? No woman would leave the protection of her friends to venture into the Gardens alone.'

'Are you saying you were not alone?' Kellford put on an affable smile, but his voice rose. 'Come now, you were not with another man, were you?' This was jokingly said, but one look at Kellford's eyes showed he was not amused.

Mariel waved a hand dismissively. 'Do stop talking nonsense. You know very well I remained here all the time. It was you who left the boxes. I saw you. If you do not wish my company, please have the courtesy to say so. Do not merely sneak away.'

Clever girl. Leo smiled.

She lifted her chin and walked away from Kellford, seeking out Charlotte, who was delighted to see her.

Kellford was left scowling in her wake, but his posture conveyed uncertainty. Her ruse had been successful.

But how many more times could she thwart him? Once married, Kellford would undoubtedly have no further need to charm her.

Leo kept his eye on Mariel the rest of the night while she continued to portray an indignant, offended woman whenever Kellford came near her. It was a brilliant performance. From time to time she caught sight of Leo, but, at such times, the displeasure on her face was not play-acting.

The next morning Mariel rose early and rang for Penny to come help her dress.

'Did you enjoy yourself at Vauxhall Gardens?' the maid asked as she pinned up Mariel's hair.

Mariel had had a miserable time, but there was no reason to explain that to Penny. Worse, she'd spent the night tossing and turning. Whatever sleep she'd managed had been filled with dreams of walking through the Gardens with Leo. They were lovers again. They were joyous.

Then she would wake.

'The Gardens were lovely,' she finally managed to respond.

'I'd like to go there.' Penny sighed.

Mariel smiled at her maid's reflection in the mirror. 'Do you not have a beau who would take you there?' With Penny's beauty, she ought to have several willing to be her escort.

Penny blushed. 'Oh, miss! There is no one I like that way.'

'Indeed?' Mariel was surprised. 'None of our footmen? Or the others who work near here?'

The girl shook her head. 'I...I cannot like their attentions. They look at me so strangely. Like a hungry cat looks at a mouse.'

This Mariel did not doubt. 'Well, some day perhaps you will find a man who is to your liking.'

Penny stilled. 'Is Lord Kellford to your liking, miss?'

It was an impertinent question for a servant to ask, but Penny spoke with so much concern that Mariel refused to chastise her.

'No,' she responded. 'Lord Kellford is not to my liking at all.'

'He is a bad man, is he not?' Penny went on. 'I heard what that other man said of him.'

Leo, she meant. They had not spoken of that day Leo walked back into Mariel's life.

Mariel nodded. 'Kellford is bad, indeed.'

'Who was the man who told you about Lord Kellford?' Penny asked, obviously emboldened by Mariel's confidences.

But Mariel could not explain Leo to her lady's maid. She could not explain Leo to anyone.

'Someone I once knew,' she said, as if it was of no consequence. She quickly patted her hair. 'Are we done here? I believe I'll wear my blue morning dress if you would fetch it, please.'

Penny curtsied and hurried over to the clothes press. They spoke no more of Leo.

After Mariel finished dressing she went to the dining room to see if her father was still at breakfast. The room was empty, although the sideboard was set with food. She bit her lip, hoping her father had not gone out.

The scent of sausages and muffins made her mouth water, but she did not stop to eat. Instead she hurried to her father's library and knocked at the door.

'Who is it?' she heard him say.

Relieved to have found him, she walked in. 'It is Mariel, sir.'

'Ah, Mariel.' He attempted a smile, but she knew he was not pleased to see her. 'What do you want?'

'I wish to speak with you.' She approached his desk.

He glanced down at his papers. 'I have much to do.'

'You may do it later.' It was difficult for her to be civil to her father. She could not forgive the situation he had put her in. Or how his lies had ruined her chance for happiness.

He balled his hand into a fist. 'Do not speak to me

again of not wishing to marry Kellford. You must do so and that is enough. Talk until you are hoarse. You still must marry him.'

'I do not wish to argue with you.' She attempted a mollifying tone, strolling to the bookshelves and pretending to peruse the titles. 'I want some information.'

He sighed. 'What is it?'

Why did you lie and trick Leo? she wanted to say. *Why did you send him away, believing I cared nothing for him? Why would you wish to cause me such anguish?*

Worse, why had Leo so readily believed you and not me?

Her legs trembled. She needed to confine herself to the problem at hand. It was too late to change what had happened two years ago.

Forcing herself to remain calm, she ran her fingers over the leather bindings of the books. 'I want you to tell me exactly why I must marry Kellford. How is it he can ruin us? What does he know?'

Her father's face turned an angry red. He looked down again and rattled his papers. 'That is none of your affair. Suffice to know we will all be ruined if you do not marry him.'

'But that will not suffice, Father.' She walked back to his desk and faced him directly. 'I want to know all. Whatever you tell me need not go beyond this room, but you must tell me the whole.'

He lifted his chin and glared at her. 'I need do no such thing. And I'll brook no further impertinence from you. I am your father—'

She held up a hand. 'And I am your daughter, the daughter you are giving away in marriage to a monster.'

Her father gave a dry laugh. 'Come, come. He is not a monster. He is a charming man.'

She leaned closer to him. 'You know all about Lord Kellford, Father. He follows the practices of the Marquis de Sade. That makes him a monster, correct?'

Her father turned pale and guilt shone in his eyes.

She met his gaze and held it. 'Tell me what this is all about. Tell me and I'll not argue with you about this ever again.'

He glanced away and carefully stacked his papers.

'Tell me,' she insisted.

He squirmed. 'I owe him money.'

She rolled her eyes. 'You owe everyone money.' He'd already sold her mother's jewellery. And hers and her sisters', replacing them with paste. He'd sold everything they had of value and mortgaged their houses to pay his gambling debts. 'What else is it?'

He lifted his head and stared with vacant eyes. 'He knows what I did.'

Her alarm grew. 'What did you do?'

He swallowed. 'I stole money from my cousin.'

'From Cousin Doring?' The wealthy Earl of Doring had paid off her father's debts several times.

'He would not give me a loan.' Her father wiped his face. 'I begged him. I had money lenders pressing me for payment. I was desperate.'

Money lenders? Had he sunk that low? Low enough to steal, apparently.

She blew out a breath. 'How much?'

He cleared his throat. 'A thousand pounds.'

'A thousand pounds!' He'd gambled away a thousand pounds? On top of the debts he'd already amassed?

'How does Kellford know you stole this money?' she asked.

He shrugged his shoulders. 'He was the one who sent me to the money lenders. I...I'd already confided in him that Doring would not give me the funds to pay. I fear he became suspicious when I paid the whole. Next thing I knew he'd discovered my theft.'

Her father embroiled himself with such despicable characters? Money lenders *and* Kellford? He was beyond foolish. A liar and a fool.

What difference if Kellford knew of the theft? Surely Cousin Doring would not want the scandal. They could strike a bargain with him.

She put her hands on her hips. 'Well, it seems to me it is Kellford's word against yours about this theft. I think we should go to Cousin Doring and confess the whole. I will write a promissory note to pay him back when I come into my inheritance.'

'It will not work.' Her father's shoulders slumped. 'My cousin has already told me he does not care if I go to debtor's prison. He said he did not care if I hanged. He washed his hands of me. He said I was never to darken his door again.'

'I will go to him, then.'

He shook his head. 'Doring told me not to send you, your mother or sisters on my behalf. He said you could not influence him any more than I could.'

'But if I made a promise to pay the money back?' she insisted.

'No.' His voice rose. 'If you tell him what I did, he'll have me hanged. He was that angry. You must believe me!'

The risk was too great not to believe him. The stakes were his life and, at this moment more importantly, the well-being of her sisters and mother.

She sighed. 'What exactly did you do? How did you steal the money?'

Her father drummed nervously on his desk. 'I forged a note on Doring's bank, giving me the money. Doring never looks that carefully at his finances. I thought he'd be none the wiser and his men of business would assume he was merely giving me money again.' He paused. 'Kellford has the note in his safe.'

'Kellford has the banknote?' Her skin turned cold.

'I do not know how he did it, but I have seen the note in his hands. He threatens to confront Doring with it—in a public place, he says—and openly accuse me of theft.' His expression turned bleak. 'I will hang!'

Worse, her mother and two younger sisters would be plummeted into scandal and poverty, and there would be nothing Mariel could do about it until she turned twenty-five. Isabel was fourteen and Augusta was sixteen, almost ready for her Season. What chances in life would they have if such a scandal were attached to their name?

Unless Mariel married Kellford. 'So you offered me in return for Kellford's silence?'

He shook his head. 'He wanted to marry you. That was the bargain he struck with me. Marriage to you and the paper would remain in his safe for ever.'

'Why would he want to marry me?' she cried.

Her father grimaced. 'For your inheritance, Mariel. Why else?'

Countless men had tried to court her, even during these last two years. Those men had been after her money, as well, but surely those men did not derive pleasure from inflicting pain and were not extortionists.

She trembled as she glared at her father. 'Do you know what you have done to me, Father?'

He raised his hands. 'I had no choice. Surely you can see that.'

She leaned towards him again and deliberately lowered her voice. Otherwise she might have screamed at him. 'You chose to gamble, Father. You chose to amass debts you could not pay. You resorted to theft and put your family in jeopardy like this. How could you do this?'

He'd ruined her life. If only he'd not interfered two years ago. If only he had not lied.

If only…

Leo padded in bare feet from his bedchamber, yawning as he entered the drawing room, then stepped back into the hallway.

'Walker!' he called. 'Are you here?'

'Mwa?' Walker staggered out of his room, still in the clothes he wore the previous day and with the ashen look of a man who'd bitten the jug. Two jugs, perhaps.

Leo peered at him. 'Where were you last night?'

Walker winced. 'Do not shout.'

'I'm not shouting.' Leo entered the kitchen. 'Do we have anything to eat?'

'Do not speak to me of food.' Walker pressed his hands against his head.

Leo emerged from the kitchen, munching on a piece of bread. 'I discovered something last night. Covendale is deep in debt. Gambles.' He took another bite of bread. 'I could not discover if he owes Kellford, though.'

'Stop chewing so loud,' Walker mumbled. 'Don't know about that. Kellford's in deep with money lenders, though.'

'What?' Leo was taken aback. 'How did you learn that?'

Walker slumped into a chair. 'Drinking. Followed his valet to a tavern. Got him talking.'

'Excellent.' This was why he valued Walker. 'What did you learn?'

Walker pressed his head again. 'The valet is unhappy. Hates Kellford. Gossips like a woman. I've discovered what you need to know, I believe. Even have a solution.' He grinned up at Leo. 'How would you like to again become a thief?'

Lord Kellford stood in the office of Mr Carter of Messrs Carter and Company, No. 14 Old Cavendish Street.

'Payment is overdue, Lord Kellford,' Mr Carter intoned.

It was a humiliation to be spoken to in such a tone. And to be required to beg. 'A month's time is all I ask.' Kellford favoured Carter with his most charming smile.

'A month is a long time.' Carter looked at him over spectacles worn low on his nose. The money lender dressed like any cit, in plain coat and trousers, devoid of the tailoring that would have marked him a gentleman. It was unconscionable that he held Kellford under his thumb, like an insect about to be squashed.

'I shall have to demand more interest,' Carter drawled.

Kellford kept smiling. 'Do not fear. I am marrying an heiress in less than three weeks. In four weeks I shall pay you in full.'

'At twenty per cent, Kellford.'

'At twenty per cent.'

Carter nodded and waved Kellford out of the office like some inconsequential underling.

Infuriating.

How he'd like to slice that man in two. No. No. Better to kill him slowly. Flail him with chains. Burn him with hot irons. Unfortunate they did not live in medieval times. Think of the pleasure of placing Carter on a rack and slowly turning the wheel.

Kellford crossed into the hall and walked out the door. As soon as he stepped onto the street, the skies opened up with rain. Perfect.

After receiving Carter's summons, Kellford had taken an ordinary hackney coach to Old Cavendish Street. It would not do for a coach with his crest to be seen waiting in front of a money-lender's door.

He was soaked to the skin by the time he reached the line of hacks awaiting riders. 'Take me to Charles Street, Mayfair,' he demanded of the first coachman.

He climbed in and settled back against the cracked leather seat, closing his eyes.

Only a few weeks more of this degradation. He abhorred kowtowing to a manipulative money lender. When the Covendale chit's inheritance was in his hands, he'd be free of the man.

And he'd have plenty of money to spare, which was as it should be. He deserved the luxuries of life.

And the pleasures.

She had angered him the previous night, making him look the fool for chasing after her in Vauxhall Gardens. After she had spoken her marriage vows, he would teach her not to make a fool of him.

Ever.

Until then, he'd play the devoted future husband. He'd make sure the *ton* all knew about the dinner he was hosting the next night, the one honouring his prospective bride and her family. Perhaps it would quiet her prickly nerves when he impressed her with the finest delicacies and wines.

He rubbed his chin. Knowing his betrothed had such spirit made him want to break her like a wild horse.

Tame her.

Chapter Six

Mariel sat at Kellford's right at the long table laden with every delicacy that might impress. Kellford, at the head of the table, urged his twenty guests to try each dish, and, as if he were a besotted lover, offered a toast to her, calling himself the most fortunate man in the world.

She inwardly scoffed. If he thought himself the most fortunate, then surely she was the least. The only good fortune he wanted was her inheritance.

Her mother, happily oblivious to Mariel's frightful situation—and her husband's if his misdeed came to light—giddily pronounced everything a delight. Her father's behaviour proved even more appalling. Gone was the miserable demeanour he'd adopted when confessing all to Mariel; he now laughed appreciatively at Kellford's attempts at humour and chatted genially to the ladies seated on each side of him.

The table included some impressive guests, making Mariel wonder how many of these titled men were fooled by Kellford's gracious facade and how many knew his true nature. Worse, were any of these men like him? Did their wives endure the horrors Leo had described to her?

Kellford continued to lay on the charm as thick as plaster on a wall. She supposed some would think him a handsome man with his fair hair and pale blue eyes; that is, if they ignored the expression of disdain in those eyes and the hint of cruelty around his mouth. He was paying for this dinner on credit, she would wager. She'd be paying for it out of her inheritance, no doubt.

Not if she could help it, she vowed.

Although Mariel tried to avoid looking at him as much as possible, she watched everything else carefully. Impatiently, she looked for the opportunity she needed. The guests were busy talking and eating, the servants, serving. Now was the perfect time.

Damping down a flutter of nerves, she leaned over to Lord Kellford and spoke in a quiet, confidential voice. 'Sir, I fear I must use the ladies' retiring room.'

He looked perfectly solicitous. 'Are you ill?'

'No,' she replied. 'But it is a matter of some urgency.'

He glanced around at his guests as if assessing their reaction to their private conversation. The guests paid no attention to them.

The corner of his mouth turned up. 'Do you need for me to show you the way?'

'Not at all,' she assured him. 'I remember where it is.'

When she and her parents had arrived at Lord Kellford's town house, her mother requested a tour of the house, so Mariel knew precisely to which room she was headed.

She stood and addressed the guests. 'Please excuse me. I will return shortly.'

Most of them did not even trouble themselves to look up.

She exited the dining room in some haste and quickly found the room set up as the women's necessary. She went inside, but only long enough to find a lighted candle. Peeking out to make certain the hallway was empty, she tiptoed to the door of the library.

Her father had mentioned that Kellford kept the incriminating paper in his safe. Her father's safe was in the library, so it stood to reason Kellford's would be, too.

She opened the library door and stepped inside, closing it behind her.

Instantly she was seized from behind. She uttered a surprised cry and dropped the candle. Its flame was extinguished by the fall.

A man's hand covered her mouth. 'Be quiet. Do not make a sound.'

How could she mistake that voice?

'Leo?' she mumbled beneath his palm.

He freed her mouth, but still held her. 'Mariel?'

'What are you doing here?' she whispered.

Another man, dressed all in black and his face shrouded by a mask, stood behind the desk. Although there was a small candle in his hand, he almost blended into the shadows.

Leo's lips came very close to her ear. 'We have come for a paper incriminating your father.'

He knew about the paper? 'You are mad. The house is filled with people.'

'Perfect time to come.' His breath was warm against her cheek. 'Everyone is occupied.'

The other man turned back to the shelves behind the desk. Mariel's eyes adjusted to the dim light and she could see the man had found the safe.

Leo pulled her away from the door to a small alcove.

He loosened his hold on her. 'Why are *you* here? Are there others walking about?'

'They are all dining. I am alone.' She turned to face

him. 'Why are you searching for the paper? I've come for it, as well. What do you know about it? How did you learn of it?'

He, too, was masked and dressed in black. He held her closer, and the darkness felt like a blanket around them. Her heart skittered.

He murmured into her ear, 'You should know why. Never mind how we knew of it. You should not be here. What if Kellford discovers what you are doing?'

'He could hardly do worse to me than what I face after the marriage,' she retorted. He and his companion were risking far more than she. They would hang if caught. 'You have obviously broken into the house. You are trespassing, Leo. And stealing. Have your wits gone begging?'

He held her so close their bodies touched and, in spite of the situation and her anger at him, her senses flamed. Feeling malleable as putty, Mariel found temptation to melt into his embrace become nearly irresistible. He again placed his lips near her ear, and she yearned to turn her head and place her lips upon his.

'I said I would help you,' he murmured. 'Leave it to me.'

Mariel trembled at the whirlwind of emotion and sensation coursing through her. The darkness of the room fuelled the illusion that they were alone.

The man at the safe put the candle down on the desk; the sound caused enough distraction to jolt her back to reality.

She strained against his arms. 'What will you do with the paper if you find it?'

He released her, but reached up to cup her face. 'Give it to you, Mariel. What else?'

Perhaps it was the darkness or the danger with which

they flirted, but he seemed to possess her with his touch, warm her with the sound of his voice. Her body ached to be held by him again.

'Mariel,' he murmured.

His hand still rested on her arm; his thumb gently rubbed her skin, creating wonderful sparks that flashed through her.

He drew her closer, leaning down so that his lips were near to hers. Memories flooded her, memories of stolen kisses, hidden from everyone's view. The impulse to close the scant distance between them and again taste his lips was hard to resist.

She forced herself to step away from him, out of the alcove to where she could feel chaperoned by the other man. He seemed to be putting keys in the safe's lock.

'Do you have a key that will fit the lock?' she asked Leo.

'Not a key. A set of lock picks.' He still spoke in whispers. 'How did you intend to open the safe?'

'I would have used a hairpin.'

He smiled for a moment, then sobered. 'You must go back, Mariel. Someone might come looking for you, then we will all be in danger.' He took her arm and led her back to the door. 'Meet me in the park at eleven tomorrow. The same place where we talked the other day. I will give you the paper then.'

'Yes.' Her heart gladdened. It would be over by tomorrow. She would be free. Impulsively she flung her arms around him.

He held her very tight, so tight she could feel the length of his body against hers. The ache grew stronger.

He released her and, his gloved hand firmly on her arm, walked her over to the door. Opening it a crack, he peeked out. 'It is safe to leave.'

She hesitated. 'The candle I dropped—'

He put his hand on her back, urging her on. 'We will take care of it. Go now.'

She slipped out and hurried down the hallway back to the dining room.

Leo stared at the closed door as if it would give him one more glimpse of her. Her appearance in the room had shocked him. Holding her in his arms, feeling her body against his, had sent his senses reeling. His desire for her was unabated, even if he had ruined long ago any chance of spending the rest of his life with her, loving her each night, waking beside her each morning.

The wrenching pain he thought he'd buried deep inside him burst forth anew. He felt doubled over with it.

And it was only worsened by the knowledge that he could have prevented it.

He glanced over at Walker, who was trying one pick after another. This escapade of theirs was fraught with danger, but Leo would do anything to save Mariel from Kellford.

Walker tried another pick. 'That's it,' he whispered. The safe door opened.

Leo walked over to him. 'Let us have a look inside and be quick about it.'

His hopes rose. Kellford's garrulous valet had told Walker about the paper. They were moments from discovering it.

Mariel would be free. She would be safe.

The next day Mariel told her mother she was taking Penny with her to shop for wedding clothes. Her mother detested shopping, but cooed with excitement at Mariel's apparent interest in the wedding.

'Purchase anything you desire,' her mother said.

Her poor mother. Had not the sale of her jewellery taught her she must practise economy?

As Mariel left the house, she turned to Penny, 'Let us hurry.'

'Yes, miss.' Penny sounded puzzled.

Mariel usually stretched out her time away from the town house for as long as possible.

When they reached Oxford Street, she turned left instead of heading towards Bond Street.

Penny looked around in confusion. 'Where are we bound?'

'To the park.'

Penny faltered. 'We are not going to the shops?'

Mariel waited for her to catch up. 'I must beg you say nothing of this. I am meeting someone. The...the man I met before.' She looked down on Penny. 'It is of great importance.'

Penny's eyes widened. 'Yes, miss.'

They walked through the Cumberland gate and down the same path where Leo had led them before. When they reached the alcove with the bench, Leo was already there, pacing back and forth. Her heart quickened at the sight of him, tall and powerful. The memory of his body against hers returned, filling her with a unique excitement. He did, indeed, look as if he could perform impossible feats such as saving her from Kellford.

He turned and caught sight of her, but did not smile. 'Mariel.'

A *frisson* of anxiety ran up her back. She spoke to Penny. 'Would you mind standing where you did before?'

Staring at Leo, the maid nodded and stepped away from the alcove.

'We must speak quietly, Leo. I do not wish her to hear.' She walked with him to the bench, but did not sit. 'Do you have the paper?'

His frown deepened. 'I do not.'

Trepidation replaced hope. 'You did not bring it? You promised me, Leo.'

He put his hand to his forehead. 'We did not find it, Mariel. There was no bank draft in the safe. No paper showing your father's name. It was not there. We searched the desk. It was not there, either.'

'No!' Tears stung her eyes. 'Then Kellford is still able to threaten my family? I am still in his clutches?'

He stepped forwards and enfolded her in his arms. 'No, Mariel. I will find another way. I promise you.'

The sensations of the previous evening when he had held her returned with full force. His arms enveloped her; his masculine scent filled her nostrils; his hard, muscular body pressed against her. Worse, she almost fell under his spell. She almost believed him.

The memory of how deeply she had once believed in him, trusted him, known in her soul that they would be partners for life, flooded her. How wrong she'd been! He'd walked away from her when she'd never have done so to him. She would have followed him anywhere, given up anything, even the inheritance that had now become an albatross around her neck. She'd believed they could face any trial, any tribulation, as long as they were together.

And he had abandoned her without a word.

Her spirits plummeted to rock-hard ground and she pushed him away. 'It is no use.'

'Miss! Miss!' Penny ran back into the alcove. 'There is a man in the bushes. He is eavesdropping!'

'Oh, no!' If anyone saw them together—heard

them—it could make matters much worse. They might make enquiries about her father. Or tell Kellford—

Leo caught her arm. 'Do not fear. He is with me.' He turned. 'Walker!'

The man emerged from the shrubbery.

Mariel swung back to Leo. 'You had someone spying on me?'

'Not spying.' His gaze was earnest. 'Protecting. Walker was looking out in case you were followed. Or in case someone strolled nearby.'

She glanced away. She'd gone from believing the best to believing the worst of him and she could not seem to help herself.

Leo's companion bowed. 'Miss Covendale, ma'am.'

'Walker is my valet,' Leo explained.

'Your valet?' Her suspicions returned. This man did not have the appearance of a valet. On the contrary, he was nearly as tall as Leo and even more muscular. His face had the battered look of a pugilist and there was nothing servile in the way he carried himself.

Leo cocked his head. 'For want of any other description, I call him my valet. I suppose if we had been in the army, he'd be called my batman.'

It suddenly dawned on her who the man was. 'Did we almost meet last night, Mr Walker?'

He gave a deferential nod. 'Very perceptive of you, miss.'

She returned the courtesy. 'You were the other man.' The man who had picks to open a safe's lock.

Walker's gaze drifted to Penny and held for a moment before he turned back to Leo. 'Did you tell her of your plan?'

Mariel's hope stirred. 'You have another plan?'

Leo gestured towards Penny. 'Do you wish your maid to hear this discussion?'

Mariel lifted a shoulder. 'She knows enough of this ugly business already. She may hear whatever you have to say.'

Leo waved a hand. 'The plan Walker refers to poses too much of a risk. You need not concern yourself about it.'

Mariel's eyes narrowed. 'It is my life that is at stake. And that of my family.' She lifted her chin. 'Tell me the plan, Leo.'

'Mariel.' Leo shook his head. 'The plan requires too much of you. It puts you in danger.'

She put her hands on her hips. 'Am I not in danger already? Do me the courtesy of including me in any discussion of what might save me from Kellford.'

His eyes flashed at her words. 'It is not a good plan. Too much can go wrong.'

'I thought it was a good plan,' Walker chimed in.

Mariel fixed Leo with a glare. 'Tell me of it and let me decide.'

'You might as well tell her, Fitz,' Walker said.

Leo flashed him an annoyed look, before facing Mariel again. 'The idea is for you to confront Kellford. Tell him you do not believe that there is a forged banknote. Ask him to produce it for you or you will refuse to marry him. Then you coordinate with Walker and me the time you arrange to meet him. We'll know Kellford has the paper and we will take it from him.'

It was a brilliant idea. 'Do you actually think he would agree to show me the paper? Would he not merely refuse?'

His eyes found hers. 'You would have to convince

him. Stand up to him. He needs your money. He will not be able to refuse you.'

She easily set her mind on it. 'I will do it. The risk means nothing to me.' Anything to free herself of this marriage.

John Walker's attention wandered away from the discussion between Miss Covendale and Fitzmanning. His gaze slid to the pretty blonde standing near him, the one who'd warned of his presence.

She must be Miss Covendale's maid, he decided, although being a mere maid seemed too confining for such a beauty. She reminded him of a portrait he'd seen in Florence, a painting of timeless, ethereal beauty.

In addition to teaching him to read and write, Fitz had exposed him to such things as mathematics, science, literature and art. He'd easily perceived the usefulness of science and maths and literature, but art? What use was art? That Italian portrait taught him.

Like the portrait, this young woman had pale skin, huge brown eyes fringed with dark lashes, lips as pink as roses. Her thick, blonde curls were too luxurious to be contained by her bonnet.

His throat grew dry as he merely gazed upon her.

She turned to him and asked in a quiet voice, 'What are they talking about?'

Walker felt his cheeks burn at this scant notice from her.

He answered her in a low voice, 'Lord Kellford has a paper that would cause Miss Covendale's father harm. If we can take possession of the paper from him, she will not have to marry him.' He was surprised he could form so many words.

She turned away again, as if thinking on this, then

glanced back at him, her lovely brow furrowed. 'Will she truly be in danger?'

He took a step towards her, drawn to her as a magnet attracts metal. 'We will protect her.'

Her face relaxed and gratitude shone in her eyes.

He swallowed and extended his hand. 'I am John Walker.'

She put her small delicate hand in his. 'I am Penny Jenkins, Miss Covendale's maid.' She looked up at him with her wide brown eyes. 'Are you really a valet?'

He tried to smile. 'Among other things.'

'You do not look like a valet.'

He averted his gaze, well aware his appearance spoke of mean origins in the East End. He could hardly remember a time there when he had not needed to fight just to reach the next morning. Walker had yearned to escape. He had finally managed it, fleeing to the Continent and making his way to Paris. But he knew only thieving and fighting and nothing had changed but the city. Until Fitz happened upon a street fight, that is. Walker had been outnumbered and was taking a beating, but Fitz had come to his aid, fighting hard for a complete stranger. By the end of it one man lay dead and both he and Fitz were wounded. They'd gone to Fitz's rooms to recuperate. Walker never left. Fitz taught him to read and to think and to behave with decorum. Walker taught Leo how to survive the seamier side of life.

When Walker turned his gaze back to Miss Jenkins, though, he felt as if every sordid act he'd ever committed showed on his face.

She tilted her lovely head. 'I thought valets were all skinny men.'

His cheeks heated. Hers had been an admiring glance?

She transferred her attention back to her lady, who was at the moment listening to Fitz.

'We need a way for you to inform us of when and where the meeting will take place,' Fitz said.

Miss Covendale glanced over at her maid. 'Perhaps Penny can carry the message.'

Then Walker would see her again? His heart beat a little faster, but the young woman looked distressed.

'Do you object to that idea, Miss Jenkins?' he asked as Fitz and Miss Covendale continued talking.

Again her expression cleared. 'Oh, no. I am just so worried about her. I heard your employer say that Lord Kellford will hurt her. I cannot bear that thought.'

'Were you to go with her if she married?'

She shook her head unhappily. 'She will not allow it.' She lifted her gaze to him. 'But, if she marries Lord Kellford, somebody has to be there to help her. She cannot go alone.'

As if this sprite would be any match for Kellford's whips. More likely Miss Jenkins would merely become another of Kellford's victims.

Walker glanced over to Miss Covendale and Fitz. They dealt together as if she was a great deal more than an old family friend.

He asked Miss Jenkins, 'Do you know what there is between them?'

She shook her head. 'I do not even know who he is.'

'He is Leo Fitzmanning, the natural brother of the Duke of Manning.'

Her eyes widened and he assumed she would comment on Fitz's irregular birth. 'A duke's brother!' she exclaimed instead, clearly impressed.

'He is a good man,' Walker commented to no purpose.

What would this beauty think if she knew of *his*

birth? Walker knew nothing of his father. All he remembered of his mother was her leaving him alone at night in their dark, tiny room, with frightening sounds coming at him through the walls. He remembered her death, a slow, wasting ebbing away of her life.

Women in service might come from humble origins, but their employers demanded their reputations be unblemished. In comparison his reputation was a festering sore.

Like the Italian portrait, Penny Jenkins was something to admire from afar, not something he could aspire to possess.

Miss Covendale's voice rose. 'Penny, come. We are finished here.'

Fitz put his hand on Mariel's arm. 'You will send word to us?'

The way they looked at each other... Yes, Walker suspected something existed between them, something now fraught with complexity.

If Miss Jenkins looked at him with that same pent-up yearning, he would do anything for her.

Chapter Seven

After parting with Mariel, Leo and Walker took a path through the park to return to Leo's rooms on Jermyn Street. Walker, typically so alert, seemed preoccupied with watching his feet.

'Is something troubling you, Walker?' Leo asked.

His friend glanced up in surprise. 'No—no—nothing.'

There was much troubling Leo.

He was becoming more and more affected by Mariel with each moment he spent in her presence. She looked beautiful this morning in the fawn-coloured walking dress that highlighted her ginger-coloured eyes and chestnut hair. He knew that he had never stopped loving her, not even when he'd thought she'd rejected him.

His yearning for her now was nearly unbearable.

Sometimes he sensed the same yearning in her, but likely that was his own desire creating an illusion.

Not that it mattered. He'd changed in these last two years. He no longer wanted the things they'd planned together, a business the *ton* were bound to respect. He no longer cared what anyone thought. He wanted to be a success in his own eyes and to the devil with everyone else. Mariel still worried about her family being ruined and he could not deny that the disdain of society could ruin a woman's life.

Besides, she'd not forgiven him for leaving her—and well she should not, although he'd forgiven her the instant he realised it was his inconstancy, not hers, that had separated them. And to think now he was putting himself and Mariel at risk merely to protect the honour of her father, whose duplicity had already done irreparable injury to them both.

He'd prefer to solve the problem of Kellford alone, but in any event, he must resolve the problem quickly and keep Mariel safe. They should have conceived a plan to procure the incriminating banknote that did not involve her.

'Walker.' Leo's voice was harsh, as if Walker were privy to his thoughts. 'You should not have forced me to disclose that plan to Miss Covendale. I told you I wished to leave her out of it.'

Walker scoffed. 'How else were we supposed to find the paper? There's little more than two weeks before she's to wed the lout.'

They exited the park through the Stanhope gate and walked through the town houses to Piccadilly. When they reached Jermyn Street, a familiar figure walked towards them.

Leo's brother Stephen.

Stephen's face lit up when he saw Leo. 'Ah! How fortunate. I was disappointed not finding you at home.' He shook Leo's hand. 'Good to see you.'

Walker stepped back as befitted a valet.

'Hope you are well, Stephen.' Leo managed to sound reasonably glad to see his brother, although his emotions were so tied up with Mariel that the last thing he needed was a brother primed to come to his aid. 'Sorry to have missed your call.'

Stephen smiled. 'Nothing's missed. I'll go back with you.'

As they entered Leo's rooms, Walker said, 'Shall I bring some whisky, sir?'

Leo could use some spirits right now. 'Whisky, Stephen?'

His brother removed his hat and gloves. 'Delighted.'

'Have a seat.' Leo tried to sound cordial. 'I assume you have a purpose in calling upon me.'

By the time they were seated, Walker had produced a bottle and two glasses. He poured them each a drink and with a bow—as if he were a typical servant—he left the room.

'So, what is it, Stephen?' Better not to tarry.

His brother took a sip and raised his brows in appreciation of the flavour. 'I don't have a particular reason for calling, except to see how you are getting on.'

Leo was surprised. 'You are not going to try to give me new stables and an abundance of breeding stock?'

Stephen's expression brightened. 'Have you changed your mind?'

Leo put up a hand. 'No! Not in the least. I told you I am never breeding horses again.' That desire had truly passed.

Unlike his desire for Mariel.

Stephen settled back in his chair. 'So... How are you getting on?'

Leo sipped his drink. 'Splendidly.'

'Nicholas said you have been attending society functions.'

He'd been talking to Nicholas. Leo could imagine

their conversation. *How can we help our poor bastard brother?*

'Not many.'

'You are welcome to accompany Mae and me any time you wish. We receive almost as many invitations as Nicholas. I know he is refusing more of them now that Emily is getting closer to her time.'

Leo felt a stab of shame. Stephen's generosity was based on deep family affection. Leo understood that.

'I appreciate the offer.' He changed the subject. 'I trust Mae fares well? And the children?'

Stephen beamed. 'They fare excellently well...' Stephen went on to describe the latest antics of his children, whose lives Leo had almost entirely missed.

His nieces and nephews were a blur. He doubted he even had an accurate count. They were part of a world into which Leo did not fit.

'I say—' Stephen lifted his glass to his lips '—you ought to come visit us in Sussex. It would be like old times.'

Leo's days helping Stephen establish his stud farm had been productive ones and Leo had learned everything he'd needed to know to establish his own farm at Welbourne Manor. They'd been productive days, but it had been like living another man's life.

'We're only in town for the Season,' Stephen went on. 'I confess, I am eager to return.'

Leo raised his glass in a toast. 'To Sussex.'

Stephen's horse farm, smelling the stable smells, hearing the stable noises, touching the horses—that was a part of Leo's past. He'd moved on to explore and conquer new worlds and experiences. He'd grown in strength and character and wealth as a result. He experienced deep satisfaction over devising an investment scheme, carrying it out and having it succeed. His associates were in trade, trafficking and manufacture, hardly acceptable in the world in which he'd grown up.

The world that included Mariel.

Leo downed the rest of his whisky and stared into his empty glass.

'Leo?' Stephen's voice jarred him back to the present.

'Sorry.' Leo cleared his throat. 'Was I wool-gathering?'

Stephen looked at him with concern. 'Does something trouble you? Does it have something to do with why you wish to re-enter society?'

'I told you before—all of you—I am not *troubled*. There are no problems you need fix for me. It is time for me to re-enter society, that is all.'

Stephen persisted. 'Are you in the market for a wife?'

'No!' he snapped, then made himself laugh. 'Good God, no. I'm not ready to be leg-shackled.'

Stephen smiled. 'You say that now, but you will change your mind when the right woman comes along.'

Except she already had come along—and Leo had deserted her.

Stephen finished his drink and stood. 'I should be on my way.'

Leo stood, as well. He and Walker had some preparations to make. It would not be the first time they'd planned an ambush.

At the door, Stephen shook his hand again. 'Let me know if you need anything. Anything at all.' He held Leo's hand longer than necessary and gave him a direct look. 'It is good to see you, Leo. I am glad you are back.'

Suddenly Leo missed those days at Welbourne Manor when he and his brothers and sisters were free to laugh and play and enjoy life.

His brother crossed the threshold and stepped into the street. A moment later he was gone.

That afternoon Kellford called at the Covendale town house, as was expected of a betrothed gentleman. It would not be all tedium. He anticipated and rather relished another sparring match with his spirited heiress.

He'd driven his phaeton—Tilbury's latest design and the height of fashion, he was told. Having the best was important to him, even if he did not care a whit about horses or carriages.

Leaving his phaeton in the hands of his groom, Kellford knocked upon the town-house door. He was admitted by a footman and escorted to the drawing room where Mrs Covendale and her daughter were taking tea.

'Kellford, my dear boy, how good it is to see you,' Mrs Covendale chirped, extending her hands to him from the sofa where she sat, a piece of embroidery at her side.

'You look as lovely as ever, my good lady.' He leaned down to give her a kiss on the cheek, before turning to her daughter in a chair nearby. 'And you look quite fetching as well, Miss Covendale.'

The mother tittered. 'My gracious, you are to marry her, Kellford, you may call her Mariel.'

An honour Miss Covendale had not yet granted him. He smiled at her as if she'd not given him a slight. 'Only with your permission, my dear.'

Her face conveyed no emotion. 'Whatever pleases you, sir.'

He laughed inside. She had no idea what pleased him, but she would soon learn.

'Mariel it is, then.' He bowed to her.

'Please do be seated, Kellford.' Mrs Covendale patted the space next to her. 'Have a cup of tea with us and tell us whatever news you have heard in town.'

He sipped tea and regaled the mother with various bits of gossip he'd heard, thinking all the while that he would have preferred to marry into a titled family. Mariel, the mere granddaughter of a second son, was quite a bit below him, but she would have to do. Still, she was presentable, she was a challenge and, most of all, she would make him very rich.

He was fully cognisant of the fact that she did not want to marry him, but that did not trouble him overmuch, not with a fortune as large as she would provide. It had been a stroke of luck when her father confided in him about his money problems. That information gave him what he needed to discover the man's crime and win the hand of this heiress.

She would eventually learn how fortunate she was to be married to a baron, but for now he would enjoy the challenge of winning her over. He was confident he could do so.

When he took his last sip of tea, he placed his cup on the table and addressed his reluctant bride. 'Mariel, my dear, I brought my phaeton and would derive great pleasure in taking you for a turn in the park.'

It was the fashionable hour and he rather wanted to be seen with her, to show the *ton* he had won the heiress, to rub their noses in it.

She stared at him, with that impassive expression of hers, before answering, 'Very well. Give me a moment to change.'

A short time later they pulled into Hyde Park and found a space among the other fashionable carriages circulating the paths. With his liveried groom standing on the back footboard, Kellford trusted his equipage showed to good advantage.

He had to admit that Mariel looked equally impressive in her dark blue carriage dress.

He greeted everyone he saw and was gratified to receive their admiring glances.

Eventually the crush of carriages thinned and there were fewer people to impress.

'Shall we leave the park, my dear?' he asked, glancing over at her.

To his surprise she replied, 'Not yet. There is something I wish to discuss with you.'

'My pleasure.' His interest was roused.

Her face turned deadly serious and she lowered her voice. 'My father told me that you have in your possession a banknote that proves he improperly appropriated money from his cousin.'

Kellford lifted his brows. Her father had told her of the banknote? How foolish of him. The man should have kept his mouth shut.

She blinked. 'Well, do you have the paper or not?'

He smiled. 'I have it, never fear.'

She shifted in her seat. 'How do I know you are not bluffing?'

He simply stared at her.

She glanced away and back. 'How do I know this is not some elaborate ruse to force me into marriage and to get your hands on my inheritance? For all I know you may have merely heard some piece of gossip and embellished it.'

She dared to question him?

His smile stayed fixed. 'Trust me on it...' he paused '...or not. It is your father and your family who will pay the consequences if you are wrong.'

Her smile matched his own. 'Or it is *you* who pays the consequences if I am right. Can you hold off your creditors until you find another heiress to coerce?'

He gripped the ribbons and his face flushed with anger. 'What do you propose, then? You want proof that your father is nothing better than a common thief?'

'That is precisely what I want,' she shot back. 'I want to see this banknote you claim to possess. I want to hold it in my hands and convince myself it is genuine and not a forgery.'

'Forgery?' he huffed. 'It is your father who commits forgery, not I!'

Her gaze did not waver. 'No, your crimes are extortion and—and—other offences.'

He forgot about the horses and seized her arm. 'You impertinent chit! You will be sorry for this!'

A tiny flash of fear appeared in her eyes. It aroused him.

She straightened. 'Take your hand off me or I shall scream. Your groom might be trained to ignore me, but there are others near enough to hear.'

A quick glance behind him revealed other carriages approaching. He opened his hand, retrieved the ribbons, flicking them to signal the horses to increase their pace.

'Will you show me the paper, or shall I break our engagement?' she persisted.

He collected himself. 'Very well.' He put on an ingratiating smile. 'I will bring it to the ball tomorrow night.'

'No.'

She dared to disagree with him?

She explained, 'It is too public a place. If this paper is real, I will not have anyone else discovering its contents.'

He feigned solicitousness. 'Shall I bring it directly to your father's door, then?'

She shook her head. 'My mother must know nothing of this. A private place, I think.' She glanced around the park. 'There.' She pointed. 'That bench over there. Meet me there at seven tomorrow morning.'

'Seven tomorrow morning?' His voice rose.

She might as well have said to meet her at dawn. Was she fancying this to be some sort of duel?

'No one will be about at that hour and it is but a short walk for me from my house.'

'Very well.' He could not believe he was allowing her to dictate to him, but she had guessed one thing correctly. He could not afford to have her cry off. Mr Carter and the other money lenders would refuse him more time, high interest rate or not.

They reached the Cumberland gate. Kellford did not even ask her if she wanted another turn in the park. He was eager to be rid of her. He drove her to her house and escorted her to the door.

Before she went in, he seized her arm once again. 'I will see you in the morning.' He spoke it as a threat.

Once safe inside, Mariel leaned against the door, taking deep breaths to stop her shaking. She'd done it! She'd convinced Kellford to bring her the paper and, even more, she'd matched wits with the man again and won. It felt extremely gratifying.

Perhaps she could succeed in ridding herself of the man and his menace to her father after all.

Perhaps she could simply rip up the paper once he placed it in her hands. Leo and his valet did not have to risk being caught as thieves.

That would be a better plan, she thought, but there

was something more satisfying about working together with Leo, even with his valet and with Penny. She quite liked the camaraderie of it all.

Besides, she would feel secure knowing Leo and Mr Walker waited in the shrubbery, just in case Kellford turned menacing, as he had today. No, she would proceed with the original plan. She was no longer alone in this.

Mariel giggled with excitement. She'd even managed to point to the exact spot Leo had suggested for her to meet Kellford.

She pulled off her gloves and ran up the stairs, removing her hat as she entered her bedchamber. Penny was not there. She pulled the bell cord and undid the buttons of her spencer and sat at her writing table to compose a note.

Penny arrived as she was finishing it. 'You rang for me, miss?'

'I have the note for you to deliver to Mr Fitzmanning, Penny.'

The girl's eyes widened. 'You arranged a meeting with Lord Kellford?'

By now Penny had overheard enough so that Mariel had filled her in on almost all the details of her situation—except those of her father's crime.

And Mariel's past history with Leo.

'They must receive it today.' She folded the envelope and sealed it with a wafer. 'Because I am meeting Kellford in the morning.'

Penny took the note and placed it in her pocket. 'When shall I deliver it?'

'As soon as possible, I think,' Mariel responded. 'But help me dress for dinner first.'

As Mariel changed into a dress suitable for dinner,

she was glad that Penny knew as much as she did. It had been so lonely handling everything by herself.

One worry nagged at her. She might adhere to the plan, but would Leo? He did not like this plan. He might take matters into his own hands somehow. Could she truly count on him to work with her?

He'd failed her once before....

Chapter Eight

Penny rushed out of the servants' entrance and hurried to the line of hackney coaches on Oxford Street.

'Jermyn Street, please,' she told the jarvey.

His brows rose and she felt herself blush. Did he think she was bound for some tryst? He was wrong!

She climbed in the coach and leaned back against the seat.

Hers was an important errand, one that might mean life and death to her lady.

When Penny had been little and living with her parents above the glove shop in Chelsea, she could often hear through the wall when their neighbour, Mr Baker, beat his wife. One day Mrs Baker's cries abruptly stopped. Her husband had killed her!

That must not happen to Miss Covendale.

So it was very important to bring the note to Mr Fitzmanning.

Penny was not sure what to think of Mr Fitzmanning. He seemed like a very formidable man and always upset Miss Covendale so. Something very bad must have happened between them in the past. Penny wished she knew what it was, but that was wrong of her. It was not her place to be curious about her lady's private matters.

She did already know a great deal. It was a very great privilege to be taken into her lady's confidence like she was. It was a great honour to be trusted with the important task of delivering the note to Mr Fitzmanning.

Would she see his valet?

Probably not, because valets usually stayed near bed-chambers. Lady's maids did, too. Mr Covendale's valet was a fussy little man who didn't like her at all. He was nothing at all like Mr Walker.

Mr Walker's face scared her a little. Not because it was ugly, though, because it wasn't ugly. He did have some scars and a broken nose, but that wasn't why, either. She only knew that she felt funny inside when she looked at him.

He stared at her like Edward, the footman, stared at her, but for some reason, it did not feel bad when Mr Walker did it. Maybe it was because Mr Walker looked sad.

She gazed out the window and saw that they were on Bond Street, not far from Piccadilly. Too nervous to even think any more, she watched out the window, counting the shops they passed, holding her breath when they turned on to Piccadilly at Burlington House.

When the hack turned onto Jermyn Street and stopped, Penny climbed out and paid the jarvey the two shillings Miss Covendale had given her. As the hack drove away, she walked slowly down the street until she came to the right door. Taking a deep breath, she knocked.

Mr Walker opened the door. 'Miss Jenkins.'

She curtsied, although she thought maybe she should not have, because he was a valet. 'Miss Covendale sent me with a note. Is—is Mr Fitzmanning at home? I must give it to him.'

Mr Walker's surprised expression remained fixed on his face. 'He is not at home—'

'Oh, no!' What was she to do? 'I am supposed to give the note to him.'

The man froze for a moment, then collected himself. 'Please come in, Miss Jenkins.'

She entered into a small foyer that led directly to a sitting room. The room had nice chairs and sofas and tables—nicer than she'd grown up with—but it did not have any decorations, except a mantel clock.

'Do be seated.' Mr Walker extended his hand towards the sitting room.

She did not know if she should or not. 'Will Mr Fitzmanning return soon?'

'I do not know.' His face had that sad look again. 'You may wait for him if you wish.'

She nodded and sat in one of the chairs as if she were the gentleman's invited guest. She patted her pocket, reassuring herself that her precious note was still there. 'I did not expect you to open the door.'

His forehead creased. 'You did not?'

'Mr Covendale's valet would think it beneath him to open the door.'

He glanced away.

She feared she had injured his feelings. 'He is a very snooty man, though.'

He almost smiled and it made her heart skip beats. He stared at her as he had the day before and she fixed her gaze on her hands.

Just when she thought she would die from her discomfort, he asked, 'May I bring you some refreshment? Tea...or something?'

'Me?' She glanced up. 'Wouldn't Mr Fitzmanning think it improper?'

He laughed. 'Fitz would not care.'

'You call your gentleman Fitz? He's your employer!'

He shrugged. 'It is an unusual situation.'

She scrutinised him. 'Where are you from, Mr Walker? You do not talk like you look.'

He lowered his head. 'I owe that to Fitzmanning. He taught me to read and made me desire to improve myself in all ways.'

She did not know what to say to that. It was to his credit, surely.

He glanced away again and was silent. Penny examined the walls, as if there was something to see hung on them.

Finally Mr Walker spoke again. 'Is the note about a meeting with Kellford?'

She nodded. 'I must give it to Mr Fitzmanning today, because it says the meeting time is tomorrow morning.'

'Tomorrow morning?' His brows rose. 'Not much time.' He rubbed his chin, then quickly composed himself again as if the gesture had been too unseemly. 'You may leave the note with me, Miss Jenkins. I will make certain Fitz sees it.'

There was a knock on the door.

'Has he come?' She jumped to her feet.

Mr Walker rose more slowly. 'He would not knock.'

He crossed the room to the foyer and opened the door.

Penny heard a woman's voice say, 'Good day, Mr Walker. Is Leo at home? We have brought him something.' The woman did not wait for a reply but walked straight in, followed by a gentleman carrying two large, flat packages.

The woman—a very pretty lady—stopped suddenly when she spied Penny. Her brows rose.

Mr Walker closed the door. 'Mr Fitzmanning is not at home.'

The lady's eyes remained fixed on Penny. 'Oh?' She turned to Mr Walker. 'Do you remember me, Walker? I am Leo's sister, Mrs Milford.' She gestured to the gentleman toting the packages. 'Mr Milford.' She turned back to Penny. 'Who is this?'

Penny executed a quick curtsy. 'I am nobody, ma'am. Merely delivering a note from...someone.'

Walker approached. 'I was about to take the note from the miss, ma'am.'

Penny gave it to him and looked up into his eyes. 'You will see to it?'

'I will indeed.' His voice lowered just a bit and his eyes—very nice eyes, actually—were quite reassuring.

'Well.' Mrs Milford untied the string around the brown-paper wrapping. 'Let me leave these with you for my brother.'

The packages were about four feet wide and three feet high and Mr Milford rested one edge of them on the floor while his wife unwrapped them.

'Oh, they are paintings!' Penny exclaimed, then clamped her mouth shut.

Mr Milford smiled. 'My wife's paintings.'

The first one was of a grand house on a river. It was made of white stone that shimmered in sunlight. The second was a portrait of a man.

'It is Mr Fitzmanning!' Penny cried.

Mrs Milford did not seem to resent her outburst. 'I have long wished to give it to him.'

She removed the rest of the paper and her husband rested the paintings against the wall.

She gazed at them with an assessing eye, before turning to Mr Walker again. 'Would you please tell Leo how sorry we are to have missed him?'

'I will indeed, ma'am.' Mr Walker bowed.

'I must go.' Penny rushed to the door before she spoke out of turn again.

Mr Walker went after her and opened the door.

Before she walked out, she turned back to him. 'Thank you, Mr Walker,' she murmured.

He bowed slightly as if she were a lady. As if she were somebody important.

She curtsied in return and stepped out to the pavement. A carriage was outside, its driver holding the horses. Mr Milford's carriage, she supposed. A soft rain started to fall and she had forgotten to carry an umbrella. Surely her bonnet would be ruined and her dress would not be fit to wear to the servants' table for dinner.

She walked quickly to Piccadilly where she hoped to find a line of hackney coaches. A carriage stopped and blocked the way for her to cross the street.

Mrs Milford leaned out the carriage window. 'Miss Jenkins, may we take you to your destination?'

'Oh, no, ma'am,' Penny responded. 'I couldn't accept.'

'Of course you can,' the lady insisted.

She opened the door and Mr Milford extended his hand to assist her inside.

She did not know how to refuse. She climbed in and sat on the rear-facing seat.

'Where shall we drop you?' Mr Milford asked.

She thought before responding. 'Oxford Street.' It was better this lady did not know she was bound for Hereford Street.

Mr Milford leaned across her and opened the little window to tell the driver.

The carriage started and Mrs Milford looked at her so hard Penny squirmed in her seat.

'Your hair, your complexion, are lovely, Miss Jenkins. I wonder if you would allow me to paint you?' the lady asked.

Penny felt her cheeks burn. 'Oh, I could not do that, ma'am.'

She was relieved when the carriage reached Oxford Street. 'I can get out here.'

Penny ducked into a shop until their carriage drove out of sight.

The morning was thick with mist as Leo and Walker, dressed in workmen's clothes with masks at the ready, concealed themselves in the shrubbery near the spot where Mariel was to meet Kellford.

Leo still could not like placing her in this situation. Kellford was a dangerous man. He was bound to be angered by Mariel confronting him. If the man lashed out at her here, Leo and Walker would make short work of him, but what if Kellford saved his retaliation for a later time?

Mist crept through the trees, lending the scene an eerie quality which did nothing to allay Leo's foreboding. The day did not promise to be a fine one. Leo only hoped the rain would hold off until Mariel was back safe in her house.

A footfall sounded on the gravel path. Mariel appeared through the mist, wearing the same dark green hooded cape that she'd worn at Vauxhall. Her step was determined, her posture courageously erect. His heart swelled with pride for her.

Mariel had once been a daring little girl, the first to respond to a challenge or propose an adventure. Charlotte was her willing follower, Annalise more likely to impose good sense on the two of them. Even as a boy Leo had had a grudging respect for Mariel's pluck. Two years ago he'd fallen in love with it. Their courtship had been a daring adventure, as swathed in secrecy as Mariel was now swathed in her cloak.

She did not pace, merely stood still as a statue, waiting. The mist melted away from her skirts as if she'd willed it to disappear. Sunlight broke through the trees to illuminate her, standing strong and determined. Leo wanted to signal her that she was not alone, but if Kellford was near, he might hear.

The crunch of gravel signalled the man's approach. Mariel turned towards the sound, and, a moment later, Kellford appeared, swinging a walking stick.

'Mariel, my dear.' He spoke as if this was a friendly tryst.

'Sir,' Mariel replied curtly. 'Do you have the paper?'

Kellford laughed with apparent good humour. 'Come, come, my dear. Is that any way to greet your betrothed?'

Mariel's spine stiffened. 'No nonsense, if you please, Kellford. No one is here but you and I. There is no need to act out this farce. If you have the paper, show it to me. If you do not, I'll bid you goodbye and you may consider yourself a free man.'

Kellford's smile grew stony.

Leo glanced at Walker. Both men were poised to spring to Mariel's aid.

'I have the paper.' Kellford stepped closer to her. 'But what is your hurry?'

She stood her ground and Leo imagined her eyes flashing in anger. 'I dislike being in your presence, as you well know. And I do not relish spending a great deal of time alone in the park.'

He moved even closer, his walking stick tapping ominously on the ground. 'Now, now, my dear. You must become accustomed to my company. We will be together often after we are married. Allow me to show you how pleasant it will be.'

Leo's muscles tensed.

'Do not be tiresome, Kellford.' Mariel's voice was impatient. 'Show me the paper.'

'The paper...' He paused as if calculating his next move. 'My dear, you must believe that I am as eager to protect your father as you are. Otherwise I would do my duty and report his crime, would I not?'

'And lose the chance to gain my fortune?' Mariel folded her arms across her chest.

'Well, a favour such as mine towards your father cannot go unrewarded, can it?' He chuckled. 'Surely you see the logic in this.'

She tilted her head. 'Perhaps my suspicions were correct. You are simply bluffing. This paper is a mere figment of your imagination.'

His smile turned cold. 'Are you prepared to see your father hanged if you are wrong?'

She looked him directly in the eye. 'Are you prepared to lose my fortune?'

To Leo's amazement, Kellford backed away, laughing as if she'd said something very amusing.

Kellford stuck his stick under his arm and reached into a pocket inside his coat. 'When we are married, I shall have to teach you how to honour and obey.' He drew out a folded paper.

Mariel reached for it.

'No, no.' Kellford wagged a finger. 'Not so fast, my dear. Let me unfold it.'

He unfolded it and gazed at it himself before turning it towards Mariel.

Again she reached for it.

He snatched it away. 'You may read and not touch.'

'I wish to hold it in my own hands to examine it,' she insisted.

'Why?' His voice turned hard. 'So you can rip it up? Now who is being tiresome?' His smile vanished. 'Come closer and examine it. You may even touch it with one finger, if you must.'

She did as he said, bringing her eyes close to the paper.

Kellford went on, 'You will see, of course, that it is a bank draft signed over to your father. You will also see that it appears to be signed by his wealthy cousin. The signature is only an approximation of Doring's signature, as is very evident when compared to other documents he has signed.'

She examined the paper in an unhurried manner. Leo admired her steadfastness. Surely it must be unnerving to peruse the object of her father's ruin, but she gave no sign of it. If her hands came too close to the document, Kellford moved it away. If she had indeed planned to rip it up, he gave her no opportunity.

'Are you satisfied now, my dear?' Kellford changed his tone to a patient one.

She straightened, facing him with a direct look. 'We are done here, Kellford.'

Without another word she turned and walked quickly away. Kellford leaned on his stick, watching her with an amused expression. Leo glanced at Walker to ensure his readiness. Simultaneously they donned their masks.

Kellford let out an exultant laugh as he refolded the paper and put it back into his pocket. As if he had not a care in the world, he strolled on to the path leading out of the park, jubilantly swinging his walking stick.

Leo and Walker had already scouted the area, finding the best place to make their move. From the shelter of the shrubbery they beat a parallel course to the appointed spot, reaching it ahead of Kellford. He made it easy for them to anticipate his approach by whistling as he walked.

As he took a step past them, Leo sprang from the bushes and seized him from behind, pulling his upper arms behind his back so tightly he could not move them. Walker jumped in front of Kellford, snatching the walking stick out of his hand and tossing it aside.

'See here!' Kellford cried, but Walker stuffed a handkerchief in the man's mouth, muffling further sounds.

In a swift economy of movement, Walker emptied the contents of Kellford's pockets, finding his coin purse and, of course, the incriminating paper. Just as swiftly, Walker placed them in his own pockets. Last of all he ripped Kellford's watch fob from its chain, the timepiece with it.

While Leo continued to hold Kellford tight, Walker produced a cord with which he quickly tied Kellford's feet. Leo forced Kellford's hands together and Walker bound them with another cord.

Then they fled, hearing Kellford's enraged but muffled cries behind them as they ran.

The entire attack, made to appear like an ordinary robbery, took less than two minutes.

As soon as they were out of Kellford's sight, they removed their masks and stuffed them in their pockets. Their escape took a zigzag route, eventually re-entering the park and crossing it to exit at Hyde Park corner. From there it was a short walk back to Leo's rooms.

On their way they passed a one-armed, one-legged beggar in a tattered soldier's uniform. He held out his hat and pleaded, 'A ha'penny for a poor old soldier. Surely you gentlemen can spare a ha'penny.'

Leo grinned at Walker. 'Surely we can spare *something* for an old soldier.'

Walker threw Kellford's coin purse, his watch and fob into the beggar's hat.

Leo leaned down to the man and said, 'Take care in fencing the watch.'

Leo and Walker quickly walked away, hearing the beggar's astonished cry as they turned the corner.

Chapter Nine

After Mariel rushed away from Kellford, Penny helped her sneak back into the town house.

'Your parents are still sleeping,' Penny whispered as they climbed the stairs to Mariel's bedchamber.

As soon as they closed the door, Penny asked, 'What happened, miss? Did he meet you? Did he bring the paper?'

Mariel nodded, breathless more from belated nerves than from running back to her house. 'He showed me the paper.'

Penny clapped her hands. 'And did Mr Fitzmanning and Mr Walker steal it from him?'

Mariel pulled off her gloves and her hat. Penny skipped forwards and took them from her.

Mariel wrapped her arms around herself, trying to quiet her skittering heart. 'I do not know. I did not see any sign of them and I left the area quickly.'

She'd stood as quietly as possible at the meeting place, hoping Leo would somehow let her know he was near, but she heard nothing, saw nothing. Not knowing for certain that they were there was the hardest part.

She'd started wondering if they'd come to their senses and decided it was foolish to risk their necks.

Surely Leo would not have allowed her to be alone in the park with a man who relished hurting women, but a single sound, a whisper, a whistle, anything would have reassured her.

'How will Mr Fitzmanning tell you he stole the paper? Is he to meet you somewhere?' Penny apparently did not question whether he had come.

But she was still young, much younger than Mariel had been when her ill-fated romance with Leo took place—and ended with so much pain.

How could Mariel believe in any man after Leo had abandoned her, her father had lied to her—so many times she'd lost count—and Kellford wished to exploit her? She hoped she was finished with Kellford.

She wanted desperately to believe in Leo this time, to believe he'd done as they'd planned together.

He'd once broken the most important promise he'd made to her. He had said he would marry her, but had so easily believed her father's lies. She did not know if she could ever trust again after that.

She swallowed the pain. 'I do not know when I will see him.'

'Should I deliver another note to him?' Penny placed Mariel's hat in its box.

Mariel ought not impose on Penny again, merely to appease her anxieties. 'No, we must believe he will contact me.'

How long would she have before she knew for certain what he'd done, before she knew for certain that he had not abandoned her again?

What would she do if Leo had not risen early and come to the park to act like a common thief? She'd played the best card she'd had, but success all depended upon Leo. Nothing was left but to simply refuse to marry Kellford and to hope he did not report her father's crime.

She pursed her lips. Likely he would derive pleasure from seeing her father hang and seeing the lives of her mother and sisters ruined.

To think her sisters were at the country house, blithely under the care of their governess, a dear woman whom her father probably neglected to pay. Her sisters were like she had once been. Carefree. Happy. Anticipating one excitement after another. Augusta would probably be chattering on about her come-out, hoping it would take place next year, although it would probably be delayed until she was eighteen, or never happen unless Mariel gained access to her inheritance. Isabel was probably thinking of little else but her horses, too expensive to keep if they were plunged into poverty. Poor Isabel. She was as horse-mad as Leo had been—

Must her mind always wander back to Leo?

She lowered herself into a chair and looked up at Penny. 'We will wait for him.'

That was exactly what she'd told herself to do two years ago. Wait for him.

Mariel was too restless to stay at home all day, simply waiting. After she had breakfasted with her mother and father as if she'd just risen from bed, she took Penny out to the shops.

They did more walking than shopping. Mariel treated Penny to an ice at Gunter's Tea Shop, to make up for dragging her up and down Old Bond Street.

When they returned from the shops later in the afternoon, Mariel had no choice but to sit with her mother and receive callers. Several of her mother's friends visited, asking countless questions about Mariel's wedding preparations and gossiping incessantly, especially about that scandalous Leo Fitzmanning who had attended the Ashworth ball the other night.

There was another ball this night at Lord and Lady Sendale's, a society entertainment promising to be more lavish, more fashionable than all that had come before. Mariel had not been looking forward to it.

At least not until Kellford sent a note to say he was unable to escort her. This had not happened before. Her first thought was that something had happened to Leo. Was it possible that Kellford had thwarted him? Or was Kellford's note a sign that Leo and Walker had succeeded? How would she find out?

Her heart suddenly beat in excitement. The ball! That was where Leo intended to contact her. At the ball.

When Penny helped dress her for the ball, Mariel found herself taking more care in her appearance than usual, choosing her prettiest white-silk gown, one Penny had altered to show off Mariel's bare shoulders as was the latest fashion. For a belt she tied a long scarf bordered in deep scarlet flowers. Its fringed ends nearly reached her hemline. Her headdress was also deep scarlet and adorned with one curling white feather.

When the ensemble was complete, both Mariel and Penny stepped back to examine it in the full-length mirror.

'You have outdone yourself, Penny,' Mariel said. 'I cannot think I've ever looked so well.'

'No credit to me, miss,' Penny responded, although she stood like an artist surveying her work. 'You chose the gown and the smaller articles of dress.'

'I felt like fussing a bit tonight.' Mariel smiled at her. 'You see, Lord Kellford is not attending. I do not mind looking my best.'

Penny's eyes grew large. 'He is not attending the ball? Do you suppose Mr Fitzmanning and Mr Walker gave him a black eye or some such thing?'

Mariel grinned. 'We can only wish.'

Penny nodded with surety. 'We will find out when Mr Fitzmanning contacts you.'

Mariel examined her image again, fussing with the belt and smoothing the skirt. It had been a long time since she had really cared about how she looked.

Since Leo had left her, she realised with sudden surprise.

When she and her parents arrived at the ball, Mariel's father lost no time in retiring to the card room. Mariel remained at her mother's side as her mother promenaded around the ballroom, greeting friends as if she'd not seen them in a millennium, although some had been her callers that very day.

Mariel engaged in the required social niceties, but mostly she anxiously scanned the room for one tall gentleman with dark, unruly hair and changeable hazel eyes.

Her mother interrupted this quest by insisting she tell one of her bosom beaux all about the wedding plans, as if she had any real plans. A church ceremony. A wedding breakfast. She cared about none of it.

The butler's voice rang out, 'The Duke of Manning and Mr Leo Fitzmanning.'

Mariel swivelled around, her heart pounding like a schoolgirl with her first infatuation.

His black formal coat and trousers contrasted with

the brilliant white of his neckcloth. While other men embraced the nipped-in waist and puffed-out coat sleeves that were the fashion, Leo's coat had an understated cut that somehow made him stand out from the others.

After he and his brother greeted the host and hostess, Leo turned and, as if he'd known exactly where to find her, their eyes met and the ghost of a smile appeared on his face.

Her heart leaped and her spirits soared to the ceiling. He'd succeeded! He was safe. She was free. She felt like running to him and throwing her arms around him. What gossip that would generate!

Slowly his gaze slipped away, reluctantly, she thought. She dampened the enthusiasm bursting inside her and watched him melt into the crush of guests. It did not matter that she lost sight of him. She knew he would seek her out again.

The moment brought back the days of their secret courtship—meeting without anyone knowing, dancing together without anyone guessing the emotions that blossomed between them. She almost felt as if those exciting, breathless days had returned.

Mariel heard a laugh she recognised as Charlotte's. A scan of the room located her one-time best friend on the other side of the ballroom.

She touched her mother's arm. 'Mama, I see Charlotte. Would you mind terribly if I went and spoke to her?'

Her mother waved her away. 'Amuse yourself as best you can without dear Kellford here.'

Mariel would be delighted to amuse herself forever without *dear* Kellford.

She wended her way through the crowd while the musicians tuned their instruments, the notes blending with the discordant buzz of conversation. She heard Wellington's name mentioned several times, but then he was the new Prime Minister and everyone delighted in speculating upon whether he would succeed or fail in his endeavours. Ireland was spoken of, as well. So much discord in Ireland; Mariel hated to think about it, tonight of all nights, when she was determined to be happy.

Finally she neared Charlotte, whose eyes lit up at the sight of her and who walked towards her with arms outstretched.

'Mariel!' Charlotte exclaimed. 'How lovely to see you.'

They clasped hands.

'It has only been a few days, hasn't it?' Mariel smiled.

Charlotte laughed and the sound lifted above all the other din. 'At Vauxhall! I am so happy to see you this evening.' She tensed and suspiciously searched the room. 'Where is Kellford?'

Mariel tried not to display her disgust of the man. 'Not attending tonight.'

Charlotte relaxed noticeably. 'Well, come join us. You may be part of our party tonight, if you like.'

'I would enjoy that above all things.' Especially if the party included Leo.

Charlotte took her arm, and together they walked to a group of more familiar faces.

'Mariel!' Charlotte's husband Drew kissed her on her cheek and turned to the gentleman standing at his side. 'Say hello to Amesby.'

Amesby squeezed her hand. 'How are you, Mariel?'

Amesby had been one of Leo's old friends, another horse-mad fellow.

His wife Mary stepped forwards. 'May I also say hello?'

'Mary!' Mariel was genuinely happy to see them all. 'My goodness, I feel as if we are at one of Welbourne Manor's house parties.'

Charlotte fanned herself. 'Except we would have more space in the manor's ballroom.'

Drew put his arm around his wife. 'We should plan a party there.'

Charlotte grinned. 'Yes! And get Nicholas to pay for it.'

As the group chatted together, Mariel searched for Leo again, glimpsing him at his brother's side. Everyone wished to talk to a duke. It took an age for them to work their way to her side of the room. She kept track of their progress.

'Nick! Leo!' Charlotte called to them as soon as they were close enough.

Leo walked directly over. Nicholas was detained.

Charlotte took Leo's arm and he leaned down to give her a kiss on the cheek. Mariel well remembered how his lips felt against her skin. She touched her cheek in memory.

'Look at us!' Charlotte exclaimed to him. 'We just said this might be a house party at Welbourne Manor.'

Leo's gaze lingered a moment longer on Mariel than on the others. 'Indeed. Good to see all of you.' He shook hands with Drew and Amesby.

Amesby's handshake was enthusiastic. 'It has been an age, Leo. It is a happy thing to see you back among us. I'd relish an opportunity to make up lost ground.'

'We must do so,' Leo replied.

He greeted Mary and, finally, Mariel.

'Good to see you again, Mariel.' His tone hinted at nothing.

'Leo,' Mariel managed, not quite erasing the expectation in her voice.

The orchestra quieted and the first dance, a quadrille, was announced, to be led by the host and hostess.

Amesby turned to his wife, a loving look on his face. 'Shall we dance, Mary?'

Her smile was his response. He took her hand and led her to the dance floor.

Drew turned to Charlotte. 'Shall we join them?'

Charlotte glanced uncertainly at Mariel. 'Are you engaged for this dance, Mariel? I cannot just leave you.'

'Of course you can!' Mariel shooed her off, but Charlotte was reluctant to go.

Leo stepped forwards. 'I will keep Mariel company.'

Charlotte and Drew hurried to join Mary and Amesby.

Mariel turned to Leo, knowing her complexion was bright. She told herself her anticipation had only to do with the banknote. 'Did you get it?'

Leo grinned. 'We did. It went without a hitch.'

She felt dizzy. 'I want to hear all the details. And we have to plan a way for you to give it to me. And I must have a safe place for it, as well—'

Leo took her hand. 'Time enough for that later. Will you dance with me?'

Mariel was ready to dance for joy—with Leo.

He closed his fingers around hers and led her to the gathering dancers, joining three other couples looking for a fourth. The other couples were as young as she and Leo had been when they'd fallen in love. The young people exchanged dismayed glances.

Leo laughed. 'Do not fear. We shall keep up.'

The music started and the figures were called. Mariel and Leo danced as if they, too, were young and full of gaiety. Twirling, skipping, performing the figures with as much enthusiasm as their younger partners.

They spoke little. What could they say where others could overhear? It did not matter. Mariel was almost too happy to speak. Leo had rescued her. She'd thought she was doomed to marry Kellford, but she was free! Leo had set her free.

They came together for a moment, and Leo asked, 'Where is Kellford?'

The dance parted them for a moment, before she could answer. 'He begged off. He did not say why. I wondered if he had become ill…or something.'

They parted again.

When they joined hands, Leo answered, his voice a monotone. 'He was well enough last I saw him.'

Mariel understood. They'd not injured him.

When Leo came close again, his eyes smiled. 'Of course, he was a bit tied up at the time.'

She laughed and put even more energy into the dance. At its end she was out of breath.

'Shall I get you something to drink?' Leo asked.

'Please.' It felt marvellous to be on easy terms with him.

He walked her back to Charlotte, who seemed to take no special notice of her dancing with Leo.

His brother joined them and greeted Mariel warmly. 'You look lovely tonight, Mariel.'

She flushed with the compliment. 'Thank you, Your Grace.'

He made a face. 'I remember pulling your pigtails. It feels silly for you to call me your Grace. Nicholas will do.'

The Fitzmanning Miscellany, as others called them, always made her feel as if she were one of them, an honour few experienced. When Leo left for the Continent, she let herself grow distant from them, rarely seeing even Charlotte, who'd been her very best friend. The reminders of Leo had been too painful. Now being among them again felt like being with family, a feeling she did not have when she was with her own parents.

She could not be more content.

Leo handed Mariel a glass of champagne and sipped one for himself. A moment later Brenner and Justine joined them, along with Mary and Amesby. The Miscellany and their friends were together again, all except Annalise and her husband Ned, but they rarely attended functions like this.

It seemed wholly familiar to Leo to be with them all again, talking and laughing. Mariel's presence reminded him of earlier days, when he and she would pass each other secret glances across ballroom floors and eventually contrive to be alone.

Other guests were tossing less-than-approving looks at them, and more than once Leo heard the word *miscellany* spoken. This, too, was familiar. He knew how these conversations went. *Scandalous family,* someone would say. Another would gesture his way. *The bastard son.*

Not the duke. Not the duke's brother. Not the earl. *The bastard son.* Soon the whispers would be about all the scandalous things he was said to have done. His flight to the Continent merely fuelled what they wished to believe of a bastard—the worst.

They did not know the worst, however. They did not know how many times Leo had been tested in the last two years, how much violence he'd been engaged in, how hard he'd fought to stand on his own and succeed.

He was no longer a mere member of the Fitzmanning

Miscellany, no longer merely the bastard son. He had changed. He was separate from this privileged ballroom set. He was his own man.

But he danced and talked with the others as if time had not altered a thing. He watched Mariel smile and laugh, the cares lifted off her shoulders. She looked as if she were in her element. At ease with all these people who scorned him.

He had danced only one dance with her. Society dictated no more than two dances with the same partner. Break that rule and tongues would wag. In the past she'd always insisted they behave with utmost propriety. She had always been careful not to blemish her family name. In private, though, they'd shared many kisses, many embraces.

Today Leo cared nothing about what these toplofty people would think of him, but he'd play their game for Mariel's sake.

And he'd have his second dance with her. He'd make certain it was a waltz.

Eventually the two of them were left standing alone while the others had paired up for a mazurka, a new, fast, Russian dance brought to England by the Duke of Devonshire.

Leo seized the opportunity. 'Would you like to get some air?' he asked her.

The ballroom was stifling. No one would look askance if he escorted her to the open doors leading to the veranda, an unusual feature in a Mayfair town house.

Her gaze lifted to his. 'I would like that.'

She took Leo's arm and he led her through the open doors. Once they would have contrived to find the darkest spot in the garden where Leo could hold her in his arms and kiss her beautiful lips. This time he led her to a place on the veranda out of earshot of the other strolling couples.

'We can speak freely here,' he said.

She grasped his arm. 'Tell me what happened? I am perishing from curiosity.'

Her touch inflamed him, but he remained controlled. 'We trailed him until we had the opportunity to seize him and steal the paper.'

'Did he see who you were?'

He shook his head. 'We were disguised and masked. We didn't speak. There was no way he could identify us. The whole business was over in an instant.'

She released a pent-up breath. 'I do not know how I can ever thank you, Leo. It was a brave and foolhardy thing to do.'

This was more foolhardy.

The night breeze loosened a lock of her hair. He reached over and brushed the wayward curl off her forehead. 'I owed you that…and more.'

Looking into her eyes was like diving into a warm, sensuous pool, plunging deeper and deeper to the yearning in his soul. His hands slid to her arms, holding her in place, not an embrace, but tethering himself to her. She licked her lips and his grip tightened, bringing her inches closer, so close he could feel her breath on his face.

She sighed. 'I am so grateful to you.'

His fingers tightened around her arms.

'So grateful,' she repeated.

He wished time could be erased, that two years could vanish, that all he had done in that time period would not stand like a wall between them. All he wanted now was to take possession of her lips, to taste her sweetness once again.

'Mariel,' he murmured.

She rose on tiptoe.

Slowly, as if desire alone controlled him, he bowed his head and touched his lips to hers. Sheer will restrained him lest the violence of his emotions erupt, the grief for all the kisses lost in two years. She quivered in his grasp and wound her arms around his neck, pressing her lips to his with a hunger that matched his own.

With a low moan, he responded, parting her lips, tasting her tongue, pressing against her.

His entire body was afire, like the gas lamps in the trees at Vauxhall. Before, he'd been in darkness; now all was light. They were again among the stars.

Laughter sounded nearby. Another couple ascended the steps from the garden to the veranda and would soon pass near them.

He pulled away, his body still throbbing for her. They moved even deeper into the shadows.

'Forgive me for that.' He still held her arm.

'Forgive you?' her voice was breathless.

'So much has changed,' he managed to say. 'I should not have done that.'

A line creased her forehead. 'Why did you, then?'

Why? Because it had been impossible to resist her. 'I was caught up in…remembering.' The ache of still wanting her pierced his insides.

'Has so much changed?' she whispered.

'I have changed.' He'd turned away from everything that was familiar to her and entered a world of which she could not be part. 'I am not the same man. I've… I've lived a very different life these last two years and I cannot go back to what once was.'

'I see.' All expression fled her face. 'Well. I should be glad, then, that you thought to come to my aid.' Her tone was biting. 'We must plan a time for you to give me the paper, though.' She pulled away from his grasp. 'After that your job will be done.'

He set his jaw, detesting the loss of camaraderie between them and battling a need to possess her lips once more.

'I do not wish to meet in the park again,' she went on. Was she afraid to be alone with him, afraid of another moment like this one? 'Meet me at Hatchards Bookshop at eleven o'clock tomorrow. I will be browsing through the novels.'

'Hatchards at eleven,' he repeated.

'And take me back to my mother, please.'

He nodded. It was for the best he not mislead her. The life he had chosen, exciting to him, would certainly be censured by her world. He might be willing to take risks to achieve what he wanted, but he refused to place her in any more jeopardy.

He still wanted her, though.

But it was too late.

Lord Kellford stepped out from where he'd concealed himself near the door and watched Mariel and Fitzmanning leave the veranda.

He had decided to attend the ball after all. No sooner had he arrived than he'd seen Mariel walking through the doors to the veranda with Fitzmanning. He'd followed them, but was unable to move close enough to make out more than a word or two of what they said to each other, not enough to glean what had transpired between them.

Was the chit cuckolding him with the likes of

Fitzmanning? A mere bastard son? She'd soon regret it if she were. He'd be no man's laughingstock.

Then the word *paper* had wafted over the wind and it all became clear.

The chit had humbugged him.

Kellford could see it all in his mind's eye. She'd convinced Fitzmanning to steal the paper, Kellford was certain of it. *That* was why she contrived the meeting in the park. Everyone knew she was a great friend of the Fitzmanning Miscellany; she'd chosen its most disreputable member to do her dirty work. One of his brothers had probably been the cohort.

Fitzmanning. The bloody prig. Sticking up his nose about a mere frisk with a serving girl, as if anyone cared a whit about what happened to a tavern maid. Fitzmanning had taken a dislike to him ever since that time. A tavern maid, for devil's sake! Where did that compare to the robbery of a peer? The man's hypocrisy was not to be outdone.

Nor was Mariel's deceit. One thing was certain. She would not be allowed any contact with the Fitzmannings after the wedding.

And he would show her what happened to chits who aspired to outwit him. She thought she could stop this wedding? Deprive him of his fortune? Let her try.

She did not know the lengths he was willing to go to ensure she would never dare to thwart him again.

Kellford glanced through the doorway. Making certain no one saw him, he made his way to the hall, collected his hat from the footman and departed.

Chapter Ten

Near the time the ball would end, a waltz was announced. Leo crossed the ballroom to where Mariel sat at her mother's side.

He extended his hand to her. 'This dance, Miss Covendale?'

Her mother waved her on. 'Oh, do dance, Mariel. Try to have some enjoyment even though dear Kellford is not here.'

Mariel flashed him a wounded look, increasing his guilt for kissing her.

But he could not resist dancing with her one more time, sharing again with her that unspoken passion, that undeniable and impossible kinship between them.

They joined the circle of dancers. He bowed to her curtsy and placed his hands at her waist. She hesitated before resting her hands on his shoulders. As at Vauxhall they twirled through the dance, the circle turning like a colourful wheel on its axle.

His gaze remained steadily on her, but it took several turns around the ballroom before she met his eye. So many emotions were visible in her ginger eyes. Anger.

Confusion. Wariness. Need. He ought to be ashamed at himself for putting her through such discomfort.

One last time.

In many ways he had become the man he'd thought she had rejected, but it had freed him to become a man he could respect. They could not find their way back to each other.

When the dance was over they stood a moment longer, still caught in each other's eyes. It was Leo who moved his hands first. Mariel blinked rapidly before dropping hers off his shoulders. He walked her back to her mother and bowed. They'd not spoken a word the whole time.

After one more dance, which Leo sat out, the ball was over. A few moments later he was out on the pavement, waiting for the Duke of Manning's carriage, still several carriages behind in the queue. The cool evening air was welcome. Leo needed cooling off after his waltz with Mariel.

He still felt the light pressure of her fingers on his shoulders, still saw the struggle of emotion in her eyes. She was not unaffected by him. Her response to his kiss proved that. He could seduce her, he supposed, if he wished it, but seduction would be unconscionable. One thing was certain: he needed to keep control of himself whenever near her.

Like tomorrow at Hatchards.

While his brother engaged in conversation with other gentlemen, Leo paced the pavement, thinking of Mariel.

She'd fallen in love with a man who wanted to raise horses on his family estate and rear his children in his family home. Now he'd cast off the chains that bound him to the past and carved out his own future through daring and risky investment. The riskier the better.

He mixed with tradesmen who were little more than smugglers. He befriended men who defied government barriers to find ways to increase a profit. Many of his dealings were clandestine. This was not a life for her.

In only two years she would be wealthy and would be able to assume control of her life. He did not wish to jeopardise that for her, not when independence was what he most wanted for his own life.

His brother walked up to him and placed a hand on his shoulder. 'What troubles you, Leo?'

Nicholas gazed at him with intense concern. Would his brother never stop being protective?

'Nothing troubles me,' he responded. 'Why do you ask?'

'You were pacing.' Nicholas leaned forwards for emphasis. 'What happened at the ball? Your whole demeanour changed. At the beginning you seemed almost happy. Then something changed.'

Had Leo been that transparent? He must be more careful.

'I merely grew bored,' he lied.

Nicholas did not look reassured.

Their carriage arrived and both climbed in.

Leo took advantage of the distraction. 'You were in demand tonight. What was of such importance that everyone needed to speak to *the duke* about it?'

Nicholas hesitated a moment before answering, as if he knew Leo was merely changing the subject. 'There is a great controversy afoot. Ireland's in an uproar with riots and other discord. Wellington favours concessions to the Irish and Lords is divided on whether to grant the concessions or to oppose anything to do with Catholic Emancipation.'

Leo well understood why the Irish would despise another country controlling them.

He asked Nicholas more questions about the matter. They managed to travel the entire distance without his brother turning the topic back to Leo's behaviour at the ball.

The next morning after breakfast Mariel dressed to go out, but this time a plain brown walking dress would do, one she'd worn countless times. She had Penny merely pin up her hair and cover it with a lace cap. A simple bonnet would go over the cap.

Leo's kiss had unsettled her. Or rather her response to it had done so. It was so clear that she remained as vulnerable to him as ever. It had been devastating to her when he pulled away and apologised for it, calling it a mistake.

For a brief moment it had seemed like two years had vanished, but she'd misread him. He no longer wanted her.

She steeled herself. She'd survived the two years without Leo; she could survive another two years, inherit her money and be free of any man's influence.

That was her plan. No more kisses. No more giddy schoolgirl infatuation. No more pretending happiness lay in partnership with a man, or comfort in a man's arms.

Even if those arms were Leo's.

There was a knock at her bedchamber door. 'A caller, miss,' Edward, the footman, announced from the hallway.

A caller? So early? 'Who is it, Edward?'

'Lord Kellford.'

Mariel exchanged an alarmed glance with Penny.

'What shall I tell him, miss?' Edward asked through the door.

'Tell him... Tell him to wait in the drawing room. I'll be down directly.' She listened to the footman's footsteps recede before speaking to Penny. 'Wait for me in the hall, Penny. I will try to dispatch him quickly and still make the appointment with Mr Fitzmanning.'

Penny nodded.

Mariel's parents were still abed, which was fortunate. She preferred they not walk in on her hopefully short conversation with Kellford. What could he possibly want? She'd thought he'd simply disappear.

The two women descended the stairs and Mariel strode straight to the drawing room.

Kellford swung around when she entered.

She closed the door behind her. 'What reason do you have, sir, to call upon me at this early hour?' It was half-past ten.

He sauntered towards her, a grin on his face. 'Good morning, my dear.'

'You must know I am not pleased to see you, Kellford. Did you come to explain why you begged off from the ball last night?'

He advanced on her and drew a finger down the length of her arm. 'Did you miss me?' He held his lips close to her ear.

Involuntarily she inhaled his cologne, the scent sickening her. She stepped back. 'You know I did not.'

His eyes flicked over her, the smile still fixed on his face.

She shivered. 'I thought you would insist upon taking me to the ball. To gloat.'

The smile faltered, but he soon recovered it. 'Do not

take me for a fool, Mariel, *my dear.* I know what you did. What you had Fitzmanning do for you.'

A stab of fear shot through her. 'I am certain I do not know what you mean. Are you talking about Charlotte Bassington's brother?' Was he guessing or did he know?

He laughed. 'Did you think I would not remember she was your friend? Although I do not think her a very proper friend for the wife of a baron.'

'You cannot control whom I choose to make my friends.' Where was this leading?

He suddenly came so close she could see where his razor had cut his chin. 'A wife must honour and obey.'

She pushed against his chest. 'Stay a proper distance, sir!'

He grinned again and moved only a step away. 'I am all that is proper, my dear.'

She crossed her arms over her chest. 'And you are tiresome, as well. With your hints and threats.'

He lifted his hands in mock surprise. 'My hints?'

'You obviously wish me to beg you to tell what Fitzmanning is supposed to have done for me. Or do you just wish to contrive a way to threaten to spoil my friendship with Charlotte?' She tossed her head. 'I would simply prefer you leave.'

Instead he seized her and pulled her closer.

'Let me go or I shall scream for a footman!' His grip hurt.

'You will not.' He pressed his body against hers as Leo had done the previous night, but the sensations were so different. 'What did you promise Fitzmanning as payment? Money? A kiss?'

He placed his lips on hers with a violence that spoke nothing of love. She feared she would retch.

She tried to twist away, but his fingers were like a

vise. She struggled against him and managed to bring her leg down hard on his foot.

'You cursed wench!' He released her and staggered backwards.

'Do not touch me again.' She backed towards the door. 'I do not know what you are talking about. Payment? For what?'

He advanced on her again, but remained an arm's length away. 'Did you think I would not discover who stole the paper for you?'

Her insides churned. He could not know it had been Leo. He and Walker were masked, Leo had said.

'What paper?' she stalled.

'Idiot!' he snarled. 'The forged banknote.'

She made herself laugh. 'You are trying to make me believe you no longer have the paper? Why would you say such a thing? Surely you know I would be delighted if that were true…'

On the other side of the drawing-room door, Penny stood with her ear pressed against the wood. From the sounds inside the room, she thought Lord Kellford had attacked Miss Covendale in some way.

But then *he* cried out and her voice became stronger. Even if he was not hurting her any more, this was still very, very bad. Kellford knew Mr Fitzmanning had stolen the paper!

Penny felt she must do something. She could not open the door, Miss Covendale would not like that, but she also could not stand by and let that horrible man hurt her lady again. She must do *something*.

Penny ran back to the hall. 'Edward! Edward! Are you here?' He was supposed to be attending the door.

He emerged from the dining room. He had probably pilfered a piece of ham. 'What is it?'

'Come with me.' She dragged him by the arm to the door of the drawing room. 'You stand here and if you hear something that sounds like Miss Covendale is… is hurt or…or frightened, you open the door and help her. Do you understand?'

He looked baffled. 'But she is in there with Lord Kellford.'

'I know.' Penny tapped her foot impatiently. 'But do it just the same. If she comes out and asks for me, tell her I've gone to Hatchards.'

'To Hatchards?' His brows rose. 'The bookshop?'

She slammed her bonnet on her head. 'Yes. She will understand. Just do as I say, will you, Edward?'

'If you like,' he mumbled. 'Seems rummish to me, though.'

'Just do it.' She hurried back to the hall.

Penny departed through the front door because it was faster than the servants' entrance. As soon as she reached the pavement, she lifted her skirts and ran, stopping only for carriages and horses to pass so she could cross Oxford Street.

She ran to the hack stand and yelled up at the first jarvey. 'Take me to Hatchards and hurry.'

The jarvey chuckled. 'First time anyone wanted me to hurry to a bookshop.'

Once inside the coach, she stuck her hand in her pocket and breathed a sigh of relief. She had two shillings for the fare.

The mile-and-a-half ride seemed much too long. When the coach finally stopped in front of the bookshop's bowed windows, Penny jumped out and handed the driver his fare.

Standing in front of the shop's door, she took a deep breath and smoothed her skirt before walking in. The clerk behind the counter eyed her suspiciously. He had probably worked out she did not shop in Hatchards very often.

She wandered around the shop until she saw Mr Fitzmanning gazing into one of the books.

She hurried up to him. 'Mr Fitzmanning, sir!'

He looked up. 'Penny, isn't it? Where is Miss Covendale?'

'Oh, sir, she could not come, because Lord Kellford came to call and I heard them arguing and I heard him say he knew you sto—' She stopped and lowered her voice to a whisper. 'He knew you stole the paper.'

'He could not!' He stiffened.

'I heard him say so…and…and I heard him do something to Miss Covendale. I think he hurt her.' She tried to talk quietly, but her voice kept rising on its own.

'Hurt her?' His eyes flashed.

'Well, she hurt him, too, I think,' Penny went on. 'He cried out awful bad. But I thought you should know right away, because she could not come to this meeting.'

He took her by the arm. 'I'm going to her.'

'Oh, no, sir, I do not think you ought—' But she could not finish because he rushed her out of the shop, to the surprised stares of the other shoppers—including Mr Fitzmanning's sister, Mrs Milford.

Leo had difficulty tolerating the slow pace of the hackney coach. When it reached Hereford Street, he opened the door and climbed out before the vehicle fully came to a stop. After helping Mariel's maid from the coach, he dropped several coins in the jarvey's hand.

If Kellford had hurt her, he'd kill the man and his

conscience would not bother him any more than the first time, the only time, he'd taken a life.

'I'll not knock,' he said to the maid. 'You admit me.'

She reached the door and opened it. He followed her inside.

A footman stood in the hall. 'There you are, Penny.' He gaped at Leo. 'What is this?'

'Never mind, Edward.' Penny waved an impatient hand at him. 'Why are you not standing at the drawing-room door?'

'His lordship left a few minutes ago,' Edward said defensively.

'Where is Miss Covendale?' Leo demanded.

The footman's eyes grew wide. 'In the drawing room.'

Leo rushed directly there, opening the door without knocking.

Mariel sat on a sofa, her head in her hands. She sat up. 'Leo!'

Penny entered the room behind him. 'He was set on coming, Miss—'

Mariel turned to her. 'Thank you, Penny. You may leave us alone.'

Penny curtsied. 'Yes, miss.' She walked to the door.

'Oh, Penny?' Mariel called her back. 'Warn us if my parents are about.'

'Yes, miss.' She left and closed the door behind her.

Leo crouched down to meet her at eye level. 'Are you injured, Mariel? Did he hurt you? If he did, I'll—'

'He didn't hurt me.' She rubbed her arms.

He moved her hand away.

Red marks, the shape of fingers, ringed her upper arms. By day's end they'd be purple bruises.

'That cur!' His blood boiled.

'It is of no consequence, Leo. I did worse injury to him.' She squeezed his hand. 'I must tell you. He has discovered you stole the paper.'

'He could not. It is a bluff.' Their disguises had been complete. 'You did not admit to the theft?'

'No, of course I did not.' She released him. 'I acted as if I believed he made it all up. But, Leo, he says he does not need the paper. He says he has the bank clerk. He's hidden the bank clerk away somewhere.'

The bank clerk. The only witness to Covendale's theft. What arrangement had Kellford made with this clerk? Had he promised the man money? Or was Kellford threatening him, as well?

It was not finished after all. 'I must find this man, Mariel.' Whatever Kellford had offered the man, Leo would offer more. 'Leave it to me.'

'There are only two weeks left.' She covered her face with her hands.

Leo moved to sit beside her on the couch. He put his arm around her.

She allowed him to hold her close and, for a moment, he cared about nothing but comforting her.

'He frightened me, Leo,' she said. 'He is a monster. I cannot bear to marry him, but I also cannot bear what will happen to my mother and sisters if I do not.'

The clock on the mantel struck the half-hour. Half-past eleven. Surely her father or mother would be up and about soon.

'Let me talk to your father, Mariel.' This time Leo would make the man heed him. 'I'll offer to help him.'

She sat up and wiped her eyes with her fingers. 'It would be no use. My father is convinced his cousin will see him hanged.'

He lifted her chin. 'Do not lose courage. Let me try to convince him otherwise.'

Leo and Walker would find the bank clerk. Leo wanted Mariel's father to be on their side when they did.

'Stay out of it, Leo. Kellford will exact revenge on you as well as on me and my whole family. He was so angry. Who can tell what he will do?' Her voice trembled.

He stood. 'I can take care of the likes of Kellford.' He touched her face. 'I'll send word to you.'

She nodded, tears forming again. She rose from her seat and wiped them away.

Even with nose and eyes red from crying, even in a simple lace cap, she looked beautiful. She had fended off Kellford by herself, brave girl. Leo admired her. No, not merely admired her.

He loved her.

He had never stopped loving her. He could run to the far reaches of the world—to China, Brazil, Africa—and it would not be far enough to change the fact that he loved her and would do anything for her.

Especially rid her of Kellford.

She walked with him to the drawing-room door.

When he placed his hand on the doorknob, she covered it with her own. 'Promise me you will not speak with my father,' she insisted.

Leo had no fear of meeting her father. In fact, there was much he wished to say to the man. Such as, how dare he come between them two years ago with his lies? And, now, how dare he sacrifice his daughter to save his own skin? 'Why should I not speak to him?'

'It will make it worse for me.' She looked so weary he did not have the heart to pursue the matter. 'Promise me, Leo.'

He blew out a breath. 'Very well. I promise.'

He opened the door, but turned back to her. 'The paper. I almost forgot.' He pulled the bank draft from his pocket and handed it to her. 'Hide it somewhere safe.'

She rolled it in her hand. 'I will.'

He gazed into her tear-reddened eyes and was tempted to draw her closer and share his strength with her. For a moment she moved nearer to him, but just as quickly moved away again.

He opened the door and walked out, not looking back.

He hurried to the hall, placing his hat on his head as he went. The footman, who had been standing with Penny in the hall, rushed to do his duty at the door. As the man opened the door for Leo, a voice from behind called after him, 'You, sir! Wait. Who are you?'

As Mariel had requested, Leo paid Covendale no heed. He exited the house and walked swiftly away.

Mariel had followed Leo to the hall to watch him leave, her head spinning in confusion. When they were together she felt powerfully attracted to him and it was so easy to melt into his arms.

It also seemed more and more impossible that he would be able to keep his promise to her.

Her father's voice sounded from the top of the staircase. Quickly she folded the bank draft and tucked it down the bodice of her dress.

He reached the bottom of the staircase. 'Who was that gentleman?' he demanded of Edward.

The footman kept his eyes averted. 'I do not know, sir. He left no card.'

Penny slipped behind Edward and hurried up the stairs.

'What was he doing here?' Mariel's father demanded.

Edward looked as if he was about to faint. 'I do not know, sir.'

Mariel stepped into her father's view. 'He called upon me, Papa.'

'You?' Her father turned to her. 'Who was he?'

'None of your concern, Papa.' She trusted he would not notice she'd been weeping. He never examined her that closely.

'See here, Mariel—' He seized her by the arm and led her away from the footman's hearing. 'I'll not have you speak to me in that tone, especially in front of the servants.'

She winced. His hand pressed into her bruises. 'You are hurting me, Papa.'

He released her.

She pointed to her arm, already turning blue. 'See this?'

'I didn't do that!' he cried. 'How did that happen? Did that man—?'

'No, not *that* man,' she retorted. 'Lord Kellford.'

'Kellford?' He squinted. 'He called, too?'

She nodded. 'He is fond of cruelty—or did you forget?'

His nostrils flared. 'Enough impertinence, girl. What mischief are you about having men call at all hours?'

She glared at him. 'You may be able to force me into this marriage for the sake of Mama, Isabel and Augusta, but I have something that will ensure you behave from hereafter.'

'I do not know what you are talking about,' her father huffed.

She looked him in the eye. 'I have the incriminating banknote in my possession. It will not be enough to stop Kellford, to my deep regret, but it will stop you from placing your family in such peril again.'

She pushed him aside and walked up to her bedchamber to find some place to hide the paper, a hiding place her father would never discover.

Chapter Eleven

Over a week passed and Mariel had heard nothing from Leo. She'd attended two breakfasts, a musicale and another ball and he'd been at none of them.

She'd assumed he would keep her informed, but again she was caught in the agony of not knowing where he was, what he was doing.

She thought she'd go mad.

Desperate for information about him, she decided to call upon Charlotte, something she had not done more than once or twice since Leo had disappeared the first time. The day promised rain, like the previous several rainy days, but that would not stop her.

When she was announced, both Charlotte and her sister Annalise were in the sitting room. Both women jumped up from their chairs and, squealing with delight, ran to her and exchanged hugs. Charlotte's dogs yapped excitedly at their feet.

'It is so delightful you have come,' Charlotte exclaimed.

Annalise squeezed her tightly. 'I have not seen you in an age. I've missed you so.'

'Let us sit.' Annalise sat with Mariel on the sofa. Charlotte pulled the chair closer to them. The two pugs leaped into her lap as soon as she lowered herself into the chair.

Mariel asked after their children and felt a pang of envy as the sisters caught her up on the children's ages and their latest antics. She'd once pined to have children.

With Leo.

'And you, Mariel,' Annalise said, her cheerful tone sounding forced. 'You are to be married, I hear.'

Charlotte's smile became wooden.

'In less than a week,' Mariel managed.

'How lovely,' Annalise said too brightly.

Charlotte stood. 'Come up to my bedchamber and see these new gowns I had made. They were delivered this morning.'

The two dogs ran along with them. Two gowns were draped across the bed—one a pale aqua, the other, rose.

'This V-shaped waist is to be all the rage, the modiste said.' Charlotte ran her finger over the seam. 'As well as the flounces on the skirt.'

'They are lovely.' Annalise laughed. 'I cannot believe my tree-climbing sister is prosing on about dresses!'

Charlotte poked her. 'I like to look pretty for Drew.'

As Mariel had once wanted to look for Leo. She had been right to stay away from Charlotte and Annalise. In their presence all she could think of was Leo.

'Where do you plan to wear the gowns?' she asked.

'I thought I'd wear one to dinner at Nick's tonight.' Charlotte fingered the cloth of one, then the other. 'If I can decide which one.'

'The rose,' her sister said. 'It will enhance your complexion.'

'Nicholas is hosting a dinner tonight?' Mariel asked.

Charlotte moved the dresses to a *chaise longue* in the room and climbed on the bed.

Annalise climbed up beside her. 'For the family. His wife is expecting, you know. She is due any day now and goes nowhere. She is starved for company.'

The pugs made several efforts to jump on the bed, to no avail.

Mariel picked up the dogs and handed them to Charlotte before joining her friends. 'Is everyone attending?'

'The whole Fitzmanning Miscellany.' Charlotte turned to Annalise. 'You should have been at Lady Sendale's ball. It was like old times, wasn't it, Mariel?'

Too much like old times, Mariel thought. 'Almost.' Her voice wobbled.

'Even Leo attended,' Charlotte went on. 'Although he was vexed about something at the end. Before that we were dancing like we were back at Welbourne Manor. Weren't we, Mariel?'

She'd danced joyfully with Leo at first. It was painful to think on their waltz together, though. 'Is Leo attending Nicholas's dinner?'

Charlotte threw up her hands. 'Who knows! None of us can make any sense out of what Leo does. I tell you, he's been quite erratic since the fire. We cannot talk any sense into him, and, believe me, we've tried.'

'I know what is wrong with him.' Annalise turned smug.

Charlotte squirmed to attention. 'What? Do tell us.'

'A woman.'

'A woman?' Charlotte laughed. 'It is about time. Drew and I have often said Leo needs to settle down.'

Mariel sat very still, as if even moving a finger would betray her pounding heart. 'Who?' she asked.

Annalise shrugged. 'I do not know precisely, but it

makes sense, does it not? A man involved with a woman always behaves oddly.'

Had Annalise seen her with Leo? Where? In the park? Impossible.

But Annalise must be speaking of her. Mariel might not know what progress or lack of it Leo was making in finding the bank clerk, but she was certain there was no other woman.

Not the way he had kissed her. Not how he had held her. Something else caused him to pull away.

'A mistress?' Charlotte cried. 'Leo? I should have known. It goes with his gambling and drinking and who knows what else he's been engaged in.'

Theft and burglary, Mariel thought. All terrible risks. For her sake.

Was he engaging in even more serious risks? Was that why she had not heard from him? The idea caused knots of fear to twist inside her. She had the right to know what he was doing. She needed to know. This was her problem and he should not shut her out. She was of a mind to march right up to his door and demand to know what he was doing for her.

Demand to see he was unharmed.

She could not call upon a gentleman herself, of course. She would send Penny with a note insisting that Leo meet her tomorrow. The park might not be a good idea. Rain was likely. Besides, who knew how tempted she would be if alone with him again?

Hatchards would do. Hatchards it would be.

Later that afternoon, between rain showers, Penny stepped from a hackney coach and knocked upon the door to Mr Fitzmanning's rooms, her insides fluttering, not from nerves but from expectation.

Maybe Mr Walker would open the door.

It was silly of her to be so excited about seeing him again. Even sillier that her thoughts so often wandered to him. While she was brushing out Miss Covendale's dresses or putting hairpins back into their silver box, he popped into her mind and refused to go away again. She'd never been a dreamy girl, not with losing her parents and having to go into service so young.

She did not know what to do with all these feelings about Mr Walker. How was she to stop thinking of him and start paying attention to her work again? She could not tell the housekeeper about this man. She would merely ring a peal over her head because she wasn't working hard enough. The other maids were likely to gossip about her and make it into something that would get her in trouble.

And it would not be at all proper to ask Miss Covendale what to do.

She knocked at the door again. Perhaps he was not even inside. She rocked on her heels, waiting, and lifted her hand to knock again.

He opened the door.

She gasped. His coat was unbuttoned and he wore no neckcloth. She could see his bare chest through the slit in his shirt, dark hair peppering it. His hair was dishevelled and his chin unshaved. He looked quite magnificent.

'Miss Jenkins!' He quickly buttoned his coat and moved aside for her to enter.

She stepped just across the threshold. 'I have a note from Miss Covendale.'

'Is anything amiss?' He ran a hand through his thick brown hair, only slightly taming it.

'I do not think so.' She looked up at him.

He gazed down at her, his expression confusing to her. She could not tell if it was admiring or disapproving.

He still grasped the doorknob. 'Fitz—Mr Fitzmanning—is not at home.'

He remembered their conversation about calling his employer Fitz. Who else thought her prattle worthy enough to remember? Except Miss Covendale, of course.

'I will give the note to you, then.' She fished it from her pocket and placed it in his bare hand.

His fingers brushed her glove as he accepted it. It made her feel all warm inside.

That confused her. She started to chatter, 'Miss Covendale wondered why she has not heard from Mr Fitzmanning for so long. There isn't much time left, you know, and she is worried.'

Mr Walker averted his gaze. 'We have been working on it. Fitz—Mr Fitzmanning—has been to Coutts Bank where the teller worked and he's spent a great deal of time in gaming hells trying to get information.'

'Are you helping him?' she asked. He said *we,* after all.

He nodded. 'My part has been to befriend Kellford's servants, particularly his valet. You can tell your lady that we believe we are getting close to locating the clerk.'

'Are you?' How very clever of them! 'She will like hearing it. I should tell her straight away.'

She took a step backwards as if to leave.

'Wait!' He cleared his throat. 'Will you wait for me to…to make myself more presentable? I will walk you back to your lady's house.'

She glanced outside. The rain looked as if it would

hold off long enough, and, if it did not, she carried an umbrella this time. She would much rather walk the mile and a half with Mr Walker than ride in a coach. Perhaps Miss Covendale would not mind if it took her a little longer to get back.

'I need the air and I would enjoy the walk…' he paused '…and the company.'

She turned back to him and smiled. 'I would like that very much, Mr Walker.'

That evening Leo planned to visit two or three gaming hells to see if any new talk about Kellford was circulating. Word was he was 'up to something,' but no one knew what. Tonight he hoped someone had discovered what it was. Walker was already out. Kellford's valet had arranged to meet Walker at the tavern where they had met before. Between the two of them they might be able to discover precisely where Kellford was hiding the bank clerk.

Leo crossed the room to leave when there was a knock at the door. He cursed. Who would call upon him at this hour?

He opened the door and the answer was obvious.

Brenner.

His eldest half-brother, his mother's legitimate son, stood in the doorway. 'Good evening, Leo. I've come to collect you for Nicholas's dinner party.'

Good God. It had slipped his mind completely.

He made a dismissive gesture. 'I cannot attend, Brenner. I have an important meeting.'

Brenner pushed past him and entered his rooms. 'You cannot mean that, Leo.'

He did mean it. Finding the bank clerk could be a matter of life and death for Mariel.

Brenner's gaze slid to Annalise's paintings still leaning against the bare walls. 'The family is already gathered at the Manning town house.' He glanced back to
Leo. 'We are waiting dinner for you.'

They were waiting for him? How like them to be
stubborn enough to wait until the food was unfit to eat
and would be wasted and then blame him for it.

'That is ridiculous, Brenner. Surely one person
should not hold up an entire dinner party.'

Brenner gave him a steady look. 'I agree. Come with
me now.'

Leo threw up his hands. 'This is precisely the sort of
pressure I despise. And you all excel at it. I have important matters to attend to, but that means nothing to you.'

Brenner's gaze remained steady. 'What important
matters, Leo? We know something is troubling you.
Tell us what it is.'

Could Brenner not conceive that there might be
something he preferred not to share with his siblings?

Brenner's voice turned low. 'Perhaps we can help
you. We all want to help you.'

Leo bit down on an angry retort. His siblings always assumed he could not handle his own problems
without their advice and assistance. If he did talk with
them about Mariel, they would merely explain to him
all that he'd done wrong—as if he did not know—and
then they'd get busy fixing it.

There was nothing they could do that Leo could not
do himself.

He made himself return Brenner's gaze. 'Some things
a man must do on his own.'

Brenner did not look away. 'A man also recognises
when he needs help.'

Leo rubbed his temples, which had begun to ache.

'I'll attend the dinner with you.' He had no wish to hurt them. He'd go to the gaming hells afterward. They'd be open all night. 'But don't tease me further about this.'

The next morning Mariel waited by a shelf of novels at Hatchards Bookshop, paging through one volume of *Armance* as if she were considering the purchase of it.

She could not even see the words.

What if he did not come?

She steeled herself. If he did not come, would it mean he was hurt? Or in danger? Or—or imprisoned in New-gate? Penny had reported no such thing yesterday, but much could happen overnight.

How like two years ago that she had not heard a word from him.

She took a breath. What was she to do if—if Leo failed—what could she do to escape Kellford? She was going to be a wealthy woman in two years. Surely some-one would lend her the money to support her mother and sisters for two years.

But paying back what her father had stolen would mean revealing the theft and that meant her father's life.

If theft meant her father's life, it could mean Leo's, as well. What if he'd been caught in another theft or some such thing on her behalf?

'Mariel?'

His voice startled her. She snapped the book shut and turned, weak with relief.

His tall frame filled the space between the shelves and charged the air, making her senses tingle. He was definitely very fit, very uninjured.

'Is anything amiss?' His gaze was intense, his pos-ture taut, as if he were ready to march into battle for her. When he looked upon her that way, she could almost believe in him again.

She mentally donned armour. 'I meant to ask you the same thing. Is there anything amiss? I have heard nothing from you and it has been an age.'

He stepped closer. 'I told you to leave it to me. Walker and I have been working day and night to learn the whereabouts of the bank clerk.'

Penny had reported as much from Walker.

Mariel lifted a brow. 'And?'

His mouth slowly widened into a smile. 'And... We know where he is.'

They'd found the man? Mariel placed her hand on his arm. 'Where is he? Have you spoken to him? What does he want for his silence?'

He covered her hand with his own. 'We only know where he is. It will take some travel to reach him.'

'Where is he?' she cried.

'We must keep our voices down.' He glanced around, but there was no one in earshot. 'Kellford has a hunting lodge near Maidstone, not far from Marden Thorn. A day's ride by coach.'

She was still touching him and he, her, she realised. She pulled her hand away. 'When do we leave?'

'We?' He shook his head. 'You are not going, Mariel. Walker and I will go.'

Oh, no. She would not be left behind this time. They were in this together.

She opened her mouth to argue, but quickly shut it again. She knew him well enough—or thought she did—to predict he would merely dig in his heels if she pressed the matter.

'Very well.' She must be craftier than he. 'Will you ride? That would be fastest, would it not?'

'We will engage a coach. We'll have to bring the bank clerk back to London. A coach seems the most secure way. We should reach Maidstone in five or six hours on good roads.'

'You will have to leave very early.' She used a cautionary tone.

'The coach and driver will fetch us at six,' he assured her. 'We will have time if we need it, never fear. We'll find the clerk and be back with days to spare. You will see.'

He took her hand and squeezed it gently.

An ache grew inside her.

She believed he would do as he said, precisely as he had done since he first learned of her problem. But that episode in her drawing room had convinced her Kellford could be very dangerous. If Leo became imperilled, she was determined to be there to assist him.

She dropped her voice to a whisper. 'I am worried.'

He moved closer and leaned down as if he were going to kiss her. Nothing impeded her moving away from him. Except she could not.

His lips hovered inches from hers, but he retreated again. 'I will not fail you, Mariel. Trust me. Leave it to me.'

The word *trust* made her flinch. It was not Leo she mistrusted. It was Kellford.

Leo smiled again. 'I had better leave now. There is still much to do.'

Unable to speak, she merely nodded.

He hesitated a moment, as if reluctant, but then turned and walked away.

Mariel leaned her forehead against the bookshelf, trembling inside, wishing his mere presence would not affect her this way.

She straightened her spine and made her decision. When she walked out of the shop, it had begun to drizzle. She hurried to find a hackney coach and gave the driver the address.

A short ride had brought her to Charlotte's house. A few minutes later a footman escorted her to Charlotte's sitting room.

The two pugs ran to her as she entered. Charlotte, still in a morning dress, greeted her with outstretched arms.

'Mariel! I am surprised to see you again so soon.' She clasped both of Mariel's hands and was too kind to mention that it was unfashionably early for callers.

'I have come on an urgent matter, I'm afraid,' Mariel told her.

'Urgent?' Charlotte gestured for her to sit. 'What is it?'

The dogs jumped up and settled beside her.

Mariel swallowed. 'I need a favour and I could think of no one else to ask.'

Charlotte laughed. 'Well, I should hope you would think of me. What do you need?'

She faced her friend. 'I need you to lie for me.'

Charlotte's brows rose.

How to tell her? How much to tell her? 'I need to tell my parents that I am visiting with you for a few days. I—I need to go some place and I do not want to tell them where.'

Her friend's expression of concern looked so much like Leo's that it took Mariel aback. 'What is this about, Mariel?'

Mariel stood and paced. 'I—I do not wish to marry Lord Kellford, but, for reasons I cannot explain, I cannot merely cry off. I must contrive it so he no longer wishes to marry me. To do that I must go away.'

Charlotte leaned forwards. 'You do not wish to marry Kellford?' She breathed a relieved sigh. 'I am so delighted. I confess, I could not like him at all. Oh, I know he is charming, but—I cannot put it in words. He is not at all the husband for you. I will do whatever you need for me to do.'

Lord Kellford looked up as the man entered his library. 'Well? What information do you have for me?'

After witnessing Fitzmanning and Mariel together, Kellford hired a man to keep watch on Fitzmanning. Fitzmanning was up to something, Kellford was certain. He'd had it in for Kellford for a long time.

Hughes, an average-size, nondescript man, faced him. 'I have good information.' His posture was not at all deferential. 'But it will cost extra.'

'Extra?' Kellford fumed. 'I am paying enough already.'

Hughes shrugged. 'I had to add some men to follow Fitzmanning's servant.'

'A servant?' This was too much. 'What has a servant to do with a gentleman's business?'

'Pay more and I'll explain.' Hughes folded his arms across his chest.

Why not? In a less than a week he'd be a wealthy man—if he prevented Fitzmanning's interference. 'Ten pounds more.'

Hughes scoffed. 'One hundred.'

Ridiculous! 'Thirty.'

'Fifty,' Hughes persisted.

'Fifty,' Kellford conceded. He lifted a finger. 'But only if the marriage takes place. If you do not succeed in that, you will be paid nothing more.' He'd already secured the man's work with twenty pounds.

'That is the agreement.'

Kellford waved his hand impatiently. 'Well, get on with it. What information do you have?'

Hughes wore a smug expression. 'Seems that Fitzmanning's man has befriended your valet, who has told him that you are hiding someone at your hunting lodge in Kent. There is a carriage hired to take Fitzmanning there tomorrow.'

'My valet.'

That was good information, indeed. Worth fifty pounds and more.

Of course, his valet would regret having big ears and a loose tongue. He had no doubt eavesdropped on an early conversation with Hughes. Well, he'd be dealt with. Turned out within the hour and given no references. In fact, Kellford would pass the word that the man had stolen from him—which he had by stealing information—he'd never work again.

Kellford turned his attention back to Hughes. 'Leave today and remove our friend from Marsden Thorn.'

He wanted the bank clerk to be in London for the wedding anyway. Hughes would merely bring the man back a few days early.

Kellford leaned forwards. 'Then deal with Fitzmanning. Hire as many men as you need. I'll pay. I want you to stop his interference once and for all.'

Hughes gave an acquiescing bow.

Kellford went on. 'I do not care how you do it, but you must stop him. Do I make myself clear?'

'Fifty quid more and I'll guarantee it,' Hughes said.

Kellford took no time deliberating that offer. 'Agreed.'

Chapter Twelve

The next morning dawned fair, warm and clear, a perfect day for travel after the rains of recent weeks. Leo was glad of it. He'd promised Mariel to return in mere days, and he wanted to fulfil that goal, to stand before her and tell her the ordeal was finally over.

He and Walker had packed quickly, well practised in doing so after their travels throughout the Continent. Each had only a small bag, now resting by the door ready to grab as they went out.

Leo paced, trying to think of anything he might have missed that would affect their success. He worried a bit about leaving Mariel alone. Who knew what Kellford would do? Although the man would be a fool to do anything to ruin his chances with only days left before the wedding.

Walker sat by the window, his nose in a book.

'What are you reading this time?' Leo asked.

Walker did not look up. 'Plutarch's *Lives*.'

'Good God. You are reading that for enjoyment?' Leo remembered it from his school days.

'It is fascinating,' Walker said. 'All these brave, ancient men either overcame their flaws or perished because of them.'

Ah, that was it. Overcome or perish. Walker had made the choice to overcome his past, to leave his criminal days behind him. He'd merely required a little help in eliminating the shackles that imprisoned him in that life.

Now that he was out of it, there was no limit to what Walker could do, what he might become. He would not be a servant forever. Leo counted himself fortunate to have Walker as a friend and companion. He wondered how long before Walker needed to strike out on his own as Leo had done.

There was a knock on the door.

'The coach?' Leo glanced at the hall clock. 'It is early.'

'Must be. I heard it outside.' Walker closed his book and rose to cross the room to the door. He opened it.

'My God!'

Leo turned.

Mariel crossed the threshold, her maid behind her. Each carried a portmanteau. 'Good morning, Leo.'

'Mariel, what the devil?'

'We are accompanying you.' She placed her bag on the floor.

'The devil you are,' he said sharply. 'You cannot want this, Mariel. Your reputation will be ruined.' Her ruin was not his biggest fear. He and Walker were heading into danger. The clerk would be guarded, certainly. Kellford was no fool.

She laughed. 'Leo. My reputation is the least of my worries, as you should realise; however, to my parents and the world, I am visiting your sister Charlotte. No one will know I am with you.'

Damned Charlotte. Still ready to be talked into folly.

Walker approached the maid and took her bag. He nodded a greeting. 'Miss Jenkins.'

The maid lowered her lashes. 'Mr Walker.'

Leo glanced back to Mariel. 'You will hamper us.'

She waved a dismissive hand. 'Trust me to know when to stay out of your way.' She faced him, looking defiant. 'I'll not wait here in London without a word from you. I endured that two years ago when I did not know where you were, what you were doing—'

'Did you think I would leave again? Is that what you thought?' She ought to know by now he would not again desert her.

She narrowed her eyes. 'Have you not shown me already that you have no wish to be with me? I do, however, believe you will keep your word about helping me. But I intend to accompany you.'

Walker and the maid watched their conversation with raised brows.

'I refuse to allow you to accompany me,' he said tersely.

'Well.' She took a breath. 'I refuse to stay behind.'

'It might become dangerous, Mariel.' This was the crux of it.

'It cannot be worse than marriage to Kellford,' she countered.

Another carriage rolled to a noisy stop in the street outside.

She glanced out the open door at it. 'Enough talk. Let us go.'

She reached down to pick up her bag, but Leo grabbed it first. 'I could force you to stay.'

'You will not!' She tried to pull the bag from his grip.

He wrenched her bag away from her and carried it out to the carriage.

Walker picked up the other bags, including the maid's, and followed him. Mariel and Penny trailed behind.

The carriage was attended by a coachman and post boy. Leo handed Mariel's bag to the coachman who threw it up to the carriage's roof.

'Thank you, Leo,' Mariel murmured.

The post boy took the other bags from Walker.

Walker turned to Leo. 'I will ride outside. It will give you more room.'

'Miss Covendale,' the maid broke in. 'May I ride outside, too? It is such a fine day.'

'If you like, Penny,' Mariel responded.

Walker looked uncommonly grim as he climbed up to the carriage's roof and reached down to pull the maid up beside him on a seat behind the coachman. Leo assisted Mariel inside the carriage.

There would have been barely enough room for all four of them inside, Leo realised. As it was, he and Mariel could not fail to touch if seated side by side. He chose the back-facing seat, which meant gazing at her and brushing his legs against hers.

The carriage started and, as it made its way through the Mayfair streets to the Strand, Mariel stared out the window. She did not move even as they reached the Waterloo Bridge.

'Do we spend this whole trip in silence, Mariel? It will be five hours or more.' Leo asked. 'We once had more to say to each other.'

She slowly turned to face him. 'We did, once.'

'How many ways must I say I am sorry?' He knew

she would understand he was speaking about two years ago, nothing else.

The corners of her eyes etched in pain. 'You cannot know what you put me through.'

'I did not know at the time.' He'd thought she'd found a better man to marry. 'Even if I had gone to you, your father would never have approved our marriage. You would have lost your inheritance.'

'You knew that did not matter to me.' Her voice cracked.

'You would have lost respectability, as well, and that did matter to you,' he reminded her. 'Defying your father and losing your money would have created a scandal.'

'I did not care about scandal,' she insisted. 'Except for its effect on my mother and sisters. Besides, my father would have given in. I certainly know now that he would not have given up any potential source of money.'

But neither of them had known it two years ago.

He leaned forwards. 'You must understand. I had nothing to offer you. After the fire, I had nothing.'

Her eyes flashed. 'I did not know of the fire on that day. You thought I would marry someone else even before I could learn of it. I read of the fire in the newspapers. The newspapers, Leo!'

He sat back, averting his gaze.

She spat out her words. 'Why did you not let me share in the tragedy of your stables burning down? Did you not know how sad I was for what happened to you? How much I would have wanted to help?'

'There was nothing you could have done.' His muscles tensed. Ashworth had everything and he'd had nothing.

'You just went off,' she went on. 'You didn't allow

your family to help you. You never allow anyone to help you.'

He felt a knot tighten inside him. 'My family helped me. They bought Welbourne Manor from me.'

Her voice cracked. 'You know what I mean! Could you not have shared your pain with me? I thought we were to share everything.'

The desolation he'd felt two years ago returned now.

Her lip quivered. 'I do not blame only you. My father is the real villain. He decided what I should want and what I should do. You merely agreed with him.' She lifted her eyes to his. 'How could you have believed him?'

Leo shrugged. 'He was very convincing. He had the special licence with your name and Ashworth's on it. He said you and your mother were visiting Ashworth's estate.' He met her gaze. 'And he showed me your note.'

'My note?' She looked surprised.

'The one that said "Father will explain it all."'

Her face paled. 'I did not mean…'

He reached out to touch her hand, but caught himself in time.

'In any event,' he managed. 'Neither of us can change what happened.'

They fell into silence again.

Matters between them were so complicated, he did not know what to say to her. He had not meant to put any blame on her for what happened. She'd been wounded deeply. Not only by him but by her father. Leo accepted his responsibility. After the fire—after his failure—he'd been primed to believe she could not love him.

But he did not want this depressive gloom to remain

with them the whole trip. He tried changing the subject. 'How did you get Charlotte to agree to your scheme?'

She gave him a direct look. 'I asked for her help.'

That took him right back to her accusation—that he never asked for help.

He could inform her that he sought Walker's help all the time, but he suspected she would say that was different because Walker was in his employ. And he'd asked for Nicholas's help, hadn't he? Of course, he'd lied to his brother about why he wanted to attend society events. He suspected Mariel would have something to say about that, as well. Truth was, the last thing he and Mariel needed was his family taking over and making matters worse.

Although Leo had to admit, at the dinner two nights ago, his brothers and sisters made an effort to restrain their intrusive questions and offers of assistance. Their restraint caused nearly as much tension as if they'd plied him with litanies of what he should be doing and how they could assist him. Nothing was worse than people treading on eggshells around him, holding back all they wished to say and do for him. It was clear they thought he would make a mess of things if left on his own.

Mariel turned back to the window and Leo lowered his hat to shade his eyes. Did she view him in the same light? he wondered. Certain he would fail unless she kept watch?

He stretched his legs as far as possible. He'd had no more than a couple of hours of sleep the past two nights—that must be why he was thinking like a schoolboy instead of the man he'd become, a man who could handle himself very nicely.

He opened his eyes a slit, just able to see she'd turned back and was staring at him.

It was not likely he could sleep.

Walker lifted his face up to the sun beaming from the cloudless sky. They'd travelled out of the city into the countryside with its green fields and rolling hills that never ceased to awe him. When he'd been a child, he'd had no idea such places existed outside of heaven.

His gaze slipped to Miss Jenkins. If the Kent countryside was heaven, then she surely was an angel.

Had she chosen to sit with him or had it been the fresh air she was craving? He did not know, but he was glad to be at her side.

The carriage hit a rut in the road and dipped suddenly. Walker threw his arm around her, holding her securely in place. She turned to him, her eyes wide, her mouth forming an O.

He released her. 'I beg pardon, miss. I feared you would fall.'

'I did not mind. I was frightened is all.' She threaded her arm through his. 'Do you mind if I hold on to you, in case it happens again?'

Her touch aroused him, surprising him and making him feel ashamed. She was a respectable young woman, not the sort he usually lusted after.

She looked around her. 'Is not the country beautiful? I remember being so surprised at all the green hills and the trees and all in the country the first time I saw it.'

His eyes widened. It was as if she'd read his thoughts—or at least his non-carnal ones. 'When did you first see the country, miss?'

Her brow creased in thought. 'It was about a year

and a half ago when I was sent from London to be Miss Covendale's maid.'

'You grew up in London, then?' As he had. He'd guess, though, that she'd not known the Rookerie. He'd also wager that he'd lived almost half his life before she was even born.

She nodded. 'My parents had a glove shop in Chelsea.' Her voice cracked ever so slightly as she spoke.

'Your parents?' he asked, wanting her to say more, always hungry to hear of what it was like to have parents.

She put on a brave smile. 'They are dead now and the shop gone. That is why I went into service.'

He took her hand. 'I am sorry for it.'

She covered his hand with her other hand. 'And your family?'

The pain of losing his mother still scraped at Walker's insides. He did not even know how old he'd been, only that he'd been very young and on his own ever since.

'Dead, as well.' He could not tell her his mother made her meagre living on her back and his father could be any one of countless men. She'd died from disease given to her by one of those men.

She held on to him tighter. 'We are lucky, then, are we not, to have such good employment?'

'Indeed,' he answered. He'd be dead without it.

'My lady worries that you will not find this man you are looking for, but I believe you will.'

When had anyone shown such blind faith in him—besides Fitz, that is?

'We will find him.'

The carriage pulled into a posting inn to change horses.

Leo broke their silence. 'You should stretch your legs a bit, Mariel.'

She nodded in agreement and he exited first before turning to help her out, putting his hands on her waist and lifting her down. From the roof of the carriage, Walker helped the maid down to the ground.

'Do you need me, miss?' her maid asked.

Mariel glanced at Leo. 'I do not believe so.'

Leo pulled some coins from his pocket and handed them to Walker. 'Would you purchase some food for all of us?'

'I'll help you,' Penny offered.

Leo turned to Mariel. 'We might have time for a quick cup of tea. Would you like that?'

'Very well,' she responded.

They entered the public room of the inn and Leo asked for tea to be served right away. A pot and two cups were quickly placed on a table. Mariel poured, remembering exactly how he took his tea. She did not seem to notice anything remarkable in that knowledge.

As soon as she put the cup to her lips, she set it down again.

'Oh, look!' She rose and walked over to the hearth.

A mother cat lay on a blanket, nursing her kittens. A yellow tabby kit toddled its uncertain way off the blanket.

Mariel scooped it up and held it against her cheek. 'Look at you, you sweet little thing.'

The other kittens became curious and left their meal to look up at her. She lowered herself to the floor and gathered them into her skirts, where they climbed and fell as if encountering some strange new land.

Leo's heart ached at the sight. He forced himself to smile. 'I remember when you and Charlotte and Annalise found kittens in the barn at Welbourne Manor. You looked much like you do right now.'

She made a face. 'I must have been all of eleven years old.'

But still a beauty. He hadn't realised it then, but he'd known that day had been a moment to cherish.

As was this moment.

Their gazes caught and held.

He spoke quietly, 'We've known each other a long time.'

A horn sounded to call them back to the carriage. He rose from the chair and offered her his hand. She scooped the kittens back onto their blanket and put her hand in his, letting him pull her up.

They came close, inches from each other, and neither moved as their gazes caught and held. He inhaled her scent, felt the warmth of her body.

The horn sounded again and they hurried to the yard.

Walker met them. 'There is a basket of food in the carriage.'

Leo asked the maid, 'Would you like to sit inside the carriage now? I can sit on the roof.'

She looked stricken. 'I—I like being outside.' Her glance darted to Mariel. 'Unless you would prefer I ride with you, miss.'

Leo watched Mariel look from Penny to Walker and back again. 'You may ride outside, if you like.'

Her maid beamed. 'Thank you, miss!'

Once Leo and Mariel were back inside the carriage, Mariel remarked, 'I believe there is romance afoot.'

'Romance?' He was puzzled.

She gestured to the outside. 'Penny and Mr Walker.'

His brows rose. 'No?'

'I am fairly convinced.' She peered at him intently. 'Must I worry for her sake?'

'Worry about Walker?' Leo laughed. Walker, for all

his rough past, would never trifle with an innocent such as Mariel's maid. 'He's a fine man.'

'Good.' She averted her gaze. 'I would not wish Penny to be ill used.'

'Neither would I.' True, he and Walker had engaged in encounters Mariel must never learn about, but all was different now—although their business was not entirely on the up and up.

She plucked cat hairs off her skirt. 'You? With your reputation?'

He frowned. 'Gossip, Mariel.' He'd not been a saint, but he didn't debauch innocent women. 'Do you believe the tales told of me?'

She cast him a long look before finally saying, 'Your sister Annalise believes you have a mistress. Shall I not believe her?'

'A mistress?' He shook his head. 'What mistress?'

She held her gaze steady. 'You must ask her.'

He could not tell if she was teasing him or not. 'Mariel.' He spoke firmly. 'I do not have a mistress. I do not have any idea what Annalise was talking about.'

Mariel lifted one eyebrow.

The carriage rolled through the village to the open country again. Pristine green hills passed by, and the rain-swollen Medway River. None of it provided enough distraction for him.

Where the devil had Annalise got the idea he had a mistress? She wouldn't have seen him with a woman. Good God, he'd not been with any woman besides Mariel, had he?

The entire next hour was consumed with reviewing in his mind everywhere he had been and whom he had spoken to. The only woman he'd been with had been Mariel.

He suddenly sat up straight. 'That's it!'

She started.

He laughed. 'Penny!'

She blinked. 'What about Penny?'

'It was driving me mad.' He leaned towards her. 'The mistress was Penny. Annalise saw me with Penny. At Hatchards. And Annalise called at my rooms the afternoon Penny delivered your note. It was Penny.'

She cocked her head. 'Well, that explains it, doesn't it?'

He could not tell if she believed him. 'I have never kept a mistress. My reputation might suggest otherwise, but the truth is I—'

She reached across and put her gloved fingers on his lips. 'I never believed you did. At least not at present. I knew Annalise was mistaken.'

He captured her hand in his. 'I will not say I've been a saint, but, Mariel, you are the only woman I ever truly desired.'

Yearning filled her eyes. 'Oh, Leo! Then why can we not forget these past two years? We could start over.'

He felt himself grow cold. 'I told you. I am not the same man as I was then—'

'I do not care if you lost your wealth,' she broke in.

He gave a dry laugh. 'It is not that. I have plenty of money.' And a small fortune coming soon by ship, God willing.

'Then, why, Leo?' Her voice cracked.

Some things were best unspoken. 'I no longer belong in polite society. As for why? It is best you do not know.'

She pulled her hand away and turned from him.

Chapter Thirteen

Hughes stood in the centre of the road watching for the carriage. How fortunate he and his men had spied Fitzmanning when the carriage stopped to change teams at an inn. They'd ridden ahead to this spot.

This perfect spot.

All was going according to plan.

The rumble of an approaching carriage reached his ears. Was their luck still holding?

'Make ready!' he called. His men were hidden from the road, obscured by shrubbery.

Hughes's excitement grew. This task was almost too easy. He wanted to shout in triumph, but first he needed to make certain this was the correct carriage.

It came into view. He kept his eyes peeled on the post boy, the coachman, the passengers seated on top. This was it!

'On my signal!' he cried, stepping out of view.

He waited until the horses reached his mark in the road.

'Now!'

His men pulled on a rope they'd strung across the road.

The rope caught the back legs of the wheelers. The

horses stumbled and the rope caught in the carriage's wheels. There was a loud snap—the shaft breaking, perhaps?—and the horses broke free of the vehicle, the post boy frantically trying to get them under control as they galloped away.

The carriage jolted and rocked and tilted on its side. Finally it fell, tossing the outside passengers and the coachman like rag dolls. Its momentum thrust it towards an embankment at the side of the road.

Hughes let out a laugh.

He glimpsed Fitzmanning inside as the carriage slid down the embankment and landed with a splash in the river.

Hughes had counted on this scheme impeding Fitzmanning's progress. If Fitzmanning were injured, so much the better. But having him lost completely in a rain-swollen river was the best of all possible outcomes. Kellford would be pleased.

Hughes watched the fast-moving current sweep the carriage away, pulling it deeper and deeper into the water.

'Off!' he shouted to his men. They retrieved the rope and scurried away, before the coachman, holding his head in his hands, gathered his wits about him. The passengers were nowhere to be seen, but they were of no consequence to Hughes. The post boy was probably a mile away by now, still fighting the horses.

The event would be written off as another unfortunate coaching accident. Its cause would remain unknown. And, for it, he and his men would be paid handsomely.

It had all happened so fast. The shout of the coachman. Mariel's screams. The snap of something breaking.

The carriage suddenly crashing on its side and sliding into the water, the cold water.

Leo could only think to grab hold of Mariel, to shield her with his body. At first, the carriage floated like a boat, but quickly water poured in through the windows.

'We have to get out of here.' He scrambled for the door, but could not push it open. The windows were too small to crawl through.

Mariel pushed at the door along with him, but the water pressed on it with a force too great for them to counter. In no time the water was up to their necks. Remnants of their food basket floated around them.

'Take a deep breath,' Leo told her. 'Get as much air into your lungs as you can.'

She nodded and her gasp for air was the last sound he heard before the water covered her and reached his ears. He took his breath and joined her underwater.

They pushed at the door again and this time it opened. Leo gripped her arm and pulled them both out, kicking hard to bring them up to the surface. He could feel the weight of her skirts trying to drag them down and the current sweeping them away from the carriage, but he kicked towards the daylight shining above the river water.

He broke through to the surface and pulled her up with him, lifting her so that she could fill her lungs with air. The river dragged them under again. Leo kicked to the surface once more and they were able to grab another lungful of air before going under again.

Leo had only one thought. To save Mariel. He'd fight to reach the shore, because he refused to allow Mariel to die this horrible death, unable to breathe, knowing life was ending.

He clasped hold of the front of her dress, gripping it

tight. He would die before he released her. One of his arms was free to fight the water like the enemy it had become. Mariel gamely did her part, kicking and adding her own strokes to the effort.

A memory flashed through his mind. Swimming in the pond behind Welbourne Manor, the boys and the girls together in their underclothes, unsupervised as usual, but innocent in their play. He remembered dunking Mariel and laughing when she came up sputtering.

In the rushing river, though, he fought to keep her head out of the water. He increased his effort, though his muscles ached and fatigue threatened. No matter. He must save Mariel's life.

The shore came closer and closer by inches. Suddenly the river pushed them towards the trunk of a fallen tree jutting out into the water. With all his strength Leo lunged for the tree's branches and grasped one at the last second. The river continued to try to sweep Mariel away, but he hung on to her and pulled her towards him until she, too, could grab hold of the tree.

He lifted her onto the fallen tree, although it took several tries. She made it finally and straddled the trunk. Leo lost his grip and the water tried to capture him again, but Mariel grabbed his coat and held on until he could fight his way back and again catch hold. Finally he, too, straddled the trunk.

Leo's muscles felt like jelly as he rested his cheek against the wet wood, savouring its solid surface. He had no idea how long they'd battled the water or how far the current had taken them. They were alive.

Mariel was alive.

'Are you hurt?' he called to her.

She turned her head to look back at him. 'No.'

His muscles relaxed in relief.

But relief was short-lived. He remembered Walker and Penny, the coachman and the post boy. What had happened to them? The coachman, Penny and Walker must have been thrown from the vehicle. Had they been thrown clear of it? Were they alive?

And what had caused the accident in the first place?

He raised his head to look at Mariel. 'We need to get on land. Can you move?'

She nodded. 'I'll try.'

She inched her way down the tree trunk to where the river became quieter. Tips of shrubs peeked up through water that had overflowed the river's banks. A breeze rippled the surface of the water and chilled his skin. She must be cold as well, he thought. Cold and weary.

But she kept on, crawling to where dry land beckoned.

The tree acted as a bridge to the dry shore. When close, Mariel stood and navigated the rest of the way on foot, until she dropped to ground that was muddy but firm.

Leo came right behind her. When his feet touched the ground, he reached for her, holding her in his arms, pressing her against him. Her life was the solid earth beneath his feet.

'Mariel.' He seized her lips in a kiss.

All his terror for her, all his relief, were poured into the kiss, as if this alone would affirm that she was alive and safe and not lost to him forever. His embrace was almost violent in its intensity, but she matched him. Her arms encircled his neck, holding fast. She returned his kiss with equal fervour, clinging to him as hard as he was clinging to her.

When they broke apart, both were trembling. He

could not release her. At this moment it would have felt as if she would be swept away from him.

He embraced her again, more gently, holding her against him, while his heartbeat and breathing gradually slowed to normal.

'Thank you,' she whispered against his chest. 'Thank you for saving me.'

Mariel wanted never to leave the safety and security of Leo's strong arms. Death had come so close and he battled it away. Emotions that she'd kept at bay during the danger now threatened to engulf her like the river water that had tried to sweep her into oblivion.

Leo had saved her. He'd held on to her and saved her.

'Come.' He pulled her away, but kept his strong arm around her shoulders. 'We need to move away from the edge.'

She needed no further coaxing.

The shore at this spot was thick with shrubbery and they had to push their way through, feet slipping on wet ground underneath. Finally they came into the open.

The clear day that greeted them at the beginning of their journey had vanished. The sky was grey. Dark rain-clouds gathered in the distance. Nothing was in view but green fields. No houses. No road. Not even a church spire poking into the sky.

Where were they?

She seized his arm. 'Leo! What happened to Penny? And Walker and the coachmen? Did they fall in the water, too?'

He faced her and looked directly into her eyes. 'They must have been thrown from the carriage when it tipped over. The horses broke free, I think, the post boy with them.'

Thrown from the carriage? How could Penny survive such a horrible event? She could have been smashed against a tree or tumbled onto rocks or—or—crushed under the carriage.

'We need to get dry. Find shelter.' Leo was changing the subject and she did not like that. 'Would you like to remain here while I look for help?'

'Do not leave me!' she cried. 'I want to go back and find Penny. They might need us.'

His expression was sympathetic. 'We do not know how far the river carried us. It might be miles.'

'I do not care,' she insisted. 'I want to find them.'

He held her again. 'I think it a better plan to find you a safe place to recuperate. Then I can go back to the site of the accident.'

'No. I'm going with you.' She could not bear it if he left her to worry and wonder about where he was and what he might find.

It took a moment for him to respond. 'Very well. We'll look for them together. There is a chance that they are safe. As horrific as our part of the accident was, we came out unharmed. Walker knows how to keep his wits about him. After all he has been through, it will take more than a carriage accident to undo him.'

'Kill him, you mean,' she said.

'Yes, that is what I mean.' He released her.

He was trying to give her hope, but she'd already steeled herself for the worst. She could bear discovering the worst better than waiting and knowing nothing.

He took a breath. 'If we walk upstream we'll eventually find the road and the site of the accident. Perhaps it is closer than I think.' He peered at her. 'But if I find someplace where you can be cared for, I will insist that comes first.'

She would cross that bridge when she came to it. 'Thank you, Leo.' She gave him a swift embrace.

Mariel pulled out the few pins left in her hair and wrung it as best she could before trying to pin it into a knot at the nape of her neck. Her bonnet had been lost in the river. Her clothes were still dripping wet and there was no sun to warm them.

'I'm ready,' she said.

Leo took her hand and they started walking.

It was hard going. Mariel's skirts were heavy and her muscles weary. Her half-boots were soaked and her feet chafed from her wet stockings. Worse, she kept reliving the carriage falling on its side, sliding into the river, filling with water. Worse still, she pictured Penny lying broken and still by the road.

'I should never have brought Penny with me,' she said as she put one foot in front of the other.

'You could not have known what would happen,' Leo responded. 'Try not to think about it.'

'What did happen, Leo? All of a sudden the coach just lurched and fell on its side.' She felt it again. The jolt of the carriage. The crash of the fall.

He shrugged. 'It felt as if we hit something in the road.'

She tried to think of other things, as he suggested.

She thought of his kiss. It spoke of loving her. She could not deny that. And of her loving him. She had never stopped loving him, she realised. No matter that he had left her two years ago. He was back and he'd fought the river to keep them alive.

She glanced at him. His face revealed the effort it took to keep walking, as did hers, she supposed. His was a strong face. The sight of it still made her breath catch.

Her mind flashed with the image of the water trying to sweep him away from the tree, right before she'd grabbed his coat. The thought that he might die had been so much worse than his leaving her two years ago had been.

Tears stung her eyes, but she blinked them away and glanced up at the sky. 'It is going to rain.'

Leo nodded. 'Yes, it is.'

Rain would only make matters worse for Penny, Walker and the coachman. 'I hope we find them before the rainfalls.'

Surely they'd walked at least three miles by now. You'd think they would have spied a village or a farmhouse, someplace where they could get help for Penny and Walker. They'd seen no buildings at all. They'd not even found the road. Mariel's feet ached. She was tired and hungry and cold.

Just when she thought she could not feel any worse, the rain started. Fat drops, falling here and there, quickly thickened into teeming sheets of water and sent them running for the shelter of a tree.

'Stay here,' Leo said to her. 'I'm going to run over the ridge to see if I can find shelter.

He sprinted away, not giving her an opportunity to stop him.

She started after him. 'Leo! Wait!'

He acted as if he didn't hear her, which was certainly possible in the roaring rain. He quickly disappeared from view. She abandoned the chase and made her way back to the tree to face the agony of not knowing where he was or if he would make it back to her.

The minutes seemed like hours and all her doubts and worries flooded her like the rains flooded the river. She wept for poor Penny, convinced the fall from the carriage had killed her. She also wept for Walker, and for the fledgling love budding between them.

Mariel also grieved the loss of all the hopes and dreams and delights that had accompanied her first romance—her only romance. She again let herself feel her love for Leo, her need of him.

She slid to the ground and buried her face in her hands, trying to stop herself weeping, trying to make herself strong and determined and self-reliant.

'Mariel!'

She looked up. Leo emerged through the grey curtain of rain and strode towards her from the crest of the hill.

She wiped her face as she stood, then hurried to meet him.

He caught her in his arms. 'I've found shelter!'

Pulling her arm through his, he led her up the hill and over another until she saw below them a small house. No signs of life around it, no smoke from its chimney, but it had a roof and, at the moment, that was more than enough.

They ran towards it, their feet slipping on the wet grass.

When they reached the door, though, it was padlocked.

'I don't suppose you have Walker's keys with you?' Mariel said, her voice catching on Walker's name.

He smiled at her. 'No, but I'm game to try one of your hairpins.'

She pulled one out and her hair tumbled down. She handed the hairpin to him. He inserted it in the lock and moved it carefully until, finally, the lock opened.

'See, a hairpin can undo a lock,' she commented. 'I was not so foolish at Lord Kellford's.'

His gaze pierced into her as he opened the door. 'You were foolishly brave.'

They walked in.

The little house was dark and consisted of one large room with a table, three chairs, a fireplace and a cot. It smelled of dust and disuse, but it was dry.

'It looks like a groundskeeper's cottage,' Leo said.

'How long before the rain stops?' she asked.

He glanced towards the window, rattling from the force of the rain. 'I have no idea, but while we wait we should try to get warm.'

She could not argue. There was no use to keep going in the rain.

He walked over to the fireplace. 'There is a stack of wood and a pail of coal.' He immediately set about laying a fire.

Mariel spied a pump and went over to examine it. 'It looks like there is water.' She sighed. 'Not that I wish to see any more water today.' She tested the pump, but its pipe must have been filled with air.

She was suddenly thirsty, even after swallowing all that river water. She found a large jug and carried it to the door. 'We'll need water to prime the pump.' She opened the door again and set the jug out in the rain. At the rate the rain was falling, it would be filled in no time at all.

Leo started a fire in the fireplace, no more than tinder burning at the moment, but a fire nonetheless.

Mariel walked towards it. 'It will be lovely to be warm again.'

He stood and, suddenly, she felt the intimacy of being in this small space, in the darkness with him. The rain pattered on the cottage roof, but she fancied the sound of her beating heart rose above its din.

He glanced from the cot in the corner back to her, moving closer to her. His hazel eyes seemed to glow in the flame's reflection. He touched her hair, a wet, tangled mass heavy on her shoulders.

Gently he combed it back with his fingers, his eyes on hers. 'Mariel, you need to remove your clothes.'

Chapter Fourteen

'**R**emove my clothes?' Mariel pulled back.

He reached for her again, but withdrew his hands. 'You are shivering. You'll never get warm unless you get out of your clothes. Turn around. I'll untie your laces.'

'But…' she protested.

'You must. You'll become ill if you don't.' He twirled his finger.

She knew he was right and did as she was told.

The knots had undoubtedly been made tighter by being wet. He struggled to undo them and she could smell the river on him. It brought back the terror of being pulled under the water over and over, fearing she would drown or, worse, she would watch Leo drown.

She trembled.

'I will hurry,' he said.

He finally undid the knot and loosened the lacings. Once she had dreamed of undressing for him on her wedding night. Never had she supposed the circumstances would be like this. She let her gown drop to the floor and she stepped out of it.

As soon as her dress was off, he started to work on the laces of her corset, a task Penny so often performed for her. Dear Penny, who took such pride in Mariel's clothing and her appearance. Was she lying dead or injured in the cold rain? Mariel shook her head. She must not think about it.

Leo loosened her corset, which, like her dress, she let slip to the floor. He walked over to the cot and picked up one of the blankets that had been folded at its foot.

Holding it like a curtain around her, he said, 'Take off your shift. You can wrap this around you.'

When her shift joined the other sodden clothing on the floor, he wrapped the blanket around her naked body like a cloak.

He dragged the cot close to the fire. 'Sit here and I'll take off your shoes and stockings.'

This seemed even more intimate than removing her corset. He rubbed her red and blistered feet to warm them, sending sensation shooting throughout her body. She forgot her chill, aroused now by his touch.

But as soon as he stopped she shivered, even under the blanket.

'Lie down, Mariel. The fire will soon warm the place.'

She lowered her head onto the pillow and he stepped out of her sight. The sounds of his undressing made her wish to turn and watch him. He took a second blanket from the bed and she heard him wrap it around himself.

He climbed onto the cot and held her close against him. 'Forgive me this liberty. It is the fastest way to take away your chill.'

This liberty? Her senses craved more than *this* liberty. She was not so green a girl that she did not know what she craved was the intimacy of a husband and wife. It immediately felt right to be enfolded in his arms, to feel his breath on her neck and the strength of his body next to hers.

'I was thinking,' he spoke quietly. 'Chances are the post boy was unhurt. Surely he would have ridden to get help. Or likely another carriage came by and found them. Perhaps at this very moment Penny and Walker and the coachman are warm and dry and well tended.'

It was the nicest thing he could have said to her. His words made perfect sense and, for the first time, gave her real hope. There were other people who would help Penny and Walker and the coachman. She could relieve herself of that responsibility and the guilt of failing at it. She could think of Penny, well fed and in clean nightclothes, safely tucked into a clean bed at a comfortable inn.

It helped her relax enough to close her eyes. She was so tired that even lying naked next to Leo, a mere blanket between them, was not enough to keep her awake.

It was enough that he held her, that they were together, that they were alive.

The surgeon stepped away from the bed and lowered his voice. 'Nothing is broken. She has a nasty cut on her forehead, but that is all. I suspect tomorrow she'll be right as rain.' He glanced to the window where rain poured down as if from buckets. 'Pardon the expression.'

Walker accompanied him to the bedchamber door and pressed a coin into his hand. 'Thank you, sir.'

The post boy and the coachman, his head wrapped in a bandage, hovered in the inn's hallway.

'She will recover,' Walker told them. 'It is only a cut. Thank you both for your help.' He shook their hands.

The post boy had ridden the team of horses to the next inn and sounded the alarm. They'd not had long to wait for help to arrive, but even that short period of time had been agony for Walker.

Miss Jenkins had been bleeding severely.

The accident had happened so fast. Suddenly the horses stumbled and the carriage lurched. With only a split second for decision, Walker grabbed hold of Miss Jenkins and jumped from the carriage at the moment it fell on its side. They landed in some bushes, barely escaping being crushed under the vehicle. They fell hard. Miss Jenkins's head struck a rock and instantly blood poured down her beautiful face. He had gathered her into his arms as the carriage slid into the river and disappeared beneath the water, Fitz and Miss Covendale trapped inside.

Walker's jaw flexed with emotion, but there was no time to grieve. Miss Jenkins needed him.

He bid good day to the two men who had shared the tragic experience and closed the door, returning to the bed where Miss Jenkins was propped up by pillows, tears rolling down her cheeks.

He sat in the chair next to her bed. 'Did you hear that, miss? The surgeon says you will be well tomorrow. It is only a cut.'

'I keep seeing the carriage.' She wiped her eyes with her fingers. 'My poor lady! What will I do without her?'

Walker glanced away. What would he do, as well? Fitz had given him his new life.

'I don't want to think of myself.' Miss Jenkins sobbed. 'It is so bad of me, but, without Miss Covendale, how will I ever get another position? There is no one to recommend me.'

Walker took her hand, still damp from her tears. 'Do not upset yourself,' he murmured. 'These things have ways of coming to rights.'

If truth be told, he shared her worries. He'd depended upon Fitz to keep him from needing to return to his former life. He could not go back to that existence.

She looked up, her eyes glistening. 'I should have stopped her from coming on this trip. She'd be alive if I did. I wish I had. She'd be alive then.'

He squeezed her hand. 'That kind of thinking gets you nowhere. None of us possesses second sight. We could not know the coach would have an accident.'

Was it an accident? He'd seen nothing amiss on the road, but something elusive had caught the corner of his eye after they'd hit the ground. A man in the wood? He could not say for certain.

He turned his thoughts back to Miss Jenkins. 'We were all merely trying to do something worthy. To help Miss Covendale.' He'd thought Miss Covendale's plight worthy of an Ann Radcliffe novel...if not for its tragic end.

Miss Jenkins nodded. 'I did think I was helping her. That's all I ever wanted to do.'

A bruise had formed beneath one of her eyes and a bandage was wrapped around her head, but she still was the loveliest woman Walker had ever seen.

He resisted the impulse to bring her hand to his lips. 'You were devoted to her.' As he'd been to Fitz. 'Think. Would she want you to worry so? Do not worry over the future. You have me to help you.'

He would see that no harm came to her. He'd devote his life to the task if she'd allow him.

Her eyes widened, but he could say no more at this moment, at least about his feelings for her.

He swallowed. 'You must think of what she would wish you to do. We must both think of what they would wish us to do.'

She blinked, but looked into his eyes again. 'Do you think Lord Kellford will still ruin her father?'

He preferred this topic. 'He might. Such men are spiteful.' Kellford would certainly be enraged that his hopes for Miss Covendale's fortune were dashed.

'My lady would not like to see her family suffer. She is very devoted to her sisters.' She broke down again. 'I mean, she *was* devoted....'

Without thinking, he moved to sit beside her on the bed, wrapping his arms around her. 'There, there,' he soothed.

A dim memory glimmered. His long-lost mother had once held him in the same way. He shuddered. When was the last time he allowed himself such a memory of his mother? If grief over Fitz was nearly undoing him, what would happen if he gave in to his grief over his mother?

He forced his thoughts back to Miss Jenkins. 'Would you like for us to still find this bank clerk? We might at least save Miss Covendale's family from ruin.'

Her face glowed. 'Could we? I would like that above all things.'

He could not help but smile. 'That is what we will do, then. In the morning. If the rain ends, that is.'

She hugged him. 'As soon as the rain ends!'

The trusting warmth of her arms almost loosed the tenuous hold he had on his emotions. His eyes stung with tears he refused to shed, but his heart wept in grief for the only two people in his life who had ever cared about him.

Leo had not intended to sleep, but the comforting sound of Mariel's even breathing had lulled him. When he finally opened his eyes he had no idea how long he'd dozed. Rain still sounded on the roof and windowpanes, but it was dark outside. The only light in the room came from the fire in the grate, now burning low. It had done its task, though. The room was warm; his bone-cold chill had vanished.

Sometime during the night, Mariel had rolled over to face him. He gently tucked her blanket around her and simply gazed at her lovely face.

She looked relaxed and peaceful in sleep. Rather than a woman who'd nearly drowned, she resembled that little girl he'd once teased and taunted at Welbourne Manor. How he wished he could recapture those innocent days.

So much had happened in the meantime, so much disappointment and heartache. He'd hoped to atone for all she'd suffered by finding the bank clerk and freeing her of Kellford. Now he feared they would run out of time.

Tomorrow they must find a village and he must discover what happened to Walker and Penny. Would they have time to hire a new carriage to take them to Kellford's hunting lodge, secure the bank clerk's cooperation, and still return to London by the day Mariel was to be married? It was cutting it close to the quick.

What would happen then? Kellford would no doubt enact his revenge. Mariel's father would be arrested and her family would be awash in scandal made even worse by Leo's name being attached to it.

In that case, Leo would marry her, although he suspected that, like his parents' own scandalbroth, the damage to Mariel's reputation and that of her mother and sisters would be long-lasting.

Leo could at least try to help Covendale fight the charges. If he failed at that and the man was hanged, he could, at least, support Mariel's mother and sisters, make sure they wanted for nothing.

Two things he could not guarantee for them: preserving Covendale's life and preserving the family's reputation. Those two things were the very reasons Mariel had agreed to marry Kellford in the first place. Would she feel any better being forced to marry him instead and still suffer the consequences she so wished to avoid?

He took a deep breath. Under no circumstances would he force her to marry him.

He sat up abruptly.

What he could do was give her the best of his efforts without requiring anything of her. No matter what, he would fight for Covendale's life. No matter what, he would support Mariel and her family. No one would have to know the money came from him. And in two years' time she would become an heiress and need no one's help.

Mariel opened her eyes and rose on one elbow. 'Leo? Is something amiss?'

His heart pounded in his chest. Even if he failed to stop Kellford, he could help her.

'Nothing,' he replied. 'A thought. That is all.'

She gathered her blanket around her. His had slipped down to his waist.

'About the accident?' She rubbed her eyes.

'No.' He waved a hand. 'It was nothing.' It was everything to him, but nothing he need speak of right away.

She turned towards the window. 'It's dark and still raining.'

'Indeed,' he managed.

He stood, wrapping the blanket around his waist as

he did so. He went to the fireplace and put more coal on the fire.

'Are you thirsty?' she asked. 'I am very thirsty.'

He'd not thought about it, but he was both thirsty and hungry. 'We could get the pump working.'

She rose from the cot. 'I'll go outside and fetch the jug I left out there. It should be full by now. Plenty of water to prime the pump.'

He intercepted her, touching her arm. 'I'll go. No need for you to get wet again.' He crossed the room to the door, but turned back to her. 'Look away, Mariel. I'm going to take off my blanket. To keep it dry.'

He could not tell in the dark whether she turned away or not, but he dropped his blanket, opened the door and walked outside. The rain felt good on his bare skin, clean, compared to the river water. He stood in the open and let it pour over him, lifted his face to it and tasted it in his mouth. He did not know how long he stood there, but it felt wonderful to wash the river out of his hair, off his skin.

'Leo?'

He turned and saw Mariel silhouetted in the doorway. 'Mariel! What are you doing?'

'I—I—you took so long. I thought something had happened to you.' She averted her gaze.

'I'm letting the rain rinse me off.' He must look deranged, standing in the pouring rain, stark naked. 'Go back inside.'

The silhouette disappeared.

He picked up the jug of water and carried it into the hut. As soon as he crossed the threshold, there she was, right inside the doorway.

'What the devil, Mariel?' He put the jug down and snatched up his blanket.

'I want to rinse off, too,' she said.

She didn't wait for him to answer, but walked past him, dropping her blanket right before stepping outside.

To not look was impossible for him, but he remained far enough inside that he would not be visible to her.

She was a mere shape in the rain, but still took his breath away. She lifted her arms to the sky and twirled around, graceful and sinuous. Her innocent abandon reminded him of their childhood days.

Her perfect beauty, though, was that of a woman and his body responded.

He could not turn his eyes away. His hands begged to slide down the curves that were merely suggested in the rainy night. His lips yearned to taste her again. His loins throbbed to possess her.

He must have moved forwards. She turned to face the doorway and she stilled. Slowly she moved towards him.

He remembered how powerfully he'd wanted her when they'd escaped the river; he wanted her even more now. He stepped outside and the rain cooled his fevered skin.

But did nothing to dampen his desire.

She walked directly into his arms and he captured her lips. Passion coursed through his veins, heightening his yearning for her. The kiss sent him back to when he'd so nearly lost her. The danger they'd endured fuelled his ardour once more.

His hands slipped down her back and rested on her derrière, so satisfyingly round and feminine. He pressed her against him, against his arousal, wanting more. Needing more.

She gasped beneath his lips.

He loosened his hold on her and looked down at her, unable to speak the question in his mind. Did she want this?

'Let us go inside,' she murmured.

Chapter Fifteen

They were standing in the rain, naked, on a chilly rainy night. He ought to feel the chill, but he was aflame.

He lifted her into his arms and carried her inside, stepping over the blankets that had once covered them. It seemed more natural that no barriers existed between them.

He carried her to the cot and lowered her onto it. She pulled him down atop her, kissing him again, sharing her tongue with him as if she, too, could not get enough.

He forced himself back to his senses. 'Mariel, are you sure you want this? There are consequences...' They could create a life by their lovemaking. He would stop if that was what she desired.

'I don't care. I don't care,' she rasped. 'We almost died yesterday. We might die tomorrow. I will not die without making love with you.'

And I cannot live without it, Leo thought.

Her hands explored him, kneaded at his flesh, urged him on. He became too fevered to think clearly. He knew he should go slow, prepare her, be gentle, but his need was too powerful and she was too tempting, too willing.

His wonderful Mariel, never one to balk, always game to do what needed to be done, fearless in forging ahead. He loved her for it.

Loved her.

'I love you, Mariel,' he whispered. 'I have never stopped loving you.'

Her legs parted for him and he rose above her, wanting to plunge into her and hasten his release. He fought for the control to slow down, to enter her slowly, letting her body adapt to him.

She gasped and stiffened when he filled her completely.

He stopped. 'Did I hurt you?'

She shook her head and raised her hips, her hands pressing on his back.

He tried to hold back, but she writhed beneath him, impatient sounds escaping her lips. The rhythm of lovemaking drove him to move faster inside her.

Sensation grew, that exquisite hunger that demanded to be slaked, but other feelings, too, because this was his valiant Mariel beneath him, surrounding him, joined to him.

She moved with him, her need intensifying, as well. He wanted to give her the pleasure he knew he would experience at the end. Nothing was more important than giving himself totally to her.

But his need took over, becoming more intense, building higher, until his release exploded within him. At the same moment his seed spilled inside her, she cried out, convulsing around him in the culmination of her own passion. Together they writhed in pleasure until sensation ebbed and languor took over.

He slid to her side and held her close.

'I did not know it would be like that,' she murmured. 'Is it always like that?'

He kissed the top of her head, her hair still wet from the rain. 'Only with you.'

She sighed. 'Promise me you will not be sorry for this in the morning.'

Be sorry for it? He would never be sorry for making love to her. The risks were all hers. 'I should ask that of you, Mariel.'

Her body was humming with pleasure from joining with him. It might have been wrong of her to seize the moment, to act without thought to propriety, without heed to the consequences. But was not propriety meaningless after facing the prospect of death? And if Leo's child grew inside her, could anything be more wonderful?

She sat up to gaze at him steadily. 'I have no regrets.'

He made love to her one more time before retrieving their blankets and filling cups with water, which they sipped as if it were the finest wine. As the new day dawned, they sat together on the cot, wrapped in the blankets, the fireplace warming them in a cocoon of their own creation. It seemed to Leo as if nothing in the world existed except the two of them.

He embraced the illusion. It was preferable to imagine these walls as the confines of the world than to think about the complications that faced them outside.

She turned to place a kiss on his bare chest, warmed by the fireplace and their lovemaking. Her fingers traced one of the scars that were reminders of the worst he could do. Or had it been his finest act? He could never be certain.

Her touch was gentle, such a contrast to the wound

that created the scar. 'What happened, Leo? How did you get these?'

What would she think if he told her? 'It is best you not know.'

She shifted and looked him straight in the eye. 'Do not say that to me. Do not put secrets between us. Not now.' Not after making love, she meant.

'I was in a fight,' he finally said. 'In Paris.'

'A fight?' she repeated.

She wanted more, he was certain, but it was not an episode he wanted to share. He did not want to place it in her memory, giving her images he did not wish her to have.

He knew too well how impossible it was to shed those images.

It involved his meeting with Walker. Walker had grown up in an East End rookery and had belonged to a gang of thieves virtually his whole life. Like Leo, though, Walker had not belonged in the world where he was born. Like Leo, Walker wanted more. He'd dared to leave the gang and the rookery and made his way to Paris, where Leo happened upon him in a three-against-one street fight. Knives were pulled and the fighting became life or death. One cut-throat slashed at Leo, causing the wounds whose scars Mariel so tenderly touched. Leo managed to wrest the knife away, but the man lunged at him and the knife plunged into the man's chest.

Leo could still see the look of surprise on the man's face before he fell, never to rise again.

The others scattered and Walker pulled him away from the body before the gendarmes could be summoned. It was only later Leo could reflect on what he'd done. He'd taken a man's life, and even though he'd do it again to save Walker and himself, it disturbed him.

He faced Mariel and tried to adopt a light tone. 'It happened to be a very a nasty fight.'

Mariel searched Leo's face. She sensed there was a great deal more to Leo's story than he had disclosed to her, something that caused him great emotional pain as well as physical injury. She waited for him to go on, but he added nothing.

'Tell me more,' she pressed. 'Why were you fighting?'

'Who recalls?' He shrugged. 'I found myself in many scrapes while I was on the Continent.'

He knew the reason, she realised.

She stared at him and finally said, 'You will not tell me, will you?'

His gaze remained steady and his voice turned low. 'The less anyone knows about those days, the better.'

His words created a leap of anxiety inside her. What had happened to him in the past two years? The rumours made it sound as if he'd turned into some sort of dissolute rake. Each contact she had with him left a different impression. He was still like the Leo she'd fallen in love with, except there was a darkness inside him, a darkness he would not share with her.

Perhaps she could learn more from Walker—she swallowed—if Walker was alive.

An image of Walker and Penny being flung off the carriage assaulted her, but she pushed it away. She could not think of Walker and Penny. Not yet. She wanted to remain cocooned here with Leo and keep all the ugliness that surrounded them at bay. If only they could do so forever.

Perhaps she and Leo should just run away to Switzerland, like the poet Shelley had done years ago with his lover, Mary Godwin. That flight had caused heartache for those they left behind, especially Shelley's children and his wife, who later killed herself.

By drowning, Mariel remembered. She shuddered, knowing precisely what Harriet Shelley experienced before her death.

A knot formed in Mariel's stomach. Think what running away would do to her family. Her father would hang and who would look after her mother and sisters?

She quickly changed the course of her thoughts once more.

'What woke you so suddenly before?' she asked Leo.

He frowned.

Would he leave this question unanswered, as well? What did he hide this time?

Finally his gaze rose to meet hers. 'I'd been thinking of the reason we came on this trip.'

'Oh.'

Most of all Mariel did not wish to think about Kellford.

But Leo continued. 'With luck we should still have time to find the bank clerk.'

She held up a hand. 'Must we speak of this? While we are here we are powerless, are we not? Let us not even talk about it.'

Their time together would soon enough come to an end. When the day cleared and their clothing dried, they would walk out this door and whatever reality they faced would cause great pain.

Leo placed his cup of water on the floor and took her hand. 'There is something I must say. We need to plan for what to do if we do not find the clerk.

At least he was saying 'we,' including her in making plans, but what was there to do if they did not find the bank clerk? All would be lost.

She pulled her hand away and used her fingers to comb the tangled mess that was her hair. 'Very well. Say what you must.'

He positioned himself behind her, pulling her between his legs, resting her back against his chest.

'In the event we run out of time...' he seemed to choose his words carefully '...I want you to know I will do whatever I can for you and your family. I will support you and your family and help your father in any way I can. I will pay back what your father stole from his cousin.' He paused. 'If you wish it, I will marry you.'

His offer was incredibly generous. He also made it sound like an obligation.

'You do not have to do such a thing,' she said.

He spoke near to her ear, his breath warming her skin. 'I owe it to you.'

She moved out of his arms and wrapped the blanket around her. 'Because we made love? I was equally responsible for that.'

He faced her. 'Not because of that.'

It was hard to look at him. 'I have no wish to be an obligation.'

His eyes creased as if in pain. 'I know it would not be a respectable marriage for you. I am aware of my reputation. If we are discovered to have been together, it will make the scandal even worse. The burden would be yours—you'd be the one with a bastard husband with a disreputable past.'

A past he kept secret. 'And you would endure the shame of marriage to the daughter of a thief.' She lowered her eyes. 'Once we did not care what anyone thought of our romance.'

His eyes pierced into hers. 'You cared enough to keep it secret. You worried about scandal even then.'

'Not for my sake!' she cried. She'd never cared about such nonsense. 'I worried that if we eloped it would reflect badly on my family, that it would hurt my sisters' chances for good marriages. I had to think of them.'

He held her by the shoulders and held her gaze. 'That is the one thing I cannot prevent. If we fail to find the bank clerk on time, I cannot prevent the scandal or gossip or the damage to your family's reputation. I cannot promise to save your father from the hangman's noose.'

She stopped breathing. Could reality be any uglier? The marriage she once dreamed of would cost her father's life, her family's reputation.

She wished she could collapse under the enormity of it all.

As if he sensed her despair, his blanket slipped off his shoulders and he wrapped his arms around her, giving the comfort she so desperately needed. She leaned her head against him, her ear against his bare chest filled with the sound of his beating heart.

He held her until her heartbeat matched his. He sought her lips and kissed her as hungrily as if they'd just escaped the river again. They lay back on the cot, she atop him, prolonging the kiss, feeding her own need along with his. Their tongues touched and explored, their breath mingled.

Flames shot through her body and she burned with desire for him once more. She needed to be joined to him. Needed the pleasure they created together. Breaking free of his kiss, she savoured him, rubbing her hands over his muscled chest, over the scars from wounds that might have cost him his life.

He slid his hands up to her breasts, his touch hot and erotic. Sensation flashed through her, consuming every inch of her. She never knew a man's touch could be so glorious.

Leo's touch.

He filled his hands with her breasts, tenderly kneading and scraping her nipples with his palms. When she thought she could not endure this exquisite thrill a moment longer, his hands moved to cup her derriére. She straddled him and rubbed herself along his erect manhood, trying to ease the aching that grew inside her.

A part of her stepped outside herself to wonder at the experience. She'd always known she wanted to make love with Leo, but she had understood nothing of the glory of it, of how freeing it would be to abandon herself to sensation, to cast off worries of the past and future and simply relish the intimacy of bare skin and secret places. In a moment she would take him inside her and be filled by him. The pleasure they would create together was unlike anything she could have imagined.

Perhaps she should be selfish and marry him, obligation or not, family or not.

She gasped. Pleasure fled as swiftly as the river's water had whisked them away.

'What is it?' His body tensed.

Tears filled her eyes. 'If I marry you, it will mean my father will die and my family will be ruined. If I have you, it means I destroy them.'

'It is not you who would destroy them,' he murmured. 'Your father and Kellford bear that responsibility.'

'But I could change it.' By marrying Kellford, she added silently.

He stroked her tangled hair. '*We* may yet change it and prevent those dire results.' He gestured to the window. 'The sun is rising and the rain has stopped. We'll be able to leave here soon. We'll find Penny and Walker and then we will find the bank clerk. We will only be a little delayed.'

His fingers and his words calmed her. Lying next to him made anything seem possible.

Her arms encircled him and she placed her lips on his. Together they lay down on the cot and she took sustenance from his kiss, as if he were breathing his strength into her. He ran his hands over her body as if she were his most cherished possession, as if he might never have another chance to touch her. She explored the contours of his muscles, so firm and thrilling. At this moment she could sweep past and future aside and relish this passion between them.

She said a prayer of thanks for his strength and his will and for the joy of touching him so intimately. Nothing separated them now. They were mouth to mouth, skin to skin, body to body, as they were meant to be. Her senses flared with desire for the pleasure they could create together.

His hand covered her breast and the need for him intensified again. His mouth covered her nipple and his tongue created new delights. She nearly cried aloud at the rapture of it.

Her fingers dug into his back. Her hips rose as his hand slid down to her feminine place. She suddenly needed for him to touch her there. How could she have guessed such a need existed? At the moment she wanted nothing more.

She pushed his hand lower and his fingers gently circled the area. She felt herself become wet under his touch. The excitation he created pushed her somewhere between ecstasy and agony, the agony of craving more.

She could bear the waiting no longer and he obliged her as if her feelings were his own. He moved over her and she opened for him. He entered her quickly and she knew, like her, he could not wait an instant longer. His strokes soothed her at first, but quickly made her desire even more acute.

This was a moment to savour, she realised, as her need was rapidly growing too strong for thought. This was a moment she would possess forever. Perfect joining. Perfect accord.

Perfect man.

He moved faster and faster and she moved with him, certain nothing could be wrong as long as she was with him, joined to him.

He drove her to her peak and she cried out with the glory of it. His muscles tensed and she felt him spill his seed inside her.

As her climax ebbed, a calmness washed over her, along with a fledgling feeling of hope. There was still time. They would succeed and she would be together with him for all the days of their lives and all their nights.

She sighed in contentment and he lay next to her, snuggling her against him.

'We'll succeed, Mariel,' he murmured, his voice deep with emotion. 'I'll make it right if it is the last thing I do.'

Chapter Sixteen

$\sim\!\!\infty\!\!\sim$

Mariel hated donning the clothing that reeked of the river, especially putting on her damp half-boots over her sore feet, but the sun was high in the sky and it was time to leave the cabin.

For one, they were hungry. The last food they'd eaten had been in the carriage before its accident, a lifetime ago, it seemed.

They tidied the cabin, doused the fire in the fireplace and put the place back to rights as best they could. Leo left a note and a few coins as payment for the coal and wood they'd used to keep warm.

Their last act was to lock the padlock.

In daylight, without rain pouring down, a path leading away from the cabin was clearly visible.

'It is bound to lead us somewhere,' Leo said.

They could reasonably expect to find a village within a day's walk, especially if the path led to a road. Neither wished to return to the river.

It was not an easy walk. Although the ground had dried somewhat, the path was riddled with puddles and their boots still sank into mud. The sky was grey and smelled of more rain. Mariel did not relish the idea of becoming soaked again.

With each step her hunger grew; she started thinking of meat pies and lamb roasts, tureens of oxtail soup, of bread warm from the oven, butter melting on a slice, jam piled atop it.

It did not take long for the path to lead to a road. There was a choice to make. North or south?

'Would you like to choose this one, Mariel?' Leo asked. 'Which way should we head?'

'I do not know how to choose.' Which would lead her to Penny? 'I have no idea where we are.'

'Neither do I.' Leo looked from one direction to the other. 'It doesn't matter overmuch. We will know how to proceed no matter what village we reach.'

He chose south.

This road led to another. East or west.

He chose east.

They'd been walking almost three hours and Mariel's feet hurt her more and more. The sky clouded over and there was a chill in the air made worse by her still-damp dress. If she had not been with Leo, she would have succumbed to a fit of weeping, but, even with sore feet, damp clothes and hunger, she preferred being with him than alone in comfort.

They'd walked this new road only a short distance before hearing the welcome sound of a wagon approaching behind them. It was a farmer's wagon making slow progress pulled by one sturdy-looking horse.

Leo stood in the road to halt it.

'Can you assist us, sir?' He asked the driver, who was dressed in the clothing of a farm worker, an unlit pipe between his teeth. 'We were in a carriage accident yesterday and we need to get to a village.'

'Carriage accident?' the man's bushy eyebrows rose. 'Out this way?'

'I'm afraid we were carried some distance by the river.' Leo put his hand on the wagon. 'May we ride with you?'

The man shrugged. 'I'm bound for Aylesford, if that will do.'

'That will do nicely.' Leo turned to Mariel, who hurried to the wagon.

'Good day, ma'am,' the driver said, tipping his hat.

'Thank you so much for helping us,' she replied. With Leo's help, she climbed into the wagon.

They were its only cargo. The driver explained he was headed to Aylesford for supplies. Mariel fancied she could smell produce from the wood of the wagon. Kale and asparagus and rhubarb, although it could very well have been her imagination.

The ride to Aylesford provided welcome comfort, even with every bump and rut in the road intensified by the hard wooden floor of the wagon. Anything was preferable to walking. Mariel began to long for the slippers she'd had Penny pack in her bag at the last minute. Her slippers—and maybe Penny—were long gone, however.

Any chance she had for happiness was gone, as well.

Leo caught the gloom that settled on Mariel's face and he feared she was giving in to worry. He put his arm around her. If only he alone could carry this burden.

She rested her head on his shoulder and he tried to savour the simple pleasure of having her next to him, but fears of how to find Walker and Mariel's maid and then seek out the bank clerk plagued him.

He tapped on her head. 'Are you worrying about your maid?'

She shifted, but remained nestled next to him. 'I force myself not to think of Penny—too much, anyway. I was thinking about the future.'

His insides twisted. 'I will take care of you and your family no matter what, Mariel.'

She nodded. 'I did not say before how generous of you that would be.'

She did not know the half of it. It meant giving up the excitement of his less-than-legal, but highly profitable trade. It placed him at the fringe of society again, at a time when he was happy to simply turn his back on it.

She sighed. 'I just wish we could run away and stay away forever and pretend none of this ever happened.'

Why not? His heart beat faster. They could live well in Belgium or France or Italy. 'Is that what you wish, Mariel? Because I suspect everyone will think us dead. We could catch a coach to Dover, change our names and set up housekeeping anywhere we like.'

She took his hand in hers. 'I had that fantasy, but I could not abandon my family. Besides, one cannot truly run away. Your past must always catch up to you.'

'It can be done,' Leo insisted. 'I did it. I succeeded.'

She squeezed his fingers. 'But I am the past that has caught up to you. And look how awful it is.'

He could not regret this time with her, even in its grim circumstances. How could he ever regret making love to her? It was a memory to cherish for as long as he lived.

The wagon rolled along for half a mile before she spoke again. 'I was thinking that I should take the first coach I can find back to London. After we discover what happened to Penny, that is. I—I should like to make arrangements for her.'

'We will find her, but do not give up hope that she will have survived the accident.' He was trying not to give up on Walker, either.

She smiled sadly. 'I have resigned myself to her loss. And to the fact that I must hurry back to London in time to marry Kellford.'

He could not believe his ears. 'No. No matter what, you must not marry Kellford. I cannot permit it.'

'It is the only way,' she insisted.

He frowned. 'Do you fear the taint of being connected to me? Because of the past? Because of my reputation? Do not tell me Kellford is preferable to that.'

'Never think that, Leo!' she cried. 'I love you. I have never stopped loving you. Did not our time in the cabin prove that to you? I cannot be with you, though. Not at the cost of my father's life and my family's reputation.'

His hand curled into a fist. 'Your father does not deserve this sacrifice of you. Your life with Kellford will be hell on earth.'

'I agree my father is undeserving of any mercy.' She uncurled his fingers and gently rubbed his hand. 'But, still, I cannot cause him to die. Most of all, I must look after my two sisters. They are innocent of any wrongdoing, surely.' She paused. 'We are back where we started about Kellford, are we not? I do want you to know that I will cherish this time we have had together. I will hold the memory of making love with you in a special place in my heart. It will be with me always.'

'Mariel—' He did not know what to say. He did not like her giving up.

He must find the bank clerk. It was more important than ever now.

They fell silent, but held hands as the vibrant green of the countryside passed before their eyes. The fields were dotted with buttercup and cowslip, daisies and dandelion. In more innocent days, he and his brothers used to chase Mariel and his sisters over fields much like these.

Soon a stone tower of a church came into view, then a peek of red rooftops.

'Aylesford.' The driver gestured.

Leo watched the village come closer and closer. More traffic filled the road. People walked by carrying huge bundles. Men rode on horses. Simple wagons, like the one in which they rode, rumbled behind finer vehicles. He ought to feel relief. Instead his tension grew. How long would it take to discover what had happened to Walker and Penny? Would they be alive? Would he have enough time to find the bank clerk?

He glanced at Mariel and saw tension pinching her lovely features. Let them at least discover good news about Walker and Penny.

The closer they came to the town's centre, the greater his trepidation. At every turn bad luck had dogged them. Would good luck never come? He tried to appear reassuring for her sake.

'Can you drop us at a coaching inn?' he called to the driver.

'Yes, sir,' the man replied.

The man stopped at an inn bearing a sign of St George slaying the dragon. Leo fished inside a pocket and handed the man some coins.

The farmer stared at the money in his palm. 'Thank you, sir!'

Leo helped Mariel out of the wagon and she winced when he placed her on her feet again.

He frowned, but she waved away his concern. 'It is not so bad. My feet do not hurt overmuch.'

They entered the inn, where the innkeeper, a round, balding man, met them.

'Good day!' the innkeeper said cheerfully, though he eyed them with more than curiosity. 'What may I do for you? Do you want a room?'

'A meal to start,' Leo said. 'In a private parlour, if that is possible.'

The man looked askance. 'Begging your pardon, sir, but do you have the ready to pay?'

They must look a sight and smell worse, with their dank and dirty clothing, caked with the dust of the road.

'I do.' Leo pulled out his still-damp purse and opened it to show the coins. 'We are in urgent need of food.'

'Come this way.' The innkeeper led them to a small parlour at the back of a public room. 'Hungry, are you?'

Leo answered, 'Very hungry. Bring us whatever is easily prepared. Some ale, as well.' He looked questioningly at Mariel and she nodded approval.

'Very good, sir.' The innkeeper left, closing the door behind him.

Mariel immediately lowered herself in a chair and removed her shoes and stockings. She rose again to put the shoes and stockings near the window, hoping they would dry.

She glanced out the window. 'Oh, no.' She turned to him. 'This inn is right on the river.'

He crossed the room to the window. The river was swollen enough that some of the inn's garden was under water. It was as if the river were reaching out to snatch them back.

He put an arm around her. 'Try not to think about it.'

She leaned on him a moment before swivelling away and choosing a chair that faced the door. 'I want to ask about Penny.'

'We can ask when he brings the food.' He sat down, as well, and unbuttoned his coat. 'I confess I could think of nothing but food.'

She reached across the table and took his hand again. 'I have been thinking about it for the past three hours. Right now I think I can tell by scent alone every dish and drink the public room serves.'

The innkeeper brought food right away. A mutton-and-oyster stew, thick-crusted bread and cheese. A tavern maid carried in ale.

While the tavern maid placed the tankards on the table, the man lingered, still eyeing them curiously. 'Anything else, sir?'

Leo held up a finger while he took a quick gulp of ale. 'We have not eaten in a day. We were in a carriage accident yesterday—'

The innkeeper's brows rose. 'That's odd. Yours is the second carriage accident in two days.'

Leo straightened. 'You know of a carriage accident?'

The man nodded. 'Heard about it yesterday.'

Mariel looked as if she might leap from her seat. 'What did you hear, sir? How do you know of it?'

He shook his head. 'A tragic thing. Two people died, they said.'

Two people died? Were their worst fears coming true?

'Tell us what you know.' Leo pressed.

The man shrugged. 'Don't know much. One of the coachmen who passes through here talked about it. Said he heard about it at the Swan.'

'The Swan?' Leo's voice rose. 'Where is the Swan?'

'West Malling,' the man replied. 'Not far from here. Two or three miles on the London Road. That's where this accident happened, supposedly. On the London Road.'

'How did the man hear of it?' Mariel asked.

The tavern maid spoke up. 'He heard it from someone who was in the accident.'

The innkeeper looked at her in surprise. 'How do you know that?'

She shrugged. 'He was a talkative sort.'

'Sir,' Leo broke in. 'We need fresh clothing. And someone who can drive us to West Malling. I'll make it worth your while if you find both by the time we finish eating.'

'A carriage to take you to West Malling?' He rubbed his chin. 'I cannot think who—'

'Charlie will do it,' the tavern maid piped up.

'Charlie.' The man nodded. 'That's right. He should be willing to do it. What kind of clothing do you want? We don't have much choice in that, I fear.'

'Any clothing will do as long as it is clean.' Leo added, 'And dry.'

'And shoes for me,' Mariel added. 'Shoes and dry stockings.'

An hour later the small carriage that carried them from Aylesford pulled up at the Swan in West Malling. Leo and Mariel lost no time in climbing out of the vehicle and entering the inn. No one was in the hall, so they made their way to the tavern. Most of the booths were empty, but conversation buzzed and tavern maids bustled back and forth.

Leo spied a man behind a bar. 'Sir! Sir!' he called from the doorway and strode quickly toward the man.

The publican continued to wipe glasses with a white cloth. 'Yes?'

'There was a carriage accident yesterday. Do you know anything of it?'

'Heard people talk of it,' the man said.

Leo turned towards the room and raised his voice. 'If anyone has information about a carriage accident yesterday, will he please come to me now. I will give you a handsome reward for good information.'

He heard someone shuffling in his seat, but he could only see the tops of heads over the high sides of the booths. One man moved out of a booth and into the light.

'By God, Walker.' Leo hurried towards him. 'You are alive.'

Leo shook Walker's hand, but relief overtook him and he hugged his friend.

'What of Penny?' Mariel cried.

'I am here!' Penny ran into her lady's arms. 'Oh, miss!'

The two women burst into tears and fussed over each other. The maid had a black eye, which Mariel tenderly touched. Her head was also bandaged.

Walker turned back to Leo. 'We had no hope you had survived. No hope at all.'

'How fared the coachman and the post boy?' Leo asked.

'The coachman hit his head, but otherwise was unhurt. The post boy suffered no harm. He rode the horses here and brought us help.' Walker blinked, half expecting his friend to disappear. 'How did you manage it?'

Leo caught the eye of the publican. 'Is there a private parlour?'

'Of course, sir.' The man ushered them to a private room and they ordered more refreshment.

Penny clung to Mariel while Leo told the story of their survival.

'My poor lady!' Penny exclaimed. 'It must have been horrible!'

'It was at that,' Mariel admitted. 'I would have drowned if not for Leo.'

'And I would have drowned if you hadn't caught me when my hand slipped from the tree,' Leo responded.

'It is sufficient that you both survived.' Walker beamed at them.

Leo and Mariel asked more questions about what happened to Walker and Penny and received more explanations of their ordeal. Walker asked where they had spent the night and Leo told about finding a cabin for shelter. Walker's brows rose, as if he suspected what had transpired between them.

'What is the story of your clothes?' Walker asked.

Leo laughed. 'Does my attire offend my valet's sensibilities?'

Walker grimaced. 'You know I never truly acquired a valet's sensibilities.'

Penny piped up. 'We have your bags! They were thrown from the carriage when it fell.' She turned to Mariel. 'There is a fresh dress for you, and we still have your brush and comb and hairpins.'

'I have been very grateful for the dress I am wearing. If you could have seen my other one…' She made a face.

Leo sat up straighter. 'Now that we know you are safe, we must attend to other matters.' He looked towards Mariel.' 'We must be close to this hunting lodge. Let us find the bank clerk. We have time.'

Walker exchanged a glance with Penny. 'The bank clerk is gone.'

Chapter Seventeen

'Gone?' Leo could not believe his ears.

'Miss Jenkins and I went in search of him today.' Walker explained. 'We just returned a short while ago.'

'You did not find him?' Mariel's voice rose in distress.

Leo drummed his fingers on the wooden table, waiting for Walker to explain.

'We found the hunting lodge with no problem, but the bank clerk was not there.' Walker's expression was grim. 'The housekeeper told us that some men called upon him yesterday morning and that the clerk left with them in some haste.'

'Did she say where they took him?' Perhaps they could still find him in time.

'She heard the men say they would take him back to London, but she did not know more than that.'

'London...' Leo curled his fingers into a fist. 'To Kellford, I'll wager. He'll use the man to ensure Mariel goes through with the wedding.'

Mariel's eyes turned solemn. 'Leo, it is as I feared.'

'It changes nothing,' he insisted. 'We still have four days. We can find him in London.'

'Three days, Leo,' Mariel corrected. 'It is too late to do anything today.'

Leo glanced to the window. 'There's still daylight left.'

But it would soon be evening. Already the sun was low in the sky. Even if they found a carriage to take them to London, there would not be enough daylight left to reach the city.

'There is something else, Fitz,' Walker broke in. 'I am not so certain that the carriage mishap was an accident.'

Leo looked at him. 'Why do you say so?'

Walker rubbed his chin. 'Well, it is nothing so clear, but after we jumped from the carriage, I saw something. I took no heed of it then, as there were other matters more important.' His glance slid to Penny and back to Leo. 'But afterwards I remembered. I saw a man in the wood, running from the accident. Why would he run from it unless he caused it?'

'Why would he cause it?' It made no sense.

'To stop us on our errand.'

'But no one knew we were going after the bank clerk.' Had Leo missed something?

Walker shrugged. 'Kellford's valet might have guessed.' He glanced away. 'Although I swear I never gave him any reason to think I considered what he told me anything more than gossip. Even so, he never showed any inclination to help his employer in any way. But it is a possibility....'

'Or someone in the gaming hells might have told Kellford I was asking about him.' A sick feeling lodged in Leo's stomach. 'Kellford would have wanted to stop me.'

Leo had made a mistake. He'd underestimated Kellford and the lengths the man would go to in order to achieve his ends.

Mariel touched his arm. 'But he would not have wanted to hurt me. What would that serve?'

'He did not know you would be in the carriage.' Leo himself had not known she would come.

Kellford could not have conceived Mariel would be in the carriage, too.

Her eyes widened. 'Leo, he tried to kill you for helping me.'

'He wanted to stop us, not kill us,' Leo said. 'No one could have planned for the carriage to fall in the river.'

'They took the bank clerk away the same day,' Walker added. 'So they could have been on the road the same time as we were.'

'Kellford must have known our plan.' There was no other explanation.

'He also must have known you could die,' Mariel insisted. 'People die from carriage accidents.'

Penny nodded vigorously.

'Likely he did not care,' Leo mused. 'He has long held me in ill favour.'

Mariel shook her head. 'But there was also Walker and the coachman. Surely he could not have had a dislike for a coachman!'

The world abounded with men who cared only for their own gratification and nothing for another's life. Kellford was but one of them.

She lowered her head into her hands. 'He is a monster.'

Leo regarded her intently. 'That is why you must not marry him.'

'It is too late,' she whispered.

Once again happiness had been within Leo's grasp,

but luck had failed him, as it had failed him before when it came to being with Mariel.

No. He refused to give up. Stone-hard determination grew inside him. He refused to give up.

He stood. 'It might be too late to reach London to-night, but we can get a great deal closer. I am going to find a carriage to take us as far as possible tonight. We might still be able to find the bank clerk in time.'

'I'll go with you,' Walker said.

'I will, too.' Mariel rose from her seat.

Leo put a stilling hand on her arm. 'No, Mariel. Rest your feet. We can move faster without you.' He assured her, 'It is only to procure the carriage. We will return very soon.'

Penny extended a hand. 'Come with me, miss. All our things are here in the room Walker got for me. You and I can pack and have our bags brought to this parlour so we will be all ready to go. We can wait for them here.'

Mariel nodded.

Leo embraced her quickly.

His resolution was strong. He'd not fought for Mariel two years ago. This time he'd fight to the bitter end.

For an hour Mariel paced the length of the private parlour, ignoring the pain in her feet. Penny sat by the window, busying herself with some mending.

The situation was worse than ever. Now her choices were to marry Kellford or risk *Leo's* death—and the death of anyone else who got in the way.

She paced faster.

Finally there was a knock on the door. Before she could say, 'Enter,' it opened and Leo appeared.

Mariel clasped her hands together expectantly. 'Leo?'

He avoided her eye, instead looked towards Penny. 'Miss Jenkins, would you mind leaving us alone for a moment?'

Penny rose and curtsied. She hurried to where Walker waited just outside the doorway.

Mariel faced Leo and instantly knew they'd not had success. 'You did not find a coachman to drive us.'

He met her gaze steadily. 'We enquired everywhere. No one was willing to transport us anywhere before tomorrow.'

She turned away. Leo would be safe tonight. If only he would never go back—

She swung around to him. 'Leo! You do not need to return to London at all. You can simply disappear.' She strode over to him, curling her fingers around his arms. 'Penny and Walker could go with you. I can hire a coach tomorrow and still return to London in time. No one would know I was with you. Once I am married to Kellford, you'll be safe.'

'No. That would never do.' He held her face in his hands. 'I have hired a horse. I will ride to London tonight and start the search for the bank clerk.'

She moved away from his grasp. 'No, Leo.'

'The horse is already saddled and waiting for me.' His voice was firm.

She could not allow him to go to London. 'Kellford will discover you. He will try to kill you again.'

His eyes hardened. 'I can handle myself.'

She gripped his coat. 'I cannot let you do this, Leo. It is too dangerous.'

He remained steady. 'My brothers used to tell me what I could and could not do, what was too dangerous. I have faced danger before, Mariel. I can conquer it.'

'Not alone, then,' she persisted. 'Take Walker with you.'

'I need Walker to stay here with you and Penny.' His voice turned low. 'I will not leave you unprotected.' He leaned down and touched his lips to her forehead. 'Do not worry over me.'

His kiss only increased her pain.

She pulled away. 'Do not leave,' she begged. 'I fear all kinds of frightful things. You put me through this once before, I cannot bear it again. This time I know you will be in danger. We may all travel back tomorrow, then. But I want you to give up trying prevent my marriage. Kellford has won.'

He stroked her cheek. 'I am not ready to give up. I'll have more time if I reach London tonight. Trust me that I can take care of myself.'

Helpless tears stung her eyes, but she refused to stop. 'This is the worst thing you could do, leaving me to worry over you.'

He swept fingers over her hair, a soothing gesture. 'I will be in touch with you as soon as possible.'

When he'd left her two years before, her imagination had gone wild with fear that some danger had befallen him. This time she knew precisely what the danger would be—Kellford. She remained unbending, even when he embraced her and touched her cheek. She was already afraid that this might be the last time she saw him.

She watched him say a quick goodbye to Walker and Penny. He glanced back at her.

Her gaze met his as she stood in the doorway, her fears abounding. She watched him until he disappeared from the public room. Despair threatened. Despair and utter helplessness.

She could see no good outcome. She could only see losing him again.

Penny approached her and put an arm around her. 'Mr Walker is ordering us some food. You should sit now.'

She let Penny lead her to a chair. What difference did it make what she did now?

When Walker entered, she looked at him accusingly. 'You should have stopped him, Walker.'

His brows rose. 'I do not tell him what to do, miss.'

'You should have told him this time,' she insisted. 'He is riding into danger; I am sure of it.'

Walker looked towards the door as if still watching his employer leave. 'He is accustomed to danger.' He turned back to Mariel. 'Do you know how he met me?'

She crossed her arms. What difference could it make?

Walker regarded her intently. 'In Paris I encountered some vicious men intent on stealing my purse. I had but a few coins to my name, so I fought them. It was three against one, but I was raised on the streets and knew how to fight. Turns out Paris street fighters fight with their legs—*savate,* it is called—and a kick has a longer reach than a punch. They were kicking me to a fair pulp, when suddenly this fellow I never saw before jumps in to help me. The other men pulled out knives, but this stranger still fought hard. We beat them off.'

The fight where Leo suffered the wounds that scarred his chest? He'd been heroic. He'd saved Walker. Despair threatened again. He would attempt to be heroic again.

Walker went on. 'Fitz and I have been in other dangerous situations. He handled himself well then, too.'

Mariel closed her eyes; all she could see was men beating Leo and no one to come to his aid.

She regarded Walker again. 'You are not there to help him now, are you?'

'Now he knows someone is after him, he'll take care. Do not worry.' Walker sounded confident.

Mariel tried to be reassured, but she knew when she lay in her bed to try to sleep this night, her fears for Leo would return.

Leo made the most of what was left of the daylight, changing horses frequently at the posting inns along the way, resting little himself. He had ridden through another bout of rain and, in the last two hours, near pitch-black darkness, hardly able to see past the horse's head. The roads were muddy and full of ruts from the day's earlier traffic. For many moments he held his breath against the chance that the horse would stumble or, worse, break a leg.

He rarely rode these days but found little pleasure in returning to horseback for such a difficult journey. Each horse he mounted showed a distinct personality. Some were adequate to the task of getting him back to London as fast as possible. Others were not.

He needed to concentrate on the road. His nerves were strained to breaking point and the darkness ahead was an oppressive void.

Dark and oppressive were his fears of failing Mariel. He simply could not fail. He must find a way to stop Kellford before Kellford married Mariel. Each mile convinced him that finding the bank clerk would be impossible. The man would be well hidden. There was no time for him to discover where. He needed another plan.

His horse stepped into a rut, stumbled and faltered

before regaining its gait. Leo drew his concentration back to the road.

Suddenly hoofbeats sounded from behind. In front of him a man on horseback emerged from the blackness and blocked the road.

'Stand and deliver!' the man shouted.

No bloody way, Leo thought. He urged his horse into a gallop and rode directly for the man.

A shot rang out, its explosion illuminating the darkness for an instant. It missed its mark. Leo continued straight for the man.

The highwayman's horse jumped away at the last minute. Its rump brushed against Leo's leg as he sped past. He heard more than one man riding after him, but Leo did not slow down until their hoofbeats faded into the night.

His heart continued to race and the exhilaration of thwarting danger pumped through his veins. From surviving the river to escaping highwaymen, Leo felt like a soldier who'd run a gauntlet and emerged triumphant.

Only one more trial to endure.

After a final change of horses at the next posting inn, the glow of London's gas lamps soon shone in the distance.

The closer Leo came to London, the more he could turn his thoughts to planning a confrontation with Kellford. If there was no time to find the bank clerk, all that was left was to face Kellford directly and convince him to withdraw from marrying Mariel.

Leo returned his horse to a posting inn at the edge of town and hired a hack to take him to Jermyn Street. Once back in his rooms he built a fire in the grate, took off his clothes and washed himself from top to toe, finally feeling clean of the river. He climbed into bed and fell into an exhausted sleep.

Lord Kellford, seated at the desk in his library, looked up from his papers. 'What news have you for me, Mr Hughes?'

He disliked having this common ruffian come to his house, but it was the lesser of two evils. It would be vastly more unpleasant to meet Hughes in whatever hovel he might dwell.

'Your clerk is safely tucked away in Covent Garden.' Hughes smiled an ingratiating smile. 'And the other... matter...will not trouble you again.'

Kellford's brows rose. 'Not trouble me again? Do not say you have eliminated the problem completely?'

Could he be so fortunate? To be rid of Fitzmanning, that self-righteous prig?

Hughes's grin turned more genuine. 'There was an unfortunate carriage accident. The carriage fell into the Medway River. I saw it disappear under the water and be swept away.'

'And he was inside?' Could this be true?

'He was indeed.'

'Ha! Ha!' Kellford clapped his hands. 'Who could have imagined it? I thought you were merely going to stop him.'

Hughes withdrew a piece of paper from a pocket. 'Here is an accounting of my expenses and the fees we agreed upon.' He handed the paper across the desk.

Ah, yes. An accounting. No doubt Hughes would charge as much as possible.

He took the paper from Hughes's hands and peered at the figures.

He gaze shot up. 'This sum is astronomical! It is twice as much as we agreed upon.'

Hughes shrugged. 'Carriage accidents come at a high price.'

How he detested dealing with these low lifes. As soon as he had his fortune, he'd pay this creature and be done with him. From then on he'd move only in the most esteemed circles, precisely where he belonged.

Kellford glared. 'Your task is not completed yet. You still have to produce the clerk at the church Saturday morning. I want my new wife to see him seated in a pew. Not too close to my guests, mind you, but where she can see him.'

'I'll tend to it personally and produce the final accounting afterwards.'

Kellford was sure putting the bank clerk in a pew at church would be quite an additional cost.

He favoured Hughes with a false smile. 'I am very certain you will.'

There was a knock at the door and Kellford's footman appeared. 'You have a caller, your lordship.'

It was much too early for reputable callers. That was why he'd scheduled Hughes at this hour. It would not do for his reputable visitors to catch him with such a man. Obviously his precautions had not worked perfectly.

'Well, who is it?' Kellford snapped.

The footman answered, 'Mr Leo Fitzmanning, sir.'

Kellford felt his face drain of colour.

'I saw him float away,' Hughes whispered. 'I swear it.'

Kellford signalled for him to be quiet. He turned to the footman. 'You may tell Fitzmanning I will see him here.'

The footman bowed and left.

Kellford, anger raging inside him, ripped up Hughes's tally of expenses. 'Unless a ghost walks in here, Mr Hughes. You failed to complete your task.' He waved him away. 'Hide yourself now while I hear what Fitzmanning has to say.'

Hughes walked to the other end of the room and concealed himself behind the curtains.

The footman appeared again. 'Mr Fitzmanning,' he announced.

Kellford fumed. It was not a ghost who walked in. Fitzmanning was very much alive.

'Surprised to see me, Kellford?' Leo's tone was sarcastic.

Surprised and acutely disappointed, Kellford thought, but he fussed with his papers and acted as if this visit was a mere annoyance.

'Nothing you do surprises me, Fitzmanning,' he drawled. 'Even calling upon me at this hour. To what purpose?'

'To discuss your wedding,' Leo growled. 'Call it off, Kellford. Before you carry this too far.'

'Come now.' Kellford made himself laugh. 'I cannot call it off. Happiness is within my grasp.' He peered at Leo. 'It astonishes me that you think this is any of your affair.'

Leo glared at him. 'I have made it my affair.'

Kellford raised a finger in the air. 'Ah, I recall. My lovely betrothed and your sisters have been friends from childhood. You are here at your sisters' behest. The famous Fitzmanning Miscellany coming to each other's aid.'

Leo looked threatening. 'Enough nonsense. I have an offer. I know you started this whole charade in order to pay your debts. I will pay the money lenders for you.

Release Miss Covendale from her engagement. Give up the ruin of her father. Stop now before you are the one taken to the gaol.'

Did Fitzmanning think *he* was behind the carriage accident? No, no, no, no. That was Hughes's idea.

Kellford raised his brows, pretending surprise. 'You are the one speaking nonsense. As to my betrothal…' he wagged his finger '…a gentleman does not cry off. Only the lady has that privilege. Miss Covendale has only to say she does not wish to marry me and I will properly withdraw.'

Not bad bluffing, thought Kellford smugly to himself.

Leo leaned across the desk. 'And then you will proceed to destroy her father and ruin her family. *That* is not the behaviour of a gentleman, sir.'

Kellford's knees started shaking, but he didn't dare show weakness. He lifted his chin. 'I hardly think one of your birth and reputation is a proper judge of gentlemanly behaviour.'

Leo's back stiffened. 'Never mind about me. This is about Miss Covendale. Release her.'

Kellford put on a charming smile, gratified that he'd got under the other man's skin. 'I shall tell you what I will do. I will forbid my wife to see you or any of your family. I must protect her from your corrupting influence.' He could not resist another barb. 'Your interference is unconscionable… But, then, what should I expect from the bastard children of a debauched duke?'

Leo's voice turned even more menacing. 'Murder, perhaps?'

Kellford could not breathe, but he managed to feign indignation. 'Are you threatening me? Oh, dear. That I cannot tolerate. I'm afraid you must leave now.' He waved the man away as if he were an annoying fly.

'Watch your back, Kellford. I mean to stop you.' Leo looked extremely lethal.

He turned on his heel and strode out of the room, slamming the door behind him.

Kellford drew in a breath. He fussed with his papers, trying to calm down.

Hughes stepped out of his hiding place.

Kellford looked up at him. 'What are you waiting for, Hughes? Follow him. Do not fail this time.'

Chapter Eighteen

Hughes hurried out of the town house onto Mayfair street. Fitzmanning was nearing the end of the street, walking at a fast pace.

Still angry, Hughes figured. Kellford had made the man spitting mad.

Hughes whistled for his men. Two of them had accompanied him in case Kellford gave them any trouble.

They emerged from where they were hiding.

'We have to nab that fellow.' Hughes pointed to Leo. 'Try to get ahead of him. He's probably going to Jermyn Street. When it is safe, we grab him.'

The men nodded and took off in different directions to get ahead of Leo without him knowing. Hughes followed behind, keeping him in sight.

His quarry strode towards Berkeley Street. It was busy with traffic. Not a good place to capture him. Not that there were any good places for it between here and the man's rooms on Jermyn Street. They might have to break into his rooms. Not good odds if his servant was in there, though.

Hughes did not see his men, but trusted they were

somewhere ahead. They'd better be. Too much money was at stake and Hughes was not about to lose out at this late date.

Leo strode into the crush of pedestrians on Berkeley Street, still angry. He'd come close to hauling Kellford out from behind his desk and killing him with his bare hands. It had been a huge gamble to try to get Kellford to listen to reason.

He was fresh out of options. He could go to Doring and beg him to accept the return of his money without prosecuting Mariel's father, but why should the man listen to him? What influence could he have?

He had no doubt he and Walker could find the bank clerk eventually, but in less than three days? It had taken them longer than that the first time and now Kellford knew he was looking for the man.

Leo resisted the impulse to push his way through the crowded street. What was he in a hurry for? It was merely anger propelling him forwards. The crowd thinned and he increased his pace again.

It had been a mistake to call upon Kellford, but what else was he to do? Where could he look in London for a man who was meant to be kept out of sight?

Leo crossed Piccadilly, wondering why he was headed back to his rooms. There must be something else he could do, something he'd not thought of yet.

When he started across Arlington Street two men sprang out. Before he could gather his wits, the men pushed him into an alley. Leo twisted out of one man's grip. He swung and landed a hard right to the other man's jaw, sending him sprawling. The first man pulled a knife and charged for him.

Leo grabbed the man's wrist and spun him around,

pulling up on the man's arm behind his back. The knife fell and Leo dived for it.

He picked it up and held it out in front of him. 'Get back!' he growled, slashing at the air, like Walker had once shown him. He inched towards the entrance of the alley.

He was about to step into the safety of busy Piccadilly Street when he was seized from behind, his arms immobilised. The first two men surged forwards. They punched him in the stomach and face. Again and again.

Leo was consumed with pain. If he did not do something, these thugs would beat him senseless.

Unless he became senseless first.

Leo made himself into dead weight, letting the knife fall from a hand gone slack. If he pretended to be knocked out, perhaps he'd have another chance to escape.

'Now we got him, do we kill him or what?' one of the men asked.

Leo felt a new surge of fear.

'Bloody good idea,' the man holding him said. He was lowered to his knees and his head jerked back to expose his throat.

He'd be damned if he'd let them get away with that.

Leo sprang to life, twisting the man, holding him into the path of the knife.

'Ahh!' cried the man who clutched his arm.

Leo ran.

'Don't stand there!' he heard behind him. 'After him!'

He didn't look back and didn't stop, even when he reached the street. He ran to St James's.

This had been no robbery attempt. He'd been the target for killing, just as he had been in the carriage accident. And how coincidental that he'd just left Kellford's.

He heard the pounding of feet behind him. He was the target, for certain. He was close to his rooms, but instinct told him it wouldn't be safe there. That's precisely where they expected him to run. He needed to fool them again.

Leo ran down Jermyn Street, letting them think they knew where he was bound, but, at the last minute, he turned into the churchyard and crossed through it to return to Piccadilly.

He entered the Burlington Arcade, surmising his pursuers would not try anything with the beadles guarding the place. Breathing hard, he ducked into a shop and received curious stares from the clerk and other shoppers. He pretended to look at the merchandise, but watched until his pursuers hurried by.

He walked out, melding into the Arcade's other visitors. He went back to the entrance, trying not to call attention to himself. He moved into Old Bond Street, disappearing from sight as quickly as he could, trying to decide where to go. Where to hide.

He'd succeeded in fighting off the three men, but he might not be so lucky if they caught him a second time. They'd underestimated him once and were not likely to do so again. Now he had a new problem—how to avoid capture and certain death and still save Mariel.

He crossed Berkeley Street again and lost himself in the labyrinth of Mayfair. He walked aimlessly, avoiding Charles Street, although he toyed with the idea of calling on Kellford again and giving him a taste of what he'd just been through.

He thought better of it.

Leo wandered to Park Lane, considering his options. Perhaps he should call upon Mariel's father, convince the man his neck was not worth the sacrifice of his daughter.

He laughed to himself. Covendale would never listen to him. If Covendale cared about his daughter, he would never have put her in this predicament. Indeed, if he cared about her, he would have accepted Leo's suit all those years ago. Besides, if Leo stood in front of the man, he'd more than likely say exactly what he thought of a father who sacrificed his daughter to a man like Kellford.

Leo had time to contemplate his next move. He walked slowly up Park Lane, glancing at Hyde Park on his left, remembering first telling Mariel about Kellford there, remembering how it felt to see her again, how unchanged his feelings had been towards her, how deeply it hurt to have lost her.

The pain of losing her again shot through him, worse than the recent blows to his gut and face. He closed his eyes until he could bear the agony. When he opened his eyes he was staring at Manning House.

His brother's house.

His throat tightened and his insides felt as shredded as if the knife had sliced into him.

Suddenly Mariel's voice came to him. *Ask for help.*

Leo sprinted up to the door and sounded the huge brass knocker with its ducal crest. This time the footman who answered the door was a man who had also been in his father's employ.

He immediately recognised Leo and ushered him in. 'Master Leo! What has happened to you?'

Leo was touched by the man's obvious concern. 'A minor mishap, Shaw. Is my brother at home?'

'I'll see, sir. Come wait in the drawing room.' Shaw moved as if to assist Leo.

Leo shook his head. 'Don't worry over me. I look worse than I feel. Just find my brother.'

It seemed a long time since Leo had been in this room although it had been mere days since his brothers and sisters gathered for the dinner party. So much had happened since then.

He heard footsteps running on the marble floor of the hall. The door flung open and his brother entered, hurrying up to him.

'Leo! Shaw said you were injured.' Nicholas examined him, then put an arm around his shoulders. 'Come sit, for God's sake. Why are you standing?'

Leo lifted a hand. 'I am not hurt, Nick. But I am in trouble. Big trouble. I just need for you to listen to me. Hear me out.'

Nicholas nodded, but sat Leo in one of the chairs. Holding up a finger, he signalled Leo to wait and went to a cabinet and produced a carafe of brandy and two glasses. As if he were a servant and not a duke, Nicholas poured one drink for Leo. Then he positioned a chair directly facing Leo and poured a glass for himself.

He didn't even speak after all that. He simply waited.

Leo took a long sip of the brandy. The warming liquid slid down his throat and calmed him. He took a breath and looked directly at his brother.

'Nick, I need your help....'

Hughes's men met him at the tavern in Covent Garden near where the bank clerk was comfortably housed. Hughes intended to be paid for all the work he'd done and that would not happen unless they found Fitzmanning.

'Well?' he addressed the men.

'We lost him,' one admitted.

'In the Burlington Arcade,' the other said.

Hughes's anger boiled. His arm ached from the gash that the surgeon had just stitched closed. He was in no mood for failure.

'You lost him? You incompetent curs!' He pounded the table with a fist. 'Go back out there and *find* him.' He summoned another man to the table. 'These dunderheads lost him. Round up as many men as you can and find him. Set some men to watch his rooms, Covendale's and Kellford's. While you are at it, have men watch the houses of his brothers and sisters. And the gaming hells, any place he might hide. I'll brook no failure in this. We find him and eliminate him or we do not get paid.'

'Yes, sir,' the man said.

Hughes drained his glass of gin. 'Do not fail me in this. I want him found.' He lowered his voice. 'I want him dead.'

Leo told Nicholas the whole story, and, for once, his brother did not interrupt.

When he finished, Nicholas poured him more brandy, and said, 'I think we should send for Brenner and Stephen.'

Leo nodded.

Within an hour Brenner and Stephen arrived, and, in the meantime, Nicholas had persuaded Leo to wash, don a fresh set of clothing and eat a generous meal. It was nearing noon. Mariel could be arriving in London any time now.

The brothers gathered in Nicholas's library under the watchful eyes of their father's portrait. Leo remembered how his father always made it seem possible to do anything he wanted to do. It was how his father had lived his life, whether what he wanted defied convention or not. It was a lesson Leo had only belatedly learned. Here with his brothers surrounding him, Leo could almost feel the optimism that had been his father's hallmark.

He repeated the story a second time for Brenner and Stephen. It was easier than before, with Nick sitting next to him, filling in details he'd forgotten.

'My God,' Stephen said after it was all over. 'Mariel Covendale? Now you say it, I can very well imagine the two of you together.'

'You are skipping over the little matter of Kellford,' Leo responded.

Stephen waved a dismissive hand. 'We'll fix that.'

Brenner leaned forwards. 'What do you want to do now, Leo?'

Leo could think of only one thing. 'I want to take away the problem once and for all.'

Stephen broke in, 'Kill Kellford, do you mean?'

'It is a thought.' Leo blew out a breath. 'Although I have no wish to hang for the likes of him. No, better to go to Doring. Compensate him for the money Covendale stole from him and convince him not to take any action against his cousin.'

'I agree,' Brenner said.

'I can put up the money.' Nicholas grinned. 'I'm good for it.'

Good for it? He was rich as Croesus.

'No, Nick. I need to pay,' Leo said sharply.

Nicholas peered at him. 'Are you certain, Leo? Because it is truly a trifle to me.'

'I know, but it is a matter of importance to me.' It was of vital importance to Leo. He owed it to Mariel.

'Very well.' Nicholas rose and poured them all more brandy.

Leo gaped at his brother. He'd expected a huge battle, with Brenner and Stephen joining in, insisting he should take Nicholas's offer.

'The problem is,' Leo went on. 'I am not even acquainted with Doring. Why would he allow me to convince him not to prosecute?'

'I have had some contact with him on a parliamentary matter,' Nicholas said.

'I know him slightly,' Brenner added.

'As do I,' Stephen said.

'We should all go to call upon him.' Brenner stood, as if they were leaving this very minute. 'Strength in numbers.'

'We may need strength in numbers if Kellford's men find us.' Stephen glanced out the window.

'Nick, you must not go,' Leo said. 'Not with Emily increasing.'

'She will understand,' Nicholas reassured him. 'Besides, a couple of days won't make a difference. She's not due that soon.'

Could they accomplish all this in time?

Leo glanced up at their father's portrait. He could almost hear his father bellow, 'Of course you can.'

Leo's brothers debated how they should travel to Doring and how to get Leo out of the house unnoticed, just in case Kellford's men were watching. Likewise they discussed how to get messages through to Walker and Mariel.

Leo watched them. He needed them, he realised. Never had he known that with such surety than at this moment.

He could be his own man and still not do it all alone.

When the brothers settled on a plan, Brenner turned to Leo. 'What do you think? Is this what you wish to do?'

Leo looked from one to the other. 'I am unused to my

brothers asking *my* wishes. I thought you would scold me for mucking up matters with Mariel in the first place and then go on to tell me precisely what I'd done wrong every step of the way.'

Nicholas touched his shoulder. 'Leo, this isn't merely some scrape you've gotten yourself into; this is your life at stake. Did you not think we could tell the difference?'

Stephen laughed. 'Yes, we never guessed it was about you and *Mariel Covendale*. Charlotte and Annalise are going to have apoplexy when they find out. They're the ones you should worry about.' He clapped Leo on the back. 'You must let me be there when you tell them. I want to see their faces.'

There was a knock on the door.

'Yes?' Nicholas said.

Shaw opened the door. 'Mrs Bassington, your Grace.'

'Seems I'll be granted part of my wish,' Stephen murmured.

Charlotte burst into the room. 'Nicky, I must speak with—' She came to a sudden halt as her brothers all rose. 'Oh, my!' She looked from one to the other. 'What are you all doing here?'

Nicholas walked over to her and gave her a peck on the cheek. 'What are *you* doing here, Charlotte? You are not even toting one of the pugs.'

She gave him an exasperated look. 'Do not jest. I am in such a pickle and Drew is off somewhere with Amesby. I could not think what to do.'

Nicholas put his arm around her shoulders and gave her a squeeze. 'Come, sit and tell us. With all of us here, we should be able to help you.'

Her expression turned wary. 'It is a rather private matter concerning someone else. I do not know if I should tell all of you.'

Brenner also approached her. 'Now, if you cannot tell your brothers, who can you trust? We have no secrets in this family.'

'Or not too many...' Stephen clarified.

Leo watched this with growing trepidation.

Her explanation came in a flood of words. 'I lied about Mariel...*for* Mariel actually—Mariel Covendale, you know—she asked me to say she was staying at my house, but her father discovered that it was not so, and now I am certain I have managed to get Mariel in terrible trouble, but I do not know what to do about it.'

'They know she was not at your house?' Leo cried. 'When did they discover it?'

Charlotte regarded him with a puzzled expression. 'This morning, apparently. Why?'

'Damnation!' He pounded his fist on Nicholas's desk. 'Could they not have waited a few more hours?'

Charlotte's brows rose so high they almost disappeared into her bonnet.

Stephen sat down next to her and took her hand. 'We have quite a tale to tell you, Charlotte.'

Chapter Nineteen

The hackney coach stopped in front of the Covendale town house. Mariel and Penny climbed out and retrieved their baggage. It was midafternoon. Would Leo have sent a message already? Mariel hoped so.

Ever since he had ridden off the day before, her nerves had not settled. Riding at night posed enough dangers, but how much worse it would be if Kellford discovered Leo was back in London and sent more men to kill him? During the long carriage ride from their inn in Kent her imagination had provided endless dire consequences for him.

She tried to block her fears, reminding herself that Leo said she must trust him, but the fears always broke through.

A message was all she desired.

The town-house door opened before she and Penny had a chance to knock.

'Ah, good day, Edward,' Mariel said to the footman. 'You must have seen us arrive.'

'Yes, miss.' His expression looked distressed.

'Is something amiss, Edward?' she asked.

'You father,' he said quietly. 'Towering rage.'

'Mariel!'

It was her father's voice, booming from the stairway. He descended, looking more than enraged. He looked panicked.

'You and your maid will attend me in the drawing room immediately,' her father ordered.

Penny looked as if she would faint. Mariel took her arm and walked her into the drawing room.

'Where have you been, Mariel?' her father demanded, his voice high-pitched.

'I left you a note. I visited Charlotte Bassington.' She kept her gaze steady.

Her father marched up to her and wagged a finger inches from her face. 'You did no such thing!'

She forced herself not to flinch. 'I assure you I did.'

His eyes looked wild and spittle formed at the corners of his mouth. 'I called there this morning to bring you back. You were not there!'

'I left early in the day,' she responded calmly.

'You are lying to me!' her father shouted.

'It is the truth.' She *had* left early, but not from Charlotte's house.

He put his fists on his hips. 'Then where have you been all day?'

This time she would lie. 'Shopping in Cheapside.'

They could have been shopping in Cheapside. A few days ago she would have shopped anywhere merely to avoid him.

Her father scoffed. 'I do not believe you.' Turning to Penny, he demanded, 'You were with her, girl? Where was she? If you value your employment, you will tell me now.'

Penny still clung to Mariel. 'Ch-Cheapside, sir.' Mariel felt her trembling. 'Shopping.'

Mariel's father pulled Penny away from Mariel and shook her by the shoulders. 'Tell me the truth. Or you are fired.'

'Cheapside!' Penny sounded terrified.

Mariel's father shoved Penny away so forcefully, the girl almost fell. 'One more chance, girl, or you will be discharged immediately.'

'No!' Mariel put a protective arm around Penny. 'Leave her alone!'

'Cheapside,' Penny rasped. 'Shopping.'

Mariel's father grabbed Penny by the front of her dress and pulled her from Mariel's grasp. 'Out!' He pushed her towards the door. 'You are discharged!'

Mariel ran to her. 'You cannot do that, Father.'

'I pay her wages. I most certainly can.' He pointed at Mariel. 'You tell me the truth and she may stay.'

'No, miss,' Penny pleaded.

'Very well, Father, I will tell you where I was.' Mariel stood between Penny and her father. 'I was with a lover!'

'A lover?' Her father turned so white she thought he would pass out. 'You fool! Who is this lover? What if Kellford gets wind of this? He'll not want damaged goods! You'll ruin everything. What will happen to me?'

'To you?' Mariel spoke in a low tone. 'Is it not time to consider me? Or if not me, my mother and sisters? You are responsible for this trouble, Father. Not I.'

'That is neither here nor there,' he said to no purpose. 'Everything was settled. Now you could ruin it!'

Mariel kept an arm around Penny, who wiped her eyes and sniffled. 'I hope I do ruin it!' Mariel said. 'I do not want this marriage.'

His mouth dropped open. 'You would wish your father dead? You ungrateful child.' He cleared his throat and spoke in a careful tone. 'This lover of yours must be prevented from causing any problems. Who is he?'

Mariel stood her ground. 'I will not tell you. It is my own affair and had nothing to do with you.'

Her father looked as if he might say more to her, but a sly expression came over his face.

He turned to Penny. 'You, girl!' he said in a mollifying voice. 'You will tell me who this man is.'

Penny's eyes widened again and she shook her head.

Her father swung back to Mariel, a snide smile on his face. 'Tell me, then, who is the man?'

'Do not do tell, miss,' Penny cried.

How could she tell? If her father let Leo's name slip in front of Kellford, it would definitely cost Leo his life. But she also could not allow him to use Penny to get his way.

'Out with it,' her father demanded, while tears ran down Penny's cheeks. 'Tell me the name of the man or you are discharged.'

'I will not tell you, sir.' Penny sobbed.

He pointed to the door. 'Then, go. Leave this house immediately. This instant!'

Mariel embraced Penny and whispered in her ear, 'Go to Walker. He will take care of you. Tell him what happened here.'

'Yes, miss.' Penny nodded.

Mariel gave her one swift hug before Penny hurried out of the room.

Mariel faced her father again. 'That was not well done of you, Father.'

Her father wiped his face. 'Tell me the man's name and she may come back.' His voice was more desperate than demanding.

She merely glared at him.

'Please, Mariel?' His breathing accelerated. 'Please do not ruin this. I'll hang, if you do.'

'At the moment, Father, I do not care.' She was still furious at him for sending Penny away. 'You have accomplished nothing but the injury of an innocent girl. I cannot stand the sight of you. I am going to my room.'

She did not wait for his permission.

By the time she reached the hall, Edward, who was just closing the door on Penny, waved her over. 'You have a message, Miss Covendale.'

Her father marched past her and snatched the paper from Edward's hand. He read it and crumpled it in his fist. 'Go up to your room, you ungrateful wretch.'

She reached for the note in her father's hand. 'I'll have my note first.'

He pulled it out of her reach. 'Go to your room.'

This was impossible to tolerate. The message was from Leo; she just knew it.

Edward approached her, standing between her and her father. 'I will carry your bag for you, miss. Penny took hers with her.' He winked, which was very unlike him.

She followed the footman up the two flights of stairs to her bedchamber.

At her door, he turned to her and leaned close. 'I read the note,' he said in a hushed tone.

'You read it!' Her heart beat faster.

He looked sheepish. 'Well, the seal broke.' He opened the door and put her bag inside her room.

She seized his arm. 'What did it say?'

'It said, *Arrived safely. Have plan. Do not worry. Take care.*' He lifted his palms in the air. 'It was not signed.'

She squeezed his arm. 'Thank you, Edward. It is enough.'

He bowed and started to walk away, but turned back. 'It was not right for Mr Covendale to dismiss Penny like that.'

'I agree, Edward.' It was abominable.

He nodded and hurried back to the stairway.

Mariel entered her room and closed the door behind her.

Bless Edward for being a busybody. The note was not nearly enough, though. It said almost nothing. Like her note to Leo two years ago. Had she written more carefully, he might have guessed her father's manipulation. But Leo's note might have been cryptic on purpose. If anyone—such as her father—confiscated it, it would tell them nothing.

But why had Leo told *her* to take care? Did danger still exist? It must or he would not have written that. She could do nothing but wait, not knowing at all what was happening outside these walls.

She lowered her face into her hands. Once again she was left waiting...and not knowing.

Penny walked through Mayfair with tears streaming down her cheeks. She was terrified. She had no employment and no references. How was she to find a new position?

Plus what would happen to Miss Covendale? Her father was so very angry. Could he force her to marry Lord Kellford, after all?

She hurried through the streets, clutching her portmanteau, all she had of her belongings. Would she even be able to get her other things from her old room at the Covendale town house—the pair of gloves from her father's shop, the garnet cross that had been her mother's? That was all she had left of them.

When she reached St James's Street, young gentlemen loitered on the corner. They made rude comments to her as she passed by. Her faced burned with shame at the words they used and the names they called her. She kept her eyes straight ahead and pretended she did not hear them.

Soon she could see the building where Mr Fitzmanning lived. She quickened her step and wiped her eyes before knocking upon the door.

There was no answer. Her nerves jangled even more. What if Mr Walker or Mr Fitzmanning were not at home?

Finally she heard Walker's voice behind the door. 'Who is there?'

'It is Penny,' she cried. 'Oh, please open the door for me!'

The door opened and he seized her arm and pulled her inside, putting her behind him. He glanced quickly out the doorway before closing the door again and turning to her. 'Why are you here? What has happened?'

He sounded angry and it frightened her. 'I—I had nowhere else to go.' Her voice cracked.

He wrapped his arms around her. 'Do not weep. Do not weep. I dislike seeing you so distressed.'

She clung to him. He was so strong and he smelled so nice and she felt so safe with him. He brought her over to a sofa and sat down with her.

Taking her hands in his, he said, 'Now tell me what happened.'

'Mr Covendale found out that my lady lied to him and he tried to make me tell where she went and who she was with, but I wouldn't do it.' She took a shuddering breath. 'So he discharged me and sent me away!'

His expression hardened. 'He discharged you?'

She nodded and tears filled her eyes again. 'What will happen to me? How will I find another position?'

He held her again. 'You do not need another position. I will take care of you.'

It seemed like he held her a very long time. He soothed her with this talk of taking care of her. She would be safe forever. She took a deep breath at the satisfaction of that thought.

Finally he released her and handed her his handkerchief. She wiped her eyes and blew her nose.

'Why were you angry at me when you opened the door?' she asked, holding the handkerchief in her hand and vowing to wash it for him.

His expression hardened again. 'I was not angry at you. There are men watching these rooms—Kellford's men, I imagine—I merely wanted to get you inside as quickly as I could.'

Her eyes widened. 'Where is Mr Fitzmanning?'

He frowned. 'I do not know. A note was here when I arrived. It had been slipped under the door. It only said he would be away.' He rubbed his face. 'Better he stay away. I'm worried that these ruffians will nab him if he comes near.'

'We can watch for him and warn him,' she offered.

He wore the nicest expression of concern for her. 'I will fix you something to eat. No doubt they did not feed you at the Covendale house.'

'We had just walked in when her father set upon her.' She rose and moved to a chair with a view of the window. 'Should I watch out the window while you cook?'

'No need. He won't be home tonight.' He picked up a piece of paper and unfolded it. *'I'll be gone a day,* it says.'

'Where did he go?' she asked.

He looked at the note again. 'I do not know.'

'He'll be away all night?'

He nodded. 'I suppose.'

That meant she would be alone with Walker all night long. Like at the inn. The idea excited her.

Kellford descended his stairs, spying Hughes waiting below in the hall, twirling his hat in his hand. When he reached the bottom step, he gestured for Hughes to follow him into the drawing room. He checked his timepiece, a fine gold watch that he had purchased after a very lucrative spell of faro. In an hour's time he had an appointment with Mr Carter. The money lender undoubtedly wanted to be assured that he'd soon receive payment.

Kellford hoped Hughes would bring him news that meant Carter would have nothing to be concerned about.

'Well, what do you have to say?' Kellford asked. 'It had better be good news.'

'It is good news, you could say.' Hughes spoke with an edge to his voice.

It made Kellford uneasy. 'Out with it, then.'

Hughes pulled at his collar. 'We have not captured him, but we have the next best thing. He will not bother you.'

Kellford's blood raced. 'Did you kill him?'

Hughes averted his gaze. 'No...but let me explain.'

Kellford waved his hand impatiently.

Hughes cleared his throat. 'I spread my men throughout the city, anywhere Fitzmanning might go—at great expense, I might add.'

'An expense you will, of course, take upon yourself,' Kellford inserted.

Hughes inclined his head. 'As I was saying, my men were watching for Fitzmanning. Lo and behold, one of them spots him coming from his brother's house. There had been lots of activity there all afternoon. Footmen coming and going; two gentlemen and one lady calling. Nobody saw Fitzmanning go in, though.'

Kellford poured himself a glass of sherry. He did not offer Hughes any.

'After an hour or so, grooms bring four horses around,' Hughes went on. 'A little while later, out he comes. Fitzmanning. The duke is with him, giving orders to everybody. Two other gents are with them. They mount up, all these gents around Fitzmanning. There was no way my men could get to him.'

'Where did they go?' Kellford took a sip, feeling his nerves jangle.

'They rode out of town,' the man responded.

'How do you know they rode out of town?' Hughes asked.

Hughes looked self-satisfied. 'My men followed them, which was not too hard with all the other carriages and such on the streets. They did not travel fast. My men were able to follow them all the way to Westminster Bridge.'

Kellford felt his cheeks flush. 'You dolt! What if they merely had an errand in Lambeth?'

Hughes smirked. 'Well, in that case the men posted at the bridge will see them upon their return.' He stared at Kellford's sherry glass. 'I also left a man at the duke's house in case they rode back another way.'

Kellford nodded approvingly. 'That might do it.'

Kellford's confidence was restored. He would convince Mr Carter that all was proceeding without mishap.

He'd also make certain there were no surprises at the church. His wedding was a mere two days away.

When it was finally dark outside, Walker could tolerate no more waiting. He decided to leave the rooms and gather whatever information he could.

'I'll be back as soon as I am able,' he told Penny. 'Do not allow anyone to enter. Do not even respond if there is a knock on the door. Pretend you are not here.'

She nodded, her beautiful blue eyes wary.

'Go sleep in my bed. I'll take Fitz's when I return.' He put on a black coat, raising the collar to better hide his white shirt.

'I won't sleep until you return,' she said in a trembling voice.

He reached over and touched her arm.

Her eyes looked into his. 'You must be careful.'

'I will.'

She then did a very unexpected thing. She rose on tiptoe and kissed him. The simple touch of her lips ignited his senses. And made him feel valued.

He now possessed a reason to be careful, so he could come back to her. No more living for the moment, not caring what came next. In fact, he no longer liked the idea of the trade he and Fitz were involved in. When this was all over, he'd tell Fitz he wanted to do business on the up and up. He wanted to be a man deserving of Penny's sweet kiss. He wanted to spend the rest of his life making hers happy.

He climbed out a back window and dropped to the ground. Soundlessly he made his way out the small yard behind the building and onto the street. Hiding in the shadows, he spied two men still watching for Fitz. He wished he could warn Fitz before he returned and walked into a trap.

Walker hurried away, bound for the tavern where he'd met Kellford's valet. He walked in the place and ordered ale, thirsty after hurrying through town. He threaded his way through the tables, looking for the valet.

'Walker!' a voice called.

It was Kellford's valet, seated at a table alone. The fussy man looked uncharacteristically dishevelled. His clothing was wrinkled and he'd not shaved.

Walker approached the man's table. 'What has happened to you?'

'I hoped you'd come,' the man said, slurring his words. 'I've been given the sack. Summarily discharged without references or prospects.'

Like Penny, Walker thought. He joined the man's table.

The valet peered at him. 'Do you work for Mr Fitzmanning?'

No sense lying about it. 'I do.'

'And you wanted information from me?' He looked wounded.

Walker nodded. 'Fitzmanning is a family friend of Miss Covendale and does not wish to see her ill used.'

'Ah.' The valet's brow cleared. 'I understand perfectly. The poor lady. But you need not have engaged in deception.'

'I did not deceive,' countered Walker. 'I merely did not tell you the name of my employer.'

The valet waved a hand. 'Makes not a whit of difference now. I'm sacked because Kellford assumed I'd been the one to tattle about the bank clerk and his where-abouts.'

'I am sorry to hear it,' Walker said with honesty. 'Do you know where the bank clerk is at present?' If he could find the bank clerk tomorrow, there would still be time to ensure the clerk's cooperation.

'Covent Garden, but I do not know precisely where. Kellford's newly hired men took care of it.' He paused. 'Those men were hired to eliminate your Mr Fitzmanning. Kellford's sparing no expense.'

'We've been made aware of that fact.' Walker reached into his coat pocket and removed a calling card. 'This has my direction. Come see me. You've helped us and we will help you.'

Chapter Twenty

The next morning Mariel requested a bath, something she longed for, but also something that provided her an excuse to avoid her parents.

Her father had made her so angry the day before that she could not think straight. To send Penny away! It was unconscionable. To have no word of her—coupled with not knowing Leo's whereabouts—was driving her mad.

Perhaps Edward would pass notes for her. He'd acted as her ally before.

Heartened by this idea, Mariel was able to relish the clean water and the fragrant French soap that was her favourite. She bathed thoroughly and washed her hair and, with one of the housemaids to assist her, dressed in a morning dress.

The maid made a great effort to see that she was comfortable. The girl did not speak directly, but Mariel suspected all the servants knew by now that she did not want to marry Kellford and that she'd been with another man. It touched her beyond measure that the servants showed her sympathy rather than censure.

Combing the knots and tangles from her hair brought back the memory of the river and how close she and Leo had come to death. How much it had changed things for her. Nothing mattered more to her than Leo being alive and unharmed, but she could not know if he were ambushed or captured or...worse.

She held her head. Her mind was spinning as it had done two years before, consumed with fears and speculation, not knowing where he was, if he was safe.

Please let him be alive, she prayed. *Please just let him be alive.*

The maid knocked on the bedchamber door and opened it a crack. 'Lord Kellford to see you, miss!'

'Kellford?' What did he want?

'Edward said he is waiting in the drawing room.' The girl's voice showed the alarm Mariel felt inside.

'This is the last person I wish to see,' she muttered.

The housemaid nodded in agreement.

She took a breath and gestured for the maid to come over. 'Help me put my hair up into a cap.'

The girl twisted her still-damp hair into a bun and secured it with hairpins.

'My caps are in the second drawer in the chest of drawers.' Mariel stuck in more hairpins while the maid ran to find a cap.

She brought back one made entirely of Belgian lace, edged in a ruffle and embellished with a pink silk ribbon. It was the prettiest one in her possession.

She would have preferred to look dowdy.

She did not want to tarry, however. She wanted to hear what Kellford had to say, hear if he would speak of Leo.

When she entered the drawing room, Kellford was seated with her mother. Her father stood nearby.

Kellford immediately stood and approached her with

arms open. 'Good morning, my dear!' he exclaimed, placing a kiss upon her cheek.

It paid to be careful. This was a man willing to kill Leo on the mere chance he might spoil the scheme to marry her. She must not let on that she knew anything about that, nor that Leo had survived the attempt.

'Why are you here?' she asked, finding it impossible to be entirely civil.

Her father sent her an anxious glance.

Kellford chuckled good-naturedly. 'Why, to see my prospective bride. Why else? Only one more day to go, my dear.'

'It is so exciting!' her mother piped up. 'Tomorrow at this time we shall be at the church with several of our dear friends to share the day with us.'

Kellford smiled. 'Are you quite prepared for the wedding, my dear?'

She faced him without expression. 'Not entirely.'

He gaped at her in mock horror. 'My goodness! You had better get busy. I do not wish to be kept waiting at the altar.'

'She will be there,' her father said reassuringly. 'I will see to it.'

Kellford's grin widened. 'I trust you will, sir. I have never doubted your willingness to give away your daughter.'

'I do think she jests.' Her mother tittered nervously. 'Her bridal clothes are ready. All is in preparation for the wedding breakfast. I cannot see what more needs to be done.'

Kellford walked back to Mariel's mother and took her hand. 'I am certain you have personally seen to every detail. I could not be more grateful to you.'

Her mother had done more fretting than anything

else, but Mariel did not care about the wedding breakfast. She did not care about the wedding clothes. She only wanted Leo to be safe.

'Mother,' she impulsively asked, 'would you mind terribly if I spoke to Lord Kellford and Father alone?'

Her mother looked alarmed. 'Well...no... I suppose not.' Kellford assisted her in rising from her seat.

Mariel's father glared at his daughter, but a twitching hand showed he also feared what she might say or do.

She walked her mother to the door.

'You will be good, will you not, Mariel?' her mother pleaded.

Perhaps her mother was more aware than Mariel thought. 'Do not worry, Mama.'

When the door closed behind her mother, Mariel leaned against it. 'I have a proposition for you.'

Her father braced himself against the back of a chair. Kellford merely smiled, as if whatever transpired would amuse him.

One last try, Mariel thought.

She walked towards them. 'As you both know, I do not want this marriage.' She glanced at her father. 'But I also do not want my father to be apprehended for theft and I do not want scandal. I have a solution for all of us.' She faced Kellford. 'I will pay your outstanding debts. I will even double the figure.'

Kellford's eyes were cold. 'You have no money, my dear, not unless you marry me.'

'I can borrow the money,' she retorted. 'In two years' time I will be able to repay the debt.'

Offering Kellford this proposition was surely a forlorn hope, but she had to try.

Kellford slithered closer to her. 'See? That is why

I must marry you, my dear. You have no idea how to manage money. It would be foolish to double a figure when half the amount would do. And where would you get such a loan? I assure you no bank would lend to you.'

She straightened. 'Perhaps not a bank, but I suspect the Duke of Manning would.' Or his brother. 'I am certain my friend, his sister, would convince him.'

Kellford's eyes flickered, but he resumed his apparent good humour. 'Not without charging interest and then you would lose even more of your fortune. And to no good purpose, I might add.' He shook his head. 'No, you are no manager of money, my dear. You must marry me and let me take that burden off your shoulders.' He turned to her father. 'You agree, do you not, Mr Covendale?'

Her father nodded. 'Of course I agree.'

'Do not be ridiculous,' Mariel said. 'You want my fortune, nothing else.'

She had known this all along, of course, but could not resist one last attempt.

Kellford's eyes flickered with malevolence. 'I assure you, I want more than your fortune.'

Mariel shivered.

Kellford slid a glance back to her father. 'Mr Covendale, it is my turn to ask an indulgence. May I have a few moments with my lovely betrothed?'

'Certainly.' Her father could hardly be more agreeable. Anything to keep Kellford from reporting his crime, Mariel suspected.

Her father left the room and Kellford turned back to her. He was no longer smiling.

She stood her ground while he came so close she could smell his breath.

'I have had enough of you involving the Fitzmanning Miscellany in our affairs.' His voice lost all its charm. 'It stops now.'

She made herself stare blankly. 'Asking my friend to make the request of the duke is not involving the whole family.'

He ran his finger down the ruffled lace of her cap. 'Do not play innocent with me, my dear. I know you sent the bastard brother after the bank clerk.'

She did not flinch. 'Bastard brother?'

He laughed. 'You know perfectly well whom I mean.' He gave her a self-satisfied look. 'But you need not concern yourself further with Leo Fitzmanning.'

Her knees weakened. Had something happened to Leo? Or did Kellford still believe Leo drowned in the river?

'Concern myself? Are you jesting?' She made her tone indifferent, but her heart pounded.

Please let him be alive, she prayed. *Let him be alive.*

Kellford smirked. 'An unimpeachable source informed me that Fitzmanning and his brothers left town yesterday.' He stuck out a prideful chin. 'Rode away, all four of them, over the Westminster Bridge. They are gone, my dear. Perhaps I had some influence over their leaving. I would fancy I did.'

Relief washed over her. His brothers were keeping him safe. She could envision it—Leo's brothers discovering the attempt on his life and spiriting him away. They could be taking him to Ramsgate to catch a packet to Calais, for all she knew. He would be safe.

He wagged a finger in her face. 'So none of the Fitzmanning Miscellany will be riding in to rescue you. And, believe me, if they are looking for the bank clerk, they will not find him. He is in town, close by in case I need him.

As the housekeeper in his hunting lodge had told Walker.

Mariel must not appear affected.

She scoffed, 'You needed my father to leave the room so he would not hear that the Duke of Manning and his brothers rode out of town? You could only tell me this privately?'

He leaned close again. 'I wanted you to know that I have ways of eliminating people who become troublesome to me. If you value your friends, you will not allow them to cross me.'

'I am so warned,' she responded sarcastically.

'And you will not cross me, my dear,' he continued. 'Recall that once I have your fortune, your value to me will be greatly diminished.'

She understood that implied threat.

'Well...' she stepped back and pasted on a false smile '...we are done, then. It has been so charming to have this little tête-à-tête with you, Lord Kellford.' She extended her hand for him to shake. 'I will remember to pass on your fondest farewells to my parents.'

He shook her hand, then scowled when he realised she had manipulated him into it. And that she had dismissed him. He walked out with an angry step.

Mariel sank into a chair. She felt faint with relief.

Leo was safe!

It was good that he'd left town, she told herself. Good that he was seeing matters her way and honouring her wishes for him to stay safe. His brothers would surely see to it that he did not rush in to stop the wedding.

This was the best solution. Everyone she cared about would be uninjured.

She alone would pay the price.

The day dawned grey and overcast over Brighton, matching Leo's mood. He wanted to feel hopeful. His brothers' support and optimism ought to have helped, but when he woke in his room at the Castle Inn, a sense of foreboding washed over him.

Leo and his brothers had ridden to find Lord Doring. Stephen had heard he'd left London two weeks earlier for his country estate near Brighton. A horse breeder like Stephen, Doring wanted to be present to supervise the foaling of one of his favourite mares.

They'd ridden hard the day before, reaching Brighton at dusk. Leo felt buoyed by his brothers' company. Their support humbled him. At the inn, they'd stayed awake late into the night, talking, clearing the air between them. He'd told them some of what he'd been through the last two years. They'd listened.

It should have been enough to hearten him, but too much was at stake this day and he'd already experienced so much failure.

At midmorning the inn's stable boy brought their horses to them. Nicholas had provided Leo with a strong mare, one that Stephen had bred. Once on horseback again, in the weak sunshine, Leo felt his spirits rise and his determination grow. This time he could not fail. Mariel's happiness—her life—depended upon it.

They rode past the Brighton racecourse. According to the direction given to them at the Castle Inn, Doring Park was nearby.

'How fitting that Doring's estate is near the racecourse,' Stephen remarked as they rode by. 'He is passionate to a fault about horses. Worse than you and I ever were, Leo.'

It was hard to believe that anyone could be more passionate about horses than Leo had been. It seemed a long time ago, but, he had to admit, that passion was gone now.

Soon Doring Park's stately white mansion came into sight. Built on a gentle rise and surrounded by pasture, it became visible when they were still some distance away. When they turned onto the long, winding private road that led up to the house, Leo lagged behind.

This was a great gamble he embarked upon. He planned to tell Doring about his lord cousin's theft and to convince him to overlook it. If he failed at this, it would cost Mariel's father his life and create the ruin Mariel feared for her family.

As if reading Leo's mind, Brenner turned around and gave him a reassuring smile. All his brothers were full of confidence and that did reassure him.

Their approach was announced by a shrieking peacock who displayed his colourful tail. By the time they reached the front entrance, two footmen had emerged.

Nicholas did not even give them a chance to speak. 'The Duke of Manning and his brothers to see Lord Doring,' he said in an imperious voice that reminded Leo of their father.

The footmen's jaws dropped. Obviously dukes did not often call.

One footman collected himself quickly and bowed. 'Your Grace. I will announce you immediately.'

'Very good,' Nicholas responded.

Leo and his brothers dismounted.

Nicholas gestured to the horses. 'Have someone tend to the horses, as well.'

The other footman hurried to hold the horses.

'If your Grace would follow me,' the first man said.

They entered the house into a large hall with dark wooden floors and a sweeping staircase. Another footman appeared to take their gloves and hats.

The first man led them to an oval-shaped drawing room whose many windows made the most of what little sunlight there was that day. None of the brothers sat, nor did they speak much while they waited for Lord Doring.

Stephen gazed out the windows, watching grooms lead their horses away. Brenner stood next to the white marble mantel, glancing at the clock.

Nicholas clapped Leo on the shoulder. 'This will work,' he told Leo. 'I'm convinced of it.'

Brenner turned back and smiled. 'I agree.'

Stephen said nothing.

It seemed an interminable length of time before they heard footsteps outside the door, although the clock's hand had not even moved halfway round the dial.

The door opened and the footman stepped in again, announcing, 'The Earl of Doring.'

Doring, a vigorous man in his late fifties, strode in and walked directly to Nicholas.

'Your Grace.' He nodded respectfully. 'Forgive me for keeping you waiting. I was just in from the stables when you called.'

Nicholas offered a handshake. 'I understand perfectly.'

Leo, Stephen and Brenner approached and stood behind Nicholas, who stepped aside.

'Allow me to present my brothers.' He gestured towards them. 'I believe you know the Earl of Linwall.'

Brenner offered his hand. 'A pleasure to see you again, sir.'

'Mr Stephen Manning,' Nicholas went on.

'We are acquainted, sir,' Stephen said.

Doring also shook Stephen's hand. 'Ah, yes. We last spoke at Newmarket, as I recall.'

'Newmarket.' Stephen nodded. 'I recall it well.'

'You may not have met my youngest brother.' Nicholas moved on to Leo. 'Mr Leo Fitzmanning.'

Leo noticed Doring's eyes narrow very slightly. The man, of course, realised he was the bastard brother.

'A pleasure to meet you.' Leo extended his hand.

Doring accepted it without hesitation. 'Indeed. It is my pleasure, as well.' His gaze swept over all of them. 'I've ordered refreshment, but do sit down. Your Grace, I am eager to hear the purpose of this unexpected visit.'

The man was affable. That was in Leo's favour.

Leo allowed himself to hope. 'If I may explain, sir. You may have heard that your cousin's daughter is to marry Baron Kellford—'

'Of course I heard, but I do not care one way or the other about the affairs of my cousin.' Doring mollified his churlish tone. 'It should be good that the daughter marries, shouldn't it? I admit I am little acquainted with the man, but he is a charming sort.'

'He acts the charmer, it is true.' Leo met his gaze. 'But he will make a cruel husband. I have seen him inflict injury on women. It is how he receives pleasure.'

Doring's brow rose. 'Is that so? Well, my cousin's daughter is of age. Her father cannot force her to marry the man. Warn her against him.'

'It is not so simple,' Nicholas said.

Doring went on. 'My cousin is an idiot. He should oppose her marrying any man. In two years she will be wealthy. She will make a fine cash pot for him then. He has more of a chance to get money out of a daughter than her husband.' He threw up a hand. 'Enough talk of my tiresome cousin. Why does his daughter's marriage concern me?'

'Hear him out,' Nicholas said.

At that moment, a footman entered with a crystal decanter and five glasses.

'Ah!' Doring clapped his hands. 'Some sherry, gentlemen?'

Leo waited impatiently while the sherry was poured and glasses handed out. Leo took one sip and placed his glass on a table.

When the servant left the room, he faced Doring again. 'I shall explain why you are involved in this, Lord Doring.' He paused, collecting his words. 'Kellford possesses some very damaging information about your cousin. If Miss Covendale does not marry him, Kellford will disclose the information and your cousin—and his wife and daughters—will be ruined.'

Doring's colour heightened. 'I should have known. What has my cousin done this time? Reneged on a voucher? Cheated at cards? I am certain it is something reprehensible.' He pointed to Leo. 'Whatever it is, leave me out of it. I told Cecil I would no longer lift a finger to help him. He is the veriest leech, I assure you. He'll suck me dry with his gambling debts. I have cut him off. Washed my hands of him! I do not care if he lands in debtor's prison. I will do no more for him.'

Leo's gaze remained steady. 'It is not for his sake we are here, but on Miss Covendale's behalf.'

Doring stood. 'You cannot hold his daughters or wife over my head! I warned Cecil that he is responsible for them, not I. I told him I would do nothing more for him or his family. Nothing! My fortune was gained honestly and I do not gamble it away. Cecil plunders his estate and throws its profits into a roll of dice. It is none of my affair.'

'It becomes your affair—' Leo also rose '—because Covendale stole money from you. Kellford has the proof—'

'Stole money from me?' Doring blanched.

'He forged your name on a banknote,' Leo explained. 'He trusted that you would not notice and that your man of business would not heed it as something unusual.'

Doring began to pace. 'I cannot believe he would stoop so low. He will pay for this! My cousin will not get away with it. I'll see him hanged first!'

Leo blocked his path. 'That is why Miss Covendale is compelled to marry Kellford—'

Nicholas broke in. 'Kellford has proof of the theft and threatens to expose the crime if Miss Covendale does not marry him.'

Doring gave a sarcastic laugh. 'Well, tell her she doesn't have to marry the man now. *You* have told me about the crime. Soon the world will know, because I intend to prosecute. Nobody steals from me. Nobody.'

'That is what you must not do!' Leo raised his voice. 'Think of the man's wife and daughters.'

Doring whirled on him. 'My cousin should have thought of them.' He looked at each of the brothers. 'Why do you come tell me all this? Why is this any of your concern?'

Nicholas explained, 'Our family is closely connected to Miss Covendale. We grew up with her. She has always been a favourite of our sister Charlotte.'

'No.' Leo caught Doring's eye again. 'The truth is that I love Mariel. I am trying to save her from this terrible marriage.'

Doring threw up one hand. 'You've saved her, as I said. You've told me. But her father is a different matter—'

Leo spoke quickly. 'I will repay the money her father stole from you.'

'I will pay you interest,' Nicholas added. 'You will lose nothing. There will be no need to prosecute.'

'And wait for what my cousin will do next?' Doring laughed again. 'Steal from someone else, perhaps? No, the man must be stopped.'

Brenner rose from his seat. 'We'll keep him under control.' He walked up to Doring. 'You knew my father, did you not, sir?'

Doring shrugged. 'You know I did.'

'Then you know that I was successful at keeping a foolish gambler in check.' Brenner's late father had nearly lost the family estate by making bad investments until Brenner took over control of the finances. 'We will accept responsibility for your cousin.'

Stephen remained seated and looked lost in his own thoughts. His detachment annoyed Leo, even though he could not think of what Stephen could do to help the situation.

Leo tried again, turning to Lord Doring. 'I beg of you, sir. Spare Miss Covendale. And her mother and sisters. They are innocent in this.'

Doring shook his head. 'No. My cousin bears the burden of ruining his family, not I. I have helped him time and time again and he continues to rack up debts. I do not need the money. It is not a matter of money, but of respect. He has treated me with the greatest disdain. He deserves whatever fate a judge and jury bestows on him. This is the last straw.'

Leo lowered himself into the chair and pressed his

fingers against his forehead. His gamble had failed. Doring would not listen to reason, would not have compassion for Mariel.

He heard Stephen mutter, 'He cares more for his horses.'

Indeed. Doring's horses would be cosseted and indulged, but his own flesh and blood would suffer.

Leo glanced out the window.

'Can we not convince you?' Nicholas persisted. 'You must know my father was a great friend of the king. If you ever need royal favour, I am certain his Royal Majesty would bestow it if we asked.'

Doring winced. 'I have no wish to offend the king, but I cannot be swayed.'

Leo ached with each word spoken. He rose again. 'It is no use, Nick. We might as well take our leave.'

Nicholas nodded. 'You are right.'

Doring looked apologetic. 'Your Grace, I do regret that I am unable to comply with your wishes. I hope you understand my thinking on this matter.'

'I do not,' Nicholas snapped. 'But I will waste no more of my time with you.' He started towards the door.

Stephen rose from his seat. He and Brenner followed Nicholas to the door.

Leo remained where he was.

'Wait,' he cried when they reached the door. 'Stephen, you once offered me a breeding pair of horses from your stable. May I consider those mine?'

Stephen looked puzzled. 'Of course you may. They are yours.'

Leo swung around to Lord Doring. 'Then I have another proposition for you, sir. This is one I hope you will accept—'

Chapter Twenty-one

Mariel descended from the carriage in front of St George's Church near Hanover Square. Even though she had not fussed about her appearance, she supposed she looked like a woman about to get married. She wore one of her good dresses, a pale pink muslin, and a hat with a matching pink ribbon.

Black bombazine and black gloves would have suited the occasion better.

She noticed a couple of men standing outside the church. Kellford's men, she guessed. Were they the ones who had caused the carriage accident? Perhaps they were there to ensure she did not run away.

The day before had been agony. The nightmare of marrying Kellford had become very real and all she wanted to do was flee. During the night her fears were magnified. What would her nights be like from this day forwards? Would she be able to make this sacrifice?

It was still the best option, the only choice.

If only they had been able to stop Kellford. They'd come so close.

At least Leo was far away. She must console herself with that fact.

Mariel's mother hurried into the church. Her father lingered behind and walked with Mariel.

As they passed between the church's stone columns, her father whispered to her, 'You are not going to do anything foolish, are you?' He looked haggard with worry.

She did not answer him. Each step made it harder to stick to her resolve. Each breath became more difficult.

They entered the church where Mariel's mother was already busy greeting the guests, about thirty friends, members of the *ton* who had been invited to witness the vows.

Mariel held back, scanning the church. Did she hope to see Leo there, or did she fear it?

In a pew, several rows behind where the guests sat, appeared another of those rough-looking men. Next to him was a thin, sallow-faced fellow. The bank clerk! It must be. She ought to have known Kellford would bring proof of his allegations.

Someone approached her from behind. Leo? She whirled around.

It was Walker and Penny.

She clasped Penny's hand and asked Walker, 'Any news of Leo?'

He frowned. 'He left word he would be gone a day.'

'A day?' He must stay away until it was safe to return. Her anxiety for him returned.

'Come,' her father demanded.

She gave Penny a swift hug before her father pulled her away.

'Who was that gentleman with your maid?' Her father's voice was tense.

She merely returned a scathing look.

Her mother hurried towards them. 'We should start now.' She quickly made her way to her seat.

The organist began playing a selection from Haydn and her father nearly dragged Mariel to the centre aisle. There was nothing to be done but to walk towards the altar where Kellford waited for her, the very picture of an eager groom.

'Do not fail me, daughter,' her father rasped.

She walked up the aisle on her father's arm. Her father handed her over to Lord Kellford. Kellford's cold eyes glittered with triumph as she took her place beside him.

The organ music ceased and the minister began, 'Dearly beloved, we are gathered together here in the sight of God...'

Mariel did not heed the words. She could not do this! She could not do this! She could not shackle herself to this despicable man.

Her heart pounded harder when the minister said, 'Therefore if any man can show any just cause why they may not lawfully be joined together, let him now speak or else hereafter forever hold his peace....'

She drew in a breath, praying some miracle would occur and someone would speak.

All was silent.

The minister went on, '...if either of you know any impediment, why ye may not be lawfully joined in matrimony, ye do now confess it...'

She should open her mouth. Tell the minister to stop.

He continued, asking Kellford, 'Wilt thou have this woman...?'

Mariel's heart pounded so hard she thought it might be heard in the back of the church. She heard a roaring in her ears. Would she even hear the minister ask for her vows?

The roar changed and seemed to come from outside the church, like muffled voices. She heard the guests moving and murmuring among themselves.

She could not do this. God help her. She could not do this.

The minister turned to her. 'Wilt thou have this man to your wedded husband…?'

'No,' she protested, her voice catching in her throat.

The minister did not hear her. '…keep thee only to him as long as ye both shall live?'

She tried to speak louder. 'No.'

At that same moment the doors to the church opened and a man's voice shouted, 'Stop!'

She turned. From the shadows at the back of the church, the man appeared.

Leo!

He burst into the church, dressed in riding clothes, followed by his brothers. Walker had joined them.

Mariel ran to Leo, caring about nothing at that moment except that Leo had come for her.

He'd come for her!

Leo gathered her into his arms. 'We've done it,' he whispered in her ear. 'All is well.'

Leo was the miracle, the answer to her prayer.

By this time the guests were all on their feet. Mariel's mother was wailing and her father had turned deathly white.

Kellford took a few steps forwards. 'See here!' he cried. 'What is this? How dare you interrupt—'

'There will be no wedding, Kellford.' Leo released Mariel.

Walker and his brothers formed a protective shield around her.

Leo addressed the audience. 'Ladies and gentlemen, I know this is alarming, but my brothers and I have come to prevent a wrong.' He pointed to Mariel. 'This lady does not wish to marry Lord Kellford. He is compelling her to do so in order to gain her fortune.'

Kellford straightened. 'That is a lie! And I demand satisfaction from you for speaking such a falsehood.' He moved around the guests. 'This man is lying, I assure you. The truth is, I am protecting Miss Covendale and her family—'

'Say no more,' Leo warned.

Kellford looked wild-eyed. 'You have forced me into this, Fitzmanning.' He pointed to Mariel's father. 'He is the villain in this! He stole money from his cousin, Lord Doring—'

A voice from the back of the church boomed. 'Stole money from me?' The Earl of Doring strode forwards.

A collective gasp rose from the pews.

'Yes! Yes!' Kellford hurried towards him, pointing to the back of the church. 'See that man there?' The bank clerk shrank down in the pew. The man who had been sitting next to him rose and hurried out of the church. 'That man can prove I am not a liar. He knows Covendale forged a signature—'

Doring laughed. 'My cousin did no such thing.' He walked up to Mariel's father and patted him on the back. 'I recently loaned Covendale a large amount of money. Why not? I have the funds and he was in need.' Doring glanced over to the bank clerk. 'Are you going to believe that fellow over me? Is he known to any of you?'

'Indeed!' Leo spoke up again. 'It is as I have said. We have come to stop Kellford from destroying the good name of Mr Covendale and his daughter. To prevent him from plundering this lady's fortune.'

Mariel's gaze went from one to the other, trying to take it all in. 'How did he do it?' she asked Stephen.

He grinned at her. 'He remembered his passion for horses.'

No more than an hour later, Leo sat beside Mariel on the sofa in Nicholas's drawing room. Nicholas's wife had taken Mariel's mother under her wing, distracting her and consoling her. Brenner stood in serious conversation with Covendale and Doring. Stephen and Nicholas laughed over a decanter of brandy.

'Nicholas has sent for your sisters?' Mariel asked him.

'Charlotte, Annalise, their spouses, Justine and Stephen's wife, as well.' He smiled at her. 'I am afraid you will be joining a rather large family.'

She took his hand and squeezed it. 'My happiest days have been among your family. I shall look forward to many more.' She sighed. 'I only wish Walker and Penny had agreed to come.'

'I do, too,' he admitted. 'Give them time. I have a feeling Walker is destined for such success he will soon find the company of dukes and earls commonplace.'

She returned his smile. 'And I suspect Penny will be at his side.'

Leo still had not settled with Mariel whether she would marry him. There were no real impediments now. His business ventures would now be ones he could shout from rooftops, if necessary. He would accept the help his brothers could provide. If a duke, an earl and a second son rallied around him, who would dare consider him scandalous? He'd had enough of danger and the only risks he was willing to take now were financial ones.

And emotional ones. He would risk loving again. He loved Mariel and would do whatever he could to see that she was happy. If that meant marrying him, his spirits would soar to the heavens. If not, he would find some other way to ensure her happiness.

She rested her head against his shoulder. 'I am still trying to believe that it is all over. What will happen to Kellford, do you think?'

'He left the church in the company of some hard-looking men. I suspect the money lenders will lose no time in stripping his house of its belongings. If Kellford is lucky, he will be left with his life and little else.'

Likely Kellford would flee to the Continent to escape the rest of his creditors. It was not punishment enough for him, in Leo's view, but at least they would not have to set eyes on him again.

Mariel stroked his hand. 'What Kellford has done will certainly be the topic of much gossip. I am sure some disfavour will fall on my family. I wonder if it will be enough to compel my father to change his ways?'

He threaded his fingers through hers, glad to be able to touch her, to know she was now safe. 'I suspect Brenner is concocting some plan between your father and his cousin to keep your father in check.'

She raised their entwined hands to her lips and kissed his fingers. 'I still do not see how you convinced Doring to forgive my father. My father insisted he would be full of wrath.'

'He was,' Leo responded. 'He was precisely as your father depicted him and I thought I had made a terrible miscalculation by going to him.'

'Miscalculation?' she asked.

He looked into her lovely eyes. 'I thought I would become the cause of your father hanging. I thought you would never forgive me.' It had been a painfully low point.

Her gaze softened. 'I still do not understand how you convinced him.'

He'd remembered Stephen muttering that Doring cared more for his horses than his family. That was the key. Leo offered him the breeding pair of horses from Stephen's stables and suddenly Doring was willing to forgive all.

Leo glanced around the room at his brothers. He could not have saved Mariel without them. Nicholas, as only a duke could do, had provided clout. Stephen had provided the solution. And now Brenner would seal the pact and prevent future problems. He said a silent prayer of thanks for giving him this family. This woman he loved.

'How did you convince Doring, Leo?' Mariel asked.

He grinned at her. 'Horses, Mariel.' He leaned down and kissed her. 'Horses,' he whispered.

Epilogue

Welbourne Manor—October 1830

The house party at Welbourne Manor was not unlike those held there when Leo and his siblings were growing up. Small children ran through the house, chased by haggard governesses. Older ones brought in dirt from the gardens or played rowdy games in the upstairs music room. As in days gone by, there was plenty of noise, the noise of a family party.

Leo and Mariel had invited the entire Fitzmanning Miscellany for several days of family enjoyment after the christening of their newborn son, John, named after Leo's father. Welbourne Manor was Leo and Mariel's home now and had been for two years, a wedding present from Leo's brothers and sisters, a return to their father's original bequest.

At the moment, Leo and his brothers were in the library, hiding from the children. Walker had arrived, providing them a great excuse to avoid the commotion. Walker and Penny brought two more toddlers with them, their twins, now just over a year old, their contribution to the din.

'What did you find in Liverpool?' Leo asked Walker as soon as the men all had drinks in their hands.

Leo and Walker were now partners. Their ship had come in from that not-quite-legal investment they'd made two years before, the one that had brought Leo back to London and to Mariel. By mutual agreement, they'd decided to remain within the law afterwards. That decision had not hampered them.

'The railroad is a marvel,' Walker told them. He had travelled to Liverpool to see first-hand how the new Liverpool and Manchester railways operated. 'It can move thousands of people, carry the mail, as well as goods.'

'Are you and Walker going to invest in railroads?' Nicholas asked.

'We have already, your Grace,' Walker said. 'We are looking to develop rail transport from London west.'

Stephen's brows rose. 'This is a far cry from raising horses.'

'I have no wish to compete with you, Stephen,' Leo remarked. 'Think of it this way. Railroads can bring more people to the races. There's money in this for you.'

Brenner spoke seriously. 'Do not sink everything into railroads. It is always better to invest in several opportunities. That way if one investment loses, you still make money on the other.'

'Spoken like the wise elder brother!' Leo laughed.

Walker provided more details, speaking so knowledgeably that one would never have guessed he once had been a thief and a valet. When Walker had left Leo's service, the man who had once been Kellford's valet took his place. Penny said he looked more like a valet than Walker.

Mariel knocked at the door. 'Leo, may I see you, please?'

He went to her immediately. 'What is it?'

'I need you to come to the nursery.' She gestured for him to come with her.

Leo's worries grew. It was not like her to interrupt like this.

Instead of the children's wing, though, she led him to their bedchamber.

'I moved the crib in here temporarily, because the nursery is so full,' she explained.

Indeed, it had been quite a challenge to figure out the sleeping arrangements for so many children, their nurses and governesses.

'Is something wrong with the baby?' He hurried over to the crib.

She joined him, looking down at the sleeping infant, this miracle they'd created together.

The baby slept peacefully.

She put her arm around Leo's waist. 'Nothing's wrong. The baby is perfect, as always. There never was a more perfect baby. I merely wanted an excuse to be with you.'

The sounds of children shrieking, their feet pounding through the halls, reached his ears. A new Fitzmanning Miscellany, Leo thought, smiling to himself.

He remembered running with his brothers and sisters through these rooms. How many priceless vases had they knocked over? Suffered how many scraped knees? It has been a happy place. He'd continue to make Welbourne Manor a happy place. How could it be anything but happy when Mariel was at his side?

'I've hardly seen you since the christening.' She sighed.

He wrapped his arms around her, realising he had

missed her equally as much. 'Were you worried that I'd run away to the Continent?'

Something crashed and shattered. A child began to wail and soon adult footsteps could be heard running to see what had happened.

She settled against his chest where she fit so perfectly. 'With all the noise and commotion, I would not blame you.'

He broke away from her so he could look down into her eyes. 'I would not leave you.'

She smiled. 'Not even if someone told you I'd fallen for an earl?'

'Especially not then.' He grinned. 'Or, at least, I would chase you down and make you explain why you would ever do such a thing.'

She laughed. 'Very good, Leo! You have learned something.'

He kissed her. 'The most important thing I've learned is that I love you. I will never leave you.'

She kissed him back. 'I know.'

* * * * *

MILLS & BOON®

Buy A Regency Collection today and receive FOUR BOOKS FREE!

4 BOOKS FREE!

Transport yourself to the seductive world of Regency with this magnificent twelve-book collection. Indulge in scandal and gossip with these 2-in-1 romances from top Historical authors

Order your complete collection today at
www.millsandboon.co.uk/regencycollection

0915_ST19

MILLS & BOON®
The Italians Collection!

2 BOOKS FREE!

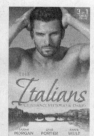

Irresistibly Hot Italians

You'll soon be dreaming of Italy with this scorching six-book collection. Each book is filled with three seductive stories full of sexy Italian men! Plus, if you order the collection today, you'll receive two books free!

This offer is just too good to miss!

Order your complete collection today at
www.millsandboon.co.uk/italians

0815_ST17

MILLS & BOON®

The Rising Stars Collection!

1 BOOK FREE!

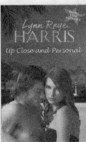

This fabulous four-book collection features 3-in-1 stories from some of our talented writers who are the stars of the future! Feel the temperature rise this summer with our ultra-sexy and powerful heroes. Don't miss this great offer—buy the collection today to get one book free!

**Order yours at
www.millsandboon.co.uk/risingstars**

0715_ST16

'A fresh new voice in romantic fiction'
—*Marie Claire*

**Everyone has one.
That list.
The things you were *supposed* to do before you turn thirty.**

Jobless, broke and getting a divorce, Rachel isn't exactly living
up to her own expectations. And moving into grumpy single
dad Patrick's box room is just the soggy icing on top of
her dreaded thirtieth birthday cake.

Eternal list-maker Rachel has a plan—an all-new set of
challenges to help her get over her divorce and out into the
world again—from tango dancing to sushi making to
stand-up comedy.

But, as Patrick helps her cross off each task, Rachel faces
something even harder: learning to live—and
love—without a checklist.

0515_ST_18